T0146673

PIONEER STREET

THOMAS LISENBEE

authorHOUSE®

AuthorHouse™
1663 Liberty Drive
Bloomington, IN 47403
www.authorhouse.com
Phone: 1 (800) 839-8640

Published by AuthorHouse 10/22/2018

ISBN: 978-1-5462-4231-4 (sc)
ISBN: 978-1-5462-4232-1 (hc)
ISBN: 978-1-5462-4233-8 (e)

Library of Congress Control Number: 2018905854

Print information available on the last page.

(for Gracie)

"Much of what we observe in nature will be due to the accident of our particular location, an accident that can never be explained, except by the fact that it is only in such locations, that anyone could live." —Steven Weinberg

Prologue

Bay Ridge, Brooklyn, 1968

It was a sticky-hot morning in August. Brooklyn suffered under a high-ozone alert. The Tet Offensive, the assassinations of Martin Luther King and Bobby Kennedy, race riots, student unrest—what had started out as leap year had become a veritable steeplechase of cataclysmic events. Yet, while chaos currently held sway at the Democratic National Convention in Chicago, irregardless of how many kids LBJ was going to kill that day, within the air-conditioned offices of the Bay Ridge Brooklyn branch of the New York City Department of Social Services, it was what Preston Stoner liked to think of as Santa Claus hour—or better said, that time before the phones started going crazy that he dedicated to filling out as many grants as he could for the poor wretches the city insisted their caseworkers refer to as "clients."

Just twenty-three years old, Preston had been a probationary caseworker for a mere six weeks, during which time he'd learned exactly two things. First, whenever new probationary units were formed, experienced caseworkers, ordered to transfer a few of their cases to the rookies, seized the opportunity to rid themselves of their most vexing cases. Consequently, in his first-ever venture into the "field," Preston found himself scared shitless, walking the mean streets of Sunset Park with an enraged young Puerto Rican—strung out on who-knows-what—trying to talk this man down from killing his wife. Then, just last week, there'd been the client who draped the front of her refrigerator with a blanket because it had no door.

"Look, friend," the landlord countered in defense once Preston finally reached him by telephone, "if you'd just taken the time to check her files, you might have picked up on how she's been frigging dead-beating you people for years. Surely, it's gotta be in there somewhere that every time I give her a new refrigerator, first thing she does is lose the door so as to balloon her electric bill. Why? So's she can use the money to buy something nice for herself. Look, pal, everyone and their cousin knows the city is prohibited by law from shutting off these leeches' electricity, and if you hadn't spent so much time standing there gawking at her goddamn door-less fridge, you'd've noticed her amazing collection of designer vodka and gin bottles, put two and two together, and saved yourself a phone call."

And that second important thing? That Manny, the owner of the funky deli downstairs that bore his name, no matter how many times a guy asked, always spooned in the sugars rather than included them on the side. And anyway, so what else was new? Merely that the goddamn union, of which he was not yet a member, was threatening to go on strike, plus the fucking peel-back tab on his coffee had come free this morning with such a fucking jerk he'd slopped coffee all over his desk like he was some sort of ham-handed klutz, with the end result that once more he found himself under the disapproving eye of his unit supervisor, Esther Schnupps.

Or *Schnuppsie*, as they called her behind her back, whose single, God-given talent seemed to be for giving fledgling caseworkers and clients an equally hard time. A real ballbuster, she didn't so much represent the welfare system. She *was* the system at its worst: heartless, indifferent, unsympathetic, callous to a fault. Her mass undeniably bovine, her personality positively crocodilian, breakfasting as usual this morning on a bagel and coffee, each savage bite wrenched into her maw, a glutinous cud undergoing noisy mastication.

Preston was weighing the possibility of repositioning his desk not to be in her direct line of sight when his telephone rang. He glanced at his watch. Too damn early for the circus to begin. Someone to see him in the Intake? Rosario Rios, a client of his? Maybe, he'd check. It took a bit of doing, locating a file with Schnuppsie's eyes drilling a hole in his back, but a hurried gulp of coffee and he was scurrying downstairs to Intake.

"Welcome to Paradise Lost," he muttered as he pushed open the door to a harshly lit, industrial-gray echo chamber arrayed with a tidy sea of battered metal folding chairs. The bane of lost souls, the place where hope rarely sprang eternal, already half full, evidently business was going to be good today.

"Rrrrosario Rrrrrios," he announced a bit louder than necessary, rolling his *r*'s a bit longer than necessary—as any bold young man full of piss and vinegar might, were he deluded by thoughts of being semi-fluent in Spanish.

When he finally located Rios (and baby?) seated behind a pillar, Preston flashed his best shop-clerk smile and motioned for her to follow him to a series of interview cubicles. According to Schnuppsie's dictum, the perfect caseworker always gave a client's file a quick once-over before coming down to Intake. But rules be damned, this caseworker had been particularly blessed in life to be Nebraska raised by an uncle who'd served as Gage County Sheriff for over thirty years, who'd gone out of his way to school his nephew in the fine art of reading people. And this lass, now seated before him, was a mahogany-skinned, extremely young, Afro-Carib mother, aged anywhere from fourteen to nineteen. Slightly built but shapely busted in a lumpen sort of way, attractively clad for the day in a summery white blouse and matching short-shorts, hair a bountiful cascade of coal-black ringlets, with eyes that tentatively reached out to him. Heavily browed eyes. Haunting, torchy, soulful but kindly eyes that reminded him of a self-portrait he'd seen somewhere of Frieda Kahlo. And her kid? Three, maybe four months old. Cute as a button in a pink frilly dress and matching bonnet.

Thinking to put Rios at ease, Preston first tried chatting her up in her native tongue, then quickly switched to English when she seemed not to understand a single word he had said.

"So, what can we do for you today, Mrs. Rios?"

"I need money … for the bebe," she said in a *muy autentico* Sunset Park, Brooklyn-Puerto Rican accent: mellifluous vowels, ill-defined consonants.

"And why is that, Mrs. Rios? Didn't you get your last check?" Preston asked, loathing the third degree that Schnuppsie called "interviewing the client." Jesus, these people were not here to get rich.

"Mai hosban' ran off wi' de money," she said.

"Where is he now, Mrs. Rios?"

"I don' know."

"Is there no one to help you in a pinch? Your mother … a sister … grandmother … an auntie, perhaps?"

"No."

The baby's listlessness was distracting. Strangely unalert. Wholly indifferent to the bottle held to its lips. "Is your child sick?" he asked.

"No."

Which he didn't believe. *Sometimes clients come to the welfare office when they are sick instead of a health clinic*, he remembered Schnuppsie once saying in one of those rare instances she actually made sense. The logical next thing for him to have done, of course, was to place his hand on the infant's forehead and see for himself. But logic be damned. This was the New York City Department of Social Services, where "Touching clients, people, is forbidden" and "Protect yourselves from lawsuits, people" was *de facto* procedural bullshit.

Instead, Preston broadened his smile, hoping perhaps to coax one out of Rios. These were the moments that were hard for him. Did he not consider himself *un hombre muy simpatico*? The caseworker with an unhardened heart who railed against the practice of social work as the avoidance of litigation? The caseworker who had not learned, nor ever cared to learn, how to separate his personal feelings from the job?

But, of course, Rosario Rios, cognizant of the *quid pro quo* that existed between them refused to grace him with a smile. Even at this tender age, it rankled in her sorrowful eyes that in exchange for paltry sums of money the state got to regulate her life.

"Mrs. Rios, let me trot upstairs and see what I can do for you. This shouldn't take long. Just make yourself comfortable." Although, he knew, just as he was sure that Rios knew, that "shouldn't take too long" within these merciless walls was more joke than fact, that the infernal cogs of the welfare machine turned with the listless deliberation of a three-toed sloth.

***

"And just where did Rios claim this husband of hers was?" Schnuppsie inquired over the half-moon rims of her reading glasses.

Preston shifted his weight from foot to foot. "She said she doesn't know."

"Come on, Mr. Stoner. Your client will have to do better than that. How do we know this isn't a scam?" she admonished with a tight little smile.

"Well …," he began, then trailed off. No use wasting his breath trying to explain to Schnuppsie that this young woman had an aura of simple goodness about her that made her incapable of deceit.

"Come, come, Mr. Stoner. To *believe* is simply not good enough. We must learn to be more skeptical. We cannot just go with what the clients say. Many of them make an art out of cheating. Our obligation to the taxpayers is to see that their money is wisely and honestly spent. I think it best for you to go back downstairs and delve a little deeper."

So that was it, for the rest of the morning. He'd be dumpster diving for more and more information until every fucking *i* was dotted and *t* crossed. Meanwhile, his phone would continue to ring and ring with this to do and that, not to mention those case notes awaiting dictation from yesterday's visit to the field.

Nevertheless, come lunchtime, Preston was, for him at least, almost a happy camper. Not only was he bounding up from Intake with what he was sure would be the last conceivable morsel of information appertaining to the Rios case that *La Bruja Gorda* could possibly require, but in between trips, he'd managed to find time enough to transcribe fully half of his field notes. Except Schnuppsie, of course, was no longer at her desk.

"She's downtown Brooklyn," Rita, the unit clerk, about to take off for lunch herself, called to him from across the room before he could ask. "A&S is having a sale. Should be back by two. And, honey, if you don't mind me saying it, I've had my eye on you all morning, so let me give you a piece of advice. In case you think she's messing with you a little bit, you're right. It in't easy being a caseworker. I wouldn't want to do it. But if you're thinking of making a career of it, you better get a little hard inside, honey. Otherwise, the job'll eat you up."

Eat him up? Bullshit. Get a little hard inside? Yea, right. He was sitting at his desk, face buried in his hands, longing for about fifteen seconds of absolute clarity when the telephone rang. Intake? Nope. Joellen, his wife.

"Preston, the mail came, and …"

"… my draft notice came today," he said, able to complete the sentence for her because, hey, it was that kind of day. Forget Schnuppsie, forget the strike. That accursed war in Vietnam was a metastasizing nightmare at best, and here he was, sound of mind and body, bereft of student deferment, the marriage deferment now a thing of the past with him and Joellen, despite the two of them having a helluva lot of fun trying yet to get her pregnant. His mouth was dry. His heart was pounding. Hell, he was fucking freaking out. *Get ahold of yourself, buster*, he could hear his Uncle Otis yelling from his grave. Preston took a long, deep breath, then exhaled. Sucked in another and realized that, hell's bells, he'd just wheezed. Yes, damn it, wheezed. Asthma. Forget all those plan B's for avoiding the draft that made him sick even to think about. Why run off to Canada or mince like a fairy through his physical at Whitehall Street, when motherfucking asthma could be his ticket out of Vietnam?

"Preston? Preston?" His wife's voice came to him laden with concern. "Are you still there?"

Oh yeah, not only was he there, he was absolutely here, there, and everywhere. "Listen," he blurted. "Get back to you later. Gotta hang up. I'm having an asthma attack. Listen. Hear that? Hear that wheeze? You understand what I'm trying to say here? Gotta get my ass in gear, find a doctor, and get it documented before it disappears."

He slammed the receiver onto the cradle. Rita looked over in surprise. But what did he care? Fuck her, fuck Schnuppsie, and especially fuck the fact that this was his day to man the unit phones during lunch hour. Rosario and cute little babykins could wait. The mantra of the moment was *thou shalt not die in Vietnam*. He took the stairs full tilt. Burst onto to Fourth Avenue dodging pedestrians. Except this willy-nilly, hit or miss search for a doctor's shingle didn't bear fruit until he switched to checking the side streets. The waiting room was crammed to bursting. He didn't have an appointment.

So it must have been the wild look he had about him that led the receptionist to take mercy on him and say she'd try and work him in.

One o'clock came, then two. He knew full well time was against him, that this *quasi* hysterical asthma attack of his might turn out to be a fickle friend. Sure enough, despite his dogged attempts to keep his wheeze on go, come half past three, when the receptionist nodded for him to go in, as near as he could tell, all physical trace of it had disappeared.

Lanky, stoop-shouldered Eric Thorensen, MD, greeted him with a kindly smile. "What seems to be the problem, Mr. Stoner?" he inquired in the learned, mousy manner of men who employed comb-overs to hide their bald spots.

Preston, sensing the delicate fix he was in, cleared his throat in order to stop himself from shouting out: *Problem? No problem, except I've been sitting in your waiting room so fucking long that my asthma symptoms have disappeared, so now, I'm going to die in fucking Vietnam!* "Gee, Doc, you see, it's like this," he finally managed to say, "darn if I didn't go off this morning without my inhaler … and this being a high-ozone day, damned if it didn't trigger another of my chronic asthma attacks … but the thing is … while I was sitting out waiting my turn … well, my symptoms pretty much straightened themselves out … and in truth, I wouldn't be sitting here bothering you … but … well …my draft notice arrived today … and I thought maybe I ought to stick around and have you check me out on the outside chance you might still be able to detect something significant enough worth documenting that I can take with me to my draft physical next month. … I mean, asthma's been pretty much a fact of life with me since I was a child."

"Remove your shirt, please," Doctor Thorensen replied, as if dealing with a borderline hysterical asthmatic seeking to avoid the draft were an everyday occurrence for him.

Preston removed his shirt and tried to remain at ease as the doctor poked around. But damn, it was maddening. The doc's stethoscope wandered here and there. Inhale-exhale-cough, inhale-exhale-cough. The sanitary paper covering the examination table crinkled every time he stirred his butt, and, pray tell, why did these guys crank their air-conditioners up so damn high? It was fucking freezing in here with his shirt off.

"Hmmmmm. And how long ago did you say this attack began?"

"About twelve thirty, I'd say."

"And you claim to have had asthma as a child?"

"Not claim—*had*, Doc—had and still do have attacks. Not every day, mind you, but often enough to need an inhaler handy around the house. Heck, when I was a kid, sometimes I had it so bad my mother had to sit up with me all night."

The doctor pursed his lips in thought. His palms were pressed into a prayer position, forefingers touching the tip of his nose. The wall directly behind where the doctor stood was arrayed with the usual assortment of diplomas—Cornell, Columbia, Johns Hopkins—along with a series of family photos taken lakeside. A sports car, a sailboat, a boy and a dog playing fetch the Frisbee, and holy shit … of all the rotten luck … last but not least, a strapping young man in Marine full-dress uniform, who, in all probability, at this very moment, was serving his country in Vietnam.

Doctor Thorensen sighed, removed his glasses and pinched the bridge of his nose. "You can go ahead put your shirt back on now, Mr. Stoner. I believe what you say. I'll write a letter for you witnessing only that when I examined you, I detected the faint traces of an asthma attack. I'll make no recommendations as to your fitness for military service. For anything more substantive, you should consult your regular doctor. To be frank, I don't think my letter is going to help much when you go for your physical. I wish you all the luck, but in my opinion, your case is rather weak."

Okay, so he wasn't getting *the* letter, he kept telling himself as the doctor clacked away on a typewriter somewhere nearby. But at least he was getting *a* letter, so he had a chance. And a chance was all he was asking for. Because while there were things in life definitely worth dying for, Vietnam, most certainly, was not one of them. Still, others were willing to risk their lives to serve, so why not he? Did he consider his life more precious than theirs? Certainly not. It was just that there was a world of difference between just and unjust wars. Just wars required a moral imperative that Vietnam lacked. Besides, if US military couldn't cotton to having asthmatics in its Army, well that was up to them.

***

Schnuppsie seemed not to notice as he slipped behind his desk—which was fine with him. Less than an hour, and he'd be out of there. All he had to do was look busy, and he could shuffle file folders and sharpen pencils with the best of them. His uncontented mind was working overtime, worrying how best to parlay Thorensen's letter into beating the draft, when Bobby Eluto—fellow probationary caseworker and weekend draft-dodging warrior in the National Guard—tapped him on the shoulder.

"Hey man, didn't see you around. Thought you were in the field. Listen, in case you haven't heard, the strike is definitely on, so don't come in tomorrow. They'll call us when it's time to come back." A slight pause, then Bobby added, "By the way, not that it's any business of mine, but don't you have someone waiting for you down in Intake?"

It was exactly twenty-three minutes past four when Preston rose from his desk. A condemned man with a colossal knot in his throat, his thirteen steps to the gallows were the four paces that separated him from Schnuppsie's desk. He was ready to crawl through shit if she asked, perform oral sex on her if it came to that, as long it put things right for that poor girl and her baby he'd abandoned in Intake.

Schnuppsie let him dangle a moment with her nose in her magazine. "Mr. Stoner," she said without looking up, "we've been wondering what happened to you. Go see Rita for the Rios check. We expected you to come for it sooner."

Oh yeah, Schnuppsie was something all right. Neat the way the bitch was able to twist the knife, treating him as not worthy of harsh reprimand and, by so doing, neatly dumping the whole day's cock-up solely on him, when she'd been as much a part of it as he. But then again, it wasn't hard for her to make him think he was a piece of shit. He had felt that way most of his life.

Minutes later, fueled by a noxious mixture of shame and despair, Preston found himself once more in Intake. Rosario's eyes refused to meet his as she tucked the check into the breast pocket of her blouse. And who could blame her? After what she'd just been put through, a guy was right in thinking she'd want to club him to death.

But it wasn't until she stood to hitch her baby onto her hip that Preston realized for sure he was destined for the lowest ring of hell. All the time he'd been out there running around like a chicken with its head cut off looking for a doctor, Rios had been sitting here with her lap befouled with baby piss, patiently waiting for the return of a pretentious, selfish little schmuck so wrapped up in himself, he'd rather disservice this mother and child than scrap his dream would not perish with him in Vietman, of one day getting a doctorate in social work from the New School for Social Research, and in so doing, crafting a thesis not only worthy of publication but powerful enough in voice and scope to set the social welfare establishment on its ear.

Returning upstairs, for some unknown reason, he paused before the grimy little window in the stairwell, as if there might be something out there he needed to see. A something that became a somebody standing next to Rosario at the bus stop. A young male Hispanic, not only holding the diaper bag, but her baby as well, so he, most probably, had to be the missing husband, who, it seemed, had just said something to crack Rosario up, something funny enough to have both of them still laughing over it as they boarded their bus.

As the bus pulled into traffic and disappeared down the street, Preston realized those few seconds of absolute clarity he'd been aching for at lunchtime had finally arrived. Never had he felt so tired. Dog tired. Beaten to a pulp, used and abused, dead-dog tired. The thought of spending one minute more in this godforsaken place sickened him. *The clients cannot be trusted.* If Schnuppsie said it once, she'd said it a thousand times, and as much as it killed Preston to admit it, no doubt about it, the old witch had, once again, been proven right. Rosario and that so-called deadbeat husband of hers had just done a number on him. And was it for moments like this that Rita suggested he was supposed to harden himself? Well, fuck that shit. Plainly, social work wasn't all it was cracked up to be—which, much as it pained him to say it, suited him just fine. Once the strike was over, if even by some miracle he did escape Vietnam, he'd not be coming back to work here again, because were he to—God forbid—tough it out in this joint the five to ten years he'd originally planned, he'd end up as case-hardened loutish as Schnuppsie and her ilk … or else go mad. And if by chance, sometime in the hazy future, he did decide to go for a doctorate, for damn sure it wouldn't be in social work. No, a few minutes from now, he'd be the one standing down there at that bus stop—just another Joe Blow freshly gobsmacked by reality. A guy who'd never once thought to ask Rosario her baby's name, waiting for the 63 bus to fetch him home to Brooklyn Heights and Joellen and whatever it was that was going to be the rest of his life.

1

Red Hook, Brooklyn, 2004

"May God bless my people, my uncle, my aunt, my mother, my good father, oh remember them kindly in their time of trouble and in their hour of taking away … who quietly treat me as one familiar and well-beloved in that home, but will not, oh, will not, not now, not ever; but will not ever tell me who I am."

—James Agee, *A Death in the Family*

It was early November of the year the Sarge was to freeze to death. An ordinary Saturday morning to be exact, one week and four days after John Kerry's baffling refusal to demand a vote recount in Ohio, when Preston Stoner, returning home from the corner bodega with a dozen eggs, six bagels, and a box of Kleenex, paused to watch a muscular, slightly paunchy black man wrestle a washing machine secured to his back by a single webbed strap into a rental U-Haul truck, with seemingly as little effort as the bodega clerk had used to fill Preston's bag with his sundry things.

"So, they're leaving today?" Preston said to this towering exemplar of manliness.

"Yes, suh," was the man's carefully enunciated reply.

"You the son?" Preston then asked—which was an easy guess since his friend Ritchie had just informed him in the bodega that the old couple who lived in this house were moving back to their roots in South Carolina, leaving the house to their son.

"Yes, suh."

"You going to be moving onto the block?" Preston then said, not only in a gesture of neighborly interest but also because he worked in advertising, and therefore, always on the lookout for camera-friendly talent his firm might use in future ad campaigns. A single gold earring, a shaved bald head gleaming in the brisk autumn air, arms the approximate girth of Preston's puny, fifty-eight-year-old thighs, had him thinking Sinbad, an ebon Mr. Clean, who honeyed his words in the Southern manner.

"No, suh."

"You up from South Carolina then?"

"No, suh. Ah lives in New Jersey."

"Well sir, I'll have you know I'm going to miss your father. He's one of my best friends on the block, you know. A very fine man," Preston enthused, only to become somewhat bemused at the son's reaction to what he had just said, which was body language 101: head held cocked slightly to the side as if someone were jerking his leg.

Ordinarily, Preston would have taken this as a hint to excuse himself and continue home. But then again, he was definitely not jerking this man's leg. The intent of his words had been innocent enough. He *did* hold this man's father in the highest regard—even though he didn't know his father's name. But then this was New York City, was it not, where people lived together in close proximity for years upon years, traded small talk zillions of times, and knew all kinds of stuff about each other without knowing each other's name?

A muffled crash came from within the house. The son's loopy grin was an exact copy of the father's. "Thank you, suh, for your kind words," he said, carefully wiping his hand on his hooded sweatshirt before offering to Preston in friendship. "Mah name's Winston. Ah'd like to stand and talk, but you'll have to excuse me. That racket inside was muh brother, Clarence. Ah better go check the damage."

Preston watched Winston ease his broad frame through the open doorway of a row house identical in facade and interior design to all the other houses on Pioneer Street. Built to house dockworkers in the 1850s and '60s. The narrow hallway inside was presently lined with packing boxes. Preston shifted uncomfortably. The very sight of packing boxes reawakened painful childhood memories that never failed to have him in a funk. His father's rocker, his mother's wingback chair, her beloved piano, their dining room china cabinet and oriental rug arrayed on their lawn, along with hundreds of people waiting for an auction to start.

Then, Winston had reappeared in the doorway, this time with a large TV cradled easily in his massive arms. Bobbing at his heels was a small girl dressed in jeans and a pink windbreaker, hair beaded and braided into cornrows, the old man's dog following close behind her.

"Your father here?" he asked Winston as he stood aside to let him pass. "I wouldn't hear of leaving without telling him goodbye," he added once the TV had been safely stowed inside the truck.

"Ah do believe he's downstairs packing," Winston said.

"Think you could get him to come out?"

Winston signaled to the little girl who stood lingering in the doorway. "Doreen, you tell Grandpa there's a man out here that wants tuh say goodbye. Now, if you'll excuse me, suh. Clarence and I got to rassle us out a mattress."

While he waited for the old man to appear, Preston couldn't resist inspecting the interior of the van. After all, he was, was he not—as his wife, Joellen, was so fond of reminding him—the packing maven for whom the proper arranging of things in the trunks of automobiles was an underappreciated art. Therefore, why should he not avail himself of this opportunity to check out the brothers' expertise at the craft?

What he beheld gave him great satisfaction. The brothers could very well have been professionals—the truck not yet half full and what was there, closely fitted in like the Inca build stone walls. But the odd thing was, while moments before he'd been misty-eyed at the sight of packing boxes stacked in that hallway, yet those same boxes, now loaded in a truck, seemingly had zero effect on him. He was pondering this oddity when he heard the door open under the stoop. The old man appeared first head and shoulders in the stairwell, then the rest of him.

"You didn't think I'd let my best neighbor sneak out of here without saying goodbye to him, did you?" Preston called, resolved not to waste the man's time and keep it short and sweet. Unfortunately, as was his wont, when he made the mistake of trying to embellish a handshake with what amounted to a very clumsy attempt at an embrace, the old man artfully sloughed it aside, leaving Preston sufficiently embarrassed to blurt out the first stupid thing that came to mind: "The old block is certainly changing, isn't it? I've been here close to twenty years. People moving out and people moving in and fixing up their houses."

The old man's dusty face formed into a wrinkled smile. "Yes, suh," he nodded sagely, an undeniable twinkle in his eyes. "Yes, indeed. Things hereabouts certainly are a-changing."

"And once you and your wife move out, that'll leave me and Ritchie as the old-timers on the block, and I'm not sure I'm ready for that," Preston said, wishing he was less a klutz at small talk.

"Yes, suh. You and Ritchie gonna be the old-timers now," the old man parroted in return. "You already been here longer than me."

Funny, Preston didn't remember it that way. It seemed forever that the old man and his dog had been making their twice daily trips to Coffey Park—sticking to the middle of the street, his dog mincing along beside him, tail between its legs. The old man always with a telescoped-out, old-time car aerial clutched in his hand. And what the heck was that aerial for anyway? To discipline the dog, for protection—and if so from whom or what?

"You best be keeping a close eye on that dog of yours down there in Carolina," Preston joked, "else it's libel to lose itself out in the woods chasing down rabbits."

"No, suh, that dog a mine, it don't like tuh travel. Winston and Little Doreen gonna take it. That little girl sure do luv that dog," the old man said, touching Preston's arm to urge him out of the way of his sons coming down the steps with a mattress.

Preston figured this was as good a time as any to say goodbye. A final handshake, a few common farewell clichés, and he was stepping for home full of goodwill for his fellow man. He smiled when he was forced to detour around three little girls chalking a hopscotch board on the sidewalk. He groaned *oh no, not again* when he noticed for the first time someone had dropped off a dumpster across the street during the night, which meant another parking space lost for months to another house undergoing renovation.

Not that he was against change or gentrification, that most certainly had brought many sorely needed improvements to Van Brunt Street: a drugstore, a pizzeria, a Chinese takeout, a quasi-spiffy Laundromat, even a couple of real sit-down restaurants where a guy and his wife could enjoy a decent meal. Still, he couldn't help but miss the early days when Jesse Jackson's Rainbow Coalition had been alive and well on Pioneer Street. Granted, the block had been undoubtedly poorer and shabbier then, but what it lacked in glitz it made up for in character and cohesion. The main problem with gentrification, Preston mused, was that for every house renovated into some newbie householder's little pot of gold, the multitude of colors in old Jesse's rainbow faded a little more. Nevertheless, onward and upward. Out with the old, in with the new. Someday, in the not so distant future, a dumpster would arrive at their house to cart off the unwanted junk he and Joellen would leave behind. He'd be forgotten. Joellen'd be forgotten. Just like that old man, as well as Ritchie and the Sarge, they'd all be forgotten. The Sarge, who'd lived his whole life in the house where he'd been born, that was until recently, when his family, finally having had it with his unpredictably violent mood swings, kicked him out, leaving him with no other choice but to take up abode, according to Ritchie, in an abandoned vehicle in the alley out behind Ritchie's house.

***

Preston held off mentioning the old man's leaving until later that night when he and Joellen would have finished watching the late-night Seinfeld rerun and would be lying on their backs, holding hands, eyes open in the dark—a custom they'd adopted recently at her suggestion because it was reputed to enhance intimacy, or so it said in one of her women's magazines. Once she gave up droning on and on about the new book she was working on and came up for, he gave her hand a gentle squeeze to let her know that he, too, had something to share.

"Hon, you know the old black guy down the block who walks his dog to the park every day?" he said.

"Sure," was her somewhat disinterested reply. "Didn't I see a moving truck parked in front of their house today?"

"So you know, then."

"Know what?" she said. "That they're moving? Why else a moving van? People on this block lately are always moving in and out." A pause, then: "Preston, is that what's bothering you tonight? I could have gathered as much. Another case of the old moving in and out blues?"

"Maybe," he said. "But I wouldn't go so far as to call it the *blues* so much as a pang of regret over losing a friend."

"A friend?" she said with a laugh. "A friend like *that old black guy who walks his dog to the park every day*? Honey, ten to one says you don't even know his name." She paused. When he failed to reply, she added: "I'm right, aren't I? Come on, fess up. You don't know his name, do you?"

"Not really," he said.

"Well, my love, I don't know about you. But when I don't know someone's name, I sure as hell don't presume to call them my friend," she said in that sassy, no-nonsense, bantering mode of hers that kind of turned him on.

"Not really my friend? And who, pray tell, has vested you with the authority to determine who is and is not my friend?" he said.

"In case you haven't noticed it, buster, nature has gifted me with all kinds of authoritative powers," she said in mock reproach, "but since you choose to press the issue, *friends*, as I understand the word, are the people one cares enough about to invite into one's home, to whom one refers to by first name or a nickname, instead of *that old black guy*. It seems to me that if this man *were* your friend, you wouldn't have been surprised to learn he was moving. You'd have been Johnny-on-the-spot, with your sleeves rolled up, helping him load that truck. Or, at the very least, offering to do so, like the way Ritchie is always over here helping you out."

"Okay, okay, enough already," he said, in hasty retreat. "Okay, so I overstated our relationship a little bit. But the man *is* leaving and I stopped to say goodbye. Granted, I don't know his name. Nevertheless, I still maintain the right to refer to him as my friend. Certainly, he's not my enemy. How else would you have me refer to him? *Acquaintance*, perhaps? Or maybe *that elderly black gentleman down the street*?"

By now, she had risen on her elbow, her face close enough for him to rejoice in the ebb and flow of minty toothpaste breath, close enough for a nose upon nose Eskimo kiss, close enough for a man to entertain the thought that what was happening here just might be a prelude to having sex, close enough to set him to wondering if maybe he ought to go re-brush his teeth and sweeten his breath.

"But, honey," she said in an offhanded way that made it plain that making love was not what she had in mind. "You're breaking my heart here. You're like the proverbial overly friendly puppy who considers every stranger a friend. How can this be, I used to ask myself, that a man who considers himself Mr. Light and Lively, insists on presenting himself to the outside world much as he bamboozles it into buying products it really doesn't want to buy? Preston, the fact that you are otherwise very precise in thought and speech, and rarely given to hyperbole, is one of the things I most admire about you. Yet I'm finding it kind of scary when you insist on telling me that people you barely know are your friends. Have you been in advertising so long that truth and illusion are now melded into one?"

He didn't bother to reply. *Truth and illusion melded into one?* He'd been down this road with her too many times. No doubt about it, when it came to exercising the fundamentals of bantering logic, she always cut him to shreds. Besides, she'd dropped her head back onto her pillow. He felt her hand squeeze his.

"Hon?" she said.

"Ummm," he said.

"When you were little, did you have imaginary friends?"

"No, certainly not. Did you?"

"Sure. Betty. Betty Goldberg."

He laughed. "Yeah, Betty Goldberg. But wasn't she one of your dollies when you were a kid?"

"Yeah, but before her baby doll incarnation, Betty G. was my imaginary friend."

"Weird," he said. "And what's up with that. A little shiksa like you coming up with a name like Goldberg?"

And now they were laughing. Laughing together. And maybe that magazine was right. It felt good lying close together, not sparring, jousting, or bantering. One could almost say that sharing a laugh in bed together with your mate was almost as much fun as actual sex—and given nearly thirty years of marriage, ever so much more spontaneous.

"I have no idea where," she said, pausing to take in a deep breath. "I must have picked the name up somewhere. But the point is, Preston, I outgrew my dolls. There are no phantom Betty Goldbergs clamoring to be a part of my life anymore."

"Meaning?" he said.

"Meaning, you big lox, you should get out more. Your social life, such as it is, consists mostly of the little interior dialogues you carry on within yourself. If you're not at work, you're moping around here. Why not hang out one of these nights with Ritchie at the Bait and Tackle? A little male bonding, as it were, might be just the thing. You know, whoop it up, trade dirty jokes with the boys, play pool, ogle women, and smoke smelly cigars. Then, when one of your *buddies* moves away, you'll have earned your tears."

"Aw, you know how I hate that barroom stuff," he said. "All reformed drunks hate bars. And in case you don't know, watching others consume alcohol's not my idea of a spectator sport. If anything, my dear, I should think you'd be counting your lucky stars your teetotaler husband prefers being home with his wife."

"Well, honey, what I think is that you have a wife who wants you to be a better person than you are, who wishes you'd stop obsessing about the minutiae of the goddamned universe and get out and enjoy yourself." Then, having maneuvered herself into sleeping position, the evening slid to a close with her muttering "gudnigh" from the depths of her pillow.

"Goodnight," he said, awed by her ability to fall immediately asleep, leaving him to lie there fully awake, pondering the lack of passion in their marriage. What once was a raging torrent was now a meandering river of sandbars and horseshoe bends. Which is not to say that they never had sex. It was getting the ball rolling, the foreplay to the foreplay, as it were, that was the rub. Still, if it was true what a wag once said, that *a marriage is over when the wife stops giving her husband correctional instruction*, by that measure, his must be in great shape—stupendous, in fact. Was he neurotic? Sure. Why not? It was a Jew who invented neurosis. Before Dr. Freud's questionable insights into the human psyche muddied the waters, ordinary people had ordinary problems. Anyway, at this late date, Preston Stoner's wife wanted him to be a better person than he was? Well, good luck with that. As for having friends, real friends in his life, next-door-neighbor-friends like the folksy sort back in his Nebraska or her Wisconsin. Well, those sorts of relationships were few and far between in a place like

New York City. Mighty cities spawn larger-than-life characters. Especially, Red Hook, as it was back in '84, when they'd first arrived. Their next-door neighbor, Virginia, with her Betty Boop tattoo, whose main claim to fame was seeing the face of our Lord in the clouds one day while hanging laundry in the backyard. Virginia, who had her husband chop down the small tree the city had just planted in front of their house, driven by the foolish assumption that the future shade it cast would encourage others to park in *their* parking space.

And who could forget Angelo and his infamous trio of junkyard GTO muscle cars that sometimes ran but rarely started? Each one stuffed to the max with old tires and less identifiable junk. The way he'd appear, regular as clockwork on alternate parking days, knocking at the door, pleading for help pushing one or another of them to the correct side of the street. "The dead car shuffle," as Ritchie used to call it. And who could forget the night Ritchie snuck out and tagged those cars. AN … GE … LO—two letters apiece, spray-painted onto each passenger-side door. Ritchie saying: "We'll know if Angelo knows how to spell or not if he ever gets them lined up in the right order again." And, sure enough, old Angelo never did.

Where are they now, the Rainbow crowd? Oscar and Willie, Edna, Crazy Mary and Hughie, with a beer belly like he was nine months pregnant, with a weakness for teenage whores? Dead or moved away. Other than the Sarge, only Ritchie remained, living in a house previously owned by his aunt. Ritchie who'd been spared a life of shirt-and-tieing to Manhattan every day because his glassed-in place of employment was perched seven stories high atop a crane on Pier Ten, wrangling containers onto or off whatever ship happened to be in. A homespun philosopher in his middle forties, artist and ardent windsurfer to boot, with curly brown hair and cleft chin, who expressed his thrill for the wild side by windsurfing close-ass to the wind at Plum Beach, who wore a red-starred Mao cap whenever he went to the Bait and Tackle because, so he said: "the babes go nuts over it."

Still, no doubt about it, when it came to the stuff from which legends were made, the Sarge had them all beat hands down. That night just after he and Joellen and the kids had moved to the Hook. It was the dead of winter and he and his teenage son, Roger, had been returning home from Atlantic Avenue with Middle Eastern takeout after a hard day of humping

9

sheetrock. The streets already dark and pretty much deserted, and lo and behold, there's this guy sprawled drunk as a skunk in the intersection of Pioneer and Van Brunt. Shit, a guy couldn't just drive on home with some poor son-of-a-bitch passed out cold in the middle of the street, so he'd told Roger to hang tight, stopped the car and got out.

Preston closed his eyes and smiled at how scared shitless he'd been at the time, thinking for sure what they had here was the end result of some sort of gangland rubout. And how relieved he'd been when he got close enough to realize it was just some drunk. So relieved, in fact, that he'd nudged the poor bastard with his foot in a vain attempt to get him to sit up. And when that didn't work, somehow, with Roger's help, they'd managed to get a man with ragdoll limbs up and swaying on his feet, except then only to have this guy's befuddled circuitry suddenly jolt awake, as he began making like Muhammad Ali on his toes, shadowboxing jabs and flailing uppercuts left and right, against an unseen opponent only he could perceive out there in the middle of fucking Van Brunt Street.

Preston chuckled, rolled over and spooned up next to his wife, his arm draped across that delicious notch where a woman's torso conjoined her heart-shaped derriere. No way in hell he'd wanted to get mixed up in craziness like that, so he and Roger had beat a hasty retreat via Richards Street. And, once home, when he'd placed a call to the Seven Six Precinct, to report a man off his rocker in the middle of Van Brunt Street, there'd been the desk sergeant's unforgettable reply: "Don't worry about it, sir. Ole Sarge's been way overdue to go off on us one of these nights. You did the right thing to leave him be. Don't worry, we'll have a car over there in no time to escort him to our drunk tank."

***

The next morning, Preston gave the old man's now-vacant house hardly a glance as he hurried to the bus stop. Because his firm had blown a few big accounts recently, not to mention the Snapple Super Bowl spot that his boss had put him in charge of, up for review by the client in a matter of weeks, it was only natural for his mind to be in an adman's version of lock and load—and would stay that way most of the day. However, returning that night, exhausted and disgruntled from yet another day spent matching wits with the clueless suits upstairs, this time as he passed the old man's house, he not only gave a glance, but did an immediate double take and stopped to check, wondering if that really had been the snout of dog he'd seen thrust between the slats of a drawn-shut venetian blind.

Sure enough, when a telltale crimp between two of the bottom-most slats suggested he might have seen what he thought he'd seen, Preston smiled as he mounted the stoop, thinking of a guy he once knew, a with sign on his front door that said: "Knock to Activate Dog."

The dog, if it was a dog, responded immediately. Nary a bark, yelp, whine, or whimper, just the clicking of toenails and a heavy thump against the door. And if that had been Hairy, Preston's dog from childhood, locked up in an empty house, it would be going absolutely nuts. But then again, he recalled reading somewhere, the old man's mutt carried a lot of greyhound in it and greyhounds were mainly a silent breed.

"Deh wen' away," a voice behind him said.

Preston knew without turning who it was, the Sarge, the only person in the neighborhood who slurred their words drunk or sober.

"Deh wen' away. Deh gae me a swader."

Preston turned around and grinned. The Sarge had the lapel of his beat-up old army fatigue jacket peeled back. The "swader" in question was a beaut—a real bumblebee of a sweater, broad stripes alternating yellow and black—without doubt, the single-most out-loud and proud article of clothing he'd ever seen the Sarge wear.

"Da dog iz'n da auwzz. Mi'dred iz'n da auwzz."

"Mildred? You know the dog's name?"

"Day tow me," the Sarge said.

"Well, it looks like somebody forgot to take Mildred with them, Sarge. You figure it's hungry? They say anything about someone coming for it?"

The Sarge shook his head. "Iz my dog. Day gay id tuh mai. Iz'n da howz."

Preston sat down on the stoop. It had been a cloudy, breezy day; hence, Pioneer Street was awash with blown trash. The temperature held steady at a chilly fifty-two degrees, and this was what Preston knew about the Sarge: Brooklyn born, Puerto Rican bred, family name Figueroa. According to Ritchie, the Sarge had been a real sweetheart of a man; drafted during Vietnam but earned his stripes in Germany instead. That was, until returning to base one dark and drunken *brathaus* night, he wrecked his jeep, scrambled his brains, and the Army mustered him out as damaged goods.

The Sarge was his usual raggedy-bearded mess: broad-nosed, bull-necked, lantern-jawed, unwashed. Shoulders hunched, unsteady on his feet, hands thrust into the side pockets of his jacket, with deep-socketed eyes that reminded Preston of photos taken of shell-shocked survivors of the Battle of the Bulge. And the pity was, this desperately dirty, mongrel man, somehow now had it in mind, that the dog inside this house was his.

"So, how's things these days with you, Sarge, now it's turning cold? You got enough blankets in that van of yours to keep you warm? Speak up if there's something I can do for you."

"Aym, okay-ee," he said.

"How about work? Been getting any lately?" Preston asked, fully aware the Sarge had spent most of the week hauling rubble out of a basement for a local scumbag contractor.

"Ay wukked som ta-dai."

"The whole day? You mean, over on Dikeman Street?"

The Sarge nodded.

"How much for a whole day?"

The Sarge flashed ten fingers twice and grinned. "Ah lot," he said.

Well, twenty bucks cash explained the Sarge reeking to high heaven of cheap booze. Preston didn't have the heart to tell the poor man he was being taken advantage of. A man his size and strength, anger and booze were a highly volatile mix. It certainly wouldn't do him any favors to rile him up. Besides, old Sarge had about him a kind of working man's swagger to his stagger tonight. Why take it away from him?

"How much of that twenty you got left?"

"Ah gun," the Sarge announced with glee, as if penury were something every man should strive for.

Preston fished his wallet for five singles, pissed off as hell because he knew that son-of-a-bitch Carnovsky paid his Mexican illegal's at least fifty a day. "Here, get yourself some coffee and a slice. Drop by next Saturday morning if you want. I plan on trimming the ivy on the front of the house, and you can give me a hand. But don't you be showing up drunk. Understand?"

Understand? The Sarge snapped to attention and flashed Preston a crisp salute, to which Preston felt obliged to reply with an answering salute in the diffident manner of emperors or five-star generals. That damn dog had already spent one night alone. Another wouldn't hurt. However, come morning, if no one had come to get it, Preston was fully resolved to step in and call the SPCA. As for the Sarge, although whatever he managed to do for him would always be too little, too late, at least he'd done something. To the rest of the world, maybe the Sarge was just another faceless bum. But he was still a man and deserved to be treated as one.

2

Beatrice, Nebraska, Summer 1952

The boy, soon to be five years old, was short for his age. He stood barefoot on tiptoe, peering over the edge of the kitchen table as his tall and slender mother spread mayonnaise on two slices of bread. Though barely past nine in the morning, beads of sweat stood out on his brow and upper lip. According to his mother, today was doomed to be beastly hot, which suited him fine, because this morning when he'd dressed himself in khaki shorts, she'd told him to forget about his underpants.

"Remember now, Preston, this sandwich is not for you," his mother said, pretty much dressed for the heat herself: sunflower print housedress, penny loafers without ankle socks, with a yellow Aunt Jemima bandanna worn loosely about her head.

"Then who, Mama?" he asked as he usually did most mornings.

"Go on now, Preston—away with your silly questions. You know full well this sandwich is for them that doesn't have it as easy as you, who come around to people's backdoors looking for handouts."

Sure, he knew that and a bunch of other things. Just like his mother, he, too, sported freckles sprinkled across the bridge of his nose. And by gum, he'd watched her do this routine so many times now, if she was ever got sick or something, he could do the whole shebang, hands tied behind his back. Spread mayonnaise on the bread, layer on a couple of slices of baloney, flop on a couple of leaves of lettuce freshly picked from the garden, cut it in half and wrap it in wax paper. And best of all, if nobody showed up to claim the sandwich today, his mother'd save it overnight in the icebox so he could have it for breakfast the next day.

"Where do the men come from, Mama?" he asked, which was another question he usually asked.

"They're just poor men down on their luck," she answered, same as every time. "Men who don't have a home and a nice bed to sleep in like you do, Preston."

The boy, of course, knew exactly the sort of men she was talking about because hadn't his father explained to him one time that whenever his mother seemed to be thinking about something else, she was probably thinking of her brother Jack, who'd passed on during something grown-ups called the Great Depression, when lots and lots of men were riding trains, his Uncle Jack one of them, wandering the country from soup line to soup line, willing to do most anything to hold body and soul together. "A regular Huck Finn he was, your Uncle Jack," his father had said. "Another unfortunate soul undone by the madness of Wall Street." Wherever or whatever this "Wall Street" was, the boy was pretty darn sure it was nowhere near Beatrice. Anyway, now that his mother was done making the sandwich, instead of waiting around to see if one those men showed up, she'd gone into the dining room to jaw on the telephone with his Aunt Lorraine.

Thinking someone ought to be on hand to answer the door, in case one of those men showed up, the boy hurried upstairs to fetch his box of clothespin soldiers his Uncle Otis had made for him so that he could play war with them while standing guard on the throw rug next to the back-porch screen door. Only this morning, maybe he'd switch things around a bit. Let Mr. Funny-Faced Potato Head be the general of the Blue Army and so that the General of the Red Army could be that ornery old stuffed monkey doll of his that his Aunt Lorraine insisted on calling J. Fred Muggs after that funny, crazy chimp she watched mornings on the Dave Garraway television show. His mother, of course, wasn't all that crazy about TV. They kept theirs in the living room and she didn't let him watch it much. Claimed it "stunted young people's minds"—whatever in the heck that was supposed to mean.

The thing was, his mother liked rules. Lots of rules. Like last night when he went to bed. "You're a big boy now, Preston," she'd said. "Big enough to stand up proper-like when strangers come calling. No more shilly-shallying around. Answer up, 'Preston Stoner, sir' or 'ma'am,' when someone asks you your name. Say it loud and proud because your father is the editor and publisher of the *Beatrice Courier-Eagle*, same as your Grandpa Peshe was before him."

But the best thing was, his mother liked to show him things. Like the time she took him out to the telephone pole in the alley to show him the secret mark one of those wandering men carved into their utility pole to let his buddies know the people who lived in this house were okay. "Used a penknife to do it, Preston, most likely just like the one your Uncle Otis has," she'd told him that day.

And if one of those men did show up today, he sure hoped he wouldn't be like the man, a week or so back, with bristly whiskers and stinky breath. His mother had called him "ripe" after he ate his sandwich and went away, which his mother told him, the time he'd asked, was a nice way of saying someone needed a bath.

Still, the single best thing about these men who came to the door was that they rode trains. Both he and his father were crazy nuts about trains. Shoot, back when he'd been just a little baby learning to talk, according to his mother, the first words he put together that made any sense were: "Choo choo train, caboose out back."

And his father knew a heck of a lot of stuff about trains. Diesel locomotives ran on fuel oil and steam locomotives on coal. Passenger trains were for people who bought tickets, freight trains were for everything including the kitchen sink. Thanks to his father, his boy could identify on sight as they rolled by: cattle cars, refrigerator cars, flatcars, tank cars, gondola cars, hopper cars, cabooses and boxcars. Beatrice, his father said, was extra special because it was something called a "division point" on the Burlington Line. Which meant, sometimes when the weather was good, he and his father would take his mother out for ice cream, and they were able to enjoy their cones parked on a bluff overlooking something railroad men called a "hump yard," meaning the place where freight cars got pushed by little switch engines up and over a little hill to coast free downhill all by themselves to form up new trains.

Other times, his father took them out to someplace in the middle of God-knows-where, to count freight cars as they passed—which was the reason his mother said, her son could already count way past a hundred even if he was only four. And sometimes, they'd be sitting there way after dark, and an open-door boxcar would pass with some men in it, and all you'd see was the glow of their cigarettes. "Like a bunch a darn fireflies," his mother said. And once, when he asked his father why so few of the men he waved at, waved at him, his father had said: "They can't, son, because they are sad ambassadors from a fallen kingdom who no longer care to abide with fancy protocols."

And the boy liked it so much when his father talked to him using highfalutin, grown-up words, even when he wasn't exactly sure what they meant, and sometimes when he'd ask, his father would laugh and wink and say something like, "*Protocol*'s a very powerful, magic word, son. Kinda like *presto chango* or *alakazam*. *Protocol* is a fool's way of setting up rules for mankind to get somewhere."

As if his son didn't already know all about the best way of getting somewhere. Riding boxcars eating baloney sandwiches was the best way of getting somewhere; and uh oh, looks like his mother just hung up the telephone, so she'll be after him to get Hairy and go outside and do something better than fool around with those clothespins. Which was fine with him, long as he was close enough around to greet the men.

Anyway, one thing for sure, that dog of theirs loves nothing better than going outside. His mother had been none too happy with his father the day he brought Hairy home. But his father had quieted her down really quickly, telling her: "Every boy needs a best friend." And good old Hairy was not only his friend, they were pals. "Just for fun," his father had said, "we'll name this feisty little mutt after that little haberdasher from Independence, Missouri, Harry S. Truman, the President of the United States, who really stuck it to the unions this spring by nationalizing the steel mills, all because of that war in Korea he's got us involved in that nobody can win."

According to his father, *haberdasher* wasn't a magic word at all. Just someone who sold menswear like hats, ties, shirts and belts. And *feisty* was someone "real hard to get along with … like your mother sometimes," his father said with a funny laugh like it was a joke that really wasn't a joke because his mother didn't laugh, and it wasn't long after that their little boy was leaving the room with his hands over his ears because his mother and father had taken to spatting again.

Anyway, the problem his mother had with Hairy was that she was a "farm girl" who didn't hold much with having them inside the house on account of them being "smelly" and "shedding" and stuff like that. Especially when the man of the house, who should have known better, brought one home suffering from something called "the mange."

One thing about dogs, they sure don't like thunderstorms. Like the other day, it was raining "buckets" and the wind blowing so hard he and his mother and Hairy had to go hide out in the storm cellar. That dog had been scared as all get out, his mother not at all, and he not so much. The main thing was, the sand in the sandbox today, after receiving a real soaking, more than likely would be just the right kind of wet for making mountains and digging tunnels today. Of course, he'd have to keep one eye peeled in case one of those men showed up looking for a sandwich. Hairy loved to chase strangers more than he did Ted Tailor's chickens. So, before taking it outside, he better give that dog a good talking to. Draw himself up, chest puffed out, hands on his hips the way his mother did when she got all business with him. Tell that dern dog to "wipe that silly grin off your face, mister" and "don't be getting any funny ideas about taking off after strangers, else you'll find yourself going straight back inside that house."

3

Brooklyn Heights, 1984

Preston was walking down Court Street on his way home from the dentist when he decided, just for the fun of it, that now was as good a time as any to stop in at a real estate office. It wasn't until the real estate agent inquired, "what size of an apartment are you interested in, Mr. Stoner? One bedroom? Two? Three?" that it occurred to him that he might be getting ahead of himself, inquiring about apartments absent the presence of his wife. After all, they had nine months left before the current lease was up. Plus, their landlord had already made it clear for them not to sweat it, that he'd be willing to cut them slack if they ran into trouble finding something else. Not that their landlord was a good guy, because the capitalist bastard was evicting them after all, via some legal loophole dredged up by some shyster lawyer on Court Street that allowed him to convert their apartment on Atlantic Avenue into two studio apartments and, in so doing, doubling, tripling—hell's bells, maybe even quadrupling—his take.

"Well, we have two kids. A boy and a girl," Preston replied with the hesitant certainty of a man recently informed by his dentist that unless he started taking better care of his teeth, he'd be a leading candidate for a mess of root canals, "so I guess we'd need three. We'd prefer to stay in the Heights."

"Who wouldn't," laughed the agent as she proceeded to rattle off several apartments with rents sufficiently high enough to take one's breath away. "When it comes to rental units, Brooklyn Heights is not for the faint of heart."

"Tell me about it," he said.

"Have you considered buying? A co-op, condo … a house?"

"Nnnnn … not really."

"Well, keep in mind, if you're willing to look outside the Heights, there are some real bargains around."

"Like where, for instance?"

"Like Red Hook," she said. "We just got a new listing down there—a whole house for only thirty-four-thousand dollars. I'm about to go see it. Probably needs a ton of work, but it's worth a look. Wanna come along?"

Come along? Worth a look? Red Hook? Was she kidding? A house in Brooklyn, in 1984, for thirty-four-thousand dollars?

"Think about it. If it's anything at all, location aside, it may turn out to be a bargain at twice the price. Who knows, Mr. Stoner, this could be your lucky day."

Lucky day? After two hours spent at the dentist, for Christ's sake. What the fuck? Does Novocain affect the brain? Everyone in Brooklyn knew *where* and *what* Red Hook was—drug-ridden, blighted, neglected, forgotten, isolated—but *no one* ever *went* there. Still, a house for thirty-four-thousand buckaroos! What the hell? Nothing ventured, nothing gained. What was there to be afraid of? A forty- to forty-five-year-old Brooklyn bagel baby real estate agent who drove a Lincoln Town Car? With wild and frizzy, salt-and-pepper hair bushed like a dandelion gone to seed? A Star of David pendant that nestled in her cleavage like a Witch of Endor on the prowl? Hell yes, he'd say yes. We're talking thirty-four-thousand dollars here.

Atlantic Avenue, right on Columbia, left on Hamilton, another quick left onto Van Brunt Street, then left again onto Pioneer, it was a quick ten-minute ride to a world wholly apart from the posh opulence of the Heights. The house in question proved to be one of many tired little brick row houses lining each side of a tired little street whose signature feature was a solitary, exceptionally gnarly but stately London planetree.

The agent seemed of similar mind. "Granted, it's a bit of a fixer-upper," she said somewhat wistfully, as they sat in her car for a moment, neither of them all that eager to disembark, "but please keep in mind. Considering it's the middle of the day, there are parking spaces everywhere, and I ask you, how many New Yorkers get to park right in front of their house anytime they want? And remember, when we go inside, houses of similar size in Brooklyn Heights currently go two million plus," she said, rubbing her thumb and forefingers together in the time-honored wise of they who paid honor to the bottom line.

Inside, Preston mustered his best poker face, lest he offend the Puerto Rican family who seemed quite proud, as they showed him around the dump they called home. So far, the only thing that sustained his interest was the asking price. Thirty-four-thousand dollars was thirty-four-thousand dollars. And the monthlies on a thirty-four-thousand dollar mortgage would be *considerably less* than what he was currently shelling out for rent! Hence, less than thirty-four minutes after he stopped into a real estate office on a whim, Preston Stoner uttered these fatal words: "My wife will have to see it first, of course, but as far as I'm concerned, we'll take it."

He declined the agent's offer of a lift back to Atlantic Avenue, saying he wanted to time the bus ride back to civilization. Exactly twelve, uneventful minutes later, he was upstairs in his apartment, brewing a pot of tea— chamomile tea, to be exact. Suitable, he hoped, for calming the churning stomach, racing heart, and whirling mind. Were this thing to happen— and for some as yet unknown reason he wanted it to happen—he needed to be at the top of his game, prepared for each and every one of those unanswerable, loaded questions his wife was bound to ask she when got home, for which he had no ready answers.

Are you nuts? You want to take our family to Red Hook? Well, he wasn't nuts. But Red Hook? Infamous in fiction as the *Last Exit to Brooklyn*? Rendered soulfully on stage in *A View from the Bridge*? The area just south of the Brooklyn Battery Tunnel, separated from Governor's Island by the quirky currents of Buttermilk Channel? The place where if you climbed to the top of the Statue of Liberty and trained your binoculars eastward, you'd be gazing at a burned-out, derelict pier at the foot of Coffey Street? A place too often singled out in the press as a Mafia playground? Yet there was truly something about the place that made him want to live there.

He had no more taken his cup of tea into the living room and sat down on the couch to sort things out, when shit, he heard her key rattle in the lock. All right. This was it. Don't panic. Act natural. Carpe diem. The guys at work claim you're at your best when you're winging it. "Hey, hon," he called, "there's a fresh pot of tea under the cozy on the table. Grab a cup, and come on in. I've got something really exciting to share with you."

"Thank you, dear … you've made tea. How thoughtful," she called back.

The rustle of things being removed from a paper bag. A fridge door that opened and closed, opened and closed. Finally, there she was, entering the room, cup in hand. He patted the cushion next to him for her to sit down.

"Well?" she said with a thank-you smile that inferred she'd prefer to stand.

"Well, what?" he said with the cheery aplomb of a man accustomed to wooing clients with bullshit artifice.

"That something *really exciting* you purport to have to share with me."

He grinned and gave the cushion another pat.

She perched herself on the arm of the sofa instead.

"Preston, what is it this time? Come on, out with it. What have you been up to?"

"You're not going to believe it."

"Try me," she said, eyebrows arched as she sipped her tea.

"Well, I know I should have talked it over with you first, but … well … today, after my dental appointment with Rosen, on impulse, thinking how we were going to be moving soon, I stopped in at that little real estate office on Court Street—you know the one a couple of doors down from Queen Pizza—and like I said, I know I should have waited for you, except it just seemed the thing to do at the time, go with a real estate agent to look at a house in Red Hook."

She studied him for a moment. Took another sip of tea. "And?" she said.

"And what?"

"Well, for starters, what's this house of yours look like?"

He took a deep breath. He licked his lips. His wife was a formidable five foot two, with eyes of blue and the Mona Lisa smile of a world-champion poker player. "Well, for starters, while the owners claim they've renovated it … to put it mildly, let's just say their choices wouldn't have been ours." He paused for her reaction. Seeing none, he soldiered on.

"There's no getting around it, dear, the house is going to be a lot of work," he said as if he knew what he was talking about, which he did not. "Right now, I'm looking at it as a fail-safe investment," he said with an assumed air of punditry, as if economics was also among his areas of expertise. "Add the cost of the renovation to the purchase price, factor in the inevitable rise in the price of real estate, if we don't like it, in just a few years we flip it and still come out way ahead." A dramatic pause, then he added, "We can go see it now if you'd like."

She reacted by leaving the room without saying a word. Then returned with her jacket in hand. "Okay," she said.

A call to the real estate agent and half an hour later, Preston was once more touring the house, only this time he was seeing it through his wife's eyes. The full bathroom, which should have been upstairs, convenient to all bedrooms, was foolishly located adjacent to the kitchen, one flight down. The master bedroom, if one could call it that, was accessible only by trooping through two smaller bedrooms. Closets, such as they were, too few and so tiny as to be nearly nonexistent. The walls throughout clad with el cheapo imitation-wood paneling. A stairway worthy of a haunted house: creaky steps, missing spindles and wobbly newel posts. Outlets too few and oddly sited. The plumbing quaintly antique and God knows if any of it was up to code.

Joellen withheld comment to the end. It wasn't until they were standing alone on the dingy wall-to-wall gold acrylic shag rug that carpeted the living room floor that she dared to whisper in his ear.

"Jesus, this place is a disaster."

"Don't worry," he whispered back. "Jesus says to get us a dumpster, redo it our way, and it'll be a gem."

But who was kidding whom here? Just as Preston expected, Joellen remained silent all the way back to Atlantic Avenue. Which was fine with him. He'd expected this to be a hard sell, that she wouldn't be able to fall crazy in love with the little house on Pioneer Street the way he had, that it was asking a lot for her to be able to embrace Red Hook for the diamond-in-the-rough he believed it to be, for her to appreciate as he did that its total lack of big-city hustle and bustle spoke of an era before traffic lights and parking meters, when utility lines were—as Red Hook's still were, as his hometown of Beatrice, Nebraska's still were—strung on poles, not buried underground.

The moment they entered their apartment, even before he could open his mouth to go into his spiel, she silenced him by showing him the hand.

23

"Preston, please. I'm well aware you've got your mind made up about us buying that old house, but … I don't know … buying an old house, after all, is not like buying a used car. It's something at least *one* of us seriously needs to think through," and, so saying, she disappeared into to the living room.

Beyond doubt, the little lady was right. One of them needed to think seriously about what was going on here. But was it his fault he was one of those guys who knew a good buy when they saw one? Consequently, here he was, the eternal husband, once again sitting on his thumbs while his wife indulged herself in her seriously-thinking thing. At first, he tried busying himself by having a go at the crossword puzzle in the *New York Times* that she'd partially filled in on the subway, only to become quickly discouraged when he discovered all the easier answers already filled in.

He had just finished sorting the day's mail and was about to fetch his checkbook and pay some bills when he heard Roger and Bunny, home from school, raising a ruckus up the hallway stairs. When he rose to let them in, he caught a glimpse of Joellen beating a hasty retreat into their bedroom—where, he knew from experience, she would, ostensibly, remain cloistered until suppertime—and since tonight was his turn to cook pasta, he might as well get started on the meatballs.

***

Conversation at the table that evening remained normal in every way. Joellen spoke of her day, and he spoke of his without once bringing up the house. The kids, of course, were their usual dopey selves. His super-serious, always-trying-to-get-to-the-bottom-of-things son, Roger, wondered aloud if medieval scholars had ever debated the number of angels that could dance on the head of a pin if their mouths were full of spaghetti and meatballs. His extremely inventive daughter, Bunny, a picky eater at best, managed to embellish the reason for the fresh Band-Aid on her knee into a hilariously droll saga.

When, at last, the kids had been excused to eat ice cream in front of the TV in the living room, left sitting there face-to-face with his wife, he was fully resolved she should be the first to speak. Should her verdict turn out to be "no" or even "I'm not sure," his next best, and probably last-gasp move, would be to plead his case to her on bended knee that every man should have at least one shot in life at shaping his abode with his own two hands. But the sound of her spoon scrapping the sides her ice cream bowl was driving him mad. He could wait no longer. "Well?" he said.

She answered with a smile. "Okay, Preston, relax. I'm willing to trust you on this one. I'm assuming you know what you are doing, but let's get one thing clear. I suppose you're going to want to try your hand at playing plumber, electrician, and carpenter, so knock yourself out. But I want things done as I want them. I want you to promise if I don't like the way something is done, you'll bust your ass to get it right."

"Of course, hon, you know I will," he said, perhaps a little too eagerly. But what the hell? He'd been fully expecting her to say no.

"What I know, Preston, is that left to your own devices, you'd hurry your work and settle for less than the best. So even if you have to do it over and over or, if needs be, hire a professional to get it done, you'll do it, because that's the way I want our house to look: professional. If you intend to subject this family to living several years amid chaos, the end product must be something of which we can be proud. Do you understand?" she said to him like the stern school marm she was not, hesitated, and then broke into a laugh. "What the hell? Who knows? It might be a fun project at that, dragging a creaky old nineteenth-century, beat-up house kicking and screaming into the twentieth century."

4

Beatrice, Nebraska, Early July 1952

Hugh Moody squinted into the glare of the late afternoon sun, searching the horizon for a row of grain elevators. Years ago, when he was a lad, his mother often teased him that his legs surely went on forever. If so, uncoiling his gnarly six-foot-three frame across the open door of a boxcar was a particularly welcoming place to stretch them.

Though he rarely traveled with a set destination in mind or, for that matter, particularly cared where he happened to be in space and time. The purpose of this trip was to fulfill a promise he'd made. He'd been just another draft dodger doing seven years of hard time in Leavenworth for refusing to do service during World War II when news reached him that his sixty-seven-year-old mother had wasted away in a poorhouse on the outskirts of Lima, Ohio, and he'd resolved then and there, that as soon as he got out, to go lay one nice red rose on the grave of the blessed little lady who brought him into an unjust and sorely troubled world.

Of course, it had to have been mid-February when they let him out. And since the idea of grieving midwinter over his mother's grave with a frostbitten rose in his hand had little appeal to him, telling himself that his mother would understand, he'd headed southwest to warm his bones for the duration of the winter in Baja, California, instead. In fact, it wasn't until mid-June that he was able to tear himself away.

Moody rose to his feet, his hands latched tightly onto the doorframe. Lima, Ohio, remained a good day's train ride away. Not far up ahead was Beatrice, Nebraska. But seeing as he was a mite strapped for cash, his mother would also understand the need of a little stopover for a day or two in Beatrice. A few odd jobs here until he had a few bucks in his pocket, and he'd be on his way. "Rich or poor," as she loved to say, "it's nice to have money."

The train he was on, which had traveled the night from central Colorado to the southeastern tip of Nebraska in one haul, was gradually losing speed. Furthermore, running parallel to the left of the tracks was a dense hedgerow of Osage orange that a guy back in Boulder had told him to be on the lookout for. So somewhere up ahead had to be Johnson's Crick, where hobo folk interested in visiting Beatrice were known to congregate. Because a night spent among smelly men was better by far than riding a train clear into the yards in the full light of day, getting jumped by a gang of railroad bulls, and ending up hungry and sore in the city jail, Moody exited the boxcar, shirttails flying. His jacket secured tightly around his waist. Kid bag clutched under his left arm, as his boots scrabbled the ballast for traction. Best of all worlds, he'd make it through that gap up ahead in the hedge and be out of sight long before the tail end of the train passed by. These days, a man could never be too careful where and by whom he was seen—especially, when that man had already had enough run-ins with the law to last his lifetime.

Satisfied to make it through the gap unseen, surprised and tickled pink to find a shady swath of cool green grass bordering the field on the far side of the hedge, Moody hung his jacket on a nearby branch, stripped off his shirt and hung it up as well, then upended his kit bag as a place to sit down. Like a seaman fresh ashore, the motion of that damn train still echoed in his legs. His aim was to put off going into town 'til the next day. And since he figured to be within easy walking distance of that crick, being a farmer's son and all, he was right at home sitting beside this field, removing his boots and socks so his feet could say hello to Mother Earth. All them cornstalks lined up in ranks and files like soldiers standing at attention, plus those coyote tracks over there to the side, put him in mind of himself as a kid, pretending to be a Kiowa scout with a Stevens twenty-two caliber, bolt-action, single-shot rifle cradled in the crook of his arm, out to track those critters down.

Yes sir, fields such as this, spoke to him of many things. Some, he'd just as soon forget. Like the time he'd been thirteen and his brother seventeen, and they'd been out in the field planting corn together, when their grief-stricken mother came running out with the news that their father had finally up and killed his drunken self, ramming a pickup truck head-on into a cement culvert. Though barely a teenager, that was the moment, Moody figured, he grew up. Up 'til then, while times had been tough, they'd been getting by quite nicely, thank you, in spite of the Great Depression. But from that day on, despite them doing their best to keep things going, the bank ended up foreclosing on the farm in the end.

Moody sighed, gathered a glob of mucus from the back of his throat and spat it into the field. Thinking about leaving the farm and moving into Lima never failed to put a crimp in his day. The sadness of them days. Able-bodied men robbed of all hope, standing in bread lines. His poor mama barely able to make ends meet. Doing most everything from cleaning houses and emptying bedpans to taking in wash. Not that he and his brother hadn't pitched in and done their share to make life easier for them and her. He and his bike running paper routes in all kinds of weather. That damned barbershop where he'd shined shoes. And worst of all, that crap job he'd had sweeping out and emptying spittoons at the pool hall. And his older brother, Nate, digging ditches and laying sewers in the summer sun—not to mention the hours put in after school and on Saturdays helping out old Ed, the blacksmith.

Still, it had come as no surprise either to him or his mother, when the summer his brother turned eighteen, he would make good on his promise to start making something of himself by joining the Navy and seeing the world. And how proud they'd all been the day his brother called home with the news that he was just about the luckiest guy in the world because he just found out his battleship homeported in Hawaii. Then, shortly after December seventh, the telegram arrived to inform his mother that her honey-eyed son was among the misbegotten drowned below decks on the USS *Arizona*.

"Love thy neighbor, Hughie, even them slanty eyed little divils that kilt your brother," was another of Edwina Moody's jewels of wisdom she gifted to her one and only remaining son. "All I'm asking is for you not to get swept up in the rush to go to war. Yer country didn't give a shit fer you, yer brother or yer family in our time of need, so ya got every right not to give a shit fer it in return."

But did he listen? Not even after she pled with him in vain, telling him he was too wild by nature to suffer soldiering for long, that surely, being her only surviving son, them draft board people would give him a break. But just as his brother Nate, he was no more out of school than he was joining up with the Marines; he figured he was set for the brawl. Except, unlike Nate, he'd finished boot camp completely soured on warrioring. Not only that, he'd celebrated his newly won buck private's stripes by picking up some sweet young thing at the USO, who, it turned out, was more than willing to whisk him back to her La Jolla apartment after he'd let it be known that for the time being he was as free as the breeze to do as he pleased because he'd managed to wrangle himself some sort of super-secret, extended furlough.

But he sure had to hand it to those MPs. No more than a couple of weeks and they'd tracked him down and under escort put him aboard a troopship destined for the South Pacific. Only the Kiowa scout in him snowed them out, faking a case of the stomach flu before giving them the old slipperoo out a filling station bathroom window. From then on it had been touch and go until he made it to the hellholes of Tijuana. And, but for *Federales* latching onto him a few months later, on the outskirts of Guadalajara, by this time he'd have been speaking their lingo like a native. Naturally, those Mexican bastards gave him a beating he'd never forget before turning him in for the reward. And this time, the MPs made damn sure to keep him leg-ironed and handcuffed all the way to Leavenworth.

Moody searched out his war surplus canteen, tilted it up and drained it dry. If war be hell, seven years in Leavenworth was hell done up in spades. But one thing about dear old mother, she never gave up on him. "Don't let 'em get to you while you're in there," she'd written to him once she learned where he was and why. "Given yer tendency for going off half-cocked and settling things with yer fists, ya got to put time spent in there to good use taming down yer wild streak or yer gonna be miserable the rest of yer life."

And sure enough, he'd done what she'd said and exited that prison not quite the same man who went in. Whether that man was now a *better* man, he couldn't say. But one of the things about him that definitely had not been changed was a fondness for freshly picked roasting ears. And, unless he'd completely lost his eye for such things, that field arrayed before him consisted wholly of sweet corn, fit food for two-legged beasts, not fodder for cows or pigs.

Moody shoved his canteen back into his kit bag, took a few steps into the field, grabbed an ear and peeled back the husk. A half dozen of these babies would do for supper that night, and if by chance, a field of watermelons should lay betwixt here and Johnson's Crick, well, as his mother would say: "Hughie, my boy, now, yer fartin' through silk."

***

The field of watermelons failed to materialize. The hobo camp at Johnson's Creek—or Crick as the locals called it—was flanked by a sorghum field and a dense stand of cottonwood trees to the west, and a bunch of willow bushes and tall grasses to the south. A somewhat muddy path led from the tracks down a steep embankment to a simple sand flat. The crick itself was heavily burdened with silt and running full to its banks. Bent weeds and grasses testified to the fury of the same rainstorm Moody figured he'd spent traveling through during the night, though thankfully not so bad as to have flooded the camp out.

The camp was presently vacant, but strewn everywhere were the leavings of thoughtless men. Still, Moody'd seen far worse places to camp out for a night. The bare necessities were there. A bunch of stones that ringed a faintly smoldering campfire. An iron-bar spit jerry-rigged between a couple of forked sticks. An upturned orange crate for somewhere to sit, and there, off to the right, a cracked hand-mirror some vain soul had jammed into the fork of a scrub catalpa tree.

To avoid soiling his boots with mud, Moody coupled their laces together so he could horse-collar them around his neck. Twenty minutes, and he'd have this place shipshape. Seeing as he'd be walking barefoot, he needed to be on constant lookout for broken glass and rusty tin cans. A foot with an infected cut among all this filth could be as debilitating as a broken leg—and far worse should lockjaw set in.

Once down, the first thing this sadder but wiser son of alcoholic parenting did was to pick up an empty whiskey bottle in disgust and send it whizzing across the crick. He carried his poison of choice stashed in his kit bag: three Prince Albert tobacco tins full of el primo Baja marijuana.

Due to the heat of the day, he decided to strip down to his BVDs, thinking that once he'd finished tidying the camp, he'd treat his dirty, grimy self to a good pre-supper soak in that crick. After all, he wanted to be looking and smelling his best when he appeared in town the next day. Clean-shaven, boots shined, hair combed, shirt tucked into pants belted an acceptable height—securing meaningful work depended on things like that. And while he was at it, he might as well rinse out his shirt and pants as well. Spread 'em to dry on them bushes nearby like his mama claimed folks did in the west of Ireland back when she was kid. "Ah, sure, the sun and wind did all that needs to be done," she'd say in that County Galway brogue of hers.

As with most hard-traveling men, Moody was accustomed to the irregular satisfaction of bodily desires. Even so, during the time spent splashing around in the crick, his empty stomach kept growling that a decent meal hadn't passed its way since the day before the day before that. Not that a bounteous feast was in the offing that night. By any standards, pickings were slim. Still, two cans of sardines, a middling chunk of dry bread, plus the six ears of corn he'd already set soaking in the crick, topped off with a cup of coffee brewed and re-brewed to its weak and bitter end, would have to do.

By this time, the sun was little better than a ruddy half disk disappearing into the horizon. Every shade of orange and red flooded the western sky. Waiting for the corn to steam, it occurred to him that as long as the light held, he ought to scout around for a place to bunk up that night. Sure enough, beneath the bridge, completely untouched by yesterday's storm, was a dry area where a rumpled blanket lay atop a couple of flattened-out cardboard boxes spread out over a bed of reeds and dry grasses, with ample space for two or three should someone else show up.

He'd returned to the fire reminding himself to take care not to spill any of the oil opening those cans of sardines so it could be put to good use greasing up the corn and dunking his bread. Once he'd teased an ear from the coals. He peeled back the husk with eager fingers thinking that while this wasn't exactly farting through silk, at least his luck had held and he was enjoying it alone. Which wasn't to say he didn't appreciate the company of his fellow men, as much as his years in prison had left him wary of their stupid, violent ways. The sad truth was, those who normally frequented these camps, in spite of having nothing but time on their hands, gulped their food, chugged their booze and gambled what little money there was among them like the casino was about to close, never to open again.

Twenty feet above his head another train rattled by. In fact, it seemed this time of day, on this section of the Burlington Line, every thirty to forty minutes another train was always rattling by. Which Moody kind of enjoyed. All his life he'd been a sucker for the lonesome wail of the whistle and the rhythmic clacking of wheels. Unfortunately, he had little fondness for the men who crewed them. In the present scheme of things, hoboes had about as much use for trainmen as feral cats have for feral dogs.

Moody smiled. They were the wage slaves, as he, decidedly, wasn't. And now that he'd finished his pitiful repast, though he'd never been much for book learning when he was a kid—and if not for time spent in Leavenworth, he might never have developed a taste for the acquisition of knowledge at all—seeing as how he'd be bunking tonight alone, the time seemed right for stuffing his pipe full of Mexican gold and maybe having another go at *Little Blue Book*, number 159, *A Guide to Plato* by Will Durant, edited by E. Haldeman-Julius, available at every neighborhood newsstand, price: five cents.

But then again, he realized, he'd waited too long. No use ruining his eyesight trying to read in tweak light. He reached into his kit bag for his harmonica instead—or better said, his daddy's harmonica—which, as was also his wont, he'd play until the fire turned to embers and it was time to go down to the crick and do as the Indians once did: smear clay mud all over his body to keep the skeeters at bay—which, washed off the following morning, cleansed a man's body as surely as using soap.

The first tune he played was "Red River Valley." Next up was "Don't Fence Me In," followed by a long, drawn-out, sorrowful rendition of "Home on the Range." After that he chose "Goodnight, Irene," which was getting a ton of radio play these days. He continued playing whatever came into his head: Everything from blues, Negro spirituals and country bluegrass to novelty tunes. However, tonight, as he did every night, the closing tune remained the same: "Big Rock Candy Mountain," with Moody singing the lyrics along in his head as he played.

One evening as the sun went down and the jungle fire was burning
Down the track came a hobo hiking and he said boys I'm not turning
I'm headin' for a land that's far away beside the crystal fountains
So come with me, we'll go and see, the Big Rock Candy Mountains.
In the Big Rock Candy Mountains there's a land that's fair and bright.
Where the handouts grow on bushes and you sleep out every night
Where the boxcars are all empty and the sun shines every day
On the birds and the bees and the cigarette trees
Where the lemonade springs, where the bluebird sings
In the Big Rock Candy Mountains.

***

The morning broke clear. Moody was neither surprised nor concerned that the other man had not returned. The stream flow had lessened considerably during the night. A ribbon of rocks defined the spot where a set of mini-rapids ran the day before. Naked as a jaybird, as he entered the crick to scrub off the crust of dry clay that sheathed his skin, standing thigh deep midstream, as his chest swelled to breathe in the new day, his nose detected the alien scent of rotting flesh. A deer most probably hit by a passing train.

Soon, he was sitting before his rekindled fire, the old blanket he'd slept under draped loosely across his still-damp shoulders, a last-hurrah mug of extremely weak coffee steaming in his hand. While he was not the sort of man likely to pay much attention to dreams, good and bad, he figured they were just nature's way of allowing a guy's mind to blow off steam. He was finding it hard to kiss off the dream he'd had last night. He and his brother Nate, back in their bar-fighting-just-for-the-fun-of-it days, going at it once more with a couple of local young toughs in the alley behind Morrissey's pool hall in Lima, Ohio. A no-holds-barred brouhaha of broken beer bottles and splintered pool cues and the rush of extreme pleasure derived from grinding the toe of one's boot into another man's groin, when suddenly reality stepped in, because the thing he'd been staring at but not seeing for the past few minutes was something he'd missed completely the previous night: twin drag marks of somebody or something being drug straight toward that far cottonwood tree. The blanket slipped from his shoulders as he rose slowly to his feet. He had the sneaky feeling that other guy hadn't gone anywhere.

It wasn't a pretty sight. The poor wretch was bare butted, lying facedown in deep grass, pants pulled to his knees, head beaten to an unholy pulp that swarmed with blowflies. Only weeks before, somewhere outside of Barstow, Moody had held in his arms a man whose leg had been severed from his body trying to hop a boxcar as he slowly bled out. But that gory death wasn't this. What he was looking at now was the product of senseless fury. Something that somebody else was going to get blamed for. Every rational fiber of his body was screaming for him to do something quick because off in the distance was the sound of an approaching train.

Heart pounding, Moody cast himself into the deep grass. He'd been pretty much screwed from the moment he'd walked down that embankment. What he was about to do in the next few minutes, his life depended on. So many trains coming and going, at least someone on one of them must have gotten a good enough look to give the police an accurate description of the person they would all suppose had done it. Guilt or innocence went out the window when the accused man turned out to be an ex-con, draft-dodger, bar-brawling bum. Still there had to be a way out of the fix he was in. There was always a way out. But hard as he tried, lying there, cheek to jowl next to a fetid, dead man, only two choices presented themselves, neither of them all that great. Either hop the next westbound freight—which was exactly what they'd expect him to do—or do something only an idiot would do. Filter himself into town and hide out under their noses in plain sight 'til the coast was clear.

The more he thought about it, the more he liked the odds of going into town. Who was to say when this body would be found? Today? Tomorrow? Hell, it could be weeks. The police were clever, but so was he. Beatrice was no one's idea of a mighty metropolis, but it was no grease spot in the road either, where everyone stuck their noses into everyone else's business. Certainly, big enough for anyone to take little notice when someone new showed up, walking its streets. To pull it off, all he had to do was make sure he was seen catching a westbound train, then *not* seen getting off a quarter mile or so down the track, circling back, then strolling into town. Of course, first, he'd have some housekeeping to do. Like sweeping the area clean of any evidence that might connect him with having been there.

Like inventorying and re-inventorying his kit bag to make sure nothing of his was left behind. Like ripping that old blanket into pieces large enough to bind his boots, so as he moved about cleaning up after himself, he'd be smudging out each and every footprint, old or new, he'd made as well. Then and only then, would he venture up beside the tracks, the brim of his hat pulled low enough to prevent anyone from getting a good look at his face. "Because," he said aloud, as he rose to his feet now that the train had passed, his face turned to the morning sun like a wolf baying at the moon:

> *in the Big Rock Candy Mountains, all the cops have wooden legs*
> *And the bulldogs all have rubber teeth and the hens lay soft boiled eggs*
> *The farmer's trees are full of fruit and the barns are full of hay*
> *Oh, I'm bound to go where there ain't no snow*
> *Where the rain don't fall and the wind don't blow*
> *In the Big Rock Candy-assed town of Be-at-tricks, Noobraska.*

5

Red Hook, 2004

The Fable of the Grasshopper, the Rose, and the Boy
Who Forgot to Cry

by Joellen Croft

Joellen sighed, clicked *save*, and logged out of her computer—not that anything she'd written that day was worth saving. Just another wasted day in the life of a clueless writer who, instead of messing around with something new, ought to have been minding her *p*'s and *q*'s, dotting the *i*'s and crossing the *t*'s, on the final draft of the latest installment of her best-selling Caldecott Medal–winning series, *The Misadventures of Mister Pickles the Cat*, that both her agent and her publisher had been bugging her for. Frankly speaking, the idea of a life spent churning out Mister Pickles stories bored her to death. Caldecott or no Caldecott, writing for preschoolers sucked.

She stretched out on the couch and closed her eyes. It had been her idea to convert the downstairs garden-flat area of 87 Pioneer into a large family room, with a smaller, second room set aside for Preston and Roger's model trains. By far, this was her favorite room in the house. Because of its low ceiling and almost total lack of natural light, she called it her woman cave. Once Bunny had cleared out for college, she'd relocated her computer workstation down here.

Her current fav reading matter, a twice-, soon-to-be-thrice, read copy of *Middlesex* lay on the coffee table nearby. A most compassionate and highly complex tale of young adult sexual transubstantiation, filled with pith, guile, and candor, this was the stuff from which real literature was made, grown-up literature, the kind of stuff she'd like to write, at the furthest remove from fuzzy-wuzzy kiddie bagatelles about cats named Mister Pickles.

When she was a child, reading even the simplest of books had been torture for her. But who understood dyslexia in those days? This, she figured, probably was the real reason she'd ended up writing children's books, because she still read much like a child, moving her finger along underneath the text to keep her eyes from jumping around, which was so unlike her speed-reading husband, who devoured books, mostly non-fiction. Ingested text in huge gulps, to be regurgitated later as blah blah blah conversation. And speak of the devil, it was nearly six, so he was due home soon. In fact, there he was now, opening and closing the front door with a clatter, calling out, "Hon, hon, hon, hon, where are you?" super excited like either he'd won the lottery or George Bush had ordered a complete withdrawal from Iraq.

"I'm down here," she called in return, highly amused as his heavy footsteps traveled the length of the hallway, then clumped down the basement stairs to plop down beside her on the sofa.

"Honguesswhat," he began, "the old man's dog. Would you believe they left it behind? Coming home from work tonight, first I thought I saw it at the window when I walked past, and when I went back to check, lo and behold, damned if it wasn't there, locked up all by its lonesome in the house."

"So?"

"Just thought you'd like to know," he said.

"And why is that?" she said, uncertain where all the dog stuff was coming from. Not that he wasn't cute when he got like this.

"Why? Well, for starters, what do you think we should do about it?" he said.

"We? You, Preston," she said, with a laugh. "You, my dear. Not me. You."

"Ah, Joellen, come on, cut the crap. I'm serious here."

"Look, hon," she replied, "all I'm saying here is for you to lighten up. So, the old man's dog has been left behind. So, it was left alone for a whole weekend. What's it to you? Surely, someone's coming for it—don't you think?"

"That's the thing, hon. I don't know what to think. I mean, you'd expect whoever it was to have picked it up by now," he said, slowly taking her hand in his, as if the answers to all things canine were encoded among the bumpy veins, wrinkles and creases on the backs of her hands.

As it wasn't like Joellen hadn't seen him this way before. An easy touch for every panhandling bum on the subway, Preston's emotive response to plight and need, even when hopelessly misplaced, was never less than genuine, so it was par for the course for his bleeding heart to get itself all worked up over somebody else's dog.

"Why don't you just call the police or the SPCA and forget about it?" she suggested, knowing full well that despite the no-more pets pact they had made after losing Tiddles the cat, *maybe we could adopt the dog* had to be lurking somewhere in the back of her hubby's mind. "Hon, here's an idea," she said, thinking her best move might be to change the subject. "Just before you came home, I was thinking about supper and realized we didn't have anything in the house. So, I thought maybe we could go to the Hope and Anchor tonight. It's karaoke night—my treat," she added, hoping somehow that his unexplainable enthusiasm for singing off-key in public might jolly him back on even keel. When he failed to reply straightaway, she playfully tugged at his sleeve. "Hey, why so low tonight, fella?"

"Take a guess," he said.

"That dog?"

"Actually, no."

"John Kerry's refusal to contest the election?"

"Wrong again."

"The war in Iraq?"

"Nope."

"Gitmo?"

"No."

"Preston," she said, "get real. That dog is none of your business, yet here you are fretting and fuming, all worked up over something you are powerless to do anything about."

His eyes met hers. "Yeah, well maybe you're right, but the idea of that poor dog stuck all alone in that house got me to thinking. Are we happy, Joellen? You and me? I mean, really happy? And what is happiness anyway? Like, there's a formula for it: a pinch of sunshine, add a rainbow or two, sprinkle in some bluebirds and butterflies, and *voila* that's happiness? I mean, does our marriage still do it for you? Is it going anywhere? Honey, it's just that I've been wondering … we don't have sex very often anymore and … well, you know what I mean."

Oh dear, she was used to him coming home from work in a funk, but this *happiness* shit was something new. She slipped her hand into his. "Honey, happiness comes to those who have a passion for life. Happiness for me is knowing I sleep each night with the man I adore by my side. Beyond that, I don't worry about it too much. Honey," she said, "you're fifty-eight years old. Thirty-plus years of marriage, and you're bemoaning to me our marriage lacks the old energizer bunny libido?"

This, at least, drew a laugh from him.

"I don't know, Preston," she continued lest he return to wallowing in misery, "sometimes I wonder about that stuff too, but then, I just tell myself that as marriages go, ours is pretty much on track. But believe you me, if and when the time ever comes that I feel this marriage is no longer working for me, rest assured, you'll be the first to hear about it. But, ah … do you remember the words I answered you with the night you proposed to me?"

"You're not perfect, but you'll do?" he said hesitantly, a trifle confused.

"Well, as I remember it, you took it as a joke at the time," she continued, "and that's certainly the way I meant it; and we both had a good laugh over it, because that was the way we were back then. But, I'm curious, just for fun, suppose our positions had been reversed that night—that it was I who asked you to marry me—what would your answer have been, or more importantly, what would you say to me, now, right here, tonight?"

"Hmmm. Wow. That's a toughie. I'm not sure what I would have said then, but I do know what I'd say to you this evening, That I'm the luckiest son-of-a-gun in the world to have teamed up with a woman like you. And if that dog's still there in the morning when I pass by, I'm not going to sweat it. When I get to the office, I'll simply make a call to the SPCA for someone to come get it. I mean, at least give me this. Someone's gotta do something, right? And speaking of doing right, if we're planning on going out tonight, don't you think we better get cracking?"

She breathed a sigh of relief as her husband took his libido off for a quick shower upstairs. She marveled at his almost Zen-like ability to flip from yang to yin. All this talk of happiness and marriage had done for her was to reawaken a secret shame she considered dead and buried years ago. An affair that really wasn't an affair—little more than a minor youthful indulgence. A tragic afternoon, in a moment of foolish weakness, a few drinks at lunch, a joint shared in a room at the Algonquin Hotel with an old high school flame in NYC on business by the name of Clark Roebeck, whom she'd let sweet-talk her into getting it on with him once more for old time's sake. A shame that resulted in pregnancy—the first three months of which she'd spent in conflict over whether to get an abortion or not and, in the end, doing nothing, trusting to fate, hoping against hope that the child she bore would enter this world the spitting image of her mother and not her mother's lover; and thank God, so it had come to pass because hadn't her husband already suffered more than enough for one lifetime, his very own mother abandoning him when he was only five? So that tonight, when the love of her life, upon whom she had perpetrated this terrible lie, leaned over to kiss her goodnight, *yes*, her kiss to him would say; *yes*, you are the one; *yes*, a thousand times over; *yes* for now and *yes* forever. *Yes* to the happiness engendered by truths that must forever remain untold.

6

Beatrice, 1952

Moody squatted on his heels, once more safely hidden behind the hedgerow. His nerves thrummed. He'd inventoried his kit bag not once but three times. Obliterated each and every footprint. Wiped clean every last thing he'd touched today and last night. He was a man on the run who'd let himself be seen casually breakfasting beside the tracks on mulberries freshly plucked from a nearby tree, as the first of a trio of westbound GP7 locomotives at the head of a mile-long train crossed over the creosote-soaked timbers of the Johnson Creek Bridge—his cap worn so low on his brow that all he could make out of the brakeman eyeballing him from the rear platform of the lead diesel as it passed were the man's scuffed work boots and the ratty cuffs of his overalls.

His plan was to lay up here, then enter Beatrice in the full heat of midday when fewer folks were apt to be out and about. However, thinking to play a tune or two to while the time, when he reached into the vest pocket of his jacket for his harmonica, it not only wasn't there, it wasn't anywhere on his person, or his kit bag as well. Still, he refused to panic. The damn thing had to have bounced out of his pocket either jumping on or off the train. Going back to look for it was out. Only a fool would risk it. And even if someone did find it, who's to say they'd be able to connect it with him? Especially since, just to be on the safe side, he distinctly remembered wiping it clear of fingerprints with his chamois. Still, that harmonica, his daddy's harmonica, was important to him. It had been the only thing of real sentimental value he took away with him when he'd left home—that and his daddy's gold railroad watch, regrettably and lamentably lost to those thieving bastard *Federales*. Playing that harmonica was what kept him sane during long days and nights spent in solitary. Of course, there was nothing to keep him from dashing out in between trains and searching the immediate area around where he'd jumped off. But then again, given a radius of thirty yards or so, who could pinpoint just exactly where his point of landing had been?

He closed his eyes to the click, click, click of a passing train. Best of all worlds, he'd get lucky, dash out unseen in between trains, and find it lying there in plain sight on the roadbed. Except, it could have just as easily ended up in among those thigh-high weeds. Then again, wasn't it for situations like this that Plato had in mind when he said: *We look for before and after, and pine for what is not*? If so, what was he hanging around here for? To hell with the harmonica. He could always get another one. To hell with irregular meals and hiding behind hedgerows, beating off horseflies, mosquitoes and no-see-ums, with chiggers feasting on his ankles. More and more, a week or two spent hiding out in plain sight was looking like a blessing in disguise.

7

Red Hook, 2004

After breakfasting like a king of sausages and eggs, Preston left home in an absolute glow of self-satisfaction, confident the day ahead was well in hand—as indeed any fifty-eight-year-old man might, had his wife come on to him with the wanton wiles of a skilled courtesan the previous night. Unfortunately, this feeling of utter delight to be alive lasted only as long as it took him to notice the police cruiser double-parked in front of the old man's house.

"What's up, officer?" he inquired of a rather petite and comely lady cop, busy making notations in her notepad. Officer P. Ramirez, her name tag said. Young Latina, Preston surmised, about the same age as his daughter, Bunny.

"Breaking and entering," Officer P. Ramirez replied in that dismissive way NYC cops have of dealing with the inquiring public. "Kicked open, from the looks of it, I'd say," she added, indicating the now open front door, hanging askew on its hinges.

"Really?" Preston said, even though a bus was due and here he was wasting time, screwing around. "Kicked open? Must have made a real ruckus. Of course, I live at eighty-seven, quite a way down the block. But we sleep in the back, so that's probably the reason neither my wife nor I heard a thing last night. But, if you don't mind me asking, is the dog still inside? The people who lived here moved out just this weekend and yesterday when I came home from work, it surprised the hell out of me to see they'd left it behind. In fact, last night I promised myself if it was still here this morning, to get on the horn to the SPCA."

P. Ramirez's pen paused above her notepad. In Preston's estimation, she was altogether too slight to be a member of the NYPD. Elfin really. Bulletproof vest, flashlight, handcuffs, nine-millimeter pistol holstered on her right hip. Overburdened to the max by the many appurtenances of the crime-stoppers trade. Try as he might, he was unable to imagine such a petite little thing chasing down perps and wrestling them to the ground.

"A dog, huh? What kind of dog we talking here?"

"Certainly not a purebred. A large, shorthaired mutt with lots of greyhound in it," he replied. "As I mentioned before, the family moved out this Saturday—an elderly couple retiring back to their roots in South Carolina. Don't ask, because I don't know their names, but they have two sons: Winston and Clarence. Winston told me he lives in New Jersey. I got no idea about Clarence … where he lives. But I do remember that the day they moved out, the father saying something about how his son Winston would be taking the dog. But, like I said, as of yesterday, that poor dog was still in that house … all by itself … can you believe it … nearly the whole weekend … I mean … abandoning an animal? If it isn't, shouldn't it be a crime?"

Officer Ramirez raised her hand to indicate she'd heard enough. "Okay, fella, you've made your point. I'll put the dog in my report. And since you're obviously the go-to guy around her who takes it on himself to keep track of things, I might as well get your name as well."

Just like that, Preston realized, he'd become a part of an official police report. "I gave that door a good rattle," he called after Office Ramirez as she mounted the steps to go inside. "It was locked when I tested it. Am I free to go? Is that all you need from me?"

The lady cop turned and smiled. "Well, Mr. Stoner, the way I see it, what we got here is a simple case of breaking and entering—which means, it's not likely, but maybe one of these days a detective might be calling around wanting to talk to you. Anyway, for what it's worth, I can assure you there's no longer a dog inside this house. Plenty of dog poop, but no dog. And if you don't mind me asking, what's all of this to you that you don't even know these people's names and you're worrying about their dog?"

Good point, Preston told himself as he squeezed onto a hopelessly overcrowded bus. Why *was* he worrying about the dog? However, as the day wore on, the answer to that question mercifully preyed upon him less and less. So that by time he returned home the whys and wherefores of an abandoned dog had receded to the furthest reaches of his mind.

That night, after he and his wife had supped like peasants on burgers and fries, he was loading the dishwasher while she was in the front room practicing "Für Elise" on the piano, when Ritchie called to ask if he'd like to join him tonight at the Bait and Tackle to watch a Rangers/Devils' game. Ordinarily, Preston would have begged off. Hockey matches were not his game. Especially viewed on TV. He had trouble keeping track of the puck. Baseball was his game and to a lesser extent, football. The Mets and the Jets were his teams. But then again, he told himself, Joellen *had* been after him lately to get out more. So, he told Ritchie to save him a seat. He'd be there in a jiff.

The game—or rather the match—was already in progress when he arrived. Ritchie sat hunched on a barstool, nursing a bottle of Bud. "No shit, Prez," he said without taking his eyes from the screen. "What took you so long? Fucking game's halfway through the first period."

"Sorry, man. Phone rang with my son on the other end. Anyway, can you believe the wind tonight? It's brutal, man. Helluva night to fly a kite. Anyway, what's the score here? I see the joint's jazzed itself up with a brand-new bar girl."

"So far we're getting our ass beat, and the bar girl, Vicki, ain't all that brand new, she's pushing forty."

As if on cue, Vicki's svelte, Danskin-clad, trophy animal haunches swung their way to ask Preston his poison of choice. Preston, not being a drinking man, instead of a bump and a beer, sheepishly ordered cranberry and soda with a twist.

"Friend of yours?" he asked Ritchie as she walked away.

Ritchie kept his eyes locked to the game. "Don't even think about getting some of that, Prez. She's married up with the stud who runs that Elite Fitness joint over on Union Street. He's six-four and the word is, bench presses over four hundred pounds."

Preston knew that would be just about it for conversation for a while. Because Ritchie, once in fan mode, apart from the occasional low moan, tended to suffer in silence—especially when the Rangers were losing, as they were right then.

Ten minutes later, Preston was wondering what was on PBS tonight. No doubt about it, sipping non-alcoholic drinks in a low-rent bar with a pressed tin ceiling and walls gussied up with rusty license plates, he was way out of his element here. Neither a sports nut nor a fanatico-late-night caller to the local sports station, WFAN, he did not find heavily padded men, wielding lethal-looking cudgeling sticks, careening about on ice skates in pursuit of a thin, hard rubber disk to be all that amusing. But what the hell, he'd finished his drink. Ritchie's bottle of Bud was a dead soldier as well, and since Richie had taken care of the first round, Preston signaled Vicki for refills.

Ritchie continued to groan and squirm. A missed scoring opportunity, an unwarranted penalty, the first period came to a close with the Rangers still on the losing end.

"Ever been to the Garden, Prez?"

"Actually, yes. Once. Back in '68. When I was working for the Department of Welfare, someone lined me up with a couple of tickets to a Rangers/Bruins game. But, I might as well admit, as a sport, I'm not too into the game. For me, the main action that night was in the stands. The crowd was fucking crazy. The place was rocking. Some scary primitive shit going on around me that night."

"I hear you, Prez. Man, sixty-eight, those were the glory days. Brad Park, Jean Ratelle, Eddie Giacomin, Rod Gilbert, Vic Hadfield. Those bastards never won the cup, but who the fuck cared? We loved those guys. Anyway, hold the fort, my man. I got to go take a piss."

Preston stood and stretched. Vicki smiled at him. He smiled back. Two guys to the left of him were discussing sports cars. Another pair to the left were comparing trips made to Cancun. Ritchie returned with the stubby brim of his Mao cap now canted to the side. "I think I know what happened to your dog," he said, apropos of nothing.

"What dog?" Preston said, temporarily taken aback, though he shouldn't have been, since it was Ritchie, more than he, who was the real fucking eyes and ears of the whole damn neighborhood.

"No use bothering to play dumb. You know fucking well whose dog I mean. The one that a week or two from now'll probably be putting an appearance in wherever it was its people moved to in South Carolina."

"So, you know," Preston said reluctantly, since he'd rather this recently discarded piece of irrelevancy not be reintroduced into his life.

"Hey, dude, I live right across the street, remember?" Ritchie said, his bottle of Bud halted midway to his lips. "Who the fuck you think called in to the police that the house had been broken into? Jesus, before Winston cut out, he made a point of coming over to let me know he'd be coming later on for the dog. Obviously, that didn't happen so something must have come up. Whatever, I'd been waiting for him to call. Shit, he must be kicking himself for not leaving me a key just in case, or at least a phone number. Anyway, it's not the dog I'm worrying about so much as maybe Winston had some sort of accident. Anyway, as I was saying, I'd give my left nut to be there to see the expression on old man Washington's face a couple of weeks from now when that mutt of his finally shows up, scratching at his door in South Carolina, wanting to be let in—because, Prez, one of the miracles of life is that when it comes to tracking down those we love, the canine nose allows them to navigate life on a significantly higher plain."

Preston winced. Navigate on a significantly higher plain? Skewered logic in the service of flights of fancy depressed him. But while it wasn't anything to write home about, at last, he knew the old man's last name: Washington. "You know what, Ritchie, believe what you want when it comes to that dog, but I pretty much gave up on the idea of bad things ever turning out right after six months of working welfare."

"Yeah, I seem to remember you saying that once. A caseworker, huh. Man, what was that like?" Ritchie said as he motioned Vicki for a refill on the peanut bowl.

"Not so bad, other than the utter hopelessness of it all," Preston replied. "Back in 1968, it was interesting for a while … in a sad kind of way. The welfare system was, and probably still is, a case of classic snafu: system normal, all fucked up."

"Man, and now you work in advertising? That must have been some weird ride: going from do-gooder to corporate con man."

"Meaning, you're wondering why I sold out," Preston said.

"You said it, not me, Prez."

"I wouldn't call it *selling out* so much as *wising up*."

Ritchie laughed.

"What's so funny?"

"The idea of *you* 'wising up,'" Ritchie said.

"What's that supposed to mean?"

"Means, I caught you out my window, going up that stoop and trying that door. The next day, there you are, sitting on the stoop with the Sarge. Not to mention this morning, you flirting with that cute cop. I know your shit, Prez, and by this time you got to be sick to death, worrying yourself over that dog."

"Concerned maybe, but sick to death? I wouldn't go that far. But you want to know what I think?"

"What?"

"It's a terrible thing to say, but Winston was putting you on. He had no intention of coming back for the dog."

"Could be, Prez. Happens oftener than you think. People dumping their pets. Especially dogs. Otherwise decent people—people just like you, Prez—do it from time to time. I ain't saying it's bad; I ain't saying it's good; I'm looking at it from the perspective of the dog. Concerning the choices between being dragged off to doggie Auschwitz by a bunch of SPCA Nazis or seizing the advantage and striking out on its own, if I was a dog, it'd be a no brainer. By the way, you're right. All that stuff I said about dogs tracking their owners down? I was just funning around. It ain't we both aren't concerned about that dog. It's just that the scenario I have in mind for it may be a little rosier than yours. The thing is, you got to admit, dogs are hardwired by nature to be part of a pack. So right about now, I figure it's already joined up with that pack of curs hanging out around the old sugar factory. I figure it to be running free as the breeze, as God meant it to, which in my opinion, is a shitload better than being cooped up all day in some crappy apartment, waiting for their dumb asshole owner to come home and take it out to pee."

Thankfully, the second period had begun. Richie had gone back into his shell. Between the beer-hall smell and phony hail-fellow bullshit camaraderie, bar life was beginning to wear thin. Preston, ready to call it a night, gave Ritchie a departing squeeze on the shoulder and stood to leave. "Catch you later, man," he said.

"Sure thing, Prez. Say hello to the wife."

However, the night Preston that stepped out to was no longer the one he'd come in from. The street was bathed in gentle moonlight. The mighty offshore wind that swept the sky clean was now a refreshing breeze. Consequently, buoyed perhaps by Ritchie's little fantasy about how Mildred, right now, was hanging out around the old Revere Sugar Factory, rather than head on home, Preston chose to stroll down Van Brunt Street, hang a left on Beard.

The old factory gatehouse stood at the intersection of Richards and Beard. Rapt to the skeletal remains of a sugar factory showcased in crystalline moonlight, it was obvious to him that—sagging beams, drooping columns, torn metal roofing, and rusted siding twisted this way and that—the night adored desolation. In the presence of such raw beauty, he no longer gave a good goddamn as to the whereabouts of Mildred. Apart from the occasional passing car, the stillness was supreme. This factory had been alive and thriving when Preston first arrived. Streetcars once transported workers to the foot of Richards Street. According to neighborhood lore, the Filipino Empress, Imelda Marcos, had been the owner of this factory at its demise. Preston was deep in mindless computation over just how many pairs of her ladyship's esteemed collection of designer dress shoes it would take to equal in value a sugar factory, when, from somewhere within the shadowy depths behind a beat-up wire fence, issued forth a dog's warning growl of such guttural intensity as to chill his spine and skip his heart into overdrive.

A feral Rottweiler, Preston was eventually able to deduce from its chunky silhouette. And not two yards from where he stood was a torn gap in the fence. Making it possible that what amounted to a living, breathing, spring-loaded killing machine, if it so wished, could easily have at him, and he, without the slightest idea of what next to do. Apart from Hairy, the beloved mutt of his youth, he'd had little-to-no experience with dogs. He and his wife, after all, were cat people—deceased cat people. Any sudden movement could be a provocation. "Hey boy," he called out, doing his best not to sound scared shitless.

The beast replied by slowly advancing into a patch of dappled moonlight.

"Easy there, fella. Don't get me wrong. I'm just a friend passing by. We got no beef, you and I," he said as he spread his arms and slowly began to back away.

For a few terrible seconds the dog took a step forward for every step Preston took back, then miraculously halted just shy of the hole in the fence. Nevertheless, it wasn't until Preston had made it to the sidewalk on the other side of the street that his adrenaline-charged brain allowed him to turn his back and fake a nonchalant stroll back to Van Brunt Street.

A near-death experience? Probably not, but for sure, the last time he'd felt this shook up was the one and only time his uncle had taken him camping. He'd been what, eight, maybe nine years, old? Some farm out by Johnson's Creek with a pigpen his uncle warned him never to go near because it contained a cranky old sow with piglets. But had he listened? Hell no. He'd snuck back and crawled over that fence because he wanted to play with those baby pigs, and the next he knew he was running for his life with an angry sow hot on his heels. Even today, he could almost repeat, word perfect, the dressing down his uncle had given him after he'd confessed where he'd been and why. "Boy, serves you right. You better believe you was running for your life. You ain't got the sense God gave a goose. If you'd stumbled and fell, that sow would've et yer guts for supper." This from the man he admired most in the world—his hero uncle who'd lost a leg in the South Pacific during World War II. Who after his LST boat was shot out from under him, had somehow, minus a leg, had the wherewithal, not only to swim himself to shore despite a fierce rip tide, but another man as well.

But damn it to hell, not just Ritchie, but everyone in the whole damn neighborhood knew this old sugar factory was where the feral dogs hung out. Yet he'd here he was. At night, no less. So, yes, maybe he didn't have the sense God gave a goose. But flipping the bird to fate, wasn't that what people do? What other choice was there? Nature abouned with perils. Like, years ago, that time in Manhattan, when he was strolling down Fifth Avenue and an air-conditioner tumbling from a window thirty stories above his head crashed into the pavement mere yards from where he stood. Not to mention, all those scary tornados that by hook or crook barely missed clobbering his hometown. The stuff presumed to happen only to the next guy. Freaky quirks of nature. Lightning bolts, volcanic eruptions, flash floods, tsunamis, earthquakes. No doubt about it, dark shadows stalk every man's daily routine. Giant meteors hurl through outer space. Terrorists who crash jet airliners into skyscrapers on what promised to be the most perfect day of the year.

Gobsmacked and humbled by the omnipresent, wholly unpredictable, on-or-off light-switch nature of the totally unexpected, a man whose childhood asthma had saved him from going to Vietnam, turned right on Pioneer Street, headed for home, wondering if he'd been perilously close to being attacked and mauled that night.

8

Beatrice, 1952

Two men stood a scant ten feet above the notorious hobo camp at Johnson's Crick, where, from the smell of things, something very large, very near, and very dead was ripening in the heat. The harmonica had been easy enough to spot: the glint of something metal lying next to the tracks, partially wrapped in a chamois skin, not far from a bunch of muddy rags.

"Fucking Hooverville," Sheriff Otis Kneebone muttered to himself, as Deputy Pru Hrenacki bent down to flag the evidence.

"How's that, Sheriff?" his deputy said.

"Goddamn bums. Pigs live cleaner. Dogs got more sense."

"You want I should go down there?"

Kneebone shook his head. "Naw, I'll do 'er ... soon as I figure out the best way for a peg-leg man to hippity-hop hisself down without busting his ass."

Pru spent a moment rooting the ballast with the toe of his boot wondering if it was worth his while to push the point. "Now, Sheriff, lookie here. You already done climbed over two barbed-wire fences, to say nothing of a quarter-mile hike through a cornfield, just to get yourself here. In my book, that says you've already done way more'n your share, so how's about you let me be the one to go down there and check 'er out?" Which, even he knew, was a pretty dumb question to ask a first-term county sheriff, four years deep into a six-year term, who was as cowboy thin and agile as a man could possibly be missing three-quarters of his right leg. Of course, the Sheriff would be the first one down that steep embankment, and just look at him go, edging his way down to that damn camp, using the old side-hill cattywampus technique—bum leg braced to the downside.

Shoot, every fool in town knew, before being elected, by any measure, Otis Kneebone had possessed scant qualifications for the job, save a Purple Heart for losing his leg and a Silver Medal for saving another man from drowning during the invasion of Tarawa. Generally speaking, the job of sheriff ordinarily went to some potbellied, beer swilling, been-around-for-a-good-long-time, wheezy good ole boy. And, but for Beatrice's crafty barber/mayor, Bat Gintzell, getting it into his head that just about any war-maimed hero who voted Republican would be a surefire shoo-in for election, right about now Kneebone would, most probably, have been selling life insurance, if not studying dentistry on the GI Bill.

It was Red LaRue they had to thank for finding the body—not to say that was much of a feat. Lordy. Anyone with half a nose could have done the same, sour as this one was growing in the heat. But Kneebone and Red? Hell, they'd played football together in high school (go Trojans). Back then, Red was a real chatterbox, but then came the war, and after being put through the wringer in Monte Casino, Omaha Beach, and the Battle of the Bulge, Red came back physically whole but so psychically wrecked that, for want of a fancier medical term, he was best described as an unnaturally silent man, which was the reason serving the Burlington Line as bridge and track inspector suited him real fine.

"How's it going down there? Something wrong? You all right? You sure you wouldn't like me down there too?" Pru called.

Kneebone smiled. Pru worried over him like an old hen. "I'm investigating. For the time being, I want you right where you are," he shouted back.

"You call that investigating, just standing there?"

"You bet. Ain't you never heard? A man who ain't quite sure yet what he's looking for is best off doing nothing."

"Yeah, but in case you haven't noticed yet, they's a campfire over to your left some fool didn't quite get put out," his squat, squeaky voiced deputy then volunteered.

Otis Kneebone grunted and shrugged his broad shoulders. Among his deputy's good and bad points was that he talked too damn much. Nevertheless, such as it was, they were a good team. Even his sister Polly had to admit that. How was it she'd described them once? A couple of guys out of one of those books she loved to read. A Don Keyhole somebody or other, with a sidekick that had some sort of Mexican greaser name—Pedro Sanchez, or something like that. But then, that was just like his sister. Shoot, they'd been ragging each other for years. No matter if it tickled her to say it; it was funny enough for him.

"Seems like Red said something about our dead man having his head stove in," Pru called down, kinda put out to be missing out on the fun.

"Well then, that don't sound too appetizing, do it?" Kneebone called back.

"And they's a mess of footprints away over there to your right."

"Yeah, well don't get your hopes up. I see 'em and they're in a sorry state. That bunch of rags you flagged along with that harmonica? Nine ways to Sunday, shortly before he left, someone had the bright idea of wrapping his feet in 'em to blot 'em all out."

"So, I gather, that's just about it for making plaster casts?"

"You got that one right. But not to worry. The thing is …"

"… is what, Sheriff?"

"I figure our killer here, if there is a killer, to be a man of passion, and generally speaking, men of passion make for sloppy killers. My guess is, this guy's left a whole lot more of him strewn around here besides a few rags and a little ole harmonica."

"But, Sheriff, how we know that mouth organ don't belong to the dead man?"

"We don't, Pru. We don't."

"Or for that matter some other bum. Hells bells, some railroad guy could've lost it off a passing train."

"Dammit, Pru, pipe down for a minute so's I can figure out how best to get myself over to where that body is without unduly contaminating the scene."

Kneebone moved slowly, pausing now and then to take a careful look. He figured to maneuvered himself into that neighboring sorghum field and approach the body with the wind at his back so the stink wouldn't be so bad. This was his first ever murder investigation, and he didn't intend to blow it. But the shits of the matter were, considering there was less than two and a half hours of decent light left, they were probably going to be stuck here most the night. And, naturally, this had to be the night he and

Lorraine were supposed to take their little nephew, Preston, fishing up to Farlington Lake, and that woman of his wasn't going to like not going one bit, seeing as she simply couldn't get enough of that child—nor for that matter could he, because that cursed bit of shrapnel he'd taken in the groin at Tarawa, while it didn't exactly rob him of his manhood, had gelded him to the point of being incapable of siring a child of his own. To make matters worse, his sister was kind of depending on them, because tonight was her choir practice night. Anyway, with the boy's father always off chasing news somewhere, it was no wonder his sister's marriage was no bowl of cherries these days. Except the fact that his sister was neither the good little homemaker nor the mothering kind didn't help things out none. Sorry to say, but she kinda depended on them to take care of that child so much, it was to no one's surprise that their little nephew took his first steps not in the Stoner house but at their house.

Thirty yards shy of the cottonwood tree, Kneebone halted long enough to tie a handkerchief, bandito-style, over his nose and mouth. Even now, with the wind at his back, his eyes and nose were beginning to smart from the stink. A few more steps and finally he had the body clearly in sight, and he sincerely wished he didn't. White male adult, pants peeled down around his ankles, arms stretched full out above his head like he'd been drug there from somewhere else.

As he bent down to make an identification, in order to get a better view of what he'd rather not see, Kneebone was forced to fan away the blowflies with his Stetson. For all the good that did, because this man's face was mushed in so bad, he had no idea in the world who it could be. About the only thing he could say for sure was that this was buzzard bait lying under this cottonwood tree. Buzzard bait that had driven Kneebone down onto his one remaining knee, his shoulder jammed against a tree trunk for support, eyes squeezed shut, mouth gone dry, because coming on hard was another of those all-too-familiar nightmare flashbacks the Navy doctors over and over kept assuring him would go away on their own someday. Because once again it was the nineteenth of November 1943, and he was at the helm of a Higgin's Boat LCVP, ferrying a load of Marines to a beachhead on the South Pacific Island of Tarawa, already chockablock with men and war machines suffering under a murderous barrage of Jap artillery, where forever it is always in the present tense for him, suddenly his boat is sunk and he's flailing in the water, one hand locked onto the pack strap of an unconscious Marine as he strives valiantly to get them both to shore against a riptide dead set on dragging them both back out to sea, mad as hell because drowning like a rat is not the way he intends to die. And somehow, against all odds, despite a soon-to-be amputated right leg, connected to his body by a few sinews and strips of skin, he and that Marine somehow make it alive to the beach, where an angel of mercy medic suddenly appears to bind his wounds, dope him sky high with morphine and congratulate him that his ticket's punched for getting out of this war, before dashing off to administer to some other poor soul, but making it only a few steps before an air burst of shrapnel neatly severs his head from his neck as the rest of his brave corpus gently humbles to the ground. Just as Kneebone knew he would be humbling to the ground, were it not for bracing his shoulder against this cottonwood tree, were it not for a voice that seemed to be coming to him from far, far away, like it was the Almighty Himself addressing him by name: "Otie, Otie, goddamn it; answer me. You all right? What's going on down there?"

Am I all right? Kneebone remembered was what he kept asking the medic. Well, he wasn't all right. He was caught in a crack between a war he needed to forget and a peace he had yet to find. He was fast becoming a part of this cottonwood tree, or it was fast becoming a part of him, except for that voice again, calling, reaching out to him: "Goddamn it, Otie, you stubborn son-of-bitch, answer me, or I swear to God I'm a coming down there." And suddenly, now that voice had a face and a name, and the truth of that fact alone helped him garner the strength to divorce himself from this tree, to stumble erect and will his vocal chords to articulate a hoarse reply loud enough to obviate the din of a passing train. "Pru, stay where you are. I'm on my way."

Which, of course, meant retracing his path through a sorghum field that he himself had made, to the spot where Pru now stood at the base of the embankment, waiting to greet him as if nothing were wrong.

"I was worried there for a moment, big guy. I figured you'd done found yourself a hole and fell in."

Kneebone did not, could not, therefore would not respond. His deputy understood only too well what was up with him. He knew he'd need time to collect himself. It was their secret, these cussed episodes of his.

Pru waited until the caboose was well down the track before he cleared his throat to speak. "So I take it, Sheriff, we got us a murder case? What's next?"

Kneebone licked his lips and tasted the salt of sweat and tears. He removed his Stetson, mopped his brow with his hand, then resettled his hat on his head. "What's next is we're gonna start beating the goddamn bushes to catch us a son-of-a-bitchin' killer. And that's gonna begin with you hiking back to the cruiser and getting on the horn to radio in the troopers. Then I want you back in town, stopping by Kirkpatrick's Funeral Home to tell Ray to git his county coroner's hat on, 'cause we're bringing one in. And while you're at it, since sure as God's little green apples we're gonna be here most, if not all, of the night, on your way back, detour by Decker's Diner for some eats and a whole shit-pot full of coffee. Could be as many as five or six of us working the scene tonight. So best we let the troopers know that Gage County treats their hired help good … and Pru?"

"Yeah … whut?"

"Try checking in with old Skip at the Burlington yards. See if he can fix us up with one of them flatcars rigged with lights they use for working nighttime on wrecks. And make damn sure he knows we want his trains running through this area under emergency conditions. Nothing faster than a man can walk, understand? Don't want anyone getting hurt here tonight. And most important of all, be sure and give Lorraine a buzz as to why I won't be home tonight. Now, you got all of that or what?"

Pru nodded, turned to leave, then hesitated. "Except, Sheriff, what I'm not getting here, is why you're messing yourself with all of this. For sure, since we're calling in the troopers, we don't need the both of us here tonight. Besides, ain't tonight's the night you and Lorraine were gonna take that nephew of yours fishing up to the lake? So, what's to keep you from going on and enjoying yourself?"

"Because they're not, Pru. The troopers are here only to help us out. Red called us first, not them, which means this sucker belongs to Gage County. You just go on and do as I said. In the meantime, 'til you get back, I'll busy myself poking around here. And one last thing: don't be getting cute on me and coming back with a bunch of marshmallows and chili dogs like this was some sort of Boy Scout Jamboree. It's gonna be a long night. Right about now, I'm a-thinking fried chicken, baked beans, and a whole bunch of Bud Decker's curly fries and onion rings."

Once Pru was on his way back through the cornfield to the cruiser, Kneebone, no keener on having the troopers in than his deputy, more than welcomed this opportunity to poke around some on his own before, as it were, the maddening crowd arrived. As for just who the killer was and the exact time of death, all he had to go on so far was a funny feeling that harmonica lying up there beside the tracks had one helluva story to tell.

9

Red Hook, 2004

Whenever Preston's cell began to vibrate the moment he stepped out of the elevator, chances were better than even that the caller was Isaac Crawford Duncan, the exulted pooh-bah of the firm that bore his name.

"See here, Stoner. Can you believe this shit? The folks at American Honda are threatening to take their account across the street. I want your ass on this right away. As the poets of yore used to say, gather ye sheepdogs as ye may and get the fuck to cracking. Have Honda back in the fold by sunset or know the reason why. We're depending on you, Stoner. You're my main man." *Click.*

Sheepdogs? Main man? Get cracking? Forty-five minutes later, Duncan's *main man* was idly marking time with the eraser end of his pencil on a yellow legal pad, upon which he'd written a reasonably accurate summation of the task at hand: *How to fake giving a fuck about something nobody gives a fuck about.* Below that were the heavily doodled names of his sheepdogs of choice: Frankie, Seth, and Arkey, who, at this moment, were supposedly hard at work, trying to put together a knock-your-socks-off ad campaign for the new Civic, while he waited for a call back from some a-hole named Jonas at Honda, on the outside chance they'd be able to see their way clear for a meeting of the minds sometime after lunch. Since the Golden Rule of advertising was to do it to your competitors before they do it to you, Preston strongly suspected Mr. Jonas of toying with him, because, were their positions reversed, sure as shit, he'd be doing the same.

"So, how's it going, my man?"

Preston looked up with a start. It was Arkey, aka Abigail Artunian—the office techie and resident genius, lesbian Armenian, whose razor wit sufficed to keep the office in stitches—on another of her not infrequent strolls to the coffee machine when she's supposed to be hard at work on the Honda account.

"Jesus, P-boy, get a grip and relax a little. You'd think I just caught you jerking off in the broom closet. Want I should bring you some coffee?"

Preston laughed and shook his head that, no, he hadn't been caught jerking off in the broom closet and, no, he didn't want coffee. "What I need," he called to her as she continued her way to the coffee machine, "is for a Mr. Jonas at American Honda to stop dicking around and call me back."

But give her credit for accurately assessing his current state of mind and, in so doing, jollying him out of his trance. The thing about this job he hated most was all the hours he devoted to just sitting there. Of course, he could always do like everyone else when they needed to look busy: check his e-mail. After all, for all he knew, some Nigerian prince out there in the ether might be in desperate need of assistance in disposing of an estate worth twenty-four million.

However, no such luck. As usual, his mailbox was stuffed to bursting with ad hominem bullshit. Which in a way seemed perfectly apt because the ad business was nothing but bullshit. And when Mr. Jonas finally called it'd be one bullshitter trying to out bullshit another bullshitter. *Why, Mr. Jonas, would you believe it? We here at Duncan/Peabody have been thinking for some time along similar lines, that Honda's current market approach has about run its course. And, of course, we here at Duncan/Peabody respect and, for that matter, fully understand Honda's interest in moving on. But the shame of it is that, here you are, about to pull up stakes when all along Duncan/Peabody's been busy working up something new and exciting for you. Surely, for old time's sake if nothing else, it's worth it for you guys to come take a look at what we've come up with. In fact, Mr. Duncan, in anticipation of your saying yes, cleared his entire schedule for this afternoon.*

Sure enough, when the call came a little past eleven, Mr. Jonas took the bait and agreed to a meeting at three. Mission accomplished, Preston figured it was time to stretch his legs and make sure the firm's resident sheepdogs were barking up the right tree.

Just as expected, the ever-sensible Frankie was gung ho for stressing the safety angle. "Put a daddy crash test dummy behind the wheel, a mommy crash test dummy in the passenger seat, with a couple of cute little crash test dummy infants car-seated in back. Put them on vacation somewhere ultra-scenic. The coast of Maine, the Delaware Water Gap, Pike's Peak, Sequoia National Park. The dummy family is beaming; they're deliriously happy because *the perfect vacation is a safe vacation spent riding in a Honda.*"

The, by this time, overly caffeinated Arkey was all for playing the eco angle. "We sod up a Civic with plants and flowers to look like a meadow. We do the shoot curbside somewhere in Times Square. We got cute baby goats standing on the hood and roof munching the vegetation, surrounded by tourists having a field day taking pictures. *Less gas means more grass: 38 miles per gallon. Honda.*"

Seth's hard-core, pot-sodden eyes, were, even for him, at eleven twenty-seven in the morning, alarmingly dilated. "Sex sells," he crooned. "Think *Sweet Charity*. Think a lust-and-desire-infused, cherry-red Civic parked late at night on Eighth Avenue, surrounded by long-legged, classy hookers soliciting tricks …"

"Okay, okay, enough already. I get the drift," Preston burst in. "Here's the way we go. Shitcan the goats, shitcan the whores, let's go with the crash test dummy, safety angle. Only it's opening night on Broadway instead. Make that Civic metallic silver, not cherry red. We got it weaving in and out of traffic down the Great White Way, hurrying to get to the theater in time. We got autograph hounds clustered behind velvet ropes, a phalanx of paparazzi snapping pictures as Mr. and Mrs. Celebrity Crash Test Dummy, resplendent in black tie and gold lamé, exit their Civic to take that proverbial walk on the red carpet every Dick and Jane on the planet would give their right arm for. We got Liev Schreiber or Donald Sutherland doing the voice over: *Talent's nice, but it's a Honda that gets you there.*" Preston snuck a peek at his watch. "Okay, then, any questions? It's a quarter to twelve already, and I'm meeting Joellen for lunch."

Hearing none, he continued. "Okay, then we're all set. You guys have been down this road enough times to know the drill. Lots of visuals and, assuming Duncan pulls another of his no-shows, I'll bullshit the rest. Just keep in mind the old man's got big-time ants in his pants over this one, 'cause the Honda account goes a long way toward keeping this firm in the black. Now, hate to leave you in the lurch, but I should be back by one. Meantime, if something comes up, ring me. You guys ordering in, or you want me to bring something back?"

"Look man," Arkey said, "don't worry about us, we'll order in pizza. And, to tell the truth, we'd rather you weren't around. Your drawing skills are laughable, your Photoshop skills are nil, so who needs you? We're the hotshot doers around here. You're merely the lowly idea man. Shit, I bet when you were in grade school, you were the kid who gobbled up the dollops of white paste the teacher doled out rather than use it to make neat things."

***

Joellen was already seated at the window table of their favorite Ninth Avenue Afghani restaurant. Preston stood for a moment admiring her from the pavement. Damn, she looked good. Nut-brown pleated skirt, long-sleeved green silk blouse buttoned at the throat, reading glasses perched daintily on the end of her nose, totally focused on that day's crossword puzzle, awaiting the arrival of a *shlumpadinka* husband who'd left his tie back at the office, whose suit wanted pressing and shoes needed shining. Undoubtedly, this lass was the classiest gal in the place.

She greeted him with her customary peck to his lips. When she inquired how his day was going, he replied by drawing his finger across his throat.

"And you, my dear? How's it these days with your editor? We all set to go to print with the latest installment of your gravy-train series, *Mr. Tiddles, the Cat*?"

"It's not *Tiddles*, Preston," his wife sighed. "Tiddles, must I remind you for the zillionth time, is or was the name of our late, lamented cat. Nevertheless, Sylvia says we're pretty much there but would like to run it past her four-year-old daughter first. Yes, I know; don't say it. The final word on my manuscript rests in the hands of a four-year-old."

He laughed, and why not? Her editor had five daughters, and they'd been milking this joke for years.

"Actually, mostly she really wanted to talk to me about future illustrators."

62

"Really? So what's up with Teddy Stern, your old illustrator? I really like his stuff."

"I thought you knew. I'm sure I told you. Teddy's in hospice. Stage four cancer."

"Bummer. Sorry to hear that. That's a real downer," he said.

"You bet," she said, reaching for the menu even though they'd eaten there so often they could recite it by heart. She ordered the chicken kabob. He stuck with the pumpkin curry. Once the waiter had departed with their orders, her quizzical smile hinted of concern. "You look stressed," she said.

"Who, me?"

"Something at work?"

"You might say that," he said.

"Want to talk about it?"

"Not particularly."

"Are you sure? Sometimes it helps not to keep things in."

Preston readjusted his napkin on his lap. They'd been together less than fifteen minutes, and already it was the old *keeping things in* routine.

"Well, for what it's worth, old man Duncan has got me babysitting a disgruntled client again because he'd rather not," he said in lieu of lengthier explanation.

"So, Duncan's got you doing the dirty work again," she laughed.

"Yeah. That's another way of saying it."

"And … you'd rather not?"

"You've got that right."

"But I seem to remember that coming up for you is that big presentation for Snapple. That Super Bowl thing you've been working on. How's that working out?"

"Pretty good," he said. "And, yes, indeed, if we pull it off, that'll be the big one."

"And Duncan put *you* in charge."

"Yes," he said, wondering why all this sudden interest, when talk of his work rarely came up at home. But then again, they weren't exactly at home, were they?

"Looks to me like your boss is showing a lot of faith in you these days," she said, refusing to let the subject die.

"Looks like it," he said a bit ruefully because, as a nine-to-fiver, he rather envied the relative freedom of a writing career.

"And if things go well, you'll be in line for a healthy bonus, right?"

"Definitely," he said. "Healthy enough to pay off the balance of Bunny's college loan, with enough left over for a dream vacation someplace we've always wanted to go. Egypt, India maybe, Africa, the Far East—you name it—Siberia, China."

"Soooo … one could say today's thing's a sort of dry run for you, you know, a little sparring match to tone you up for the main event."

"Well, I guess you could look at it that way, although I wouldn't consider our firm's concern over losing an account like Honda's exactly a minor event."

Mercifully, their food arrived, giving Preston the chance to effect a change of subject by launching into one of his good-natured rants. "Tell me, for God's sake, what's up with Middle Eastern restaurants, anyway. The table's always too small for the myriad of tiny dishes that constitute a complete meal. Would it kill the waiters to at least strike the bud vase?"

"Lower you voice, dear. People are staring. If you insist on doing *shtick* in restaurants, you really must keep your voice down."

He glanced around. "Yeah, well, you must be seeing things because no one's staring now," he said delighted to think that his ruse had worked.

"Well, they *were*," she said. "But that's neither here nor there. You know what, I ran into one of those supposed neighborhood *friends* of yours today at the bus stop," she said.

"Who?" he said, hip to the twinkle in her eye.

"The Sarge," she said, "… and he wasn't alone."

"Oh yeah, who's he hanging with now?"

"Someone I've not seen around before. An Afro-American gentleman about your height. Roger's age maybe. Extremely muscular. Middle twenties. Bulked, you know, like he works out. With skin so beautifully black it takes your breath away."

"Oh. Then you must mean Snowball," he said as he slopped a dollop of pumpkin curry onto a neatly truncated cone of jasmine rice, taking notice as he did so that his dear wife's lips were now clenched tight. "Hey," he added, sensing a misunderstanding. "What's with the sourpuss? I'm not being disrespectful here. That's what the man calls himself. I'm sure I've mentioned him in the past. You know … that time I was outside using a sledgehammer to break up a portion of our sidewalk that had gone bad because the previous owners of eighty-seven had been spreading too much salt on it during the winter since forever? And this black guy who kind of hung around doing the sidewalk superintendent thing? Well, we got to talking, and when I asked his name, I swear to God that's the name he gave me: Snowball. At the time, I guess I must have done the same sort of double take you just did. 'On account of I'm so black,' the guy then said absolutely deadpan, and I swear to God, I didn't know what to think or how to react, until suddenly his face lit up with a smile and we both broke up."

"Still, didn't that make you feel weird?"

"How so?"

"You know, a black man, making a joke of his skin color to a white man?"

"Jesus, Joellen, lighten up. What's with you? I fail to see the big deal here. It was a fucking joke. *His* joke, not mine. A joke we *both* laughed at, so how's degradation fit in? Black is beautiful, in case you haven't heard, and as far as I'm concerned, if an extremely black man has the cheek to call himself Snowball, Snowball's good enough for me."

"Maybe, Preston, but …"

"But what? Come on, Joellen, give me a break."

"Never mind."

"No, what? Go on. Say it. I want to hear what you got to say."

"No, you don't. You never want to hear what I have to say."

"Come on, Joellen. Don't start. You know that isn't true. Come on; try me."

She dabbed her lips with her napkin and forced an icy smile. "Preston, I don't see why I should have to explain my point to you. Because if you don't already get it …"

"Anyway, the two of them are not exactly friends, you know," he interjected, slopping another dollop of pumpkin curry on his rice. "Sometimes you see them hanging around together. Sometimes they get drunk and fight. Hey, the next time you catch the Sarge walking around looking like he got the worst of it in a fight, rest assured, he's probably been fighting with Snowball."

"How in the world do you know such things, Preston?" she said, a forkful of chicken kebab halted three-quarters of the way to her mouth.

"How do I know? How else do I know most of what goes on in the neighborhood? Ritchie's the man," he said with a sigh, because they were fighting in a restaurant, because, now, people really had a reason to stare.

Oddly enough, *Ritchie's the man* seemed to do it for her. Her jaw relaxed. She chewed contentedly. Or was it that she had something weightier to discuss with him?

"Bunny called today from Quito," she then said as if on cue. "Says she's okay and has a new boyfriend. Some guy from Arizona she met in an Internet cafe in Quito, just returned from the Galapagos Islands. She wants to bring him home for Thanksgiving. Won't that be nice?"

Nice was the huge forkful of curry he'd just taken into his mouth that allowed him to substitute a nod rather than hazard a verbal reply. After all, as Uncle Otis used to say: *whenever a man opens his mouth to his woman, the best he can do is break even*—which was not to say that Bunny's coming for Thanksgiving wasn't great news. But bringing home an interloper boyfriend he'd never met? For this, fathers on Thanksgiving should bow down and give thanks? But as he might have known, a wife who leaves no stone unturned wasn't about to leave it at that.

"What *is* it about men, anyway," she then inquired as she poured each of them a cup of tea, "that their initial reaction when they hear their daughter's new boyfriend is coming for Thanksgiving is to get themselves all worked up. And please don't try to deny it, my dear, because right about now you got male rivalry oozing out of every pore, and for the life of me, I fail to see how this young man's presence in our home for an afternoon and evening or two could possibly constitute a threat to you. Whenever has our daughter not brought home someone wonderfully interesting for us to meet? Preston, in case you've forgotten, the name of the holiday is Thanksgiving. Promise me now, you're going to bend over backward to be nice to this young man."

"Of course, of course. What are you talking about? Don't be silly. Look, little Miss Marple, you're reading me all wrong here. Hey, you can count on me. Nothing I love better than to snow a man by turning on the old charm."

"We'll see. We'll see," she replied.

Preston, however, when he reached for the check did so with this caveat in mind: after thirty years of marriage *we'll see, we'll see*, delivered in an icy toned couplet, was wife-speak for a line drawn that he dared not cross. Oh yes, he'd be a fool not to be on his best behavior this Thanksgiving. Otherwise, sure as hell, Bunny and her mother would conspire like thieves to make sure he'd never hear the end of it for the rest of his days.

10

Beatrice, 1952

Like most of his wandering brethren, Moody held to a strict no-fuss, no-bother regimen of sticking to the alleyways whenever he introduced himself into strange towns. The marks on this telephone pole identified the folks who lived in this house as welcoming and generous. A poorly laid brick pathway led past a bedraggled, drought-stricken garden to a two-story, gray, asbestos-shingled house. A backyard strewn with a small child's toys, a rudely constructed sandbox shaded by a large maple tree, and, uh oh, a doghouse. Generally speaking, dogs and hoboes were not a good mix. But seeing that for the moment, at least, the doghouse was empty, he decided to give it a try.

The lady of the house greeted him with a wonderfully welcoming smile.

"Please ma'am, have you work available for a hungry man?" he said.

But rather than answering directly, this apparently quite friendly woman suddenly turned to confront the small boy standing slightly behind and to the left of her, whose only sin as far as Moody could see, was holding fast to the collar of a little mongrel mutt, barking hysterically, straining to get at this stranger.

"Preston, did you hear me?" she snapped. "Didn't I tell you to put Hairy in the basement?"

Moody's heart, of course, was with the kid. What kind of mother was this, losing control of herself in the presence of strangers? But, maybe, he'd just caught her at a bad moment. A yellow bandanna worn Aunt

Jemima style on her head, maybe she was one of those women who worked themselves into a tizzy doing housework. Then again, it could be that her kid was just a royal pain in the butt. Whatever, now that the boy had disappeared with the dog, when she turned back to him, there it was again: that million-dollar smile.

"Sorry about that, sir. Small dogs always think they're a whole lot fiercer than they are."

"Don't we all, ma'am? Don't we all," Moody said to the woman, rather tallish for her sex. Late twenties, he estimated. A tiny mole on her right cheek not unlike the phony ones they paint on movie starlets. Not that anyone would ever mistake this woman for a starlet: her features too rugged, bosom too slight, eyebrows too thick, nose too sharp, and jaw kind of weak. Still, like the homemade crazy-quilt patterned apron she wore, Moody found her quite pleasing, almost fetching.

"So, work is it?" the woman said, her hand secure on the latch, her eyes taking full measure of him. "Hmmm. Well, let's see. My husband *did* promise to wash the downstairs windows tonight after work, but I'm sure it would more than make his day to come home and find them already done. How about that?"

"Certainly, ma'am," he said. "And, yew know, if yew've got tools, I can fix things. A toaster that don't work. A sewing machine. I grew up on a farm, see. I'm handy with my hands. I fix most anything."

"Well, you've certainly come to the right place if you're looking for things in need of fixing, but why don't we leave it just the windows for now," she said, the screen door now eased open far enough to lodge her hip and shoulder against the doorframe. Her head close enough to his that her breath came to him all sweet. "But before we get started, how about we give a hungry man something to eat? A sandwich maybe?"

"I don't want to put you out none, ma'am, but now yew mention it, a sandwich sure does sound nice," he said, taking care to shade his mouth with his hand, since his teeth hadn't been brushed since he couldn't remember when. "I haven't eaten at all today," he said, though of course he had—less than an hour ago: the last of the sardines and stale bread, in a small park he encountered on the edge of town. But telling lies to nice people didn't pain him none. Nice folks liked the good feelings they got helping out those they considered lesser than them.

While he waited for the lady of the house to return with the sandwich, he looked around for other things to do that might fatten his fee. Certainly, that garage needed painting. A rusty rain gutter needed replacing. And there was the garden. There were always things to do in a garden. In addition, the handlebars on her kid's tricycle could use straightening. That sandbox, over there as well, sadly in need of some bracing. And will wonders never cease, speaking of curiosity killing the cat, that little kid of hers was back, nose pressed tight to the screen, eyeing him like he was a creature from outer space.

He couldn't resist tossing the boy a wink and would have asked the boy his name were it not for his mother returning not only with a plate loaded with a sandwich, but a couple of sweet gherkins and some potato chips as well.

"Something to drink, perhaps?" she asked. "Water? Milk? How's about a nice cold bottle of soda pop?"

"A bottle of pop sounds great."

"So what is it: Pepsi, Dr. Pepper, Dad's Root Beer? Take your choice," she intoned like the pleasure really was all hers.

"Dad's, ma'am, if it's not too much trouble," he replied, taking note of her long, elegant fingers wedded to broad, meaty palms, remembering how his mama always used to maintain that a lot could be told about somebody just by looking at their hands, which made him wonder what his hands might be saying about him to her, save here was a man with frayed shirt-sleeves, who'd nicked his cheek this morning using a dull razor, whose grimy mitts would take a heap of soap, hot water, and a month of Sundays to get as citified as hers, so maybe he ought to avail himself of their outside water tap, splash a little on his face and neaten up his hair so that when she returned, she'd think him more a man and less a bum.

She was waiting at the door with his soda pop when he returned from the tap. Her laugh, when she turned to go inside, reminded him of the little bells little girls used to tie in the laces of their shoes back when he was a kid. Much as he coveted the sandwich, much as he longed to chug the pop in one long draught, he first turned his attention to the plate—which he suspected was one of those new unbreakable plastic thingamabobs that were all the rage—which he'd heard tell of but never seen. He fondled it between forefinger and thumb. *Melamine*, he remembered they called it.

Maybe before he blew this burg he should spring for one and get rid of that old tin thing he'd been carrying around in his kit bag.

The sandwich was also a thing of beauty. Constructed with care from store-bought bread as soft as it was white. And inside, instead of the usual slap-dab glob of peanut butter and jelly, were a couple of slices of baloney, garnished with sliced tomato, crisp garden lettuce, and mayonnaise. Certainly, she couldn't have thrown it together during the brief time she was away fetching it. He imagined her kitchen not unlike his mother's: neat as a pin, well-worn linoleum floor scrubbed immaculately clean, a vase of fresh-cut flowers atop a drop-leaf oak table.

But as wonderful as this sandwich was, far and away, the supreme delight of the day was the bottle of ice-cold Dad's resting beside him on the step, a treat rarely enjoyed by men who rode in boxcars. Moody pressed it to his cheek, rolled it back and forth across his forehead several times, then and only then, did he touch Dad's carbonated elixir to his lips.

He addressed the sandwich with equal respect, chewing slowly as he considered the to-ing and fro-ing of everyday city life. Somewhere, someone was push-mowing a lawn. A couple of workmen across the street were shingling a house. Shouts of joy from boys hunting sparrows with BB guns.

He took another pull on his Dad's. He was almost of a mind to join in with the old capitalist stampede called making money and be like everyone else: deaf, blind, and dumb to the abysmal plight of them who had too little of it, when he noticed that the boy had come back, nose pressed to the screen like he'd rather be outside than in.

Moody leaned forward, and out the cheeky little fella came, with something in hand that Moody recognized immediately as a harmonica. And about the best that could be said for the god-awful sound that issued forth when this little bugger put it to his lips, was that it set Moody to remembering himself at this boy's age and the hiding he'd received for sneaking his old man's Marine Band special-edition Hohner Harmonica outside behind the barn to have a toot—the very same harmonica he'd just gone and lost at Johnson's Crick.

Moody held out his hand. "Hey, boy, wanna give me a shot at playing that thing?"

But he might as well be talking to the wind. The boy persisted on with what might best be described as the wheezing throes of a dying asthmatic.

Moody felt his pants pocket for his switchblade knife. It was easy to see, to strike up a deal, he'd have to up the ante. Something with a nickel-brass handle, filigreed with mother-of-pearl, purchased off some old senora street peddler in Guanajuato, Mexico, for one American silver dollar that a small boy would go for like sunfish go for big fat worms. Moody leaned down and half-whispered into the boy's ear.

"See here now, this is the thing. If I can't coax a couple of choruses of 'Pop Goes the Weasel' out of that weenie harmonica, this here knife'll be yers."

As easy as that, a saliva-soaked harmonica dropped into Moody's hand.

"Okay, boy, then we got us a deal. But listen up. The trick of tooting this thing is as simple as knowing which hole to blow on when. But lookie here, 'fore we can get started, see how I'm giving this thing of yers a couple of knocks against the heel of my hand? Yew got them reeds all slobbered up with spit. Yew do know what reeds are, don't ya, boy?"

The boy shook his head. *No. Of course, I don't know. I'm only four.*

"Them reeds are things inside them holes," Moody said, "so when yew blow through 'em, out comes the music. Yer daddy ever showed you how to crow a blade of grass?"

The boy nodded: *Yes. Of course, sir, my father knows everything.*

"Well then, there yew have it. Crowing a blade of grass is akin to vibrating a reed," Moody said, beginning to wonder about the child's reluctance to speak, like maybe something was wrong with him.

No matter. First time through, Moody made sure to keep the tempo confined to a slow adagio. Kind of easing note to note, pure toned, no vibrato. But the further along in the tune he got, the more the boy got all *gosh* and *by golly*, such that if Moody wasn't God incarnate to this boy right then, surely, he was the next best thing. Big named artists like John McCormack, Jenny Lind, or Enrico Caruso never had half it so good. So much so, that when it came time for the "pop" at the end of the tune, darned if the boy didn't chime in with an enthusiastic clap of his hands.

Moody, sensing an encore performance to be in order, decided to extend his theatrics to the brick walkway, the better to introduce a jazzy soft-shoe shuffle into what he hoped for the boy, would be a rousing repeat performance, during which, to his great delight, he noticed out of the corner of his eye, the boy did a little choreography of his own as well.

Clapping and hopping up a step, down a step, up a step, down a step, so that Moody's soft-shoe shuffle became a full-blown Irish jig, not unlike the ones his father and mother used to do in their kitchen on Saturday nights—that was, before the pair of them became too drunk to fun around anymore and began to fight. Moody, running out of gas and collapsing onto the steps beside the boy, instead, the two of them buddy sharing what was left of the sandwich to eat—Moody, taking extra care to wipe the lip of the bottle clean each time he passed it on to the boy, lest he communicate some vile disease—who knew but there might have been another, even more rousing, chorus in the offing.

All this time, the knife had lain, all but forgotten, on the step. But it now occurred to him that should the mother reappear right about then, she might not be all that happy with it being there. When he reached to take it back, the boy's face went sour and his lower lip turned out. Moody realized he'd made a horrible mistake. The terms of their bargain had been way beyond the little guy, and before his mama came out, he'd better do something quick to defuse the situation.

He flipped the blade open and teased his thumb across its super keen edge. "Bet yew'd like to touch it, wouldn't yew?" he said to the boy, whose eyes were hazel-nut saucers. "But yew also know how I can't let yew, 'cause mamas don't look too kindly on little boys who fool around with sharp things."

The boy nodded vehemently: *Yes, "fooling around" were the exact words his mother used.*

"But see here, son, look how I've folded the blade back up inside, so now it's okay for yew to touch it. Here, I'm even going to let you hold it in your hand, but only temporary like, 'cause just in case you forgot, we struck us a bargain, didn't we? That if I couldn't play a tune on your harmonica just like I said I could, it'd be yours. But since I did as I said, that means this knife still belongs to me. Now, yew okay with that? Boy, don't just sit there nodding yer head. Answer me? Boy, yew got a name?"

The boy, who up to this moment had seemed utterly transfixed by the forbidden object that lay across his palm, carefully returned the knife to the step, then popped up to his feet with the saucy bravado of a little blue jay. "My name is Preston Stoner, sir, which was also my grandpa's name. I am four years old. Next week I will be five. My father is the editor of the *Beatrice-Courier Eagle*. My address is 203 North Osage. My telephone number is 416 …"

Moody cut short the boy's obviously by-rote recitation with a laugh and reached out to introduce himself. If there was anything on planet Earth cuter right now than this young man, Moody had no idea who or what it would be. "A pleasure to meet yew, young Mr. Preston. Hugh Moody's my name, but yew can call me Moody."

But apparently the boy's mother might have been watching them all along, because there she was, standing at the screen door, bucket in one hand, a jar of vinegar in the other and rolled-up newspapers under her arm.

"Preston, that you playing the harmonica?" she said.

Her son shook his head, then pointed to Moody.

"So now, you're the talented one, are you, Mr. aaah … Moody, as I believe I just heard you say? And a bit of a hoofer to boot at that, from what I've just seen through the windowpane. And since it's introductions all around, they named me Penelope but called me Polly, and I do be wondering if it isn't high time for this boy to come inside for his nap so you, Mr. Moody, can get on these windows of mine. Here's stuff to get you started. As I remember, you're already acquainted with the tap where you can draw your water."

She reached for her son's hand to take him in the house. When the boy refused to budge, Moody, not all that eager to see this young mother with quick temper lash out at her son again, decided it was worth the risk of speaking out of line. "Ma'am, if I may, please," he said. "With all due respect, if it's all the same to yew, far as I'm concerned, young Master Preston here is free to help me with the windows if you like. He won't be no trouble. I gather yew saw our little show, so yew know we're a pretty good team."

Polly hesitated, looked from Moody to her son, then back to Moody again, then broke into a smile and threw up her hands in mock surrender. "Oh, go on, the pair of you! In cahoots are you? Or is it, Mr. Moody, that you're nothing but a lowdown schemer, aiming to fatten your wages with a babysitter's fee?"

"Yes, ma'am. I mean, no ma'am. I mean, don't worry none. Yew can trust yer boy with me."

To his surprise, this seemed to do the trick—even though once the mother disappeared inside, Moody knew she'd be keeping careful watch on them. She'd be daft not to, considering some of the lowdown sorts who went around knocking on people's back doors, looking for handouts those days.

***

Polly gave them fifteen minutes, and this time she meant it when she ordered the boy inside for his nap. Oh, she'd been keeping watch all right. Peeking from behind the curtain as her son showed Moody where Daddy kept the stepladder and helped him fill the bucket by manning the tap, even though she'd already satisfied herself that she had nothing to fear from this man.

As expected, her son awoke at three, raring to rejoin Mr. Moody. Still, she insisted on keeping him in, if only to keep him out of the poor man's hair. However, come four thirty or so, Moody was at the door with a laundry list of the things he'd managed to get done once he'd washed the windows. Everything from re-bracing the sandbox, straightening the handlebars on Preston's tricycle, and weeding some in the garden to fetching the long ladder from the garage in order to check out a section of leader pipe that turned out to need replacing—which, he said, would take most of a day, including a trip to the hardware store and, depending on whether there was wood rot in the eave, maybe a trip to the lumberyard as well. By this time, Polly felt confident putting herself in this can-do man's hands, so she told him to "come around tomorrow and take care of that leader pipe then, that is, providing you're free. But for now, let's you and I settle today's wages."

"For as long as I'm in town, ma'am, I'm your man anytime you need me. As for today, I figure a couple of dollars will do," he said.

"Nonsense, Mr. Moody," she replied in mock seriousness. "Two dollars for a half day's labor? I won't hear of it. I'll have you know that the Stoner household frowns upon the exploitation of the workingman. Either you take ten for the work you did today or you'll never work for us again."

"Well, ma'am," he replied with a shy grin, "seeing as you put it that way, I guess I'll make an exception in your case and go the ten."

She liked Mr. Moody's dimpled grin almost as much as the way he took his leave, whistling down the garden path to the alley. She listened until to the sounds of him faded away. Even with her son at her side, tugging at her wrist and pleading to be pushed in the swing for the umpteenth time, even though she had better things to do inside. Then again, she'd been unduly harsh with him several times today, so she owed him at least that. Her son, who was once so tiny she could encircle her hands around his waist, whom she used to carry around like a football, his little head cradled in the palm of her hand—now here he was, an undeniable miracle of procreation, almost five and clamoring for his mama to push him higher and higher as if rehearsing for the day he'd be off on his own, flying through space. Her brothers, Otis and Jack, used to take turns pushing her like that, because truly, their parents had never had time for such things. Would Moody return the next day to fix the leader pipe as promised? She thought not. She couldn't remember a single one of these men ever coming back. They were wandering men after all. Men who blended in but didn't belong. They were camouflage men who melted into their surroundings. Men, for whom, coming and going was all the same.

***

However, Moody did return. By the time little Preston's birthday party took place Saturday of the following week, he'd become a regular fixture around the place. But, when Polly asked him over to, first, help with the setup, then stick around for the fun, Moody begged off, saying he had a bunch of other things that needed taking care of, but maybe he'd drop in later.

In fact, it was just as well he wasn't there when little Preston's aunt and uncle showed up, considerably more than a little late to their nephew's birthday party, because halfway there Otis had decided to give his aching stump a break and returned home to trade his prothesis for his crutches. Nevertheless, with the Stoner backyard now aswarm with kids batting after balloons with flyswatters, Polly welcomed them with open arms. That poor husband of hers could use some help in restoring law and order to chaos. Not to mention that due to her severely limited culinary skills, she desperately required Lorraine's aid in icing the cake.

Otis, of course, rallied to the task. Under his steadying guidance, balloons and flyswatters quickly gave way to blowing bubbles using Polly's bent-wire rings and homemade bubble stuff. Mission accomplished, Simon reassumed command by inviting Otis to come inspect the circular bench his new handyman had built around their backyard maple tree earlier that week.

"Yessiree, Otie, the man cobbled it together out of some scrap lumber I've been storing forever above the rafters of the garage, using nothing but hand tools, a yardstick, and a piece of string."

Duly impressed, Otis tucked a fresh pinch of Red Man chewing tobacco betwixt his lower gum and lip, propped his crutches against the bench, did a little hop to ease himself around and down, then crossed his arms and leaned back. "Yes, sir, I do believe you got yourself one nice piece of handyman-crafted outdoor furniture here, Sy. Prime yellow pine, beautifully stained. I'll have you know I spotted its prominence the minute I walked into your backyard, telling myself that surely this wasn't my brother-in-law's handiwork, 'cause when it comes to making things, that boy's no handier than the usual pinko egghead. Yes, sir, this bench is so comfortable, I do believe, when it comes time for cake and ice cream, you'd best let the little ladies know to come looking for me right here."

"Well, Otie," Simon said, as he plopped himself down next to his brother-in-law, "what I believe is that the major portion of said ice cream belongs by right to the man who's turned the crank."

Otis snorted. He didn't believe for a minute his candy-assed brother-in-law had turned the crank of that freezer long enough to make ice cream. No, he must've conned one of the neighborhood boys to come lend a hand. "That so," Otis responded, "if that's the way you feel, here's something else to put in your pipe and smoke it. You damned socialists rarely practice what you preach."

"Otie, coming from a damn Republican, I'm gonna mistake that for an ill-intended compliment. But excuse me, I'm a trifle confused here. What in the heck has socialism got to do with ice cream?"

"You're confused? My, oh my, will wonders never cease? I thought you socialists had every twist and turn of the economy figured out by now, and now here you are, telling me you're a 'trifle confused'? You seem to forget that according to the dictums of Herr Marx, it's from each according to his or her abilities, to each according to his or her needs. So, in case you've failed to notice, dear brother-in-law, my working life is that of a very active man—unlike some deskbound, pasty-faced editors I know. Hence, since my energy needs far exceed yours, by Herr Marx's reckoning, the lion's share of today's ice cream rightfully goes to me."

"I suppose that's gonna hold for cake as well?"

Otis, always one for the dramatic flourish, put off his answer by turning his attention to his hat. Like most men of his day, he was deeply given to wearing hats even in the ungodly heat of mid-July. A gen-u-ine, cream-white Texas Ranger Stetson, brim gracefully rolled to a buckaroo wedge, it was first thing he put on in the morning and the last thing he took off at night. It was not only his surefire all-weather friend, it was the absolute best thing about being sheriff, because, according to his wife, it was the place where her man stored his brains. Why, even his wishy-washy brother-in law wore a hat—or, rather, hats. In Sy's case, the straw Panama he had on today that once winter set in, he'd switch out for a pressman's snappy fedora.

"Actually, my boy," Otis said as he repositioned his beloved hat on his head, "in case you've failed to note, the hardworking man has been in the ascendancy ever since the dawning of Mr. Roosevelt's New Deal. And for my part, I say God bless the socialist safety net that apportions hardworking persons such as myself extra servings of cake and ice cream. Truly, it's an exciting and wondrous new world we're living in these days."

Simon groaned. If not for the fact they were family by marriage, odds were heavily against the two of them sitting next to each other on a bench for any reason whatsoever other than discussing the weather.

For the next minute or so the two men sat in silence—if it could be called that, surrounded as they were by kids chasing bubbles. Unbeknownst to each other they were both thinking about the same man. While Sy sat basking in the craftsmanship of his new handyman, Otis wondered if something his sister had let slip the other day about that same handyman being an itinerate, frequenter of freight trains, who apparently happened into town the very same day that he and Pru were busying themselves out there at Johnson's Crick. While the wisdom of the moment included sworn testimony to the fact that their killer had skedaddled on a westbound train, he, as Gage County Sheriff, was duty bound never to take as gospel that which had not been fully proved. Which was why he'd been wondering ever since Polly opened her yap, if there weren't a whole lot more to the Stoners' new handyman than Sy and Polly were making him out to be. And while his nephew's birthday party was hardly the time or the place for pressing such an issue, surely, that didn't mean he couldn't get in an innocent question or two.

"So, Sy, tell me more about this Mr. Fixit you got working for you these days."

"Nothing much to say. Showed up at the back door sometime early last week, looking for work. The man's right handy, no doubt about it. The things Moody can do with the simplest of tools!"

Otis leaned forward to spit into the old Campbell soup can he'd brought with him today for that sole purpose. "That so," he said.

"Well, sir, got our car running better than it ever did coming out of your cousin Joey's garage."

"Sy, considering your car's a Packard, that ain't saying too much. That old heap of yours is in my cousin's shop so often it's worth a new paint job," Otis opined with the absolute surety of a confirmed Buick man.

"Paint job? Nothing wrong with the paint job I got now. Car looks practically brand new. Besides, I like my cars black. Why? What kinda color you got in mind?"

"Lemon," Otis hooted, slapping his only remaining knee, "'cause there ain't no Packard in the world worth half the money spent fixing it."

But dang it all, Otis's fun was cut short when his sister put in an appearance at the back door, signaling for them to put a stop to the bubble stuff and corral those kids into a more or less civilized circle, because she was bringing the cake and ice cream.

Simon, of course, ever the dutiful husband, rose immediately to do his woman's bidding. When Otis reached for his crutches, he stopped him short by saying: "Stay put, Otie. I'll take care of it. But while you're sitting here doing nothin' see if you can get this through your thick head. If you're thinking of appointing yourself official disher-outer of ice cream, forget about it. Polly says the last time she let you get near the scooper, you like to hogged it all for yourself."

Which wasn't true, Otis told himself, as he watched Polly and Lorraine march a cake with five lit candles down the steps. He'd never intended to eat all of it. Just a little bit more than everyone else, but hell, what did they expect? For him to sit there and watch it melt?

From then on, Otis waited patiently as the birthday song was sung, the candles blown out, the gifts opened. But by the time the serving of the cake and ice cream rolled around, his limited attention span had settled on a grasshopper perched midway up a weed stalk, nigh on six feet away. Since it was an accepted fact at Hallacy's Pool Hall that the sheriff of Gage County was an acknowledged master when it came to long-distance targeting of spittoons, Otis was calculating the odds of being able to hit that critter broadside, when he noticed Simon walking his way, an equally monstrous serving of ice cream and cake in either hand. Whether it was preordained fate, divine intercession or plain old-fashioned cussed orneriness, Otis's jet of tobacco juice walloped the poor hopper senseless just as the goodies arrived.

"You're disgusting," Simon said.

"Are both them plates for little old me?" Otis replied, swiping the back of his hand across the corner of his mouth to neaten away any residue spittle. "Tell the truth now, Sy, ain't I something worthy of mention in *Ripley's Believe It or Not*? I can see it now, spelled out in bright lights: *Otis Kneebone: the Chaw Spittin' Champeen Sheriff of Gage County, Nebraska.*"

"Otie, what you *are* is *alarmingly* disgusting. And by the way, Polly says you got some nerve chewing tobacco at your nephew's birthday party."

"Ah, yes, my sister. Anyway, point taken, brother-in-law," Otis replied. "I grant you that chewing tobacco is indeed a vile habit particularly disgusting for the little ladies. Yet, for all its vileness, for them who choose to do it, it's a mighty enjoyable way of relaxing. However, out of respect for and fear of my sister's wrath, I willingly acknowledge that like oil and water, tobacco, ice cream and cake don't exactly go together."

And, of course, when it came to eating cake and ice cream, these two did so from opposing sides of the proverbial fence. Otis saved his cake for last, lest his ice cream go soupy on him. Simon pitched in willy-nilly, heavily laden spoonful after heavily laden spoonful. Nevertheless, when they managed to finish together, Otis's hope of having seconds immediately disappeared when Simon gathered up their empty plates and took them with him into the house. Meaning, as birthday parties go, this one had pretty much shot its wad. Parents were arriving to collect their kids. Polly, now in attendance at her son's elbow, making damn sure that boy of hers spoke up loud and clear as he thanked each and every guest lined up to say goodbye. Not so long after that, Simon was going to the garage to haul out his recently purchased set of Sears and Roebuck rainbow-hued canvas sling-back once-you're-down-in-'em-it's-hard-as-hell-to-get-back-up lawn chairs. Otis watched as Sy arranged them in a circle, waiting until his brother-in-law, sister and wife were comfortably seated before forsaking his seat on the bench and crutching over to join them.

"Now that was one great party," Lorraine murmured contentedly, her ample bulk wedged deep into her chair.

Polly sighed, kicked off her sandals and wiggled her toes in the grass. "Forget the cleanup, we'll do it tomorrow."

Simon lit a cigarette. His son was playing in the sandbox with the brand-new red-metal dump truck his uncle and aunt had picked out for him.

"My arm's sore from turning the crank on that freezer," he said.

Otis was on him like a cat. "I knew it, you sissy. And you quit too early. That ice cream of yours was too danged soft."

"We haven't played bridge for ages," Polly then said, in an obvious effort to change the subject.

"Count me in," Simon said.

"Yes, let's," Lorraine said as all eyes turned to Otis.

"All right, all right," he said, "providing, that is, the fish ain't biting at the lake, there's no ballgame on the radio, and it don't conflict with poker night at the jail."

Otis then scooched his butt deeper in his chair. "So, what's up, Sy? This guy Moody so good at yard cleaning you promote him to working at your print shop? Things so bad at the paper these days, you're reduced to hiring bums?"

Otis knew he was on thin ice, but darn if he didn't love the little rhetorical games lawmen got to play. Simon had gone into a little stalling routine: pursed lips, stroking his Adam's apple, a questioning glance flicked Polly's way.

"Well, Otie, the deal is this," he finally said. "We had us a recalcitrant linotype machine down there at the paper that was one malingering son-of-a-bitch, so not knowing what else to do, I gave your man a shot at fixing it."

"And?" Otis said.

"And damned if he didn't zero in on the problem like he's been repairing linos all his life. Goes to the blacksmith, gets a new part made, comes back, slaps 'er in, and that son-of-a-gun machine is running smoother that Polly's brand-new just-off-the-factory-floor Singer sewing machine. Man like Moody's invaluable, Otie. Something rare, I'd say."

"Hmmm," Otis said. "Rare you say? Rare like he just happens to appear in town the same day we find us a dead body out there at Johnson's Crick?"

"Otie," Simon drawled, trying hard not to sound as angry as he'd suddenly become, "if I'm a hearing you right, what you're saying here is that without one shred of evidence to back you up, you're insinuating Moody is your killer and, frankly, that scares me a whole lot. And I have to ask, whatever happened to the version you gave us that we printed in the paper? The one where you claimed with certainty that the killer had been seen hopping a westbound train? You're a helluva fisherman, Otie, but I got to say, this time you got your line dangling in the wrong pond. So what is it—just between the girls and us, off the record—you talking serious here or just pulling my leg?"

"Ummmm," Otis grunted.

"What's that?"

"Ummmm, I was just thinking as how your man Moody's quite the harmonica player."

"Otis," Polly interrupted, "stop horsing around. Seeing as I'm the one who told you all about Moody playing "Pop Goes the Weasel" on my son's little toy harmonica, I have the right to wonder what in the hell it is to you whether the man can play the harmonica or not? For the life of me, I can't see what harmonica playing's got to do with your precious little murder out there at Johnson's Crick."

"Well, Polly, this ain't for public consumption, but I do believe I found me one of them mouth organs out there, lying up side the tracks."

"Really?" Simon exploded. "That's what you got to go on? So what if the man plays the harmonica? Lots of people in town play harmonicas. Who's to say who that harmonica belongs to?"

Lorraine cleared her throat the way women do when they want their mate to shut up. "Otie, I do believe Polly's tired. I'm tired. Simon's tired.

We're all tired here. You promised me in the car not to start up with this. Let it go, dear. You can be sheriff another day."

Otis tilted his Stetson forward and eased back into his chair. Right she was. He could and would wait for another day. After all, this *was* his nephew's birthday, and he hadn't been a law officer long enough to be completely at peace with interrogating members of his own family—especially when one of them was his sister Polly, capable of flying off the handle just like that. So, until the damn skeeters told Lorraine it was time to pack up for home, he'd just settle back and enjoy his nephew, who was having a whale of a lot of fun chasing down fireflies with a mason jar, as well as the Lang kid practicing his cornet two doors down. It *had* been a good party; and, come to think of it, he'd been way out of line criticizing Sy, 'cause there was nothing wrong with his ice cream. Nor with Polly, who for the first time in her crabby, messed-up, mixed-up life, had finally succeeded in baking herself an almost decent chocolate double-layer cake.

11

Red Hook, 2004

In general, Preston did not consider himself a prideful man. Nor, for that matter, a man of many beliefs. Adopting *less is more* as his motto, he scoffed at superstition, thought astrology a joke, fate mere coincidence, and the possibility of there being an almighty, all-knowing puppeteer of whatever stripe or hue, wielding the cosmic strings somewhere out there in the great beyond, a concept laughably beyond logic. Yet, on this, the morning of the Snapple presentation, game face on, competitive juices stoked to the max, dressed to the nines in his Barney's best, he was finding it hard to believe that some arcane, djinnic force was not in play that enabled the man who just saved the Honda account for Duncan, Peabody, Wilhelm, and Cochran, to catch a ride in an empty elevator—at 8:51 in the morning, no less—and ride by his lonesome all the way up to the thirty-fourth floor. Unfortunately, much to his displeasure, the powers that be had also arranged for his rise to glory to coincide exactly with his boss's decent from his thirty-fifth-floor aerie.

"Just the man I wanted to see, Stoner," his boss—an ex-Marine Corps, Paris Island drill sergeant after doing a hitch in 'Nam—all but barked into his face. "We're depending on you for a good show today. Quadrozzi's people are asking for razzamatazz, so jam it down their throats and stick it up their asses. You know the drill. We're talking smashmouth football here. Ground and pound. Clothesline the wide receivers. Horse-collar the running backs. Sack the goddamn, fucking quarterback. Got that, Stoner? Hell, yes, you got it, because that's why I put you in charge."

Preston gazed in horror as his boss took his Knute Rockne sports clichés off to terrorize other cubicles. Simply put, there was no such thing as a small dose of Duncan. *Got that, Stoner?* lingered like a mushroom cloud in his wake. One second in this man's overbearing presence not only underscored how stupidly trivial the world of advertising was, but Klieglighted the embarrassing fact that this "Stoner" guy was actually one of his favorites, with the end result being that the false bravado he had worked so hard to cultivate during the subway ride in, to better face this dreaded day, Duncan, ever the tragicomedian, had just succeeded in bloviating away.

But Preston had only himself to blame. "Hey, hon, here's something that probably pays well that any idiot can do," he'd chortled to Joellen, waving the *Times* classifieds in her face that fateful day he'd arrived home sick to the gills of being a paralegal for a scumbag Court Street law firm, little realizing that the joke would soon be on him once he discovered to his amazement that his true gift in life seemed to be an abstruse talent for creating slick facades that artfully masked deceit.

Of course, at the time, Joellen had been riding his ass to go back to school. "Cooper Union or Columbia," yadda yadda yadda. "If you're not going to be a sociologist, capitalize on your math skills. Computers maybe or engineering." But did he listen? Hell, no. He'd set himself up to get sucked in, because as his dear Aunt Lorraine used to say: "The easiest pacts you make in life, my dear, are those you make with the devil."

Even so, in the beginning he'd found advertising work not only easy but highly amusing. He, an earthling, as it were, adrift among harmless space aliens. Thinking up catchy slogans paid well, very well, too well— well enough that eventually he'd be able to put two kids through college without going into crushing debt.

But when Duncan first proposed saddling him with the Snapple account, he'd considered begging off. And probably would have except for Frankie: "Man, don't take a pass on this one. After the setbacks this firm has suffered recently, Duncan's salivating multi-gazillions, man. Pull this one off, and the bastard'll be on bended knee, begging you to name your price."

"But what I don't get is why he wants a lowly slob like me in charge, rather than some suit upstairs?" he'd told Frankie.

"Why?" Frankie said after he'd finished laughing. "You stupid fuck. You never pay attention in staff meetings. You ask dumbass questions from out of left field. Don't you get it? Duncan's got you tagged as a creative nut job, same as him. You got a blank slate here, my man, so go for it, baby. Think Los Alamos. Duncan is General Leslie Groves, and you're Robert fucking Oppenheimer. Besides, what's to worry about? It's not as if you'll be winging it alone. He said 'assemble a team' … so now we're all in this together: you, me, Seth, Bobby Dee, Jamal, and Arkey."

Preston checked the clock. No two ways about it, Armageddon was nigh. According to the doomsday watch on Robert fucking Oppenheimer's wrist, they were two fucking minutes shy of *bombs away*. And directly ahead, down that corridor, behind that door, clustered at one end of a long, dark-as-sin mahogany conference table, waiting for the master of festivities to appear, would be Lord Duncan himself, together with a few other suits from upstairs, killing time, trading small talk with multimillionaire Ignacio Quadrozzi and assorted quislings, and then clustered around the far end, his disgruntled team of plebeian misfits: Frankie T (cool and levelheaded, as most of their Mad-Ave colleagues in slime were not); Bobby Dee (Mister Just-Give-Me-Space-and-Let-Me-Do-My-Thing); Seth McClintock (wonderfully clever, out loud and queer); Jamal Washington, who once confessed: "black may be beautiful but I'd rather be a *New Yorker* cartoonist"; and last but not least, the brains as well as the balls of the team, the firm's resident electronic gizmo wizard, the one and only: Arkey Artounian. Reminding himself that the amount of time it took to run the Snapple spot was about the same amount of time the Enola Gay spent over Hiroshima, Preston assumed a broad smile and pushed open the door. "Good morning, everyone. Kill the lights, Bobby. Let's get this show on the road."

Preston could—and certainly had many times over—run the spot in his sleep: thirty (he hoped) magnificent seconds that opened with seagulls aswirl about the Verrazano Narrows Bridge, that jump cut to a tugboat escorting a monster ship loaded with containers stacked six and seven stories high, then that same ship now moored at dock, seen over the shoulder of the man operating a crane—Ritchie's shoulder, Ritchie's leather-gloved hands. Gears grind, cables wind, a container is lifted and deposited on the dock; then a medium-range shot of said container sitting all alone as a Homeland Security Officer on routine inspection walks up and makes a call on his cell, which suddenly gives way to an overhead shot of what amounts to a twenty-first-century version of an old Wild West cavalry charge. Sirens shriek, tires squeal, tinted-windowed SUVs swerve to a stop and disgorge men dressed in black. The background music is Edgard Varese's Ionisation amped up with a Peter Gunn beat. FBI, ATF, and NYPD arrayed in tactical formation as the container door slowly swings open to reveal the seedy confines of the Sons of Padua social club in Carrol Gardens, where five hairy chested professional Italians from Central Casting, resplendent in boxer shorts, muscle shirts and gaiters, gold chains, pinky rings, shoes polished like mirrors, are playing poker and smoking Cuban cigars; the background music, now 1950s luscious, languorous make-out music, à la Jackie Gleason and Bobbie Hackett. The alpha-male capo of the gang, some manly dude Seth picked up cruising Chippendales, a veritable Adonis right down to his ponytail and a dimpled, chiseled chin. But the one the camera really drools over is the knockout babe tending bar—Bobbie Dee's latest heartthrob, last July's Playboy centerfold. She's an earth angel wearing stiletto heels, a skintight white tee shirt and a black leather mini. Her braless silicone tits displayed like cantilevered melons as she enticingly strolls toward the camera. And whatever does she have in her hand? Yes, oh yes. It is, it is. A bottle of Snapple, airbrushed to ever-loving Snappliciousness, showcased in eye-popping close-up with her right areola and nipple.

"Lights," Preston called, despite the slight catch in his throat and a mouth that had gone dry. That the nipple print was there at all was shear happenstance. All but unnoticed during the shoot, it was only later that Arkey questioned its propriety. At first, Preston's instinct had been to respect her strongly feminist bias and Photoshop it out. But once Bobby Dee caught wind of it, he put up quite a howl. "For Christ's sake, leave it in. What're we worrying about here? This won't be the first Super Bowl spot jacked up with the sex angle. Besides, fuck public reaction. Duncan will love it!"

They'd argued about it among themselves for what seemed like hours, until Seth stepped in with the clincher, pointing out that Duncan had no moral compass. He'd love anything the client loved. That Bobby Dee's sex-crazed, adolescent brain was exactly the kind of brain we're trying to reach here. And suddenly, everyone was on board, so sure of themselves they hadn't seen any reason to run it past Duncan. Only now, sourpuss Quadrozzi seemed to be getting quite an earful from one of his lackeys at the other end. To make matters worse, Duncan, who didn't look any too happy either, had just mouthed down to their end of the table: *what the fuck, don't just stand there. Run the spot again.*

So, Preston ran it again, and just as he expected, the moment the spot hit second twenty-six, Duncan roared, "Freeze it. What the fuck we got here?"

"I believe that's a bottle of Snapple, Mr. Duncan."

"No, dammit, her tit."

"Oh yeah, sure. Is there a problem here?"

Arkey, Seth, and Jamal, even Frankie, looked like they wanted to be someplace else. Bobby Dee, however, remained undismayed, positively enjoying himself. Preston didn't know what to think. At the other end of the table, Quadrozzi continued to hear it from that aide. That was, until he silenced the matter by slamming the palm of his hand on the table, and the entire Snapple crew rose as one and trooped out of the room. Duncan remained seated, but hunched over, head in hands, shoulders atremble like he was, which, laughing or crying? Preston couldn't be sure.

"Look, Mr. Duncan, I've no idea what's going on. If it's the tit, call 'em back. We can Photoshop it out."

Duncan looked up. "Who said that?"

"I did sir. The tit, the nipple, we can Photoshop it out."

"You loveable idiot! You shitting me?" Duncan roared. "Quadrozzi loved it. Absolutely loved it."

"But …"

"But fucking nothing, Stoner. Jesus, do I ever feel sorry for that poor bastard who kept ragging his boss's ear, insisting they take it out. Ten gets you twenty; this time tomorrow that prude'll be wearing cement shoes at the bottom of the Hudson. What I wanna know is which one of you fucking brass-balled geniuses thought this one up? That you, Stoner?"

"No, sir," he said, indicating Bobby Dee. "It was kind of an accident that went unnoticed until we started editing. Some of us were all for airbrushing it out, but credit Bobby Dee for leaving it in."

"Ser-en-dip-i-ty," Duncan crowed, now on his feet, pumping his fist in the air. "Goddamn it to hell, the divine jerk in the sky still smiles on

Duncan, Peabody, Wilhelm, and Cochran. Well done, you motherfuckers, well done."

Duncan turned as if to leave, then paused. Was that Bobby Dee he was motioning to come speak with him? No, Preston realized, he was the guy Duncan wanted to drape his arm around and speak privately to.

"Dammit, my boy, you scored big time today. Now, I know you've got some sort of infernal hang-up about being promoted up to the thirty-fifth floor. And you've always turned me down in the past, so I suppose you'll do the same this time as well, but for fuck's sake, consider it at least, because the offer still stands … and will stand as long as I'm part of this firm. But hell's bells, I'm seventy-seven years old, for Christ's sake. How much longer you think I'll be around? You know as well as I do how things'll shake out once I'm no longer on the scene. Sure as shit, whoever's the new chief honcho'll start shuffling the deck under the guise of getting rid of dead wood. Stoner, you're no spring chicken either, especially in this game. What I'm saying is, the golden parachutes are reserved for us guys on the thirty-fifth floor. So, if and when, the ax starts falling, if you're still down here, as our Hebrew friends say, you can expect to find yourself out on your ass with *bubkes*. Anyway, it's up to you. For now, rest assured that you'll be well taken care of come time for the Christmas bonus. Plus, for your stellar efforts today, you got an extra two weeks of vacation coming to you anytime you want it. Come to think of it, you're looking a bit pale, my boy. You could use a little sun. Take your wife. Go visit your daughter in Peru or Ecuador or wherever the hell she is. And, while we're on the subject, let's take care of this crackerjack team of yours as well. For starters, tell 'em to knock off the rest of the day. Take 'em out somewhere nice and party up on the firm."

***

Bobbie Dee being the man of the hour, they let him choose the restaurant.

"Little Italy, the Blue Grotto," he replied with consummate aplomb. "I'm down with the waiter there."

Whatever *down with the waiter* was supposed to mean, theirs was a joyous ride downtown, clustered around the center pole of a crowded subway car, hashing and rehashing the glorious success of the day. Preston, however, while he remained at one with his colleagues in collective joy, found himself somewhat constrained by the thought that he and his colleagues could be losing their jobs in the very near future. Not that turf wars and personnel upheavals weren't pretty much the norm in the what-have-you-done-for-me-lately ad biz. Still, pounding the pavement and looking for a job comparable in pay and benefits to your last one was no one's idea of fun. In truth, he was amazed he'd lasted with Duncan Peabody as long as he had. Still, while being a hired propagator of sleazy propaganda was bad enough, the act of accepting a move upstairs just to get a golden parachute would be to grievously sully his soul for all time. He didn't know about the others, but golden parachute or no golden parachute, he'd protected himself by investing his money wisely. Anytime he wanted, he could tell the boss to go fuck off.

Preston knew of the Blue Grotto only by reputation. Number 177 Mulberry Street. *La Grotta Azzurra*, where Caruso once gobbled pasta after performing at the Met, where Frank Sinatra and his rat pack were reputed to have whooped it up. A tasteless, pseudo-ancient Neapolitan ambience with nothing held back. Plastic ferns, splashing fountains. *Fugazi* plaster statuary of cherubs, satyrs, and nymphs. A Muzak, tape-looped sound system featuring yesteryear's favorite Italian pop hits sung by yesteryear's favorite Italian pop singers.

Needless to say, Bobby Dee was riding high like he'd hit the trifecta at Aqueduct. *He's a Leo. He's an out-of-control wannabe actor*, Preston told himself as he tried to make sense of the ridiculous production number Bobby was making out of the ordering and tasting of the wine. Thumb and forefinger daintily circled tip to tip. His gently pulsating wrist as he Godfather-rasped *E bene* to the black-jacketed and white-aproned waiter that Preston assumed was the waiter Bobby assumed he was "down with," whose features bore the faintly amused countenance of one who suffered many such idiotic performances daily.

Dean Martin was crooning "That's Amore" in the background as Preston rose to give the toast. "Kudos all around, for a job well done. To Arkey, for her laptop witchery, and especially Bobby, for his appropriately dirty mind. To Frankie, for keeping the wheels from coming off the bus. To Seth and Jamal, for superb casting and production."

Bobby, who insisted on ordering for everyone, made sure that the meal was served family style even though this option was not listed on the menu. The food arrived in capricious waves that spoke to an afternoon of wanton gluttony: a massive tureen of *minestrone*, two immense wooden bowls of *ensalada mista*, heaping platters of *antipasti* and fried *calamari* for starters, followed by mounds of *escarole*, *veal parmigiana*, *osso buco*, *spaghetti marinara*, *penne arrabbiata*, and *pasta con le sarde*, served with carafes of red wine and mounds of garlic bread. It was a rowdy feast where, against all odds, Preston somehow managed to hold his own, right down to the *baba au rhum* and *espresso* that concluded their meal. If this was what *down with the waiter* meant, Preston was definitely down with Bobby Dee being down with the waiter.

But as with all good things, all too soon, the bacchanal was over, and they were saying their goodbyes in front of the restaurant. Arkey and Frankie were sharing a taxi uptown. Bobby Dee, Seth, and Jamal were off to a nearby billiard parlor to shoot eight ball. This being an unseasonably warm, near-perfect day, Preston decided to walk his dinner off by hoofing it back to Pioneer Street via the Brooklyn Bridge.

Tie loosened, collar open, suit jacket slung over his arm, he swung a hard right at Lafayette Street and headed downtown. Squinting into the sun, stepping quickly, soon, he had City Hall in sight. Another hour or so, he'd be in Red Hook. With zip in his stride, he continued merrily on his way. He wasn't winded in the least when he reached the middle of the bridge and paused to enjoy the view.

And what a view it was. He knew it like he knew the palm of his hand. To the south, a series of antiquated, once heavily used piers stretched past Red Hook into the reaches of South Brooklyn. Buttermilk Channel, Governor's Island, Staten Island, Ellis Island, Bedloe's Island, the Verrazano Narrows Bridge where the Hudson ended and the mighty ocean began. Far to the right were the fledgling, wannabe skylines of Jersey City and Hoboken. While harbor traffic today was nothing like when he first came to Brooklyn in '68, there was still lots of action. Ferryboats water-bugged to and fro. Tugboats nestled nose-to-ass with behemoth flat-bottomed oil barges struggling against the tide on the East River that was not a river. And there, far out into the bay, Pete Seeger's Hudson River sloop, the *Clearwater*, straining under full sail. Yet, on a day such as this, how could he pause to admire the picture-postcard skyline of lower Manhattan and not yearn for what was no longer there? The Twin Towers. The World Trade Center. Oh sure, when they were first built, he'd been among those condemning them for being a constant eyesore, a grotesque monument to rapacious capitalism. "Glass-and-metal filing cabinets," Lewis Mumford termed them. But then came 9/11 and suddenly, a terrible beauty became a family snapshot with Mom and Dad airbrushed out. That terrible day— that terrible, never-to-be-forgotten day. A day in scope and horror equal to Pearl Harbor or the day JFK was shot in its ability to sear the mind.

That year had also been the year he and Joellen closed on their getaway home in Pennsylvania, hoping that in the not-so-distant future it would be their retirement home. He could no longer remember why he'd taken off work to be there that day—something to do with getting his Pennsylvania driver's license or the car inspected, perhaps. Or for that matter, why Joellen chose to stay in the city, rather than accompany him. Or why, on that morning of all mornings, he failed to turn on the radio as he usually did the moment he awoke so that when the telephone rang, he'd hadn't had a clue of what was up.

"Are you watching?" Frankie said.

"Watching what?"

"Turn on your TV, any channel."

"Oh, my God."

"Terrorists?"

"For sure," Preston remembered saying; then neither of them spoke for the longest time because they, together with the whole damn world, were watching in horror as people ninety-plus stories in the sky chose to leap to their doom rather than burn alive. That photograph he would never forget of a man and a woman, who may not have known each other's names, falling gracefully hand in hand to the plaza below, with already grizzled body parts. Nor did it enter his head that either of those towers would fall. But after the first tower pancaked into dust, he could bear to watch no more because the other was sure to follow.

"Listen, I'll call you later," he remembered telling Frankie as he clicked off the TV, sick to his stomach from what he'd just seen and sick with fear as well because Joellen and one of her friends, not often, but now and then, met at the Windows on the World for early breakfast. Then, when he'd tried to call her, the phone circuits were already hopelessly snarled—indeed, it wasn't until late the next day that he succeeded in getting through to her. How long he'd sat brooding in the kitchen that day was anyone's guess, torturing himself until he finally rose and took his misery outside, as if the answer to all prayers might be found sitting on a hillside beneath an apple tree, arms wrapped around his drawn-up knees, embracing himself because his wife was not there to do it for him.

And, yes, that morning, just as on every other gloriously sunny day since, there had to have been tourists on that bridge, like those carefree Japanese tourists over there, posing for each other, using the skyline and bridge cables as a backdrop—one of whom, surely by chance, might have captured the very moment the first tower was struck. And also much like today, the prevailing wind was of the northwest so that Red Hook, being situated less than a mile as the crow flies from what now and forever will be referred to as Ground Zero, was only minutes away from becoming a virtual Pompeii, engulfed in a horrendous, swirling, noxious cloud made up of industrial debris, atomized human flesh, and scorched shards of office paper—one scrap of which Joellen would retrieve from their backyard to later mount and frame. *Memo from the desk of Irene McAndrews*, it read. The *o* in *Memo* rendered as an emoticon smiley face. And poor Joellen remaining inside 87 Pioneer Street the rest of the day, doors and windows sealed off with masking tape. The entire city sealed off as well. No traffic in, hardly any out. No telephone, no TV, but at least she had the radio. It wasn't until a day and a half later that he was able to enter Brooklyn via Staten Island, only to find Red Hook still suffering— as it would continue to suffer almost daily for the next few months—the evil, windborne aftereffects of what seemed to define for all time, the cataclysmic decline of humankind.

But then again, what was he doing dwelling on the past, a man from Brooklyn with tears welling in his eyes, when the summer breeze that lured him onto this bridge now had a menacing bite to it? Preston slipped on his suit coat. And those Japanese tourists? Probably scared off the bridge by that fast approaching, great blue-black cloud, looming on the New Jersey horizon. So stop dawdling, already. If he picked up the pace, he stood an outside chance of making the 61 bus stop on Atlantic Avenue before it started raining.

Yet, when he reached the Brooklyn side and the exit to the street below, thinking of his friend Cass who lived then and now in a loft not all that far from the former site of the World Trade Center, and the remark she once made to him about the crazed behavior of the neighborhood pigeons whenever the memorial light shafts were activated, wheeling into and out of the light like driven souls in merciless frenzy, he couldn't resist slowing his steps and taking one last look.

He knew what he was about to do was a futile act of childish sorcery; still, he persisted in doing it anyway: a quick last look, then close his eyes and count to three as if when he reopened them, the forever-fractured skyline might suddenly have been made whole again, and every child who lost one or more of their parents that day, would have them back again so that they need not spend the rest of their lives dwelling upon faded images in family albums as twilight objects of endless desire.

12

Beatrice, 1952

Nebraska, the thirty-seventh state in the union. The Otoe word for "flat sea." And such a sea it was back in its day. A tall grass sea as unpredictable and demanding of respect and full of misadventure as any mighty ocean. The whole of the Great Plains a vast chunk of real estate approximately twenty-five hundred miles long by six hundred miles wide—the short-grass prairies of Nebraska but a small part of them. Before statehood, before the Homestead Act of 1862 unleashed the invasion of the white man, this unfenced land-sea was the dwelling place of tribal nomads: the Otoe, the Pawnee, the Ponca, and the Lakota-Sioux populating the banks of the Missouri, the North Platte, the Elkhorn, and the Little Blue. A sea of such vastness that when the first settlers arrived, a person could travel any direction for days on end without encountering a single tree. Where loneliness was often referred to as prairie madness. And while those days of fruitless toil and solitary desperation were long past, for Polly Stoner (née Kneebone, cornhusker born and cornhusker bred), this morning this lonely soul was merely folding laundry, but those *were* real tears streaming down her cheeks as she toyed with the ridiculous desire to stick her head into the oven and turn on the gas—or, at the very least, were her son not playing within earshot, scream aloud "goddamn it to hell" and start smashing things around because wasn't that what women did, faced with a life of diminishing returns, trapped between the devil of staying put and suffering an insufferable marriage in silence, or the deep blue sea of running off and leaving her precious child behind? Because this much she knew for sure, if she ever dared to do such a thing as run off with her patriarchal husband's blessed son, without a doubt, he'd team up with her brother and stop at nothing to track her down, if only to restore honor to the family name. And it wasn't like this was the first time she'd felt this way. She'd been suffering her own special version of prairie madness most of her married life. But as for running off? For starters, she hadn't a clue how to go about it. Certainly, in this town of wagging tongues and busybody eyes, there was no one safe for her to even counsel with—least of all the pastor of her church, where she'd served as organist and choir director these past two years, the Reverend Mr. Digby, whose belief in the sanctity of marriage was too cussedly monolithic for his own good. But then, just this weekend, lost in thought, half listening to her husband go on and on about "this Moody fellow" of theirs, who spent his lunch hours on a bench in the Courthouse Square, "whittling all sorts of doohickeys and thingamabobs for the kids— guns, boats, cars, tops, whistles—you name it. Leaves 'em wedged in the bark of a tree, low enough down for even the littlest kids to find." "Amazing man, that Moody of yours," her husband had said, fairly gushing with enthusiasm. And suddenly it all became clear. *Yes, that amazing Moody*— of hers, no less. Rational, thoughtful, considerate, and especially, quiet by nature, he was all the things her husband was not. And being not of this town, perhaps he was just the kind of person for a woman in her sort of pickle to appeal to for help in sorting things out; and seeing as how she'd finally been able to badger her atheist husband into allowing their child to attend her church's Vacation Bible School so he wouldn't grow up totally ignorant of Christian mythology; and since lunchtime today coincided with the exact hour her boy's first session; and because Digby's Church of the Nazarene had been using the basement of the First Presbyterian Church for their functions ever since their church burned down earlier this spring, availing herself of Moody's counsel was as easy as dropping off her son and strolling two blocks south to the Courthouse Square.

***

Indeed, she found him sitting on a park bench just as her husband said he would be. So engrossed in curling elegant shavings from a block of wood, he neither stirred nor looked up when she sat down on the far end of the bench. Or was it just that he was uncomfortable being seen with *her* in public? Surely, he must know by now that it was common knowledge around town that he worked weekdays for her husband at the paper and weekends doing odd jobs around their house. And it wasn't like the two of them had anything to hide. For goodness' sake, this wasn't a tryst. Then again, maybe he was naturally shy around women. Lots of men were peculiar that way. But she had come for a reason, so she might as well get on with it. "Terribly hot weather we've been having, Mr. Moody," she said.

"Yes, ma'am," he replied without lifting his eyes from his work. "It's all of that, ma'am, and then some. Hot every day."

"My husband informs me this is where you make things for the little kids."

"Just my way of passing time," he said.

"If I may ask, what is it you're working on now?"

"I do believe this is going to be a whistle, ma'am."

"A whistle? That sounds terribly complicated," she said.

"Not really, ma'am. I do it the old Indian way."

"The old Indian way? Go on now, you're not part Indian, are you?"

"No, ma'am. Sad to say I'm not. But to tell the truth, I'm not too sure about me doing it the Indian way. It's just something I learned to do from my Irish-born daddy, and his tale of picking it from some Indian could be just a bunch of blarney."

"Anyway, Mr. Moody, we missed you at the party. If you'd a been there, you'd a had some great ice cream. You do like ice cream, don't you?" she asked, because she'd yet to meet the man who wouldn't cozy up to the subject of ice cream.

"Sorry, ma'am. As I said before, I was otherwise detained."

"Well, this afternoon I'm thinking of having the neighbor boy over to crank us up another batch. It's not like we're having a party or anything, but this evening if you feel up to it, you're more than free to stop by anytime after supper and join us on the front porch."

"Ma'am, that's sure nice of yew, but … well, I guess I'd best take a rain check, seeing as how I got me a ton of things that need tending to."

"You sure? My husband would be so pleased. You know the old saying, 'all work and no play makes Jack a dull boy.' Well, that may be so, but it also means poor old Jack'll probably be missing out on a whole lot of ice cream."

"Well, Mrs. Stoner, *my* mother used to tell me that 'idle minds and idle hands do the devil's work.' When a boy grows up on a farm, the first thing he learns is that seeing to the chores comes before ice cream."

"Don't I know *that* life! You aren't the only one around here raised on a farm, you know," she said with a little laugh, realizing that he clicked the knife shut and laid it beside him on the bench so that now she had his undivided attention. "And if I may be so bold, I'd say you've got yourself a regular little business here," she added, indicating with a sweep of her hand the multitude of things already made, wedged into the bark of the elm tree that shaded their bench.

"If it's a business, it ain't much of one, ma'am," he chuckled. "Why, I do believe, were I to close up shop today, I'd be no richer or poorer than I was the day before a whole bunch of other days. Surely, now, for any man that's more than enough."

She kept her hands folded loosely in her lap, hoping he'd think her relaxed when she really wasn't. Judging by the stilted nature of his replies, she had to wonder if the possibility of her getting around to all the things she needed to say in the brief time left to say them before she had to hurry off to pick up her son that maybe, for today, she'd gone about as far as she dared, this being the first time the two of them had ever engaged in real conversation.

"Mr. Moody, I have to confess, in the past, I've always considered whittling little better than a rustic craft, but now, watching you at work has changed all that. Your skill with the knife is that of an artist. Tell me, how is it you come by your ideas for making things?"

"Ma'am, yew really want to know … or yew just asking?"

"Why, yes, Mr. Moody. I really would like to know," she said because, well, she really did.

"You have a curious nature, Mrs. Stoner. I like that. And since yew asked, I find me a piece of wood agreeable to being whittled on 'til whatever's in there wanting to get out is all that's left." He paused, chuckled and rubbed the back of his neck. "Actually, to tell the truth, them's not really my words, Mrs. Stoner. Just something I read somewhere said by some fancy-pants arteest by the name of Row-dent."

She covered her mouth with her hand. She didn't want him to see her smiling at his mangled attempt to articulate Auguste Rodin's last name.

"Ma'am, go ahead and grin if yew want," he said. "Don't hurt my feelings none. I never do say foreign names good. Heck, wasn't 'til I was in Mexico and learnt me some Spanish I found out my homefolks back in Lie-maw, Ohio, don't even know how to say the name of their town. Or is it that yew find a man of limited means such as myself knows a thing or two about art?"

"Well, to be honest, I suppose it's a little bit of both. Mr. Stoner has never once mentioned that among your many remarkable accomplishments, sir, is that you are highly knowledgeable in the field of art."

"Begging yer pardon, ma'am, but there's a whole lot about me that yew and Mr. Stoner have yet to figure out," he said.

She watched as he withdrew three small paperback books from his hip pocket and spread them out beside him on the bench. She recognized them immediately.

Little Blue Books. Of course, I might have known. Simon has a whole collection of them. Published by E. Haldeman-Julius. And Mr. Moody, are you aware that Mr. Stoner's father once worked for this man? Down in Southeast Kansas—Girard, Kansas, back in the days when they used to publish Eugene V. Debs's *Appeal to Reason?*" She picked one up and read the title aloud: "*Golden Sayings of Marcus Aurelius.* Why, Mr. Moody, you must be a philosopher," she exclaimed.

"Philosopher's going some, ma'am, but the life I lead doesn't mean I'm not curious as to the whys and wherefores of things. I'll have you know books like the one you're holding there get passed around a good deal among men like me. They're just the right size, see? Small enough to fit the pants pocket of yer average traveling man. Yew'd be surprised at some of the highbrow talking that goes on in boxcars these days—that is, when some folks aren't too liquored up on booze."

"And you, Mr. Moody, are you sometimes liquored up on booze, as you put it?"

"No, ma'am. After growing up seeing what drinking corn liquor did to my ma and my pa, I got my vices, but drinking's not one of them."

Vices. She whispered the lascivious, tantalizing word to herself—a word that slithers the tongue. Of course, he had vices. Everyone had vices. In a manner of speaking, it could be said that it was a vice of hers that had prompted her to come see him in the first place. She opened the booklet at random to page twenty-four, curious what Marcus Aurelius might have to say for himself: "Be not ashamed to be helped," she read, "for it is thy business to do thy duty like a soldier in the assault on a town. How then, if being lame thou canst not mount up on the battlements alone, but with the help of another it is possible?"

The day's temperature hovered in the high nineties. Beads of sweat stood out on Moody's brow and upper lip, just as they did on hers; nevertheless, what she just read had sent chills up her spine. *Be not ashamed to be helped.* And was not fear of the shame she was about to bring upon her family exactly the reason she had come to seek this man's help today? A man in whom she was more than ever willing to place her trust. A man she suspected, not too sure he wanted to place his trust in her, because as he must be aware by now, her brother, Otis, strongly suspected him of being the person responsible for that killing out at Johnson's Crick. Overwhelmed as she was by the desire to unburden herself to him right then and there, thank the Lord, he'd returned his attention to his whittling, because she strongly suspected that the time for dumping her woes on him was not now.

She made a show of consulting her watch. Yawned and stretched her arms above her head and stood up. "Well, then, if you don't mind, I'll leave you to your work. Much as I'd like to continue this conversation, I must go fetch my boy."

Moody grinned and he stood up too because she realized, he'd just put the finishing touches on that little whistle he'd been working on. And when he raised it to his lips, the sound he drew from it was neither nasal nor shrill but more the soft cooing of a dove.

"Here, ma'am," he said, holding it out to her, "a belated birthday gift for our little harmonica player."

Be not ashamed, she repeated to herself as she accepted this unexpectedly meaningful-beyond-measure gift for her young son. "Why, thank you, Mr. Moody. How kind. Little Preston will love it."

"Enjoy your ice cream," he called after her as she walked away. She wanted to but was afraid to look back. Afraid if she did, she'd run back to him and bury her face in his tanned, leathery neck and blubber things in his ear she was sure he would never understand.

***

Moody was on his way to the *Courier-Eagle* building when the sheriff's cruiser pulled up beside him. Deputy Hrenaki, riding solo, motioned him over to the curb.

"How's it goin' there, Moody? I do believe yer just the very man the sheriff sent me out looking for. Needs to know if yer as good as they say at fixin' leaky faucets."

Moody had been wondering when this moment would come, ever since he'd arrived in town. "Guess so. I fix most anything," he grunted. "Pity is, officer, I already got me a full-time job working over at the paper."

"Yeah, but seeing as yer boss's wife and my boss is kin, seems like we ought to be able to work something out. Hey, it's not like I'm talking about hiring ya for a whole week's work here. Just an itty-bitty leaky faucet that a clever man like yerself most probably can take care of in no time at all. Tell you what, hop in so's I can ride yew to the jail in style."

"Yew don't seem to understand, Deputy, I already got me a job."

"Come on, now. A few extra bucks for doing practically nothing? Think of it this way: it never hurts a fella that's fresh in town to get on the sheriff's good side. Besides, if I do say so myself, that jail of ours is one nice place. Why, I do believe the last man who checked in liked it so much he ain't checked out."

Nothing displeased Moody more than a man who laughed at his own jokes. Hrenaki's cackle was particularly irksome, a country bumpkin mixture, part mule, part crow, and part rooster.

"So what'll you say, Moody? Yew in or out?" Pru said, his fat little thumb thumping itself against the side of the cruiser.

While the practical, ex-con side of Moody's brain was telling him that what he ought to do is say no, the ornery, fun-loving part of it was telling him it might be kinda amusing at that, making like Daniel poking his nose into the lion's den.

"Tell you what, Deputy. I'll trade you fifteen minutes of my time for five bucks cash up front—no more, no less."

"Deal," Pru said.

The ride to the jail consisted mainly of Pru singing softy to himself, horribly off-key. As for the jail, it was nothing to write home about.

Except for someone decorating the ground-floor windows with flower boxes full of pansies and geraniums, Gage County's house of confinement was pretty much the same old red brick shithouse fortified with heavily barred windows. And once Pru escorted him through the big iron door that separated the freshly painted, split-pea-green public area from the cell area, the farther they proceeded down a long corridor, things got sorrier and sorrier.

"Here we are, the master bathroom," Pru announced before a dingy gray dinged-up metal door, so true to its kind that once he opened it and flipped on the light, a bevy of pony-sized *cucarachas* broke for cover under the sink. "Them's my tools there lying next to the crapper."

Tools? A tack hammer, an oversized plumber's wrench, peashooter-sized vice grips, Phillips screwdriver, recently abandoned in disgust? *If the tools are wrong, the job'll take twice as long*, Moody whispered to himself as he pretzeled down for a look-see under the sink.

"Actually, what we got here is two leaks. One drippin' down below and t'other weeping up above in the sink," Pru said.

"Do tell," Moody said, beginning to feel he'd been had, because, all things considered, about the best to be said so far for having fun in this lion's den was that the lion himself—for the present at least—was nowhere around. Then again, a few turns of a wrench down here, flip and reseat the faucet washer up above—given it wasn't chewed up to hell—and he'd have his butt out of there in no time. Except, what the heck?

"We got us a problem here," he groaned to the deputy up above. "Damned if some eejit ain't stripped the threads on the trap. Now, I don't suppose yew got any idea who that'd be."

"Well, sir, I have to confess to being the guilty party. But ya know, there's some things some men do, others can't. Me, I claim no kinship with pipes," Hrenaki confessed. "Thing is, I love dickering around, trying to do stuff, but run out of patience real fast. For what it's worth, my ex-wife—bless her sainted heart for putting an end to our miserable marriage by running off to Omaha with Farley Lamonski— she tended to keep my plumbing tools hid away from me."

By now, Moody had reconfigured his legs and torso into a more or less comfortable sitting position: back to the wall, right of the sink. "Pardon me for asking, Deputy, but why in the world don't the county spring for some money to fix this place up?"

Hrenaki begged off answering the question by jigging a small cloth bag of Bull Durham tobacco out of his breast pocket, together with a packet of rolling papers. "Roll your own, Moody?"

"Nope. Can't say as I do. 'Tobacco, booze, and wild, wild women,' as my daddy used to say, 'poisons the soul.' And my daddy should know, seeing as to the alarming extent he excelled in overindulging himself in all three."

"Shoot, yer daddy sure got that one right," Hrenaki said as Moody watched Hrenaki roll a homemade cig with one hand. "Back in the day, didn't our daddies know stuff?" Hrenaki went on to say, once he'd licked the paper to set the seam. "My daddy had himself a motto too: 'Women are slicker, but liquor's quicker'; but ex*cuse* me. Ain't things kinda getting off track here? Yew done give up down there or plumb tuckered out? If so, yer more than welcome to go nap in one of our cells. Shoot, when the sheriff's away, I'm not above doin' it myself. Or maybe yer just thinking about calling it quits. If so, that's fine, long as yew give Gage County its money back."

Moody smiled. Pru's jaundice free take on life appealed to him. But apart from that, he was wasting his time here. Mr. Stoner's got to be fit to be tied by now, wondering where in hell his new help had gotten off to. As far as Moody was concerned, he'd just as soon give back the money and get the hell out of here, except the heavy metal door they'd passed through on their way in had just clanked open and shut and coming down the hallway were the footsteps of an unnaturally gaited man.

Hrenaki hoisted his leg, scratched a match against the seat of his pants and grinned. "Well, now, will wonders never cease?" he announced as he lit his cig. "I do believe that be the sheriff."

Moody steeled himself for what he was sure would come. The Gage County Sheriff was peering down at him over his deputy's left shoulder like he was truly surprised to see him there.

"Well, now, Pru, if it ain't the famous Mr. Moody, paying a visit to our humble jail. Cozy yer fat ass on over onto the crapper. I swear, ain't room enough in this doorway for two."

Moody, realizing he was being cut off at the pass, skewered his legs to the side so Hrenaki could crowd into the room, slap down the toilet seat and sit down—making it three men and a whole mess of bad plumbing crammed into a tiny six-by-four-foot space. From past experiences with the law, Moody was well aware how this little deal was supposed to play out: *make 'em physically uncomfortable as possible, go easy on 'em at first, get 'em thinking you're their best friend, then once you got 'em off guard, start peppering 'em with stupid questions for which there were no easy answers 'til they're suitably riled and confused enough to trip themselves up.* Well then, Moody told himself, let the fun begin. There was no way in hell they'd ever get his goat.

Kneebone yawned and scratched his crotch. "So, Moody, what's the deal here? You gonna be able to fix that leak for us or what?"

Moody countered by tugging idly at his earlobe like it itched or something. As his mama used to say: *when you act the truth, you are the truth.* "Can't rightly say, Sheriff. A body can't be knowing for sure when a job is gonna get done 'til it is done."

Kneebone tapped Pru knowingly on the arm. "Ya hear that? This here's a man what knows things, the sort of man persons such as yerself would do well taking after."

"Tell me about it, Sheriff," Pru hee-hawed, "'fore you walked in, me and Moody were discussin' women."

"Women? Well, do tell. And what pearls of wisdom did our man have to pass on to ya concerning the fairer sex?"

"Well, Sheriff, seems as we was just getting at it when yew showed up. But my guess is, he likes them right enough. For sure, I don't think we got us no queer sitting here under our sink."

Moody remained deadpan. Hreneki's hyenic laugh and Kneebone's ice-water grin could kiss his ass.

"So, according to Pru here, yer a lady's man are ya, Moody?" Kneebone then said. "If so, I am sure as shit glad to hear it 'cause, as ya may well have heard by now, we recently had us a man murdered out there at Johnson's Crick. But what ya may not have heard—mainly because we been kinda keeping it on the hush-hush—was that just before our killer done in his man, he most likely pleasured himself, inserting his pecker into the victim's bunghole, which, needless to say, is the sort of thing good folk around here take a strong disliking to. And I, as their sheriff and humble servant, charged as I am by the law to leave no stone unturned when there's a killer on the loose, and seeing as how my sister says you blew into town the same day as we found that body and that you being a hobo and all, like many of your boxcar buddies, most likely used Johnson's Crick as your hopping off point prior to coming into town, I can't help wondering if ya just might not be in possession of some vital piece of information that might help us wrap up our case."

"What I think, Sheriff," Moody replied, steadfast in his refusal to rise to the bait, "is that this here waste pipe yer deputy dragged me over here to fix is one lost cause. What you need is a brand-new setup—trap and all."

Kneebone paused to insert a fresh pinch of tobacco under his gum. "Hear that, Pru? Man claims your best efforts were all for naught. So what ya waitin' for? Ya heard him. Don't just sit there. Hustle yer ass on over to the hardware store and get the man what he needs. In the meantime, me and Moody here'll just continue on with our delightful conversation."

One less person in that bathroom, however, did nothing to lessen Moody's feeling of being boxed in. Once Kneebone shifted his considerable bulk from the doorway to the shithouse throne—making sure in the process to leave that prosthesis of his stretched out like a log across the doorway, he had no other choice but to sit with drawn-up knees.

"So, Moody, tell me about yourself. We both look to be about the same age. Where'd you do your soldiering during the war?"

"I did my time, Sheriff, like most everybody else. But I guess you could call me one of the lucky ones. Did all my duty stateside," Moody said, determined to stick to the accused man's golden rule: *the less said the better, and don't volunteer anything.*

Kneebone rapped an especially hairy knuckle a couple of times against his prosthesis. "That so? Me, I was in the Navy. Got mine at Tarawa, bringing in a load of Marines. I was lucky too … came back minus only a leg."

Kneebone bent forward to spit in the sink. Moody scrunched his head to the side.

"If ya don't mind my asking, exactly what was it yew were doing stateside anyway?" the sheriff said as he ran the tap.

"Not much. This and that," Moody said, wishing he was anywhere but where he was. He'd been interrogated both by professionals and amateurs, and the best to be said for this yokel sheriff was that he was by far the hairiest one of the lot. Head to toe, this man's ability to sprout hairs was positively Neanderthal. It cropped out of him everywhere—eyebrows, knuckles, backs of this hands. Heavy case of five o'clock shadow at half past twelve in the afternoon.

"No, I should think 'not much,'" Kneebone chuckled, "'cept for all of that running ya did from the MPs. Anyway, yew all right down there, Moody? Ya strike me as looking a little peaked. Can't be much air stirring down there. How's about a glass of water? Or better yet, what say we adjourn ourselves to my office where a neat dresser such as yerself can converse in style, seated properly, upright in a chair, soothed by the breeze of an electric fan?"

But, to Moody's way of thinking, it was more to his advantage for them to stay right where they were. "I prefer not," he replied, suspecting that Kneebone was a whole lot less comfortable than he was.

Kneebone leaned his head down within a foot of Moody's ear. "Tell me, Moody," he said, his voice a guttural whisper that reeked of pool halls and Bud Decker onion rings, "what's it like riding day after day in them boxcars? What do yew bums do for entertainment when yer not cornholing each other?"

Moody made sure to keep his eyes focused on the tops of his knees. He was pretty darn certain Kneebone had something fisted in his far hand. What exactly that something was, he couldn't be sure. A gun? Surely not. Blackjack? Maybe. Still, given the chance, considering the maneuverable space available to him, there might just be enough room, if he moved sudden-like when he went for it, for him to get the hell out of there.

"Now," the sheriff continued, "I'm not much of one for playing games, so I'm just gonna lay my cards on the table. Back in my office, we got us a rap sheet with yer name on it. And, oh my, all of that running away from the Army yew did … all that time yew spent in Leavenworth, atoning for your cowardly sins. Truth is, I don't know how yew can live with yerself, yew being such a coward and all—and I'm here to tell ya if I'd a been yer commanding officer, I'd a had yew shot. But what I'm a dying to know is, why'd ya do it, Moody? What made you stave a man's face in so bad I couldn't recognize a person who's been a more or less regular guest in this hotel's drunk tank? Sam Gerkin, or Old Sam Pickle, as he was known in

fairer times—a harmless old coot with no more than the usual weakness
for booze, who because his daddy had beat him so often when he was
little boy, he'd grown up a little light upstairs, incapable of looking after
of himself just like all those other dimwits out at the State Developmental
Center, which yew might be interested to learn, is located just outside of
town, no more than a whoop and a holler from Johnson's Crick."

"We about done here, Sheriff?" Moody said, looking Kneebone directly
in the eye, determined not to be the first to blink or look away.

Kneebone responded with a jet of tobacco juice that bounced off the
wall to the right of Moody's ear. "Done?" he hissed. "Yer a lot closer to
being done than ya think, partner. Ain't ya wishing right now, Mr. Moody,
for a big old rock so yew could smash my face in to make me shut up? What
kind of man does the things you do? Tell me, Moody. Tell me, before I
wipe that sorry, stink-ass grin right off yer face."

Moody burst to his feet, hurdling Kneebone's outstretched prosthesis
with a suddenness capable of startling tobacco juice down a man's windpipe.
A tragic event, of undeniable comic value that prompted Moody to pause
in the doorway at the sight of the almighty Sheriff of Gage County sitting
on the crapper, shoulder slumped against the wall, tears running down his
cheeks, as he retched his guts out.

"Sheriff, I do believe yew oughta be more careful now. Tobacco juice,
don't ya know, is a terrible thing once it gets down yew the wrong way."

Kneebone struggled to speak. The best he could do was hardly more
than a wheeze. "Go on. Git on outta here. But don't be thinking that it's
over for yew, 'cause what I got in my hand's something that says yer ass
belongs to me."

Moody, having finally got a peek at whatever it was the sheriff had
been hiding in his hand, laughed long and loud. "A harmonica? Yew
kidding me? A harmonica's no proof of anything, let alone me killing
somebody, which is why yew got no choice but to let me stroll out of here.
And oh, before I go, one last piece of advice—from now on out, yew and
that numbskull deputy of yers can fix yer own goddamn faucets."

***

His hot Irish blood jacked to the max with adrenaline, Moody managed
the ten-minute hike to the *Courier-Eagle* building in less than five. Gifted

with sense enough to know he was in no fit state for making nice with the office help—much less with Mr. Stoner—he detoured around to the back door via the alley. Once ensconced safely inside the miserably small, windowless storage space that Mr. Stoner was letting him call home, before presenting himself up front, he needed to wait a bit until his insides calmed down, and while he was at it, tend to his sweaty outsides as well. He sat down on his cot to change his socks. He peeled off his tee shirt and hung it to dry in the breeze of the small oscillating fan his boss loaned him the day he moved in. Later that night, he'd go shower over at the YMCA. But a good soaping of his upper body with a washrag, paying particular attention to his armpits, would do for now. Of course, if he had his druthers, he'd be out of his skull in Merida, Mexico, smoking weed with a bougainvillea-scented senorita. If he had his druthers, he'd have never given his word to Mr. Stoner not to smoke back here—*it's a fire trap … all that paper and dust.* Even though, what Mr. Stoner had in mind was cigarettes. Still, he couldn't risk it. Especially not now. Not with marijuana's telltale smell. Just imagine the fallout if he were caught smoking dope back here? He could see the headline in the *Courier-Eagle* now: "Dope Fiend Arrested for the Murder at Johnson's Creek"—and the march to the gallows would begin.

And as if that weren't enough, what was up with Mrs. Stoner coming on to him today? Her nature normally sweet as honey, yet today she'd come to him with a trapped animal look in her eyes. Not to mention the way she'd accepted that whistle from him, flustered and all aflutter. Or was it that she'd come there to warn him about her brother—all that talk about sin and vices—then, for some reason, decided to keep it to herself. And speaking of her asshole brother, what kind of a joke of a lawman was he, losing control of himself like that?

Moody sighed. He had only himself to blame. Stuff like this seemed to happen every time he stayed too long in one place. And he hadn't exactly done himself any favors today at the jail, getting smartass with the sheriff in a way the man wouldn't be apt to forget anytime soon. Except there was always that kit bag of his peeking out from under his cot. Less than forty minutes, he could grab that thing and be on a fast freight bound for Pocatello, Orlando, or Tuba City. Of course, suddenly hightailing out of here with his tail between his legs was exactly what the sheriff was hoping he'd do. Because innocent men got no cause to be running away. Innocent men make sure their boss hears their version of what happened at the jail today *before* their boss hears it from his brother-in-law. As for Mrs. Stoner, bless her heart, should push ever came to shove, he was pretty darn sure he'd at least have her on his side. And whatever it was that she seemed to be needing from him, for that perhaps he'd best wait and see, hoping against hope, not to get sucked in too deep.

Moody finished washing up and pulled on a clean tee shirt. On his way up front, he met Mr. Stoner's young secretary, Nancy Puffinberger, on her way back to use the restroom.

"Oh, so there you are. We've been looking for you," she said as if she suspected he'd been goldbricking on his cot. "Mr. Stoner couldn't wait around. He's off to meet someone at the train depot, don't you know. Pretty much discombobulated at that, since it's the famous E. Haldeman-Julius himself who's on that train. Anyway, he told me to remind you, if and when you finally showed up, that if you haven't already, you need to get cracking on ordering up the stuff you're gonna need to build that platform for tomorrow night's debate."

Ah, yes, the debate. The Reverend Julius Watson, distinguished Pastor of the First Presbyterian Church, speaking for those who believe the Almighty, versus E. Haldeman-Julius, speaking for the lowly Heathens. It was hard to believe. That debate was the talk of the town. But given the tumult of the past few hours, it had slipped his mind. Moody gently tapped Nancy on the chin.

"Yew know what, Nancy? I been all over these United States. Put me in that there debate, and I'd set 'em straight on churches and religion. Tell every man-jack there that if he wants to walk with God, go pay a visit to Yosemite National Park. The rest of this planet is just Sodom and Gomorrah."

"Oh, Mister Moody," Nancy said, batting her refreshingly young, baby-blue eyes, "go on now! Sodom and Gomorrah. Surely not here in Beatrice."

Moody admired Nancy's youthful exuberance. He adored her nut-brown hair that was an overcoifed masterpiece of frozen waves and twirls. He treasured her little moon face and scrunched-up button nose, her ruby-red fingernails, narrow waist, perky breasts, and ample hips. Ah, to be young again, as he was not. But a lass such as she, a young woman barely out of her teens, at his stage in life, was forbidden territory for him. For girls her age, sexiness and personality were one and the same. Charm for her was the thing young ladies used to get boys to do naughty things to them. Given her tender years, she must be aching to latch on to a real man. Meaning, should he so desire, he could coax her back to his cot for a quickie anytime he pleased, teach her to smoke weed, show her that Sodom and Gomorrah was a heck of a lot more fun than the Good Book cracked it up to be. Of course, if he were so foolish as to do the nasty with her, it would have to be a one-time event. Otherwise, a heifer such as Nancy would likely start fancying herself *in love*, dreaming of marriage and children and settling down, when to him she'd be just another fuck.

For all these reasons and more, Moody limited his charms to placing his hands firmly on her comely shoulders and bestowing a grandfatherly peck upon her forehead as if he were her very own Grandpa Puffinberger. "Now, listen here, yew sweet young thing, we both got us a passel of work to get done before we knock off for the day. But my, I have to say, yer hair. It don't look the same. My bet is that yew had it done up fresh, just for me, last Saturday at Nadine's."

"Oh, Mr. Moody, you say the nicest things. But I think you must have me mixed up with somebody else 'cause I've always worn my hair this way. At least since we've known each other."

"Why, then, it must be the light. Or maybe a new shade of lipstick? But Nancy, I've got to tell yew, and one thing I never do is lie to a woman, yew never looked more beautiful than yew do today."

"Oh, Mr. Moody," she sighed, "flattery will get you everything."

Her eyes were closed. Her head tilted slightly upward. Her lower lip quivering ever so slightly in anticipation of a kiss she was never going to get. Not from him anyway. "Go on now, girl. I'll follow yew up in a minute," Moody said as gently as he could, to dispel any funny ideas she might be entertaining about the two of them ever becoming a pair. The simple truth of the matter was, while Nancy would never be taken for the prettiest flower in anyone's bouquet, for sure, she'd make some young man a great wife someday. Her rustic beauty was like something out of Zettl's bakery. Hidden beneath the frills and frostings of youth, lurked a solid piece of devil's food layer cake.

13

Red Hook, 2004

The Fable of Gary Grasshopper, Rosita Rosebush, and
the Little Boy Who Never Cried

by Joellen Croft

*Gary Grasshopper was sad. Oh, so very, very sad—sad
that it had not rained in a very long time; sad because he was
afraid his friend, Rosita Rosebush, was dying of thirst; sad
that the Little Boy Who Never Cried ran and skipped and
played each day, thinking only of himself and never once of
Rosita Rosebush.*

*"If grasshoppers could, I would go to the well myself and
bring you some water," Gary sighed.*

*Rosita struggled to raise her droopy head. "Don't be hard
on him," the poor bush said, "he's only a little boy."*

*"But he's not too little to carry a pail of water. Is that too
much to ask?" Gary Grasshopper said.*

*"Oh, shush," Rosita Rosebush said, because she knew not
to expect from others what they were unable to give.*

*Gary Grasshopper cleared his throat. What could he say?
What could he do? He did not understand …*

111

Joellen sat, chin on hands, in front of her computer screen. What a load of crap. What was it that dumbo grasshopper of hers didn't understand? Whoever said writing was fun? The previous week, when she'd met with her editor lo these many years, Cynthia had really let her have it. "While I love most of your first draft, for fuck's sake, my dear, until you yourself understand what it is this dumbo grasshopper doesn't understand, your narrative goes nowhere."

So, all right already. As they say in writing class: *Every first draft stinks. Never despair, the art is in the rewrite. Keep at it. Sooner or later, lightning will strike. If not today, then tomorrow.* Anyway, enough with writerly platitudes and back to real life. Her overdue husband had said that depending on how the Snapple thing went, he might be a little late. Not to worry, she had a seafood casserole waiting for him in the oven and a fresh load of laundry to stuff the washer. Look at you, girl, at least you accomplished something today.

On her way to the kitchen to check on the casserole, she was astounded to find her husband already home, sitting on the sofa in the faded light of the living room, seemingly unaware of her standing there. She hesitated to go in. Even in the best of spirits, her husband's posture was never good. Tonight, the curvature of his spine suggested a question mark in peril of being swallowed by a sofa. Had the Snapple presentation gone so badly that Duncan had fired him on the spot? If so, then hooray, hooray, oh happy day. As far as she was concerned, he'd spent too damn many years in advertising. Besides, when it came to money, for now, they were more or less set. Their ample savings, plus whatever royalties of hers that rolled in, would more than tide them over until he found something else.

Nevertheless, sitting alone in the dark was one thing; sitting head slumped chin to chest, as if the world had passed him by, was something else. Maybe all he needed was a little mothering. Some seafood casserole, say, followed by a bath hot enough to soak the blues away, a vigorous toweling off before being tucked into bed. She entered the room, sat down beside him and began to gently massage the back of his neck. "Honey, what is it?" she asked.

"I love you," he replied as if speaking from the depths of an elevator shaft.

"I'm sure you do, dear, but that doesn't explain why you're sitting alone in the dark."

"I wish I knew," he said.

She stroked the back of his head. Of course, he *knew*. For him, keeping everything bottled up inside was old hat. A trait, had she known about at the time, that might have kept her from marrying him. June the third of nineteen hundred sixty-eight. She'd been a shop girl in Meuniers on Montague Street when he, a New York University student with a million-dollar smile, swaggered in, seeking to buy a birthday gift for his Aunt Lorraine. Something clicked between them at first sight. Their first date that very night at Mr. Souvlaki's, a little Greek bistro kitty-cornered across the street, where she'd mistaken the nervous chatter of a closet *chaleria* for glib volubility. Truly, theirs was a whirlwind courtship. Two weeks later, he was springing the question as if it were already a done deal, as if inquiring whether she preferred peas to carrots.

"You're not perfect, but you'll do," she'd answered in a matter-of-fact tone equal to his because, at the time, being twenty years old, getting married was a kind of jokey thing to do, a stupid act of rebellion, because she'd known in advance what her parents were going to (and did) say: "You're too young" and "You're going to drop out of school" and "He'll get drafted and forget all about you" and "He wants to be what? A social worker?" and "What sort of name is *Stoner* anyway? What is he, a Jew?"

Well, except for the Jew part, he'd wasted no time proving her parents wrong on all accounts. He'd avoided getting drafted by the skin of his teeth, slick talking himself into a IIA classification when he went for his physical at Whitehall Street. And she'd never once considered dropping out of school—not even when she had Roger. Oh, those were the days: married less than a year and he working for the Department of Welfare for only a few weeks when his draft notice came, which ironically was the day the caseworkers' strike began, so that day he'd come home an absolute wreck—pathetic really—down on himself and the world because, in addition to being certain he was going to die in Vietnam, talk about the impenetrable, cataclysmic silence that lurks within, he was totally overwhelmed by something terrible that had happened at work that day he still refuses to speak about.

Undoubtedly, PFC Preston Stoner marching off to war would have been a huge mistake. But then, wasn't negotiating the huge mistakes together what marriage was all about. To be there for each other like he'd been for her when she'd gone through menopause. Maybe his demeanor tonight simply indicated he was going through a similar changing of the skin. Perhaps what he really needed right now was a few minutes of me time to collect himself. Maybe if she gave him something useful to do while she dashed downstairs to load the dryer, like making them both a pot of tea.

She returned to find two steaming mugs sitting on the coffee table, and his posture improved into something measurably less likely of being ingested by a piece of furniture; and hello, were those tears welling in his eyes? She caressed his cheek with the back of her hand. He took that hand in his and touched it to his lips like returning prisoners of war buss airport tarmacs.

"I love you, hon," he said in a voice a few floors farther up the elevator shaft.

"And I love you," she said, resolved to simply sip her tea and wait. Because it was Mike Kropsky—regrettably deceased and sorely missed neighborhood psychiatrist and friend—she had to thank for knowing what to do when her husband got down on himself like this. Or maybe better said, *The New Yorker* cartoon that showed her, depicting a man marooned on a tiny desert island, answering a telephone and saying, "I'm sorry, but he's not home right now."

"There's nothing to get upset about when you look for him and he seems not there," Mike had said. "We all have coping mechanisms. You do it your way. I do it mine. Spacing out is a perfectly normal way of dealing with things. Enduring love is a matter of balancing conflicting parameters."

Well, whatever balancing conflicting parameters meant, her husband's attention at the moment was focused somewhere across the room where their rarely played upright piano—purchased years ago, with the expectation that their remarkably talented children would soon be filling their house with music—now served humble use as the final resting place for family pictures and tchotchkes.

"Hey you," she said, "what's up?"

"I walked home over the bridge …," he began, then trailed off.

Oh dear, was it that he'd been mugged? Surely not. *She* was the one who feared lonely city streets. *He* was the one who encouraged the children that they had nothing to fear as long as they walked around like they knew what they were doing. Naturally, he would feel like that. For him, image was always the thing. Unfortunately, the image he projected tonight was that of a gray-haired, worn-out man.

"How did the Snapple thing go today, dear?" she asked

"Fine," he replied in a voice as flat as the Great Plains State of Nebraska. "Quite well, in fact. Duncan gave us the rest of the day off; told me I could expect a sweet bonus at the end of the year; gave me the usual song and dance about moving in with management upstairs. The guys and I celebrated at the Blue Grotto. The day being so nice and all that, I decided to hike home over the Brooklyn Bridge. Naturally, rain caught up with me at Tillary Street. But wouldn't you know it? Only in New York. Some umbrella guy had already set up shop at the exit under the bridge."

"Wow. So the Snapple thing went really well. That's great. I'm so happy for you. But why so down? For a second there, from the looks of you, I figured you to be either fired or, God forbid, mugged."

"Naw, nothing like that. It's just, crossing the bridge, when I paused to enjoy the view, suddenly I couldn't get it out of my mind, all the little children whose parents were lost that day," he said in a voice unmistakably brokenhearted.

Well, Mike Kropsky had warned her that until his mother issue was put to rest, there'd be occasional bouts of extreme melancholy. Unfortunately, among Preston's various pluses and minuses, when it came to getting one's mental house in order, he was—and probably always would be—a confirmed, unrepentant do-it-yourselfer.

For sure, Mike had him to a tee. In Preston's eagerness to seek the Way, he'd flip-flopped through the self-help world as if he were Toad in *The Wind in the Willows*. At one time or another, he'd come under the sway of everyone from Gurdjieff, Alan Watts, the Maharishi Mahesh Yogi, Karl Jung, Ram Dass, and Eckhart Tolle, to pop psychologists such as Deepak Chopra and Dr. Phil.

"Preston," she said as kindly and firmly as she could to a man who once spent an entire weekend trying to recreate one of Wilhelm Reich's orgone boxes, "this has to stop."

"Stop what?"

"Stop whatever this is. Listen, I too feel for those children. My heart aches for them the same now as it ached then. Nearly everyone felt that way. We were all in tears. But I have something to suggest that I want you to promise me to at least consider."

"This is about my mother again, is it?" he scoffed. "As if she had anything to do with 9/11."

"Those children," she said, determined once and for all not to let him off the hook, "most of them are going to be all right. Because, unlike back in the day when you lost your mother, most of these kids will receive some sort of guided therapy, if only a session or two—albeit some might need much more than that—that will help them to made amends with the great sadness they are doomed to carry inside them for the rest of their lives."

"So?" he said.

"So this," she responded. "I'm sure your Aunt Lorraine and Uncle Otis did their utmost best in raising you, maybe better than most aunts and uncles in their position would and could have done, but there were obviously things you needed to hear from them back then but didn't. Things that could and should have helped. My suspicion is that they lied to you some, and the subject of your mother's disappearance was rarely, if ever, directly addressed. Right?"

"Yeah," he mumbled.

"So," she said, "though I fervently believe you should, I know you're averse to going to therapy, so I'm not going there. But you're fifty-eight years old; don't you think it's about time you got a handle on this? *Just suck it up and get on with it.* How many times have I heard you tell the kids that? And for most things in life, sucking it up is pretty darn good advice. But what we are talking about here is a very big thing, Preston. We both know that. No, what I want to suggest is this: You like your little projects. After all, your mother could still be alive, so why don't you do a little research on your own and try to find her? That's all I'm asking. Just try. In the end, even if nothing comes of it, just the act of trying to find her might do you a world of good. Heck, you could start out by searching the Internet."

She paused, wondering if she'd gone on so long she'd lost him—or if he'd been listening at all? It was impossible to tell. His facial expression suggested the brainwave curve of a dial tone. "You're a do-it-yourselfer, so get off your duff and *be* a do-it-yourselfer," she then added with a little laugh, hoping to jolly him out of his funk. "How old was your mother when, she, as you so often put it, 'ran off' from you? Twenty-five, twenty-six years old? I mean, we have a daughter only slightly younger than that. Your mother was in the bloom of her life, for Christ's sake. Just think about it. I don't know about her, but just think how colossally unhappy she must have been with her *status quo* to pull a disappearing act on her husband and child like that. I mean, have you ever considered that maybe she left intending to be gone only long enough to teach your father some sort of a lesson, except, due to some colossal fuckup, things didn't go as she'd planned. A horrible accident maybe. Amnesia. Or maybe it's as simple as finally meeting Mr. Right. Whatever ... my point is … what is it, fifty-three years since the day your mother left you? Don't you see? You weren't weeping for those little kids today. You were weeping for yourself."

Preston sat up straight, finally able to look her in the eye. "You're probably right," he said, and by the way he'd said probably, she was sure he had taken to heart most of what she'd said, "but what you suggest simply requires too much effort. I sincerely doubt the Internet will be much help. Too many years have passed. Besides, apart from Googling her name, I wouldn't know where to start."

She laughed. "But, dear, Googling her name *is* the start."

"Yeah, that may be," he said, "but let me be frank. What you're suggesting here sounds to me suspiciously like a crusade. I don't have the energy for crusades. You talk like I've never thought of finding her. For your information, all my life I've thought of little else. You want to know the real reason I ended up in New York City? Because I once overheard my uncle say to my aunt that if my mother were still alive, NYC was probably where she'd ended up. In fact, for years (though lately not so much) you could safely say finding my mother has been a closet obsession of mine. As for why, up 'til tonight, I've never discussed it with you—or for that matter physically and psychically got it together enough to try to find her for myself—your guess is as good as mine. Maybe what I am is just a hopelessly flawed Parsifal, a not so pure and innocent fool, too hip to the ways of the world to be able, at this late date, to start chasing after his mother like she were the Holy Grail. A mother who never once tried to get in touch with me, who, if still alive, most probably prefers not to be found."

"Parsifal? Preston, let's not go overboard. As I recall, in Wagner's opera, Parsifal leaves his mother on a quest for the Holy Grail, not the other way around, and it was Amfortas, King of the Grail Knights, not Parsifal, who suffers from a wound that refuses to heal. But highfalutin, Wagnerian metaphors aside, all I'm saying is, the time has come for you to straighten up and make a mensch of yourself."

"Okay, okay. Enough already. Look, I'm more than willing to accept what you say, that today has everything to do with my mother. However, I don't agree that she adversely affects my life. As far as I'm concerned, I think I *have* made an accommodation with her disappearance, that I've already *done* what you claim the little kids of 9/11 will someday do, made myself into something of which my parents would have been extremely proud. I earn a nice income. I have a wonderful wife and two extremely gifted and lovely children. I obey our nation's laws, pay my taxes, and respect my fellow man. Believe it or not, Joellen, warts and all, I'm perfectly content being who I am."

She had expected as much. She'd tried encouragement. She'd tried cajoling. The time had come to rattle his cage.

"Preston, our children are grown. We're empty nesters now. Both of us, closing in on sixty years old. This means that as a couple, we may well have twenty to thirty years of living together ahead of us. Think of it. Just you and me, the two of us, alone in a house on Pioneer Street. Now, you may consider that a blessing, but I'm not so sure. It all depends—"

"What depends? What's going on here? I thought we were talking about finding my mother?"

"'What depends,' Preston, is you and me; 'what depends' is the continuance of our marriage. When you married me, you married a young woman whose idea of marital life was a sort of feel-good sitcom experience minus the commercial breaks—joy and laughter with a few tears along the way. A simple life dominated by pronouns: *he* loves, *she* loves, *they* love *their* children; *their* children love *them*; a life together in which a satisfactory makeup made right every spat. But, as the years drift by, reality sets in and the delusional 'we' we started our life out together with hardly exists. Preston, what I am trying to say is that our relationship hangs in an emotional balance fraught with what-ifs and but-who-cares. Now, if you want to go on imagining me as the same starry-eyed shop girl you married so long ago, be my guest; but after an adult lifetime of living together, absent a relationship that is truly for better or worse, in sickness or in health, I'm afraid I can no longer play the let's pretend, we're still in love, game."

Preston shook his head in disbelief. "So, what are you saying here? You don't love me anymore? You want a divorce?"

She sighed. Of course, she didn't really want a divorce. She still cared intensely for this man—and probably always would.

"Preston, what I desire is to live out the final years of my life married to a man who is not emotionally five years old, still tied to the apron strings of a phantom mother. Whether you do it on your own or seek therapy from someone else, do something, Preston—not for me or yourself, but for us."

He took a sip of tea. Ran his fingers threw his hair. Looked across the room, then back to her.

"Geez, hon. You put it like that, and I guess I'm just going to have to get out there and hire me a private detective, because the one thing I know for certain in life is, that I don't want to lose you."

His eyes pleaded for reassurance. The poor thing, his childhood had left him with a tough row to hoe. It was perfectly understandable, almost saddening really, over the years in his eagerness to please, how quickly he capitulated to her will. She was debating her reply when the oven timer dinged for her to please come rescue the seafood casserole. She smiled. "There you go, Preston. You must be living right. Saved again by the bell."

The seafood casserole, naturally, turned out great. However, they both picked their way through supper. He ascribed his lack of appetite to pigging out with the boys at the Blue Grotto. She said something about watching her weight. Conversation was confined to quotidian things— mainly Thanksgiving things: what size turkey, whether mashed potatoes or wild rice. When she inquired if he preferred pumpkin to apple pie, he suggested both. They discussed Bunny's flight information and the fact that Roger and Cheryl were still dead set on traveling on to Cheryl's parents in Scarsdale the following day. After supper, Joellen returned downstairs to fold and sort the rest of the laundry. Her husband, as was his wont, saw to the clearing of the table and the washing up of their supper things.

***

A glance out the window confirmed yesterday's AccuWeather forecast: light rain during the night, cloudy, mid-forties today. Taking care not to wake his wife, Preston dressed quietly for a day with early winter written all over it—heavy wool socks, paint-splattered sweatpants, NY Mets hooded sweatshirt. He was eating breakfast wondering if the Sarge would really show up today, when a faint rattling sound coming from out front, suggested someone or something was messing around with his garbage can. Assuming it was either a feral dog, the neighborhood raccoon, or the Sarge, he went to the front of the house quite surprised to see Adam, gaunt and dissipated crack-addict Adam, another character from the block's early days, who, the last Preston heard, was supposed to be doing time on Rikers Island instead of rifling their trash for recyclables.

Preston returned to his breakfast chuckling softly to himself. How many years had it been, since he'd glanced out that same window and seen Adam stopped astride a bicycle in the middle of Richards Street, clumsily trying to rebalance a thirty-six-inch TV set on the bike's handlebars? It wasn't until later when Joellen suggested that TV was probably stolen, that he realized that when he'd rushed out to give Adam a hand, he'd probably been guilty of abetting a crime. Still the two of them had had a hell of a lot of fun, trying to get the darn thing rebalanced long enough for him to give Adam a little push to get him wobbling on his way like a fatally wounded bomber struggling to stay aloft long enough to get back to home base.

Two eggs scrambled, a mess of home fries, a bagel and cream cheese and one very strong cup of Café Bustelo later, thoroughly sated and eager to get at his ivy with or without the Sarge, Preston took another peek out the front window and there the man was, sitting on the stoop waiting for him. And miracle of miracles, he didn't appear drunk. In fact, highlighted by a shaft of early morning sun that somehow, on such a gray and desperate day, had managed to pry its way into Brooklyn, the Sarge, blowing into his hands for warmth and the collar of his army fatigue jacket hiked up against the cold, looked to be in complete harmony with himself, almost noble.

Of course, Preston knew the correct humanist, atheist, Jewish, Christian, Muslim, Buddhist, Zoroastrian, and Bahaism thing for him now to do would be to invite the poor man inside for coffee. However, because of the Sarge's unfortunate tendency to mercurial mood swings, this was also something he knew he would not do. Rather, he'd fix up something warm and take it out.

He was layering lox onto a buttered Kaiser roll when Joellen entered the kitchen. "For me?" she said sweetly.

"The Sarge," he said with a nervous nod toward one of their innumerable and rarely used automobile travel mugs he'd just topped up with hot coffee. "He's outside, waiting on the stoop."

"But it's cold out," she said. "Why didn't you invite him in?"

"You've got to be kidding, right? We're talking the Sarge here. Christ, he lives most of his life outside. Compared to you and me, when it comes to acclimatization to the cold, by now he's a virtual Eskimo. Anyway, not to worry. I'm gonna fix him up with an old scarf and gloves."

Except, negotiating a twenty-foot ladder from the backyard and out the front door in a house filled with your wife's treasured things was a two-man job, so the Sarge had to come in anyway. *Don't worry. He's not drunk*, Preston mouthed to his woman, as they Laurel and Hardy'd the ladder past her as she stood guard over her china cabinet. A few minutes later, after the Sarge had wolfed down his bagel and coffee, the ladder fully extended and set to the house, Preston now stood on the third from the top rung; humming to himself, he clipped and stripped ivy vines from the brick face above a second-story window, when it occurred to him to ask the Sarge if he knew anything about the missing dog.

"Yo, Sarge. You know the break-in last weekend? Any idea what happened to your dog?"

But the Sarge persisted in stuffing downed ivy into a thirty-gallon garbage bag.

"Sarge," Preston repeated, considerably louder. "I said, any idea what happened to your dog?"

The Sarge's impish grin brought Preston clambering down the ladder.

"You? It was you?" he said, his voice reduced to a harsh whisper, because, if what he was suspected was true, no need broadcasting it to the whole neighborhood. "You broke into the house? That's breaking and entering, man. The police were there. Shit, you could do serious time. Where you got it?" he demanded.

"Iz mai dawg."

"Yes, I know, but where?" Preston insisted.

"Iz okay. Iz in mai van."

"Iz not okay. Iz crazy," Preston whispered through clenched teeth. "What were you thinking of? You live in an abandoned car for Christ's sake. How are you going to feed it?"

But Preston realized, he'd forgotten who he was talking to. Even on the best of days, the Sarge's doomsday clock hovered a tick or two shy of nuclear Armageddon. And now, look at the man: glowering, hands balled into fists. Preston eased back a step, took a deep breath and smiled. "You know what, Sarge? What say we take a little break here and go see if that dog of yours needs anything."

Situated in the back alley between Pioneer and Visitation Place, the derelict Chevy van that constituted the Sarge's squat was the ransacked remains of some homeboy's pimped-out primo ride. Matching beach scenes of palm trees and coco-skinned hula girls spray-painted on each side, milk crates shoved under the axels for support, transmission gone, engine stripped to the block, the neighborhood midnight auto service had worked it over pretty good.

The Sarge slid open the side door. To Preston's surprise, the interior was miraculously intact. A veritable fuckmobile done up in pink acrylic shag, with Mildred making like a queen of leisure, luxuriating in glorious squalor, atop her master's newly acquired bumblebee sweater and a raggedy old quilt spread out over a four-inch foam mattress.

Touching, Preston told himself, as the Sarge threw his arms around his dearly beloved's neck and tumbled into the van. While the world might think such an arrangement insane, for these two at least, it was nothing if not home sweet home. And far be it for Preston Frankel Stoner to deny these two the unalienable right to the pursuit of happiness—even though he himself wasn't all that certain what happiness was, other than the antidote to something Hegel once described as "the night that rendered all cows black."

Preston took a ten-dollar bill out of his wallet and passed it to the Sarge. "Look, Sarge," he said as he turned to leave, "I think we've packed enough ivy for the day. As for your dog, as much as possible, keep your mouth shut about how you came by it. If anyone asks, tell 'em you found it running around loose. Any time you find yourself running short of food for that dog, or say, it needs a vet or something, come see me, and we'll fix you up."

14

Beatrice, 1952

Lorraine's car bottomed out so hard it set her teeth. For the umpteenth time, she'd forgotten the dip where the Stoners' driveway met the street. One hand on the wheel, the other flung out in a desperate attempt to keep Polly's grocery sack upright on the passenger seat, it was not she, but her husband, Otis, she cursed for the few terrible seconds it took to keep from plowing head-on into Polly's newly planted mimosa tree, because the new set of shock absorbers that her good-for-nothing, blankity-blank husband should have installed by now, still lay in their packing boxes on the floor of *his* garage.

She took a moment to catch her breath after switching the engine off. At least, no damage had been done. She'd avoided the mimosa, and Polly's eggs were safe. However, her own two sacks of groceries stored in the trunk? As for the possibility that her onions, oranges, and potatoes were now strewn among the junk of inconvenience usually carted around in the trunk of his precious Electra, not to mention the unimaginable mess if one of her breakables, such as a jar of pickles or mayonnaise, got smashed, she'd wait 'til she got home before taking a look-see so as not to aggravate herself.

As if she wasn't already aggravated enough. Downright embarrassing it had been: little Tony Dechario from Police Brother's Market trying to make room for her grocery things amid Otis's personal cornucopia of man stuff best kept out of sight. The last time she'd bothered to take inventory, in addition to the standard stuff, like a spare tire and jack, fishing tackle, and a phony Indian blanket for her to sit on when he took her fishing up to the lake, had been a ball-peen hammer, a small shovel, a rope and tow chain, and a war surplus ammunition box crammed full of car tools and jumper cables, plus a case of 3.2 beer that he'd gone clear to Kansas for, because while it may be the 1950s everywhere else, when it came to the consumption of alcohol, prohibition still ruled the roost in good ole Gage County. And, of course, in addition to those damn hub caps that he had the filthy habit of picking up off the roadside as he went about his day that he'd add to the fifty-five and counting already tacked up on the outside rear wall of their garage, was his latest nut-ball acquisition: a brand-new softball bat and glove, because he claimed he aimed to organize a softball league. "Crazy ball," he said he'd call it. "For guys like me, who ain't all there."

Not all there? Otis couldn't find the butter in the icebox. And God forbid she ever attempt to neaten up that trunk or take something out— like, say, shitcan the ball-peen hammer, for starters—Otis would be on her quicker'n she could say *Sears and Roebuck shock absorbers*. The man was *exhausting*. Only one leg, and who could keep up with him?

As she leaned in to take out Polly's sack, she heard the back-porch screen door open and slap shut. By the time she had swung around with the sack in her arms, Polly was already halfway down the walk, coming to meet her, with her nephew, as usual, dogging at her heels.

"Here, I'll take that," Polly said, reaching for the sack.

"Nonsense. I already got it. It's no bother," Lorraine said as she shifted the sack away from Polly's grasp.

"Really, Ranie, you've done enough now just bringing it," Polly insisted. "Here now, let us have it."

"Don't be silly, child. I toted it here, might as well finish the job."

"Now, Ranie—please. I insist," Polly said like she wouldn't take no for an answer.

"Really, it's all right," Lorraine countered with equal insistence, because this little California girl had lived long enough among Nebraskans to know that, while it may look to somebody, say, from one of those big cities back east, like the two of them were squalling like a couple of little kids over who got to carry a stupid sack of groceries, in Nebraska, playing out this little ritual was just the way favors got done: the favorer and the favoree squalling in fun over who got to do what and when to whom.

"Well, then, at least let me carry the eggs," Lorraine said because, really, this silly little farce had gone on long enough. "They're on top and could fall right out. I do believe I told that girl in Police Brother's to pack 'em separate, but nowadays nobody seems to listen when you tell them things."

"That clerk heard you right, Lorraine," Polly said, her sack now hitched on her hip, the better to hold the door open. "That's the way it's done these days. Making one sack do the work of two. Pinching pennies to maximize profit."

Both of them laughed. Well, at least Lorraine. Polly barely chuckled because, as Otis always said: "I'm the one in our family blessed with funny bones. My sister Polly does math and reads well."

That may be, but Lorraine had to hold the eggs raised over her head to squeeze her ample self past Polly. Which definitely wasn't funny. Because as her husband also loved to say: "Put my Ranie through a wringer, she'd come out looking like Polly: a six-foot-tall, two-by-four stood on end." Indeed, Lorraine thought to herself, compared to her, Polly came off like a giant. And altitude and lack of bulk weren't the only large-scale attributes she failed to share with her sister-in-law. Take Polly's hands. "Man hands," Otis called them. Spider-fingered, broad-palmed, big-knuckled hands such that Polly never had to pester her husband away from Saturday afternoon sports TV to come open a jar for her—or for that matter think twice about being stranded alone at night, hoping some big strong man would come along to change a flat for her. Polly was a real tomboy, for sure. Otis claimed she was some sort of whiz at doing tricks on a bicycle when she was a kid. And even to this day, Polly and her bicycle were pretty much a fixture round town, like she had no idea she was supposed to be too old for such nonsense as sometimes on real hot days, on those rare occasions she wasn't wearing shorts, pedaling around with her skirt hitched up over her knees.

"Take a seat, Lorraine," Polly said. "Once I put away my things, I'll pour us some iced tea. There's something I've been wanting to talk to you about."

Lorraine knew full well what sitting down to drink iced tea in a Midwesterner's kitchen, coupled with something I've been wanting to talk to you about, meant—in the middle of the day, no less—the better part of an hour about to be wasted sitting in the presence of Polly's brand-new

Amana refrigerator. Not that Lorraine had an envious bone in her body. It was just that old Kelvinator she and Otis had was so out of fashion the cooling unit was perched on top. But at least, unlike folks on the poor side of town, she had a refrigerator. Gone for good were the days of putting a card in the window for the ice man twice a week. Otis bellyaching his beer wasn't cold, or worse, like the two of them coming home to find a big puddle in the middle of the kitchen floor because somebody like her husband had forgotten to empty the darn water tray, not to mention those emergency runs to Louie's Locker for an extra fifty-pound block of ice every time they were expecting company.

But Polly's glorious Kelvinator aside, the one thing about her sister-in-law Lorraine felt she would never be able to understand, envy, or abide was sure on full display today. Crouched as Polly was, stowing eggs, bacon, a few peaches, and a head of iceberg lettuce into that refrigerator and wearing shorts as she was were those skinny legs of hers thick with silky black hairs.

"European woman don't shave," she'd once said to Polly, thinking it high time her sister-in-law came to grips with the fact that her failure to shave her armpits and legs made her the talk of the town. "Don't they now," Polly had replied with one of those tight little warning smiles that said, that's enough, don't go there.

But really, about the only other woman ever heard of in Beatrice who didn't shave her legs and underarms was that war bride Bobby Purkey's uncle had carted home with him from Italy. That was, until Gloria in Nadine's took that girl aside one day and set her straight. The thing was, excess body hair seemed to run natural in the Kneebone family. Minus his shirt, Otis was a virtual woolly bear. And God forbid Lorraine should ever so much as mention his sister's hair business to him. With his knack for putting his foot in his mouth, he'd pick the most inopportune spot to say something only he thought clever that'd end up embarrassing everyone but him.

By this time, Lorraine had averted her gaze out the window to the next-door neighbor's cherry tree. Lord, it was hot. Dressed in her flimsiest cotton sundress, sweat balls were streaming down her freshly shaven legs. Shoot, on a day like today in San Diego, everyone'd be at the beach.

Polly closed the refrigerator door, placed a couple of glasses of iced tea on the table and sat down. "Lorraine, I swear, you looked like you was a million miles away out that window,"

"Sorry, dear," Lorraine said, as she spooned in two and a half sugars. "I was just thinking how I got me a ton of things to do today. But my, I see you've added a sprig of mint to our tea. I love mint. Adding it's such a nice touch."

"A ton of things, you say?"

"Well, you know, mostly stupid stuff, but stuff just the same."

Polly had retrieved a pack of Kools from the little glass shelf above the sink. She was in the act of lighting up when in came little Preston, tugging the little wooden pull train his uncle Otis had made for him.

Lorraine spread her arms and wiggled her fingers to lure him in. "Come on now, child! Get on over here and give your aunt Ranie a great big kiss."

But the lad made straight for his mother. His indifferent mother, one arm folded across her waist supporting the elbow of the other. Cigarette smoke curled up beside her ear. And it just drove Lorraine crazy whenever Polly held herself aloof from her son like this.

"Come on, honey. Get over here to your poor auntie. I'm all alone by the telephone," Lorraine gushed, hoping to envelope the boy in a big bear hug. And how delicious it was, the way he finally snuggled in, his little face screwed in disgust as she planted a big wet smacker on his cheek, the way he giggled with delight as she licked her fingers and slicked his cowlick down. His gritty scalp an unholy mixture of Wildroot Hair Tonic and frequent visits to his sandpile; if she were this boy's mommy, she'd see his hair got washed every day.

"I do believe he loves you best, Lorraine," Polly said.

"Now, honey, don't be giving me none of that. A boy always loves his mother best; don't you, Preston?" Lorraine replied, ever so grateful the boy had the good sense to nod his head that *yes, indeed, he loved his mother best.*

Normally, Lorraine held her tongue when her sister-in-law said stupid things in front of her boy like that. But lately, this kind of stuff was getting to be practically old hat. No doubt about it, Polly seemed a little more frayed around the edges these days. And that something her sister-in-law had said she wanted to talk to her about? Lorraine was really beginning to wonder. And would have continued to wonder but for Hairy, the Stoners' overly energetic, yappy little dog, suddenly bouncing into the room, up from the basement to visit his water bowl; and once the dog finished lapping its fill, both it and the boy off in a mad dash for the living room.

"You know what, Lorraine?" Polly said as she doused her cigarette under the faucet. "Those two got the right idea. What say we follow suit. Take our teas and bask in the breeze of the floor fan."

And certainly, with the shades drawn on the sun side of the house, plus the floor fan, apart from its doom-and-gloom atmosphere, it was much cooler in the living room. Lorraine eased herself into Simon's bentwood rocker. The wingback chair, as always, belonged to Polly. Hairy the dog lay on his back beside the sofa, legs poked straight up in the air. Her always-busy nephew playing something he called "parking lot" nearby, burrumping and vahrooming toy cars into neat rows. A compulsive habit she'd watched the child indulge in for hours. But Polly's enigmatic smile, the way she kept crossing and recrossing her legs, the ticktock of Grandpa Stoner's mantel clock, Lorraine broke the silence by saying the first thing that popped into her mind. "Love what you've done with this room— especially your new walnut console TV. Nineteen-incher, I do believe. What is it, a Muntz?"

Polly delayed her reply by taking a sip of tea. "Yes, it is. Simon says Beatrice ought to be getting a station of its own one of these days."

"About time, I'd say," Lorraine more than agreed. "As it is, no matter how you cut it, reception from Omaha or KC stinks. Viewing *Milton Berle* in a snowstorm ain't all that funny most of the time."

Polly set down her glass of tea and lit another cigarette. "Lorraine," she sighed, "I did my best."

Her best? Best what? This room? The TV? Or, maybe she was referring to her new drapes. "Yes, you certainly did," Lorraine answered just to keep the ball rolling. "I seem to recall you sewed all them drapes yourself. Love that blue material. Harmonizes real nice with the green in your rug. And, come to think of it, I've forgotten exactly how you came by this rug. Estate auction, was it? If so, whose estate would that be? Someone here in town?"

"No," Polly replied. "Got it when the old Jochim place went up for sale. Turkish, I believe. Or maybe Armenian. Something old Kurt came back with after serving in the First World War. Purchased in France, I heard tell, for less than fifty bucks. Worth, Simon swears, easily ten times that. I really should roll it up for the summer. But I can't bear to, seeing it's about the only thing in this house that doesn't spell Nebraska."

Lorraine smiled. Here was a subject on which she and Polly always agreed. Except Polly's beef with her home state was mainly cultural, while hers was mostly all about missing Southern California. The thing was, she'd come east wholly unprepared. Not that she hadn't gone to the public library in San Diego to bone up on what it was she was about to say yes to. Nebraska had seemed exotic enough. Willa Cather, rippling waves of grain, gorgeous sunsets, corn-fed beef capital of the world. Pictured in an encyclopedia, Omaha's busy streets hadn't looked all that different from San Diego's. But looking like and being like were something else. Not long after arriving in Beatrice, the thing she was missing most was enjoying a morning cup of coffee on a patio overlooking the sea. Yes, indeed, all that stuff they left out of books. Like the ungodly, merciless heat of Nebraska in summer, the howling blizzards of winter, the spectacular Nebraska sunsets due mainly to dust borne aloft by a westerly wind so constant that if it wasn't blowing, you must be standing in the eye of a tornado.

Polly coughed and cleared her throat. "Your car all right, Lorraine? Heard it bottoming out clear in the kitchen. Sorry about that. I've been after Simon to get Mr. Moody to do something about that dip. If it makes you feel any better, every now and then I forget and do the same."

Hmmmmm. Mr. Moody? Now, there was a name lately too much on Polly's lips. Though Lorraine had failed to attach any particular significance to it at the time, just the day before, Otis was mentioning something about Pru catching the pair of them sitting together on a bench in front of the courthouse, in a way that maybe they shouldn't have.

Polly coughed again. "Don't say it, Lorraine," she said as she ground out her half-smoked cigarette in the ashtray. "I know I've got to quit. It's just that things have been bothering me lately. Actually, quite a few things. You've got to promise me something."

"Sure, honey, anything. You know me."

Polly arched her eyebrows and leaned closer. "And you can't ever speak of it to anyone, not even my brother. Especially my brother. Understand?"

"Sure thing. Shoot, don't I know! Tell Otis something, come sundown it's out in the street running around on legs. You can trust me. You're twice the sister to me than that damned Otis is a husband."

Polly chewed her lip a moment. "Lorraine, I want you to promise that if something ever happens so that if I'm not around anymore, you'll see to caring for little Preston."

Oh, Lordy, Lorraine thought to herself, the poor dear's got some incurable disease. "Of course, honey," she half whispered, out of fear that the boy, a scant six feet away, might overhear. "If something ever happened to you or Simon, heck, you know me and Otis would be there to step in. But, honey, pardon me; you're scaring me to death. Why you talking like this? What's so wrong you're wanting me to promise you something like that?"

Polly mouthed her reply. "Something personal. Very personal."

"Something personal? Honey, I'm sorry, but that's not good enough. You can trust me. Come on, out with it. Cancer? Leprosy? Tuberculosis? Impending financial disaster? Is Simon horsing around with somebody else?"

When Polly shook her head *no* to each of these, Lorraine loathed to go where logic directed. Because, if Simon wasn't the one fooling around, then it had to be Polly. A circumspect Polly, capable of horsing around with another guy. A Polly she barely recognized. A Polly wholly unlike the woman she'd grown to love and adore, who, through thick and thin, no matter what, took what life dished out straight backed and chin up. A Polly she needed to motion over to the farthest corner of the room, where they stood a better chance of conversing without being overheard.

"Polly, child, I got to talk plain. This is way too mysterious to me," Lorraine half whispered, after they were huddled up beside a far window. "You're kind of talking riddles here. And if you want to keep the details to yourself, fine. But I think I ought to say that whatever it is that's bothering you, I'm sure between the two of us we could get it worked out. Or at least take an honest stab at it. But the only way for us to do that is for you to level with me straight: Are you or are you not in love with somebody else?"

"Lorraine, truth is, I'm not sure I know how to answer you. What is love anyway?" Polly said, unable for the first time since they had known each other to look her sister-in-law in the eye.

"Honey, I guess you just know," Lorraine answered, somewhat disheartened by Polly's evasive reply. "Anyway, Otis is my first and only, so when it comes to speaking of love, you just might be asking the wrong lady here. But if you're wondering if any of that stuff you read about in romance magazines goes on in my house, well, you've got to be kidding.

Honey, near as I can tell, falling into and out of love with your spouse is part of the regular scheme of things. Shoot, sometimes me and Otie break up and make up three or four times a day."

"And that's what you call love?"

"If it isn't, then I don't know what else to call it."

"That doesn't make you sound too certain."

"Certain? Honey, where you going with this? Everyone knows what love is, but nobody but a poet or a fool ever tries to define it in words. For sure, love ain't no bowl of cherries and it doesn't make the earth move under your feet, but rare is the wounded heart that fails to heal. Maybe your problem is that you entered into marriage with inflated expectations."

Polly's response was as rudely abrupt as it was unexpected. All further talk of love bit the dust when she summarily gathered up their tea glasses and marched them into the kitchen, leaving her sister-in-law slack-jawed and seething in her wake. And all that stuff about loving the things Polly had done to fancy up her living room? Nothing matched. The Stoners' new TV was ugly as sin. Polly's new drapes did nothing for a room devoid of pictures, without so much as a mirror. The stark truth was, Polly could care less whether her house looked pretty or not. She didn't have fancy mirrors hanging on her walls because she didn't want to see herself living here. And about the only good thing Lorraine could say about this room was that, at least, since the boy had been busy parking those damn cars of his off on the other side of the room, together with the whirr of the floor fan, mercifully, the poor child's ears had been spared.

Lorraine took a few deep breaths to calm herself down. By now, it was obvious Polly had no intention of returning to the living room. Therefore, Lorraine knew she had to go to her, because that was what one did, when someone cared deeply about someone who was in pain.

She reentered the kitchen to find her sister-in-law in distress, fighting back tears. "Oh, honey. Please, don't worry," she said as she gathered her into her arms. "You aren't alone here; you've got a friend. No, you've got more than that. I've got to say it. I love you, child. Ain't nothing on God's green earth gone so wrong that the pair of us, teamed up, can't put right." But even as she spoke, Lorraine knew nothing could be further from the truth, that there were tons of things in life that all the wisdom in the Good Book couldn't put right.

15

Thanksgiving, Red Hook, 2004

For reasons Preston preferred best kept to himself, negotiating heavy traffic was easier when Joellen wasn't riding shotgun in the car. What a relief it had been this morning when she-who-must-be-obeyed, claiming she had too many pots to look after on the stove, had begged off accompanying him to Kennedy Airport to pick up Bunny and her current Mr. Wonderful. Because, simply put, urban man's truest castle *was* his car; hence, sans the little woman, it was undeniably easier to maintain a state of cheerful calm while doing battle with the idiots on the road. To be, verily, a man behind the wheel with brass balls, who brooked no shit. A Mr. Super Cabby, as it were, hip to the primal traffic patterns of the highways and byways of NYC, eschewing the GPS to navigate by the seat of his pants, anticipating possible congestions, actualizing crucial lane changes. And this morning, of all mornings, his little wife had had the temerity to suggest that the best route to JFK was the Van Wyck via Atlantic Avenue. Atlantic Avenue? Atlantic Avenue was for idiots in love with stoplights. For the *cognoscenti*, the Belt Parkway via the Gowanus was the only way to go.

However, barely fifteen minutes after departing Pioneer Street, tooling along on that elevated section of the Brooklyn/Queens Parkway known as the Gowanus Extension, Mr. Super Cabby was forced to set his hazard lights to blinking some forty feet above Third Avenue in order to maneuver his car into the right lane, then ease it to a stop. His right rear tire had gone flat.

Okay, so what? he told himself. Only a minor screwup. No cause for alarm. As was his custom, he'd left early enough to provide ample cushion for unexpected delays. Call Triple A? As they say in Brooklyn: fuggadaboutit. Who needed them? Just a call to Joellen to assure Bunny, if she should call, to sit tight and that he'd be there soon. Except, was his cell phone in his jacket pocket, where he thought it to be? No. It was on top of his dresser, being recharged, so get out and change the tire already.

Except changing a right-rear tire on that particular stretch of elevated highway, where ongoing construction had shrunk three lanes to an extremely narrow two, leaving his car squeezed six inches tight to the guardrail, made it not only physically impossible to change that tire, but to exit his car, for any reason whatsoever, would be to endanger his life.

Surely, a tow truck would be along soon. On heavy traffic days, especially holidays, tow trucks were out in force like vultures seeking carrion. Therefore, all he had to do was hunker down, restart the engine every now and then in order to stay warm, crack a window occasionally to let in fresh air, and worst of all worlds, Bunny and boyo could take a cab. In fact, now that Preston had wholly resigned himself to his plight, he, the dumb shmuck with a flat tire, settled back to amuse himself by turning on the radio.

However, his finger hovered before the preset for the Pacifica Station, WBAI. Come on, man. Did he really want to compound this vexing moment with the latest reporting of the criminal misadventures of Messrs. Bush, Rumsfeld, and Cheney? So, he hit the neighboring preset for the jazz station, WBGO, instead, where, to his great relief, the cut currently being aired just happened to be a golden-oldie fav of his: "Lover Come Back to Me." Breakneck tempo. West Coast cool school, early to middle fifties. Messrs. Art Pepper, Shelley Mann, and Andre Previn jivin' in the groove—and was that Leroy Vinegar on bass?

Preston angled his seat back and closed his eyes. Lover came and went. He was lolling in Chet Baker's lush world now. Trumpet man turned songster crooning "Blue Moon." Bringing with it drowsy remembrances of the Dechario boys back in Beatrice, Nebraska, who were the ones who had turned him on to such all-world jazzers like Bird, Diz, Miles, Shorty Rodgers, Marty Paitch, and, yes, Chet Baker. Word had it that both Joe and Tony made it big as professional musicians. Next chance he got, he really ought to check Amazon for their CDs. Those two, how he had envied their artistic abilities. Even had a brief go himself at trying to learn the trumpet, going for lessons faithfully each week for most of six years; but no matter how great the desire, there was no substitute for talent. And speaking of talent, how about the hot dog cut they were playing now: Diz's "Perdido," as rendered by Chico Hamilton's Afro-Cuban big band?

Driven by the toe-tapping, high-octane angularities of a jazzed-up mambo, Preston popped his seat back up to check his rearview mirror for a tow truck. And suddenly there it was, as if it hadn't been there all along, affixed to the side of a building adjacent to where he sat, a billboard advert no less, for a detective agency. A ginormous grandma figure in a deerstalker hat, magnifying glass held before a hugely magnified eye. *MUMS the WORD* emblazoned below in *sans serif* lettering five feet high. Preston rummaged through the glove compartment for a scrap of paper and pen to copy down the phone number, imagining what he would say if only he had his cell phone:

Ring ring ring.

"Hello, Mums?"

"Yeah, speaking. Wajaz want?"

"I got a flat tire. I'm stuck in traffic on the Gowanus."

"Listen, kid, getta life. Mum's don't do flat tires."

Well, Mum's may not do flat tires, but five to ten they were finders of lost mommies. Oh, happy day, kaloo kalay, as Duncan said the other day, serendipity ruled. A man who needed to hire a detective to find his mother gets a flat tire, and *voila*, fucking serendipity fucking ruled.

"And hahaha to you too, motherfucker," Preston shouted aloud to a passing Escalade bearing a dumb-bunny vanity plate inscribed with those very words. Because what did the occupants of that car care of his plight? Who was he to them but a Hindu *dahlit* with a fucking flat tire listening as John Coltrane disassembled Rogers and Hammerstein's "My Favorite Things"? Trane's kaleidoscopic soprano sax, McCoy Tyner on piano, Steve Davis on bass, Elvin Jones on drums, tripping it out in three-quarter time.

Preston was feeling good. Very good indeed. So good that the next time he checked his mirror for a tow truck, it took a second or two for it to register that a minor fender bender had just taken place behind him.

For him to then lower his window, crane his head out, thanking his stars that his Subaru wasn't one of them.

Naturally, he sympathized with drivers A, B, C, and D. Despite what it was eventually going to say in the accident report, he was really the one at fault. But at least, the guys behind the wheel in cars C and D had their cell phones out, presumably calling in their predicament. So that whoever showed up to help them, could also help him. But drivers A and B? Complete idiots, both of them. Having left their cars to go toe to toe on the roadway, they've brought traffic to a complete halt so they could play the blame game. Especially, driver A. The one doing all the shouting. Coatless, hatless. Maroon velveteen tracksuit unzipped to the naval. Snow-white tee shirt stretched tight over a barrel chest on a very chilly day. One of those pretty-boy types given to facials and pedicures when he wasn't snorting cocaine, lifting weights, who went ballistic whenever someone dared visit damage upon the precious rear end of his late-model 700 series BMW. Driver B, on the other hand, was a whole other kettle of fish. Fur-brimmed hat, black satin coat and knickers, patent leather shoes, and white silk stockings? A Satmar, Preston deduced from his natty attire. Another of those Hassid fruitcake menaces of the road, driving a Windstar crammed full of wife and kids. Meek as a mouse, lips barely moving like he was muttering some arcane Talmudic blessing for auto accidents.

Still, at least traffic had managed to improvise a way to get moving again. Preston, having seen enough, rolled his window up to better enjoy Diz and Bird's crazy-wild improvisatory romp through "Night in Tunisia." Even so, with the volume cranked up high, conflict resolution Brooklyn-style was proving impossible to ignore. Such that, when Preston lowered his window once more, Beamer Boy had become a virtual one-man klavern of the Ku Klux Klan, his neck cords standing out like Roebling's steel cabling for the Brooklyn Bridge.

"Fucking Jew. Fucking motherfucking Jew. You've fucked up my new car. This for you," driver A screamed as he wrenched open the Windstar's door, grabbed the keys out of the ignition and sent them arcing over the guardrail to the street below.

The rebbetzin shrieked as her rebbe stood slack-jawed, frozen in place, and whether or not it was Diz's sizzling trumpet that issued the clarion call or simply Preston responding to his inner bugle, the moment he saw

135

Herr Beamisher seize this humble man of God by his shoulders, slam him into the side of his van, and begin to pummel him with his fists, without thought for his person, Preston Frankel Stoner stirred forth from his automobile like there were springs in his shoes, a veritable Übermensch super-stud whose righteous mission in this life was to go forth and rescue the Jews. Real-life action that turned into a slo-mo dream the moment Preston grabbed Signor Beamerini from behind. A deft spin movement, a right cross aimed straight for Preston's eye that was such a thing of grace, each knuckled finger the bearer of a runic tattoo: L for the forefinger, O for the bird finger, V for the ring finger, Mr. Pinky with an E. And the next thing Preston knew, he was seated behind the wheel of his car, hands on the steering wheel properly spaced at ten and two, without the foggiest notion why a policeman would be telling him that in the event he didn't want to press charges, he was still required to make a statement.

And yes, he made a statement—albeit a little light on the details. And yes, he didn't press charges. And no, he didn't think he'd need to take the patrolman's advice to get himself checked out for a possible concussion. What he did was to mutter something aloud about his flat tire.

Officer Robert Lowery pursed his lips in amazement. "Whatever, mac. It's up to you. Either sit tight and wait for a tow truck or rim it down to Thirty-Ninth Street. There's a Mexican flat-fix place nearby on Fortieth Street that's usually open 24/7. But I'm curious, pal. Why didn't you do that in the first place? It's Thanksgiving for Christ's sake, and you got traffic backed up behind you for miles, way up past the Kosciusko Bridge."

Preston deemed it best to treat this question as rhetorical. Tail suitably tucked between his legs, he rimmed it down to the flat-fix place, where they graciously permitted him use their landline to call Joellen.

"Come on home," she said after he finished a highly redacted version of where he was and why. "Don't worry about Bunny and Joe. They just called to say they're standing in line for a cab." A short pause, then "Honey, are you okay? You sound a little funny to me."

Funny? Not really, unless a growing lump above his left eye was funny; or a humongous traffic jam reaching clear to Queens was funny; or a Hassidic family more or less stranded in place for want of their car keys was funny; or the sad case of driver A, visibly chastened, cuffed and stuffed in the rear of a patrol car, who in all likelihood, was normally a really nice guy, with only the occasional tendency to road rage, whose family was waiting Thanksgiving dinner for him at home, wondering what was keeping him, was funny.

***

Preston returned home to find Joellen vacuuming the living room.

"Preston, good God …? Flat tire, my eye. Or, better said, *your* eye, because from the looks of it, you've either been in a fight or an accident," she exclaimed.

"Don't worry, hon. You're right. There was an accident, sure, but it didn't involve our car. As for the flat, the tire was ruined, but the rim's okay. As for my eye, youse otta see da udder guy. The main thing is, I'm home all in one piece and none the worse for wear," he said, hoping to postpone the lurid details for later, much later, like maybe never.

"Okay," she'd replied, only a little less put out, but still concerned. "Tell me later. Right now, get yourself upstairs and tidy up best you can. The last I heard from Roger and Cheryl was that they're stuck in traffic on the Brooklyn/Queens expressway. Bunny and Joe, however, are due any minute. I'll have an ice pack ready for that eye once you come down. But," she said with a *boy, are you ever on my shit list* look in her eye, "I have to say, Preston, I'm deeply disappointed in you. I mean, yesterday, I send you to the store, and you return with half the things I sent you for because you forgot to take the list. Then, you swear to me that you're going to have the house presentable for guests, yet I've spent half my morning cleaning up the places you missed. And then you leave the house to pick up our daughter at the airport and come home sporting a black eye, acting like it was nothing? Jesus, God, man, what next?"

Thankfully, rather than wait for his reply, Joellen trundled her ire back to the kitchen, leaving Preston aswirl in a vortex completely of his own making. He had no more gone upstairs than he was running back down to greet not only Bunny with her Mr. Joe in tow, but Roger and Cheryl as well. Which, he figured was all to the good, now that his home was festive with welcoming chatter and good-natured banter.

Indeed, an hour or so later, Preston found himself almost lighthearted, sitting cross-legged on the living room rug near the coffee table. Surrounded by family, bathed in shimmering light of what seemed like a gazillion candles, he relished his small-child's viewpoint of the room as he waited for the turkey to cool enough for him to carve. And that mini spat he'd just had with his wife concerning the particulars of his incipient shiner? Not altogether forgotten but far enough removed from the present glorious moment as to seem not all that important anymore. The magnificent tray of hors d'oeuvres that Joellen had set out for them on the coffee table, along with the nearly empty bottle of sherry from which he'd filled everyone's glass for the evening's toast, now sat deliciously and gloriously ravished. And his ploy of making fun of himself as a means of explaining away his black eye? As he suspected, getting everyone (even Joellen) laughing together had been not only a surefire beginning to, what he hoped would be, a truly memorable Thanksgiving, it set the stage for his inimitable, irrepressible, much loved younger child Bernadette (aka Bunny), true to the Germanic roots of her namesake, fiercely loyal and brave as a bear, to be presently holding forth center stage with the learned fervor of the college professor her father yet imagined someday she might become— whose subject at hand was the appalling misjustices wrought upon the Amazonian *indigenas* of Ecuador by a world gone mad for oil.

"Thanksgiving, a day devoted to gluttony, indolence, and too much football, a day for capitalist pigs to celebrate their God-given right to consume more than their natural share of planet Earth," she had just finished saying, blue eyes flashing, brandishing a hunk of torn-off pita in her right hand as she jabbed each point home. And how beautiful his younger child looked that night—spectacularly tanned and suitably fit. Clad for the evening in a red and white, horizontally striped rugby shirt, stonewashed jeans, and black beret *como* Che Guevara, a gringa sorceress yet to dip her pita into the hummus.

And then, seated to Bunny's left, perched side by side on the sofa, his pair of love birds, Roger and Cheryl, down from visiting her parents in Stamford. Married three years and they still held hands! Roger, Bunny's older brother, also had a temperament to match his name. *Hrodgar*, the old Norse word for spear. Truly his sturdy philosopher-cum-man-of-the-cloth son gloried in penetrating to the hearts of things. Very much of the proletariat tonight, dressed in basic workman's denim shirt and jeans, Day-Glo green suspenders, and a fiercely red bow tie. And his wife, Cheryl— deliciously full of pep, a classy but not stuffy society babe. The always appropriate, exuberantly delightful, thoroughly secular eldest daughter of the grandson of the founder of Wolf's of Scarsdale Department Store. Dressed, as usual, to the nines tonight. Neat as a pin, putting the rest of his crew to shame. Red and black silk scarf worn casually over the shoulder, white silk blouse, gray linen slacks. Yes, like his son, she had extremely good taste. And then, there was Joe. US Border Guard Joe from Nogales, Arizona. Joe, the mystery man his daughter picked up in an ex-pat coffee bar in Quito, sitting quietly by his lonesome on the piano bench opposite the coffee table, no doubt wondering what was up with a family who was wondering what was up with him. Then, hovering like an archangel in the doorway, stood his radiantly beautiful Joellen, bewitching mistress of the kitchen, the wooden stirring spoon in her hand freshly stained by whatever exotic stew she was brewing up for them that night.

Except, look out, world, because Bunny had just made the fatal mistake of pausing mid-screed for a sip of sherry, leaving herself wide open for another of Roger's brotherly digs: "Bunny, it sounds like what you're up to in the Peace Corps is fomenting revolution," he said to great laughter all around.

Bunny, of course, responded to her brother's taunt by wrinkling her face and sticking out her tongue because that had been her way of getting back at brother ever since the time they had been visiting Uncle Otis and Aunt Lorraine in Nebraska and Roger hoodwinked his baby sister into taking a bite of a green persimmon, Bunny too little to strike back and too angry to cry. And though Preston had thought it cute at the time, it certainly would not have been the way *his* mother would have reacted had *she* been around. Among the few, faded memories he had of his mother were those chilling glances she had thrown his way whenever he broke one of her dictatorial rules … and certainly, *thou shalt not stick out thy tongue* would have been one of them.

Preston shifted uncomfortably. A child's viewpoint of things was not that easy for old bones to maintain. He had growing pain in his lower back. The burgeoning knot above his eye measured each heartbeat. And worst of all, he'd just profaned the spirit of Thanksgiving, resurrecting the shade of a mother he almost wished he hadn't promised to hire a detective to try to find, because he wasn't all that sure she'd turn out to be a mother he wanted to find. As far as he was concerned, his real mother had been his

Aunt Lorraine. His aunt and uncle must have had good reason for their little conspiracy of things left unsaid.

Another burst of laughter. Roger had just cracked another joke. Although Preston missed the quip, he couldn't miss Joellen's mouthed message to him from the doorway to *stop daydreaming and pay attention.* Except, what Bunny was preaching was so old hat. Her generation, like his, wishing the old folks to step aside so their generation could get down to the business of setting the world straight. Iraq/Vietnam, Bush/Nixon: it was the same old tune. Only the names of the notes changed. Just like Bunny's hunky boyfriends. To a man, each needed something from her: the Irishman, a green card; the visiting Nigerian, a convenient place to crash in NYC. Sooner or later it'd be one of those Inca guys with braided pigtails that play panpipes in the subway. *Quechua, quichua?* She *was* learning their language, wasn't she?

It shouldn't have, but it did, bother him a lot, Bunny announcing the moment she walked in, that she and Joe would be flying back to Nogales the next day. But apparently his wife was better than he at taking disappointing news in stride. Hell, she'd met them at the door all aflutter over a blonde and blue-eyed, square-shouldered, square-jawed man with a toothpaste-ad smile. Well, Mister Joe's under the Stoner microscope now, for wasn't that what this was all about? A daughter bringing her latest trophy boyfriend home to show off to her father, the way she used to bring him childhood drawings on tenterhooks for his approval. Nevertheless, for certain, if Joe had been riding shotgun with him today, that bozo in the Beamer would be the one growing a black eye right now.

"In Ecuador, we're talking eighty percent," his daughter then declared with a surety that had tiny drops of spittle bouncing in the air. "What Americans fail to grasp about Ecuador, Bolivia, and Peru is the depth of the poverty there. We're talking a once-noble people reduced to a bare-bones, hardscrabble existence. We're talking a family of six in a one-room stone shack with guinea pigs squeaking underfoot on fucking dirt floors. We're talking people under forty looking ninety years old."

"Amen, you tell 'em, sister," Preston whispered under his breath as Bunny signaled she'd finally shot her wad by raking the hummus with her pita, top teeth perched à la Bugs Bunny on her bottom lip, the very reason Uncle Otis had saddled his grandniece with that nickname in the first place.

But now that she'd had her say, spontaneous conversation seemed to have walked the plank. Roger and Cheryl no longer holding hands, stared dumbly into space. Joellen and wooden spoon gone back into the kitchen. And Joe, hopelessly lost in that little fuzzy space reserved for the smitten, as his beloved Bunny, having opined the evils of the world, now plied her happenstance suitor with olives, dried figs, and hummus-bedaubed pita.

"So, what am I supposed to do if it turns out he's a fucking Nazi … or has tattoos?" Preston had asked his wife last night prior to putting out the light. Well, speak of the devil. Joe had just removed his sport jacket, and now, Preston didn't know whether to chortle in disgust or weep for joy. Clad in a short-sleeved white shirt, each of Joe's chunky biceps revealed a tattoo: the head of a weeping Christ wearing a crown of thorns on the left and a screaming eagle with an American flag clutched in its talons on the right.

"Don't get excited if he has a few," Joellen had counseled him last night, making a zipping motion across her mouth to show what she expected him to do tonight. "They're all the rage among the young. Get used to it. By this time, even Bunny probably has one hidden somewhere. My God, I seem to believe your much-beloved, war-hero Uncle Otis, like most sailors during WWII, sported a burlesque cutie tattooed on his arm."

Yeah, but so what? Joe was likeable enough, but damn it all, blame it on those movies he'd seen at the Cozy Theater when he was a kid. Back in his day, tattoos were something worn by menacing, volatile motorcycle crazies itching for a fight, like that creep who'd clobbered him today on the Gowanus. What kind of sickness drove a man to tattoo *LOVE* on his fist?

Nevertheless, much as Preston would have loved to unburden himself to Joe on the subject of tattoos, discretion remained the better part of valor. He had no other choice but to talk to the man. Roger had disappeared upstairs to use the john. Cheryl and Bunny had gone in to volunteer their help in the kitchen. Considering that the turkey was still a good ten minutes away from being ready to carve, maybe now was as good a time as any for him and Joe to get better acquainted, that was, if and when, Joe stopped searching his damned Blackberry for messages.

"So, Joe, tell me, how was your flight?"

Joe shoved his cell phone into his pants pocket and smiled. "Don't ask. You know: long lines at the airport, smooth flight, crowded plane, lousy movie, lousier food. And you, Mister Stoner, how'r things going here for you in Red Hook?" he said with a gorgeous smile that dominated the lower half of a beautifully suntanned face.

"Well, Joe, you know how it goes. Gentrification means lots of young rich people moving in. Other than that, things about the same. City planning regarding this part of Brooklyn is hardly worthy of the name. The local mafioso continue to obstruct anything and everything that doesn't have something in it for them. Big box stores like IKEA and Fairway may, to an outsider, seem like a good thing—and in a way, they are, a viable something where there was worse than nothing before—but it's the same old story: progress to profit the few with no regard for those who pay the price."

"The price?" Joe said, helping himself to a dried fig.

"The social misfortunes that befall a neighborhood beholden to the 'dark side,' as our Darth Vader-ish vice president might say."

"You mean, disaster capitalism?" Joe added in an uncannily accurate imitation of the vice president's deep, gravelly voice, which had Preston laughing, even though the subsequent rise in blood pressure caused his eye to ache even more.

"So, Joe," Preston replied once he regained his composure, "my daughter tells me you're a border guard, right? So, how's riding fence patrol these days?"

"They keep us busy, Mr. Stoner. There are easily a hundred million people south of the border waiting to sneak over to our side. The border always has and always will leak like a sieve."

"You work day shifts or nights?"

"A little of both," Joe said. "We trade off."

"How many men per mile can Immigration post out there, anyway? All those miles—you guys must be stretched pretty thin."

"Sir, I'm afraid Homeland Security won't allow me to get into that."

"I'll bet they won't," Preston snorted with a derisive shake of his head. "Mr. Stoner?"

"Yes, and Joe, please can the *sir* and *mister* crap. We're non-military in this house. Call me Preston. Hell, call me anything, long as it's not formal. This is family night, and while I really don't have any idea how tight you are with my daughter, as far as I'm concerned, you're official family tonight. So, that said, what can I do for you?"

"Nothing, only I was wondering about that eye. Why don't you put some ice on it? I'm not trying to play doctor or anything, but by morning, if you don't ice it, it might be swollen shut."

"And you're a medical student too, you know so much about such things?" Preston asked, cautioning himself not to sound testy.

Joe grinned and pointed to something Preston hadn't noticed before: a nose slightly off-kilter—the only flaw on an otherwise perfectly sculpted face. "I'm just an amateur but I love to box," he said.

Preston's eye be damned, he couldn't help breaking up again. Joe Palooka had been the moniker of a cartoon character out of the Sunday funnies of his long-ago youth. A boxer with a heart of gold. A gentle knight who made a point of sticking up for the little man. But before Preston could explain to Joe that *yes* he *had* iced his eye, and *thank you very much; I intend to do it again before I go to bed*, the ladies burst laughing into the room. Bunny, wriggling onto the piano bench next to her man, whispering something into his ear, that Preston strongly suspected might have to do with Bunny suddenly remembering that night not long after 9/11, when her father had lost it completely with that idiot rock climber boyfriend of hers from Seattle, a lamebrain who was all for nuking the entire Middle East back to the Stone Age.

But surely, his daughter must have clued Joe in about her family's values, that her Grandpa Stoner back in Nebraska had been an ardent, word-slinging socialist and her great-grandfather, a real-deal, card-carrying commie. That, as politics went, her father was about as far left of center as a man could get, and her mother not only Quaker by birth but a staunch supporter of PETA as well. Not to mention, her brother was a Unitarian minister—or studying to be one anyway. That the members of her family worshipped—if that was the word for it—the anti-war trinity of Noam Chomsky, Howard Zinn, and Cindy Sheenan. That if a tattooed man were to come into this house espousing right-wing bullshit, he'd be entering the lion's den.

Except, he told himself, what he was grousing about, when Roger just returned from upstairs, was warming to some sort of joke having to do with Judgment Day and God wondering to St. Peter why in the world some of his good people insisted on hanging around just outside the pearly gates, sipping coffee, instead of coming in. To which, Roger said, "St. Peter replied: 'Lord, these are the Unitarian Universalists who, by the way, remain none too happy about all of those wars that have been fought in your name. But rest assured, once they finish debating your existence, I'm sure they'll be right in.'"

Border Guard Joe's belly laugh stirred from his gut decibels far beyond Preston's estimation of the usual amount of laughter accorded jokes about Unitarians. But the saints be praised, as quick as that, Thanksgiving, the holiday with the least strings, where all you had to do was show up, make merry and eat, had managed to right itself on keel. And Joe, no longer content to play the outsider sitting quietly on a piano bench, now very much in the flow, recounting a tale of his own about a Jewish bride-to-be back in Arizona and the Navajo boyfriend whom she intended to marry. How, when she'd insisted on having a traditional Navajo wedding in buckskin and beads, her Navajo groom, unbeknownst to her, made a three-hundred-mile round trip to the nearest Judaica store so he'd be wearing a yarmulke and prayer shawl when he slipped the ring on her finger.

Preston traded winks with his son, who seemed equally pleased with Joe. In the Stoner household, the ability to tell a cracking good tale ranked right up there with the desire to sort out the deeper side of life. But then, what did he expect from Joe? As they say in baseball, battin' five hundred ain't bad. Still, Joe had a way to go before excelling at tale telling like his son.

Looking back, it ought to have been predictable that a little boy who'd spent his childhood starting every sentence with *why* or *what*, who'd been raised to be a religious nothing, had grown up to become a Unitarian. Especially, considering the night he'd poked his nose into Roger's room, thinking the boy had gone to sleep with the light on again, but found him instead, a high school junior no less, not attempting but actually reading—and understanding—Sartre's opaque existential masterpiece, *Being and Nothingness*.

That was the night when the subject of Unitarianism first passed between them, and their discussion had been lively. A real back-and-forth tussle, contrasting the transcendentalism of Emerson, Thoreau, and Channing with Sartre's existential, sour-grapes view of life, which inevitably led to a heated discussion about faiths that fancy themselves based on reason. "Religion demands faith," Preston remembered insisting to his son, "and what is faith but the antithesis of reason?" Roger's comeback had been as immediate as it was sure, as amazing then as now. A Chinese proverb his son actually quoted from memory, so profoundly beautiful his father remembered it to this day: *Knowledge without wisdom is useless; wisdom without spirituality is not possible.*

Such an answer from a boy so young! Any father worth his mettle would have gracefully admitted defeat on the spot, turned out the light, and left it at that, but no this father had to lose his cool. "Spirituality is not religion," he'd snapped in retort. "It's a state of existential wonderment that requires no prior leap of faith," he'd said, rapping his knuckles for emphasis on Sartre's weighty tome, lying open and upside down on his son's chest, as if his brilliant retort was the final word, because it was late after all and the boy should have been asleep. But Roger refused to yield. Lips clamped firmly shut, his peach fuzz moustache bristled with teenage rebellion. "Speaking of faith, Dad, we're not really Jews, are we?" he'd snapped back, resorting to his mother's favorite oratorical ploy: the sudden non-sequitur. "Despite Grandpa Stoner's menorah, there hasn't been a Jewish mother in this family for at least three generations, so why do you keep kidding yourself that our family is Jewish?"

Well, he hadn't then, and certainly wouldn't now, forfeit his sense of Jewishness to dime-store logic. Okay, his mother wasn't Jewish, and he'd never had a Bar Mitzvah. It didn't matter that he was far from learned when it came to the Talmud and the Torah. His sense of Jewishness was simply a way of proclaiming respect for, and pride in, his father's heritage. A position that Sartre would most certainly have approved of, since somewhere in *Being and Nothingness*, it plainly stated that things were best defined in terms of what they are not. Still, there'd been no call for him to turn on the boy as if he were debating some stranger on the subway. "Try telling that, buddy boy, to the Nazi Germans in 1942. You and your sister and I, Jewish mother or no Jewish mother, would have been marched off to the ovens with the rest of them."

Preston raised his head. Dear God, his wife was standing over him, peering down into his one good eye.

"The turkey, dear," she said, for what he suspected was the third or fourth time. "It's Thanksgiving, remember? So, carve the bird already. We're starving here."

His cramped-up left leg, which was all pins and needles, gave way beneath him when he attempted to stand. Joe chuckled and steadied him to his feet. And this time it was not by design that he felt himself the addlepated butt of a slapstick joke as he limped into the dining room. The others seemed to think it funny as well.

Joellen had the carving knife, honing rod, and corkscrew laid out beside the bird. A seasoned celebrant of the rites of plenty, his first task was to open Joe and Bunny's primo bottle of Moldavi Zinfandel and set it to breathe. From then on, he'd be worshipping in Uncle Otis's church: truing the blade against the rod just so, testing its keenness with his thumb so that cardboard-thin slices of turkey would daintily fall onto his waiting palm.

"A dull knife is a dangerous knife," was among his uncle's favorite truisms, as well as the excuse his uncle had given his aunt the time he'd been caught red-handed showing his nephew the proper way to go about putting an edge on the little penknife the boy had received that day as a tenth-birthday gift—a penknife that his nephew harbored upstairs, in a dresser drawer, to this day.

Indeed, his uncle had considered himself quite the connoisseur of lethal cutlery. His love for knives, like the authors he favored—Zane Grey, Mickey Spillane, Erle Stanley Gardner—as cussedly existential as a trench shovel and mess kit. Unfortunately, for his uncle, Aunt Lorraine didn't hold much with bowie knives, scimitars, dirks, and pole axes lying about the house. Poor guy, apart from the Japanese sword his uncle claimed to have won from some Marine in a poker game back during the time he spent hospitalized in San Diego, which hung for years on the wall behind his desk at the county jail, all the rest of his prized stuff was forced by his wife to suffer confinement in a locked steamer trunk in the garage. So that, other than a formidable set of kitchen knives, about the only physical evidence of his uncle's lust for tempered steel with honed edges was the knee-high stack of well-thumbed issues of *Blade Magazine* kept beside his recliner. *Nothing's worth doing if it's not done right.* How many times had his uncle told him that? Yet, today on the Gowanus, his nephew had done nothing but screw up.

He stood leaning forward, eyes closed as if lost in thought, hands bridging either side of a half-carved bird, when his wife approached him from behind and whispered in his ear, "Let it go, dear. I know you must have been frightened today."

"I'm sorry …" was as far as he got, when he noticed a platter heaped high with meat that, for the life of him, he couldn't remember slicing.

"Shuss," she said, nodding toward the living room. "Just look how beautiful they are."

And yes, they were beautiful, his children: Bunny with Mr. Joe, Roger with Cheryl, blissfully revealed in waning candlelight.

"It's Thanksgiving," Joellen said, her singsong voice hinting of something she knew that he did not. "In that room, there's someone who has something to tell you. Just ask Roger to give the blessing," she twittered as she bounced into the kitchen.

He went to the doorway to usher them in. Laughing and joking among themselves, they had yet to notice him. An oven door opened and closed. The scent of pumpkin pie blossomed in the air. Four young adults in the shank of their lives. Who cared if his camera was upstairs? The picture he was treasuring this moment could never be rendered in bytes or pixels. It was Bunny who noticed him first, followed by Joe, Roger, then Cheryl.

"So *nu, vos gibs*," he said, stretching his command of Yiddish to its outer limits, assuming an accent he had never heard but imagined many times, of his long-dead-before-he-was-born grandfather, Peshe Stoner, née Steiner. Then, as if easing his tired and aching bones into a warm bath, it all became clear. He could be so thick when women started talking riddles. What his wife had been alluding to was *being* arising from *nothingness*: the Stoner family was about to have a Jewish mother in it at last. Not only that, he realized, he too had a secret to share. After the meal, he'd take his son and daughter aside and confess to them that, finally, after all these years, he had decided to hire a detective to find out, once and for all, the truth about what had happened to their grandmother.

He ushered them in with a grand sweep of his arm, put his arm around his daughter-in-law's shoulders as she passed and gave her a gentle hug.

"And you, young lady? Except for saying hello, we've scarcely exchanged a meaningful word all night."

"Are you okay, Dad?" she said with a smile that hinted of concern.

"Of course, my dear; why do you ask?" he laughed.

"I don't know. I've had my eyes on you. At times tonight, you've looked … well … how to say it? Not quite yourself … like maybe something else besides that black eye of yours is bothering you."

"Really? Well, for your information, young lady, aside from my recent war wound … or, maybe, better said, *because* of my recent war wound … I'm very much myself tonight … and *tonight* … I want *you* sitting next to me. We'll let Roger do the blessing."

16

Beatrice, 1952

The alley behind the *Courier-Eagle* building baked in the afternoon sun. "Engine runs rough," read the scribbled note that Mr. Stoner's delivery driver had left for Moody on the dashboard. And rough wasn't the half of it. Now that Moody'd finally got it started, this old clunker belched blue smoke like a hungover Saturday-night drunk enjoying his first cigarette of the day. Not only that, considering the incident between himself and Kneebone this morning, the similarities between this truck, himself, and that stray dog over there, scrounging Zettl's trash barrel, were all too plain: each of them trying their best to see it through one more goddamn day.

Moody popped the hood. Providing the distributer cap wasn't cracked, he'd try pulling the plugs, cleaning 'em and resetting the gap. If it turned out that what this baby needed was a valve job, and maybe a ring job as well, given the tools he had at hand, Mr. Stoner would have to send it out for a complete overhaul.

Forty-three minutes and one skinned knuckle later, Moody was back in the cab listening to the motor purr, congratulating himself that he had this decrepit old piece of junk running twice as sweet as any woman he could think of right now. He depressed the clutch, slid it into gear, and revved the engine a couple of times like he was fixing to go somewhere. Hell, this old baby had miles in her yet. He was sitting there thinking all he had to do was ease out the clutch, drive it to the nearest train track, hop himself a freight and all his troubles would be solved, when Nancy poked her stubby little nose out the back door to tell him, in no uncertain terms, that the boss was back from the station and needed him up front *right now*. Meaning who knew what? Lately, Mr. Stoner had him hopping from here to there doing A to Z. *Right now* could be as simple as toting Haldeman-Julius's valise over to the hotel—or as complicated as agents of the law coming to arrest him.

He switched off the ignition and stowed the keys behind the sun visor where he'd found them. No need to panic. *Right now*, the only thing Kneebone had on him was that damn harmonica. *Right now*, he needed to make himself presentable before going up front.

The bare-bulb bathroom that Mr. Stoner was letting him use as his own wasn't much. A couple of boxes of office supplies stacked against one wall, a commode with a spent bottle of Airwick and a roll of toilet paper atop the tank, a sink and a bar of Lifebuoy soap, a hand towel hooked on a rusty nail—that Nancy did and didn't change once a week—and a cracked mirror that hung cockeyed over the sink. While these amenities were far from what most folks called the comforts of home, they were still better than the outhouse he'd had to use back when he was a kid.

In them days, they didn't call them *shithouses* for nothing. The miseries he'd endured. Winters, holding it in as long as he could, crossing his fingers when he did have to go that it'd be a quick trip. Summers, flies and spiders galore and that god-awful smell. And whatever the season, corn cobs wrapped with pages ripped out of old Sears and Roebuck or Monkey Ward catalogues in lieu of toilet paper. No wonder, that first Halloween after they'd moved to town, he and his brother snuck out where the city of Lima's sewer line didn't yet run, intent on trick or treating themselves to knocking over shithouses.

"Don't bother locking up, Hughie. Ain't nothing left in that old house that ain't broken or fit for making rags," were his mother's parting words the day they'd left their farm for a skimpy, two-bedroom apartment above Umphenauer's Grocery Store in town. That little woman, still able to put on a happy face in spite of it all, grinning ear to ear like she'd just won a ham playing bingo at the county fair.

"Sorriest excuse for a home in all of Ohio" was the way his mother had put it, once it was just the two of them sitting alone in the kitchen—his brother already lit out to the nearest pool hall—with what little they'd brought with them from the farm still downstairs in the bed of a pickup truck lent them by a kind neighbor.

"No more getting up with the chickens for us," she'd said, like it was something to crow about. "Them farming days is over. And first thing we're going to do, once we get us a little extra money, is outfit yew and yer brother into something more citified than barnyard clodhoppers."

The poor woman. If he'd have known then where that damn banker who foreclosed on their farm lived, swear to God, he'd have gone over and burned the son of a bitch's house to the ground. And she must have known that too, because once they got the truck unloaded and his hand was on the doorknob ready to join up with his brother at the pool hall, she'd stopped him in his tracks with one of her *hold 'er right there, buster*, because she wasn't about to let her youngest son leave the house half-cocked, without him promising first not to go scrapping with the town kids. "Yer not like yer brother," she'd said. "He's got brains enough to know when to make nice and wag his tail. But yew, yer a whole 'nother kettle of fish. Too much like yer father, bless his restless, drunken soul. Unable to straighten up and fly right even when it's fer yer own good. Willing to scrap with the whole damn world just to prove yer right and they're wrong. So, 'fore yew set one foot out that door, yew got to promise to count to ten and take at least two blows before swinging back," she'd screeched like a crazy old hen, "'cause if and when yew do, yer swinging not just for yerself, son, but for me and the sorry soul of yer dearly departed arsehole of a father as well."

Moody stared at his image in the mirror. The crack in the mirror ran like a scar across his cheek. He and his brother had been in top form that day. Hugh and Nate Moody taking on what seemed like a sizeable portion of the Lima High School football team, just to show the world how pissed off they were. And when their mother came to fetch them at the jail, though battered and bloodied in defeat, they'd greeted her, grinning like a couple of victorious jack-o'-lanterns. Moody inserted a stick of Dentyne gum into his mouth to freshen his breath. Slicked back his hair with the rat-tailed, nylon comb he'd recently purchased for himself at Walter Wayland's Five and Ten and turned out the light. Time to go up front.

***

Nancy greeted him with a smile. "Go right in, Moody. They're waiting for you."

The door to Mr. Stoner's office swung open as Moody reached for the knob. To his great relief, the "they" in question were Mr. Stoner and a burly stranger in the act of stepping forward and introducing himself.

"Mr. Moody, I believe. Emanuel Haldeman-Julius here. Simon speaks highly of you. Sir, it is a grrrr-eat pleasure to make your acquaintance."

Unaccustomed to being theatrically addressed by men who roll their *r*'s, whose bear-paw grips equal in strength to their bombastic voices, Moody wondered if he should blanch in disgust, run for the door, or laugh in this man's face.

Emanuel Haldeman-Julius stood hands on hips, the master of all he surveyed. "Mr. Stoner informs me that you are a man of grrreat skills who possesses the ability to fix most anything, and in my humble opinion, the world has too few men who fix things, otherwise it would be a much better place."

Unaccustomed to unwarranted flattery, Moody thrust his hands into his hip pockets. The rich and famous publisher of the *Little Blue Books* was a solidly built, but tending to the corpulent, man of medium height, in his late fifties, whose breath spoke of sour mash. And there, over in the corner of the room, sat a well-worn, alligator-skin valise. The reason, Moody figured, he had been sent for.

"Sir, fixing *things* is easy. Fixing the *mess* the world has got itself into is something else. Strikes me that not getting along and screwing each other to get rich might just be what mankind does best."

Haldeman-Julius shot Mr. Stoner an approving glance. Mr. Stoner replied with a highly satisfied nod and grin.

"By George, Mr. Moody, indeed you are as Simon says, a singularly rrremarkable man. A gentleman after my own heart, I might add. A verrritable Johnny Appleseed, as it were, capable of someday going forth into the world to sow the seeds of truth and justice."

At this point, Moody was wondering how long he was going to have to listen to the flashy pearls of questionable wisdom that spilled from this man's mouth. What could Mr. Stoner have been thinking, bringing such a man here to argue against the existence of God on behalf of the atheists? "Sir, not to skirt the issue, but I never did buy into all that malarkey about

Johnny Appleseed roaming the land sowing apple trees. Seeing as how I'm a farm boy, I can't say as I've ever seen baby apple trees sprouting on their own beneath the parent tree. Yet every year the ground underneath thick with spent apples gone to seed."

Haldeman-Julius's unrestrained guffaw revealed several missing molars. "Touché, Mr. Moody. Rrright you are about your spent apples. I most heartily agree. I have six apple trees on my farm and underneath, never a single baby tree. Still, if I may, according to my frrriend, Simon here, you're an avid rrreader of my *Little Blue Books*. So tell me, sir, which among my many titles do you find most appealing?"

"I'm not sure I can say, sir. There's been a whole bunch of them. But now that yew mention it, strictly by coincidence, my first just happened to be *Little Blue Book* number one: *The Ballad of Reading Gaol*. So, yew might say I've been one of yer readers from day one. Anyhow, seeing as I was in prison at the time, that book of Mr. Wilde's brought tears to my eyes," Moody replied, wondering as he waited for Haldeman-Julius's response how it could be that despite all the fights he'd been in, not to mention a lifelong weakness for candy and sugared drinks, to say nothing of an aversion to dentists, that he still had all his own teeth—which was a great rarity among persons of Irish decent—while Mr. Haldeman-Julius, the Jew, did not.

"And would you be interested in knowing why I decided to publish *The Ballad of Reading Gaol* as my first issue, Mr. Moody?"

"Please," Moody said.

"Because as a young man, rrrreading that poem touched me much as it seems to have touched you. That poem inspired me to become the man I am today, to take on the challenge of making a difference in this world. Hence, I wonder if you agree with me that these words of Mr. Wilde get the plight of the working man exactly right? *With mop and mow, we saw them go / Slim shadows hand in hand / About, about in ghostly rrrout / They trrrod a sarrraband / And the damned grrrotesques made arrrabesques / Like the wind upon the sand!*

"You see, Moody, I grew up in a poverty-stricken, Jewish section of Philadelphia, and is not extreme poverty by itself not a kind of jail? And since, as I understand from Simon, your family suffered considerably during the Grrreat Deprrression, I'm most curious, how did these lines read to you? *With mop and mow, we saw them go / Slim shadows hand in hand?"*

Moody paused. Yes, those lines were familiar to him, but he'd never attached particular significance to them. "Well, sir, as I see it, that poem's about a man about to be hung for killing the thing he loves. And I can't help wondering, when Jesus tells us to treat each other the way we would like to be treated ourselves, why we need prisons at all. Nothing good comes of a man when yew lock him up and throw away the key. It seems to me like there ought to be gentler ways to get folks to straighten up and behave. The thing that Mr. Wilde was trying to get at was that jails are the place where bad men get better at being bad and good men get worse at being good. As for Mr. Wilde himself, though I've never read or seen any of his famous plays, I hear tell, they're little more than froth and shallow fun, mostly a bunch of witty jokes told at other folks' expense. I do believe it wasn't until Mr. Wilde was pulled up hard for his deviant behavior by that same highfalutin society that enjoyed his plays that he finally woke up to the fact that all along, the joke was on him. These are just my personal opinions, of course, but I have to say for all its beauteous language, this poem of his yer so in love with is just one long whine that brings to mind something Nietzsche once said, in that dialogue he wrote between himself and the Buddha, that, if I remember rightly, went something like this: *Why go about sniveling because trivial people suffer? Or for that matter, because great men suffer? Trivial people suffer trivially, great men suffer greatly, and great sufferings are not to be regretted because they are novel.*

The very mention of Nietzsche's name caused a shadow to pass over Haldeman-Julius's face, and seemingly shift his attention to several photographs that hung on the wall behind Mr. Stoner's desk. "I do not think that particular quote was gleaned from one of my little books," he then said as if he were addressing a picture of Mr. Stoner's father and himself standing together in front of *The Appeal to Reason* printing plant in Girard, Kansas. "Where, may I ask, did you come by that particularly scurrilous bit?"

"Sometimes, sir, when I can, whenever I'm in a town that has one, I search me out one of them Carnegie libraries. I believe the book I was reading at the time was called *Beyond Good and Evil.*"

Haldeman-Julius suddenly turned about, jaw hardened, his reddened, rheumy eyes now fiercely alive. "A Carnegie librrrary, did you say? For your information, Moody, those librrraries you frrrequent are built with guilt money. Guilt money, Mr. Moody. Never was there a capitalist worm more despicably loathsome than that rrrapacious, union-busting midget, Andrew Carnegie."

Moody glanced at Mr. Stoner, hoping to be rescued from such tomfoolery. But his boss merely shrugged, as if to say: *What can I do? The man's given to sudden theatrics.*

And sure enough, Haldeman-Julius's ferocious outburst proved to have no more staying power than an early spring snowflake. His voice, now level and calm, he almost smiled when he then added: "Nevertheless, Mr. Moody, I must admit, I cannot help but admire the flare you seem to have for committing to memory obscure texts."

"Well, sir, I don't know as I'd call it memorizing. It's more like whenever something I read strikes my fancy, it kinda gets stuck in my brain somewhere. For me, it's not exactly like recalling something as I'st being able to see it exactly as it was on the printed page."

Again, another pause, in which Moody once again looked to Mr. Stoner to tell him where to take that bag. But his boss just stood there grinning at him, like a farmer whose prize bull just won a blue ribbon at the State Fair.

"Still, Mr. Moody, I do find it curious. If indeed it is so that *trrrivial men suffer trrrivially and grrreat men suffer grrreatly*, I can only say that's one bleak example of philosophic balderdash. Nietzsche was mad, you know. One quotes him at one's peril. His enthusiasts come in many distasteful flavors. Are you a nihilist, Mr. Moody, an anarchist … or a Nazi?"

Nazi? At one's peril. Moody decided to let this fool have it with both barrels. "Well, sir, whether I'm a Nazi or not is not for me to say. I consider myself a simple hobo by trade, a humble tramp who knows enough about the ways of the world to understand *yer* game. Not to sound disrespectful, but yer one of them do-gooder socialists, aren't yew, sir? Well, yew can take your utopias and stuff 'em in a sack. Trust me, when yer history is writ, yew and yer kind aren't going to come off any fairer than the scalawags yew strive to replace. Palmer's raids to root out the anarchists were a liberal Democrat's hysterical response to having his house blown up.

Robespierre and Stalin, oh boy, oh boy, the horrors they unleashed in the name of justice for the little man. Though I do grant you this: Nietzsche was definitely some kind of nut. But then again, most of them geniuses are, are they not? Sometimes a touch of insanity does wonders for seeing things as they actually are. As for me, now Darwin, he's my kind of nut. *Survival of the fittest* was just another way of saying us down and out folk don't stand a chance less we make ourselves into one of those *slim shadows* that Mr. Wilde was writing about. Can't pin nothing on a shadow. Can't hate 'em. Can't frame 'em. Can't lynch 'em. Can't love 'em to death. Which brings us back around to killing the thing yew purport to love again, don't it, sir?   "Just remember, during the depression, there were a whole bunch of folks like me standing around, hungry for something to eat and wishing for a job. 'Blessed are the meek, for they shall inherit the earth,' the Good Book says, and ain't that a joke? All I'm trying to say here is that maybe yew well-meaning commie-socialists, who presume to have the beeswax answers to everybody's social problems, ought to wake up and question yerselves as to just how much of this newfound prosperity us poor, meek folk have really inherited? For one such as yerself, when yew see someone down and out, do yew really do for him as if he were your own kin? My favorite Bible verse paints the world picture in just two words: 'Jesus wept.' Yes, sir, Jesus wept, just like Mr. Oscar Wilde wept, and yew socialists still weep, and in spite of all them crocodile tears and hand-wringing promises to do good, the poor are still poor, and it's always going to be that way."

Moody could have gone on and on and had, many a time, preaching into the night from the open door of a boxcar. But one thing for sure, he'd run down the curtain on this little dog and pony show. Mr. Stoner's attention, for all practical purposes, had flown somewhere out the window, and Mr. Haldeman-Julius had taken up studying that photograph again. And what was it anyway, that these learned men lacked the eyes to see? The tumbleweeds of modernity on parade: a prairie load of cigarette butts and candy wrappers, adrift in a hot, dry wind.

Moody cleared his throat. If Mr. Stoner wouldn't say what needed to be said, then he'd do it for him. "Sir, should I tote Mr. Haldeman-Julius's bag on over to the hotel?"

Yes, Mr. Stoner nodded. *You go ahead and do that.*

17

Red Hook, 2004

In actuality, it is not possible to find in every single body, intelligence and mind. Joellen's steady breathing measured the beat as Lucretius's stately iambs trooped through Preston's mind. Originally, he'd assumed that as long as he'd be keeping watch in the background, the Sarge and his dog were a win-win situation. Mildred had a home of sorts and the Sarge, someone to snuggle the night with in the van. True to his vow, Preston had kept up his end of the bargain, stopping by now and then to drop off a fresh bag of chow, making sure everything was all right.

But who could have guessed that one dog would multiply into so many in such a short time? And now, here he was, springing for at least two big bags of chow a week … and worrying, even then, it might not be enough. And it wasn't like he couldn't afford it or had something against dogs. That scruffy little Jack Russell terrier, that was the latest addition to the Sarge's pack, was actually cute. Nevertheless, as of yesterday, the count was now up to seven, including three that were more ferocious than cute: a German shepherd, a pit bull/collie mix, and, worst of all, that same Rottweiler he'd encountered at the Sugar Factory the other night. Which more or less went to show how right Lucretius had been when he suggested that it wasn't possible to find intelligence in every single thing, particularly when the thing-beast in nominal charge of this growing pack was a minimally functioning drunk with a weakness for adopting feral dogs.

Was the Sarge the alpha dog or not was the question that had Preston tossing and turning tonight. Because he was the guy who was supposed to be keeping an eye on things. The guy who had surfed the Internet for a better understanding of the hierarchical nature of the pack. Checked out episode after episode of the *Dog Whisperer* on late-night cable TV. Who'd rode home on the bus after work today, listening to a couple of old-timers from King Street, seated behind him, reiterate the worst of his fears.

"I'm only saying, dem mutts is a menace to da neighborhood."

"You said it. Put it in the books: sooner or later, someone's gonna git bit."

"Like, you know, someone otta do something."

"Like what?"

"Like, maybe next meeting of the Civic Association, tell McGettrick to get the city off its ass and come take dem K-9s away."

"Yeah. Like the neighborhood's just beginning to show a little class, and we got a drunken, no-good bum roaming our streets with a pack of mutts, making us look bad?"

As loathsome as Preston found this conversation, as much as he'd wanted to turn around and set those two straight, somehow, he couldn't do it. Because for the last week and a half, he'd done quite a bit of thinking about *Amores Perros*—a movie he'd seen a few years back. Made up of three interlocking stories, one of which centered around a hit man disguised as just another harmless old street bum called El Chivo who roamed the streets of Mexico City with a raggedy-ass pack of mutts not unlike the Sarge. The dogs were happy. El Chivo was happy, until he fucked up by taking in and nursing to health a trained-to-dogfight, badly wounded, and left-to-die Rottweiler. How El Chivo, after he'd nursed that dog back to health, returned home one night after one of his hit jobs to find out his, now, heathy Rottweiler, as true to its viscous nature as he was to his, had methodically done in the rest of his dogs while he'd been away. It was the possibility of a real-life re-enactment of that scene of utter carnage that had Preston lying awake tonight, ruing the day he'd suckered himself into playing grandpa deep pockets to a scruffy man and his pack of street dogs—which, in itself, seemed more and more an act of lunacy worthy of his hotshot social worker days, when every good deed he set his hand to, every decision he made on behalf of others, as if he really knew what was best for them, seemed to turn sour.

So then, what was it, pray tell, that was keeping him from calling the SPCA? What was he waiting for? For some little old lady or child to be attacked. But just suppose he were to make that call? The Sarge was a highly volatile man endowed with great physical strength who would never willingly surrender his dogs. Those dogs were his only family, and he'd fight 'til he dropped to protect his own. Since, in all probability, the SPCA would have the good sense to call in the cops as backup, the NYPD would no doubt automatically react to the slightest provocation, first, by tasering the Sarge—which would have about the same effect as pissing on a forest fire. So, they'd end up gunning him down, because shoot 'til they drop was the way the members of the NYPD wolfpack were trained to behave. Small wonder then that Preston was sick to his stomach, torn between what logic said to do and loyalty to the Sarge. Still, *Amores Perros* was just a movie, plotted, scripted, and highly manipulated by a director for maximum dramatic effect. However, since potential threats in no way were the same as clear and present dangers, since it was way too late in the game now for him to stop feeding those dogs and occasionally ferrying one of them to the vet, since, *in actuality, it is not possible to find in every single body, intelligence and mind*, then perhaps the best he can do is cross his fingers and sit and wait.

18

Beatrice, 1952

Playing hostess was never Polly's cup of tea. Consequently, she considered it a blessing when Simon informed her that his exalted highness, Mr. E. Haldeman-Julius, would be staying at the hotel rather than with them. Goodness knows, it had been trying enough to have had the man over for supper last night—the menu, by his request: baked ham, mashed potatoes, green beans, and cherry pie—and never had she seen a man so given to talking about himself with his mouth full. The saving grace being, pleading exhaustion, at least, Mr. Haldeman-Julius had excused himself at half past ten to return to his hotel.

His excellency, of course, had not showed up empty handed. He'd arrived not only bearing ample wine for their meal, but cognac and cigars for the boys to enjoy afterward in the living room, leaving it to the little woman of the house to clear the table and see to the cleaning up. Simon, of course, never much of a drinker, had stumbled down to breakfast this morning in no mood to be questioned by his wife one last time as to why, in a backwater town, where believers in God outnumber atheists at least a thousand to one, was he willing to jeopardize his paper's already dwindling advertising revenue by holding a silly debate over the existence of God?

"Enough already, Polly," Simon had roared in reply. "Give it a rest. It's not that I don't appreciate your concern, but I don't give a good goddamn what you think. My old man didn't send me to Columbia for nothing, you know. So what if we end up with the paper going in the tank— which I don't think it will. I can always move us back to New York City anytime I want, because I got an in with both the *Times* and the *Trib*. For your information, the *Courier-Eagle* has never once yielded to backroom pressure or bowed down to public opinion, and it's not about to start now. It's going to continue giving the people the unvarnished truth, whether they like it or not. The business model of our paper is and forever will be, to educate this town to the facts as rational men see them or go down trying."

But, of course, her husband *did* care what happened to the paper. It was his obsession, his passion, his mania. As for actually moving them all to New York City? If only, because that would truly be the answer to her prayers, delivering her to the very place she'd been dreaming of going to these many years, because then it would make leaving him once and for all, a breeze. Not that it was any skin off her nose, but once he was rid of her, he'd be free to take up again with Esther whatsit, that little Jewess ex-girlfriend of his from Brooklyn he'd never stopped crowing about.

"Every day, regrettably beautiful. From Texas to North Dakota, the Great Plains wilt under a merciless sun," Polly muttered to herself, as she pushed open the screen door. Her desiccated lawn crunched beneath her feet as she made her way to the garage to take out her bike. She'd never thought of it before, but the only decent rain for weeks occurred the day before Mr. Moody had come knocking at her door. A real doozy of a storm that highballed into town like a runaway freight howling the end of days. Not unlike the storm earlier that spring that spawned the lightning bolt that triggered the fire that burned her church down. Cannonades of thunder and lightning fissuring the sky. Air so charged with ions the hairs on her arms and the back of her neck stood on end. Little Preston squeezing her hand, his teddy clutched under his arm, the damn dog with its tail between its legs, as she hurried them out of the house. The three of them ducking inside the storm cellar just as hail the size of jawbreakers started pelting down.

Rather than sit in the dark on little campstools, she'd let her son be the little man and light the stubby candle—the poor dear terrified by the thought that their house was going to blow away; but the only thing she'd been afraid of was that the clammy, dusty air underground would trigger another of her son's asthma attacks, and she'd be stuck sitting up with him again most of the night.

But the town *had* been there miraculously intact when they emerged, hailstones crunching underfoot, with downed limbs large and small all over the place. But hardly any damage to speak of. Except for the Lang house, three doors down, that took a large limb across its front porch. Simon taking the photo that ran the next day in the *Courier-Eagle*: "It Could Have Been Worse," his headline read.

"Worse than what? Mr. and Mrs. Stoner's miserable marriage?" Polly snorted to herself as she retrieved her bicycle from a bunch of things arrayed in military formation against the back wall of the garage, because her husband was a stickler for keeping things neat.

A top-of-the-line, lady's model Schwinn, purchased with money saved from her choir director's job a few months after giving birth as a sort of reward for surviving, she'd fallen in love with it the moment she spied it in the window of the Western Auto store. Olive green with gold piping, chrome wire baskets mounted front and back, plus a headlight, rear reflector, and a delightful little bell, her bike had seemed the logical next step for someone suddenly cast into the throes of early motherhood. After all, riding a bicycle was all about maintaining one's equilibrium, was it not? No wobbling, no weaving from side to side allowed. Astride that bike, she was Katherine Hepburn with a Lady Marlboro dangling out the side of her mouth, pedaling around town not giving a damn who thought what about whom. And oh, the way Reg and those other store clerks had come outside to gawk when she'd insisted on taking the bike for a test-drive whiz around the block. Reg with a big grin on his face, calling out: "Mrs. Stoner, you're some kind of humdinger," when she returned pedaling ass-backward on the handlebars.

Polly wheeled the bike out of the garage. Humdinger or no humdinger, ever since she'd been a kid, bike riding was her thing. Just like no one had to teach her how to play the piano, nobody, not her father, nor her brothers, Otis and Jack, taught Polly Kneebone how to ride a bike that was little more than a sorry bunch of used parts cobbled onto a full-sized frame, salvaged by her father from the town dump.

At first, up until her legs grew long enough to manage the saddle, she'd ridden butt cheek perched on the crossbar. But it couldn't have been all that long before she was showing off to her brothers how to trick ride "no hands," facing backward sitting on the handlebars, just like the young woman in spangled tights they'd seen, the one and only time their father managed to scrape enough coins together to treat his family to a matinee performance of the Cole Brother's Circus—minus her mother, of course, undoubtedly left behind to scrub floors or do the wash.

Polly pulled down the garage door thinking of the look on Simon's face the day she brought the bike home. "Why?" he'd demanded to know, angry as well as perplexed. He'd claimed it wasn't the money even though they'd both known at the time that it *was*. Circulation at the paper had been falling even before little Preston was born, and with the slush fund that Simon's father had carefully amassed to ease the paper through lean times mostly gone, why her stubborn fool of a husband still had his heart set on that debate was totally beyond her. The problem was, her husband had grown up self-centered and spoiled rotten by a meddlesome excuse of a father who lived too long and a good-hearted, servile mother who died too soon.

Because Moody had recently spread fresh gravel on the drive, Polly was forced to wheel her bike to the street. In her opinion, from what she'd seen and experienced so far, somewhere along the way, good parenting became a lost art. She and her two brothers were fine examples of what happened when kids were left to raise themselves. Otis, the undisciplined middle kid, who loved to bully everyone around, now a local war hero turned sheriff. Her older brother Jack, the wildest, most studious, and cleverest of them all, despite all his many talents, reduced to picking oranges in Florida during the Great Depression, did himself in at age twenty-two by drinking pure alcohol. And what sort of humdinger was she, with her crazy plan to up and leave her child and husband behind?

Halfway down the drive, Polly paused the bike beside her honeysuckle bush. One story above was her bedroom window. She plucked a blossom and sucked the sweetness from it. Its fragrance had kept her awake much of the night … along with her husband's snoring. That the bush remained a green and growing thing at all was thanks to daily doses of her dishwater. "Where the bee sucks, there suck I," her husband had whispered into her ear the previous night. Poetry, lush poetry, calculated to get an unwilling woman to spread her legs. Poetry, she supposed, her husband thought erotic, like those cheap pulp novels he kept hidden in the garage that gloried the lurid sex life of lesbians. Far be it from her to tell him to his face, but his sweet talk, his sweet nothings, were exactly that: nothings. In truth she wouldn't have given herself to any man last night, not even whispered to by Shakespeare himself.

Don't worry your little head about it, dear. Your husband will show you everything you need to know about making babies. Just don't expect too much. Doing it with them isn't all it's cracked up to be had been her mother's womanly advice to her bewildered twelve-year-old daughter, the day her first period arrived.

Well, at least her mother had spoken the truth. That night Simon took her to a square dance, and she'd said yes to a rather hasty proposal of marriage. She'd been a starry-eyed virgin of twenty-two and he, a dashing young man of twenty-eight, recently returned home with a master's degree in journalism from Columbia University in his hip pocket, ready to assume the editorship of his ailing father's ailing newspaper. No doubt about it, that night she'd known the mechanics all right—whose thing went where and did what to whom. She was a farm girl after all, who once spied on her older brothers screwing a sheep. Even so, though she hadn't exactly expected fireworks or the earth to move all whistles and bells that night, she'd been certain coitus with one's future husband would be something considerably more exciting than a nightmare at worse or, at best, a crashing bore. And the way Simon had panted and rutted over her, it seemed cruel to just lie there stiff as a log, her heart not in it, faking orgasm after orgasm. Of course, what she didn't have to fake were the nine months of nonstop nausea and retching prior to the birth of her son, which turned out to be an event that she, a narrow-hipped woman, wasn't likely to repeat anytime soon. Dr. MacNaught, naturally, had warned her that labor might be rough. But twenty-five hours of rough? Except, what was she doing, wasting time commiserating her past miseries to a honeysuckle bush, when the man with the possible solution to her problems, at this very moment, might be enjoying his lunch on a park bench in the Courthouse Square?

Polly coasted her bike through the dip where the drive met the street. Never had she felt so alive. Never had the phrase *on the road* had so much meaning for her. Every telephone pole and fire hydrant she passed, every tree and bush, a supporting friend, cheering her on her way. And up ahead, at the end of the block, no doubt on her way home from Mass, was her next-door neighbor, Mrs. Bacacci, approaching the intersection.

Polly pedaled faster. Mrs. Bacacci. Frail, arthritic, half blind, and stooped with scoliosis. Hobbled by bunions and varicose veins. Her spindly, Ace-bandaged legs sheathed in sagging knee highs. It was a wonder that a Sicilian widow clad all in black would be out and about on such a terribly hot day. Fearful that the old dear might step off the curb into traffic without looking as if it were still the horse and buggy days, Polly arrived just in the nick of time, calling out "yoo-hoo!" and sounding her bike bell to arrest Mrs. B's progress.

"*Si, si.* That a-you, Mrs. Stoner?" the old woman called, her Magoo-lensed eyeglasses slipped to the tip of her nose, forehead and upper lip covered with sweat. "Is a-hot enough a-cook a-egg on a-side-a-walk, I'm a-think."

Next to Lorraine, Mrs. B was little Preston's favorite babysitter. "Mizbukaka," he called her still to this day. And what a lifesaver this lady had been, faithfully coming over every afternoon so that a mama cursed with a colicky baby might get some sleep. But much as she'd like to, Polly couldn't waste time talking with her neighbor today. Not when with her alive to a sense of adventure she'd never experienced before. No, she paused only long enough to see this kindly woman safely across the street.

Traffic was light. Polly pedaled anew with a now-or-never sense of urgency. She sped through intersections looking quickly left to right. Insignificant things took on unexpected relevance. Such as little Jackie Pyle, costumed as Batman, along with some unknown chum costumed as Robin, taking turns flinging themselves off the front porch to set their capes billowing. Because little boys loved their comic-book heroes about as much as the pastor of the church she played organ for hated them for being the work of the devil, distracting little minds from the only true superhero of them all: the Lord Jesus Christ. And little Preston's current cartoon favorite was Mighty Mouse. And only last week, when they'd been waiting in line at Monty's for Preston's monthly haircut—her clever boy hard at work sounding out to himself the sayings of Donald Duck—looking to pass the time, she'd picked up a comic for herself, to discover to her amazement and surprise, that yes, there was a superhero for women like her too: Wonder Woman. Yes, Wonder Woman. Athletically trim, magnificently and brazenly independent, a cartoon rehash of Diana the Huntress, mythic twin sister to Apollo, revered by the Greeks as the virgin goddess of childbirth and women sworn never to marry. Wonder Woman, among whose amazing panoply of superpowers were an invisible airplane, bullet deflecting bracelets, and a magic lariat with which to corral the baddies and compel them to tell the truth. Wonder Woman, who consorted mainly with females who referred to each other as *girls*, saying and doing whatever entered their heads, eating bonbons and deciding the important things in life for themselves, wholly indifferent to the clumsy pomposities and silly machinations of men.

Polly eased her bicycle to a stop. At last, she had arrived. For there, across the street, sat the only man among men in whom she could trust, blessed with the practical know-how necessary to put her plan into action. "Ye must be born again before ye can enter the kingdom of heaven," she muttered not to herself but to her newly found alter ego. "Crossing this asphalt Rubicon, my child," she murmured, "will be to rebirth thyself unfettered and liberated from all struggle."

***

Moody gently worked his knife against the grain of the small block of wood he held firmly in his hand. He wore the sleeves of his tee shirt rolled up. The bitch dog seen yesterday skulking around Zettl's trash was pictured in his mind. The old St. Louis Cardinals baseball cap that shaded his eyes was a loaner for the day from Mr. Stoner. Traffic, such as it was, remained ragged and sluggish like it refused to come awake, like even things moving seemed rooted. Stowed under the bench to keep it out of the sun was the ham and cheese sandwich to go he'd just picked up at Decker's Diner. While a man had to eat, this man hadn't quite got around to it yet … and not so sure he ever would in this heat. But hello, who, pray tell, could that be across the street, sitting astride her bicycle, waiting for a truck to clear the intersection? What craziness now had Mrs. Stoner out and about rather than holed up somewhere cool inside? Surely, not to see him, because that'd be two times in as many days.

He set his whittling knife on the bench beside him, hoping that during the time it took him to bend down and pretend to tug up a fallen sock and retie a bootlace, by the time he'd straightened up, she'd have passed him by. And when she didn't, and definitely seemed headed his way, since desperate times often beget desperate acts, he folded his arms across his chest and leaned back, legs stretched out before him, as if he hadn't seen her yet and was aiming to take a nap.

His eyes reduced to slits, he watched her cross the street and bump the bike over the curb. Eyes now fully shut, he measured her approach by the rattle of something on that damn bike he was supposed to have fixed by then but hadn't. And since Mrs. Stoner was a faithful user of Lifebuoy soap, it was his nose that detected the exact moment of her arrival. And though the woman weighed hardly more than a keg of nails, he felt the slats of the bench shudder as they accepted her weight. And when she cleared her throat as if about to speak, his abiding thoughts no longer dwelled with the bitch dog, but with the fact that he'd been jinxed from the moment he'd stepped into that hobo camp, that of all the possible doors he could have knocked on in this town, he had to pick the one where the lady of the house was not only the wife of the editor/publisher of the town newspaper, but sister to the goddamn county sheriff, and now here she was, hopefully come to fetch him because something needed doing around her house, like weeding the garden or cleaning the furnace.

"Okay, Mr. Moody. Stop pretending, You're not fooling anybody. Look, I know you're due back to work soon so I'm not going to mince words. I'm here to request your help in leaving Beatrice."

Hoping he'd misheard what he'd just heard, Moody opened his eyes, hauled in his feet and sat up. Mrs. Stoner sat military erect on the far end of the bench, hands folded ladylike in her lap. "Well now, ma'am," he replied with a sheepish grin, "most folks that got some leaving to do, just up and buy themselves a bus or train ticket."

"Mr. Moody, I'm not here to waste your time. The reason I've come to you is because when I leave Beatrice, I aim to go for good, and to do that, I have to make it as hard as possible for my husband and brother to come chasing after me because I suspect that right about now, you might also be thinking along similar lines."

Moody wasn't all that sure what the proper rely was to what he'd just heard. "And just when and how yew planning to pull off this disappearing act?" he finally said. "Yew surely don't look like yew're fixing to leave today: gym shoes, blue denim cutoff shorts, man's short-sleeve white dress shirt worn shirttail out, open collar hiked up in back, and about the only gal for a hundred miles around with balls enough to forgo Nadine's Beauty Salon for one of Monty's rock and roll, ducktail hairdos? If you were to up and leave, wherever you went, you'd stick out like a sore thumb."

"Never you mind how I'm dressed," she replied. "As for the time of my departure, the sooner the better. Like maybe tomorrow or the day after tomorrow."

"Ma'am, I admire directness in women, but …"

"But what, Mr. Moody?"

"Well, you coming to me with this … all in all, ma'am, you know next to nothing about me," he said, stalling to collect his thoughts, because in the past, when the housewife who answered the door turned out to be a bee looking for a little extra honey, being a man of natural sexual urges, it'd be a onetime quickie, right them and there. But then again, Mrs. Stoner wasn't the usual housewife was she? In fact, she was about the last person in this world he could think of he'd want to run off with. But then again, Mrs. Stoner wasn't your usual housewife, was she?

"You're right. I may not know much," she replied with a slight smile, "but I do know some things … and my brother Otis claims he knows a whole lot."

"How so, ma'am?"

"Such as how you're a draft dodger who's served time in Leavenworth rather than fight the Japs like he did. That you got a record of petty theft and drunk and disorderliness in almost every town within walking distance of a railroad track. Says he strongly suspects you to be the sick bastard who killed that man out at Johnson's Crick, for which he aims to get you the electric chair." She paused for effect. "So you see, Mr. Moody, I *do* know some things."

Moody removed his cap and spent a moment running his fingers through his hair. "Well now, seems like that list of my supposed peccadillos might be a trifle short," he joked in an effort to keep this little tête-à-tête from spinning out of control. "I do believe that sheriff brother of yers seems to have missed some things. But who cares what he thinks? What interests me is what you think."

"What I think, Mr. Moody, is that you're a whole lot more than you seem."

"A whole lot more? Do tell. I'm all ears."

"It means that my husband and I consider you a remarkable man. That you have an innate, commonsense view of life that puts philosophy and psychology books to shame. That I consider you a good enough man for a woman like me to put her trust in."

Trust? He'd been come on to by the opposite sex many times over without the word ever once coming up. "Begging your pardon, I was never drunk, ma'am. Disorderly? Maybe. But never drunk. I may have my weaknesses, but I never touch the curse of the Irish, seeing as how both my parents possessed a terrible weakness for it."

"Weakness? You, Mr. Moody? Truly? I can't imagine," she said with a little laugh like she was flirting with him.

"Full of 'em, ma'am," he responded in kind. "As yew may have guessed by now, I don't suffer fools gladly. If pushed, I've been known to push back—push back hard—but never so far as to kill a man. Still, there's them who says there's a kernel of truth to every lie, which makes me curious as to why in the world a person such as yerself would want to include a tainted soul such as I in this disappearing act of yers?"

"Mr. Moody, I am given to understand, that normally, you do your traveling by rail?"

"That's way too kind a way to put it, ma'am. What I am, begging your pardon, is a bum, a hobo, a lowly tramp who goes from here to there riding the occasional boxcar. Anyway, excuse me for asking, but I can't help wondering why yew'd be thinking this particular bum would be burning to leave Beatrice right about now, especially since the only thing he's ready to plead guilty to is the crime of being poor. But all kidding aside, surely yew must understand that if the two of us were to up and light out together, this brother of yers, yew say has a burning desire to lynch me, would view my sudden exit as an all-out admission of guilt and head up a posse to come after me, which would be pretty much it for either of us getting away clean. Besides, it looks to me like yew have a right fine life for yerself here in Beatrice: nice home, upstanding husband, and if I may say so, a gifted child. So what is it shaking yer tail that has you considering such a thing?"

Mrs. Stoner chewed thoughtfully on her lower lip, staring straight ahead. Moody gazed at a squirrel frozen in place, halfway up a tree. A couple of old-timers on a nearby bench bemoaned the price of soybeans.

"Mr. Moody, just how old were you when you decided to make your break and take to the road?"

"Not too long after Pearl Harbor, I'd 'spect. Right after I graduated from school. Barely nineteen."

"And at the time of your leaving, could you have articulated an intelligent answer to the question you just posed to me?"

"I get your point, ma'am. But those days, I was just a kid. Far be it from me to be prying a woman about her age, but yer a good deal older and wiser right now than I was then. Besides, I didn't have me a life yet—not settled in the way yew are—and it just strikes me as kinda curious what yer aiming to do. Which is not to say I think yer the sort to go off half-cocked. No ma'am, a woman such as yerrself, there's no doubt in my mind but yew've done a whole lot of thinking about what it is yew say yew want to do."

"Thinking about it? Yes, of course, I've done a whole lot of thinking. Probably too much, if you know what I mean. But sometimes, things like this are a little hard to articulate. It's just that all my life there's been this little something gnawing at me that something wasn't right. Lately, I guess you could say I've been doing so much thinking I'm pretty nigh at wit's end. But then, you showed up and the next thing I knew answers started dropping into place. I guess what I'm trying to say here is that love is the reason I have to leave Beatrice—love for somebody other than my husband."

The two old-timers had turned to discussing pigs. On the far side of the square, Herman Pennyworth eased his Cadillac Coupe de Ville into the space reserved for him in front of the First National Bank. Moody hooked the ball cap over his knee. "Ma'am, before we go any further here, I think we need yew to explain yerself a tiny bit. Love's a mighty big word, bandied about in prose, poetry, and song in a whole complicated mess of ways. An overused and misused term that expresses anything from 'I love the way yew look tonight' to 'I'd love to stomp the shit out of yew'—if you'll pardon my French. And, on a hot day such as this, when I think of love, I think of skinny dipping in Johnson's Crick, water up to my chin, bare butt squishing in the mud, and somehow, Mrs. Stoner, I don't quite think that's the kind of love yew had in mind."

Mrs. Stoner replied with the same impish laugh she used the day they met. Her brother be damned, Moody now found himself sort of fancying the idea that the two of them one day skinny dipping together in Johnson's Crick might not be all that far-fetched, like perhaps a hobo honeymoon and seeing the world together from the open door of a boxcar really might be in the offing for the two of them.

"Indeed, Mr. Moody," she said. "There is truth in what you say about love's myriad facets, especially in this narrow-minded, hypocritical town. But before we speak further of love, I must ask if you are familiar with the works of Oscar Wilde, works such as *De Profundis* or *The Ballad of Reading Gaol*?"

"Only with *The Ballad*, ma'am. And funny thing is, just yesterday Mr. Haldeman-Julius told me hisself that a reprint of that *Ballad* was the very first book he ever published."

"Are you familiar with the quote: 'The love that dares not speak its name'?"

"Yes, ma'am."

"Do you know what it means?"

"I believe, ma'am, Mr. Wilde was a queer. Excepting, if I may be so bold, that quote was not something said by Mr. Wilde but by his no-good boyfriend."

"Ah," she sighed. "Right you are. I stand corrected. Nevertheless, there you have it, Mr. Moody. For what it's worth, the love that dares not speak its name is the reason I must leave Beatrice. Because the person I love, who has no idea of the depth of that love, is my brother's wife."

Moody watched Paul Sell leave his store to go next door to O'Reilly's Drugstore for a box of aspirin. He watched the two old-timers cross the street for an iced coffee and a doughnut at Zettl's Bakery. For the first time in he didn't know how many years, he found himself fumbling for the appropriate words to say what he wanted to say. "Well, ma'am, if that don't beat all. I got to confess: yew really had me going there for a minute. Here I was, just thinking yew might be of a mind to run off with me—and for what it's worth, yer contrary sexual proclivities to the side, I did and still do find yew a mighty fine and appealing woman, but yew got to understand, if hopping freight trains is what yew got in mind, even for them that's done it before, it's no la-di-da thing. People end up getting killed that way. As for me helping yew out by coming along as some sort of escort—assuming that's what yew have in mind—given the pickle I'm in, with yew being the wife to the editor of the town's newspaper and sister to the county sheriff, as I do believe I've mentioned before, the two of us departing this town together would serve only to worsen both our situations. As for you going it on your own, well, I think I know yew well enough by now not to waste my breath trying to talk yew out of it. Still, for what it's worth, when it comes to riding trains, I'm only too glad to let yew pick my brain. The main thing is that the best way of protecting yerself is ride alone and trust nobody no matter how friendly they seem. If yew got to snooze, and yer not alone, make sure to do it with one eye open. Assume anyone yew meet capable of forcing themselves on yew and stealing your stuff. And if yew don't mind me asking, since I don't figure yew to be riding trains the rest of yer given days, where yew planning to head anyway?"

"No, Mr. Moody, I certainly do not intend to ride trains the rest of my life," she responded with a carefree toss of the head. "I'm headed to the only place I know where people like me have an even chance of blending in: Greenwich Village, New York City. How long you think it'll take me to get there?"

Moody grinned. New York City? He'd been there once … didn't stay long … too noisy, too many people … but she was right … a perfect place for someone who didn't want to get found. "Well, ma'am, that depends," he said, resolved not to overburden her with details … except they just kept spilling out: the perils of getting on and off slowly moving trains. How best to scope out which trains might be going where, the proper way to sneak into and out of a freight yard. That she should consider wiring the bulk of whatever money she'd be taking with her on ahead, care of Western Union, New York City. That to do herself a big favor by traveling light. A quart jar of water, say, a handful of Slim Jims, a couple of oranges or apples, unsalted nuts, a few candy bars, and a little luck should see her to New York City, give or take three or four days.

He'd no sooner done with his why and wherefores than Mrs. Stoner surprised him by saying she'd brought something for him in the basket of her bicycle. It was while she was fussing around for whatever it was, that Deputy Pru drove slowly by, all by his lonesome in the cruiser, leering at the two of them sitting there like they was up to more than just something. However, since he was the one her brother aimed to fry in the electric chair, once Mrs. Stoner returned with her handbag, Moody decided to keep mum about what he'd just seen. Really, he figured, he ought to be on his way. By all rights, he should have been back to work at the paper ten minutes ago. But then he remembered one other extremely important detail that was probably none of his business, but still he ought to bring up. "You *are* planning on leaving a note, aren't you, Mrs. Stoner?"

Mrs. Stoner sort of collapsed in on herself and shook her head that *no, she was not.*

"Look," he said, aiming to press the point as gently as he could, "I may be way out of line here, but yew leaving yer folks high and dry, like they mean nothing to yew, is not natural, ma'am. Leaving 'em like that is asking too much of them—most especially if, as yew say, yew don't want them moving heaven and earth chasing after yew. Just a few chosen words that lets them off the hook so they won't spend the rest of their lives holding themselves responsible for yew doing what yew had to do."

Moody was all too aware that such a note was as important to him as it was to her. A mysterious, unexplained disappearance could well trigger Kneebone to conclude that the homicidal monster of Johnson's Crick had done her in as well.

Mrs. Stoner, however, was buy rustling around for something in her bag, which turned out to be a fine-linen handkerchief with the initials *PS* hand embroidered in one corner, surrounded by a cluster of rosebuds, with which she proceeded to dab the corner of her eye. A special gift, he concluded, from her lady love. "Please, forgive me," he said, "I should have asked. The person who gave yew that hankie—any chance she'll be heading out with yew?"

Oh no, Mrs. Stoner replied once more with a shake of her head. *She's not like me. I'll be traveling alone.*

Moody pitied this otherwise strong woman, head bowed, handkerchief cupped to her mouth, fighting hard not to become undone. He was sorely moved by the sorrow in her eyes. He'd been around enough queers in his day to know that they were what they were through no fault of their own, because they'd just been born that way.

"Oh, Mr. Moody, yes, yes, of course, I'll take your advice and leave a note. But you must realize, if the real truth of my situation ever leaked out, the scandal would utterly crush my family." Then, as if he hadn't had enough surprises for one day, she went on to add: "I suppose you heard tell about the fire at our church this spring?"

Curious, he decided to play along. "Yew mean the one I heard tell was struck by lightning and burned down?"

"It was Wednesday night," she said almost as if she were talking to herself. "Choir practice as usual scheduled for seven o'clock. Except this particular evening, not one or two of us, as usual, but every last one of us, including myself, for one reason or another, was running late— else we'd all have been there. Now, please understand, when I initially began my duties as choir director, I did so as a confirmed non-believer, a simpleminded agnostic, not quite the ardent atheist my husband claims to be. And as you may or may not be aware of, ever since Smithworthy's bank began monkeying around with the *Courier-Eagle*'s line of credit, the Stoner family has too often been short of ready cash so that even the few bucks I pulled in as church organist helped a lot. But here's the thing: right about this time, my feelings for Lorraine had grown so intense I felt in a terrible bind. Now, I know that when I say what I'm going to say next, you're going to think I'm talking crazy. And I won't hold it against you if you do. But these are the facts as I saw them then and see them now. The thunderstorm that spawned the lightning that burned our church down struck a little before seven. Simon, of course, had the car, which left me stewing on my heels back at the house for the twenty minutes or so it took for the storm to pass and I was able to head out for the church. Anyway, suffice it to say, by the time I arrived, the church was already a raging inferno, with me and a few other choir members gathered around, struck dumb, watching the town fire department watch our church burn down. Because for some weird, unexplainable reason, the pumps on the fire truck weren't working as well as they should, leaving what little water pressure there was scarcely adequate for keeping the surrounding houses safe. Not only that, it seems that bolt of lightning struck, as I said before, more or less around the exact moment choir practice was scheduled to begin. Maggie Gillard saw it herself out her kitchen window. Even Tubby Frakes, our local fire chief, was left scratching his head because he'd never seen anything big as that church reduce itself to cinders so fast, and we all should thank our stars that we'd arrived late, else we'd have burned to death. That's the thing, Mr. Moody. We'd have all been reduced to cinders but for the grace of God.

I saw it with my own eyes; that steeple came crashing down, showering sparks like Hades on the Fourth of July. And yes, yes, I know you've got to be wondering by now, what in the world has any of this got to do with my love for Lorraine? Well, you know how it says in the Good Book that there's a corner in hell reserved for perverts and queers? Well, the Sunday before that fire, all the time Reverend Digby was sermonizing about the Lord casting His wrath upon Sodom and Gomorrah, I'm sitting there at the organ, waiting to segue into the next hymn, telling myself that surely something was amiss with what that reverend was preaching. So, I decided, right then and there, to put the Good Lord Jesus to the test. So all the while the choir was singing the necessary umpteen verses of "The Little Church in the Wildwood" to get that week's worth of sinners down the aisle to the front of the church so Digby can bless their sins away, here I am, praying hard to the Almighty Lord to either put up or shut up, to either get Lorraine out of my head once and for all or give me a sign that there's nothing wrong with me being in love with her to the inexplicable degree that I am. And darned if the following Wednesday Jesus didn't up and burn Reverend Digby's church down. I mean, freak storm … everybody late … bolt of lightning … fire pumps not working right. No two ways about it. The good Lord burned that church down just to let me know that in his eyes, lesbianism was okay and that homosexuality was neither a disease nor an unspeakable abomination."

Moody was only too familiar with the disjointed state of mind that prompted such craziness. He'd been visited with similar episodes doing solitary back in Kansas, his mind in shambles, questioning the truth of ever last thing he'd ever believed. But to Mrs. Stoner's credit, her present state of mind, confused though it may be, seemed not so far gone as not to be able to get a handle on herself. In fact a couple of deep breaths later and she was returning that little handkerchief to her handbag and turning to him with a smile.

"You know, Mr. Moody, in his magnificent essay *De Profundis*, Oscar Wilde speaks almost biblically of *having grown tired of the articulate utterances of men and things,* of a *society that has no place to offer people like us*. He speaks to *the Mystical in Art, the Mystical in Life, the Mystical in Nature, whose sweet rains fall on unjust and just alike*; of *nights hung with stars*, so that persons such you and I *may walk abroad in the darkness without stumbling; of winds sent to erase our footprints so that none may track us to our hurt; of secret valleys in whose silence we may weep undisturbed; of cleansing waters and bitter herbs that will make us whole.*

"If only the Bible had put it that way," she said, wistfully touching her fingers to her breast, "how different things would be for outcasts like you and me. But alas, the world is as it is, and my family, particularly my son, will be so much better off upon my going away. The boy is young yet, so the shock for him will be slight. I'll bet when he grows up, he'll barely remember me. And my husband, Simon—he'll hardly miss a step before he's back in the flow of things, trumpeting lost causes, which is what he loves best." Then, she hesitated, as if gathering strength for what she needed to say next. "Whatever comes to pass, I know I can depend upon my sweet Lorraine to see that little Preston gets all the mothering he needs. In fact, I'm pretty sure my son already loves her more than he loves me. As for my brother, Mr. Moody, don't worry about him. He can be trying, but whatever his faults, despite his bluster, beneath it all is a just man. So, you see, in answer to your earlier question, I have done a considerable amount of thinking about the possible consequences of what I'm about to do." She paused before gracefully asking: "Mr. Moody, what do you think? Don't you agree that it's best for everyone involved that I just disappear?"

As if he should have a voice in the matter. If this woman believed in anyone, it was Oscar Wilde. And the shame of it was that anyone could see she was the sun and the moon and all the stars for that little boy. Anyway, now she was rooting around for something else from her bag, something carefully wrapped in chamois skin that she held out to him.

"Here, my brother has taken to carrying this about with him lately. He claims it's something of yours he found at Johnson's Crick. I thought you might like it back."

And now he fully understood the rules of her game. Tit for tat. He'd help her, and she'd help him—except this only too familiar thing she was offering him was something he no longer needed to possess. "How did you come by it?" he asked.

"I'm the kid sister, don't forget," she said. "Let's just say he's all a dither these past few days, thinking he's misplaced it."

"Well," Moody said as he passed it back to her, "what I think is that you should hang on to it. Call it a memento or something like that. Something that someday might end up bringing you good luck."

"There's a name for something like that," she said.

"What?"

"A talisman," she said.

"So let's call it that," he said and knew for certain that sadly the time had come for them to part. And as he stood to leave, a lively banshee reel his father once claimed he learned from an old Galway fiddler popped into his head so that instead of hemming and hawing around for the proper words to say goodbye, he took his departure whistling a merry version of "The Maid Behind the Bar." And once he reached the curb, before stepping into the street, he turned to see her standing ramrod erect beside the bench. She waved to him. He replied with the timeworn thumbs-up sign for *you can do it, babe*, all the while thinking *bless this woman* to himself, just in case that whimsical fool God of hers might be listening in. Because wherever it was this cocksure woman was fated to end up, be it New York City—providing she made it that far—or some nicey-nice, dullsville-backwater, grease-spot-in-the-road along the way, this sorely troubled young woman, for sure, was going to need all the help she could possibly get.

19

Flatbush Avenue, Brooklyn, 2004

Viewed curbside, 3246 Flatbush Avenue showed faint evidence of occupancy. Indeed, the entire 3200 block seemed long past better days, and given the inordinate size of their ballyhoo billboard that he'd spent altogether too much time staring at on Thanksgiving Day, Preston had expected the storefront signage for MUMS—aka Mitchik, Uribe, MacDonnell, & Shumsky, Private Investigators—to be emblazoned, at the very least, in throbbing Times Square neon. Anyway, Preston, being a sucker for irony, chuckled to himself as he switched off the ignition to the Subaru. Admittedly, he was nervous as hell. His wife, of course, was of the opinion that coming to these people for help was nothing less than a wild goose chase. But he told himself, who better to solicit for help in finding one's mother but a detective agency with the deliciously acronymic, quasi-palindromic name like MUMS? Providing, of course, they were still in business. That sign of theirs looked pretty beat up. But what the heck, he'd wasted gasoline getting here, so he might as well get out and knock. Only the question was which door, the one smack-dab center or the other offset to the left?

He decided to try the center door first since it was closer. The person who finally answered was a blue-eyed, redheaded, wispy bearded, *yarmulke* clad, twenty-something Hasid who informed him that this was the print shop for Jacobi Printing, whose business offices occupied the storefront next door. "MUMS," he said, is the other door, upstairs."

Yet there was something about the distinct musk of paper stock and ink, something about the chunky, asymmetric, clitter-clatter of two working offset presses that made Preston reluctant to leave. He was that little boy again, escorted by his father to the offices of the *Courier-Eagle* to see the linotype men at work on their cacophonous machines. Burly, hairy knuckled, rough-shaven, square-jawed men who reeked of cigars, wore eyeshades and black-sleeve gaiters. Men, his father claimed, who read right to left better and quicker than most people read left to-right. Men in regal command of an almost diabolical assemblage of cogs, cams, and wheels, turning molten slugs of lead into reversed typeface sentences and paragraphs, their fingers fairly dancing, clacking away on a ninety-character typeset keyboard. And but for his mother running off and his father dying of a heart attack, and the family newspaper business burning down virtually all in a day, this world would have been a fate far sweeter than the one that commands him to go next door to ascend what he was sure would turn out be a dark and rickety stairway, to a gut-clawing truth he had spent nearly all his life trying to avoid.

Yet the hallway next door was neither shabby nor dim. The stairway was secure underfoot, and the dread in the pit of his stomach he arrived with was suddenly replaced by a manic desire to bound the steps two at a time. Even if it meant arriving at the second-floor landing, heart pounding and horribly out of breath, momentarily afraid that in his haste, he had provoked a fresh episode of A-fib tachycardia, and then be relieved when it had not. His heart was racing because he was horribly out of shape. And were Roger or Bunny here, they'd be dogging him again to join a health club, and he'd be telling them that he wasn't doing this for himself, but for them so that when the day came that their old man was dead and gone and the subject of their grandmother's unexplained disappearance inevitably came up, they would be unable to find fault with him for never once trying to find her.

Mitchik, Uribe, MacDonnell, & Shumsky. Elegantly wrought gold letters upon a frosted glass door. So far, so good. Preston pushed the button to be buzzed in. He wasn't there to hire or commit, only to scope these guys out.

The reception area was crudely lit with neon lighting. China white walls were festooned with travel posters touting paradise as palm trees and empty beaches. Preston was not impressed. An overstuffed faux-leather sofa, a chrome and glass coffee table out of the seventies, a matching pair of wooden captain's chairs of the sort used as barroom props in spaghetti westerns, the furniture looked like stuff dragged in from the street. And Jesus H. Christ, hung on the wall behind the receptionist's desk, was one of those humongous, aluminum-framed, black-and-white photographs of Marilyn Monroe lying prone on a workout bench, pumping barbells, often seen for sale in tawdry Times Square tourist-trap gyp joints back in the seventies.

Preston was vacillating between staying and going when the receptionist, who until then, had been too wrapped up chewing gum and doing her nails to take notice, deigned to look his way. "May I help you?" she said, and for one brief, acetone- and cologne-infused moment, Preston's tongue wallowed for words.

"I'm … ah … sorry … ah … gee … I don't have an appointment … ah … the name is Stoner … ah … what do you think … should I have called ahead?"

"Well, that depends, Mr. Stoner. Whom do you wish to see?"

Yes, exactly who? he thought, as he quickly ran the firm's names. *Mitchik, Uribe, MacDonnell, and Shumsky; Mitchik, Uribe, MacDonnell, and Shumsky: an Irishman, a Carib, and two Jews*. "Mitchik," he decided. When in doubt, always go with a Jew.

"Then take a seat, Mr. Stoner. Mr. Mitchik will be with you in a minute."

His eyes continuing to roam the room for details, Preston selected a magazine from the coffee table and sat down. As far as he was concerned, the only thing worthy of more than a passing glance was the sinfully beautiful, twenty-something receptionist herself. Brook Contini, her nameplate said, who wore neither engagement nor wedding ring. Raven black hair streaked auburn, Gina Lollobrigida tits, Sophia Loren lips and eyes. Oh where, oh where, had this sweetheart been during his firm's exhaustive "babe search" for the Snapple spot?

"Just a few minutes more, Mr. Stoner," Miss Contini said, with a smile that seemed to say: *I love it when men ogle me*, which set Preston's mind awhirl.

After all, he'd notified his office the previous day that he'd be coming in late and working late. Coming in late, like he and Miss Contini slipping off to spend a couple of hours at one of those day-rate motels on Route 9 in New Jersey; she, his Venus, and he, her cloven-hoofed, panpipe-playing satyr, the two of them lolling together in a heart-shaped Jacuzzi, sipping champagne from long-stemmed plastic glasses.

"All right, Mr. Stoner. Mr. Mitchik will see you now. You may go right in."

His triple-X daydream now in smithereens, Preston rose and did as he was told. A slim-hipped man of normal height, with exceptionally broad shoulders, stood with his back to the door, fussing with a cranky venetian blind. "Come on in. Have a seat," he called without so much of a turn of his head. "This freaking thing's some kind of fucked up."

Preston eased himself into the well-worn leather armchair centered before Mitchik's desk. He was determined to maintain an attitude of wait and see, but every nook and cranny of this office seemed crammed with sports stuff. Beside the door he'd come in: a large cardboard box filled with old sneakers, plus a set of golf clubs and a tennis bag. Crammed into the space between the farthest wall and three gray metal filing cabinets—the middle drawer of said middle cabinet sagging open like a lapping tongue—were in-line skates, a hockey stick, a basketball, a rack of dumbbells, and a bag of either tennis or softball things. Furthermore, on the wall, directly behind Mitchik's desk was a blown-up action photo of a New York Mets fan favorite of the late sixties and early seventies, Ed Kranepool, notorious for his muscled homers and being slow as molasses afoot, caught in the act of achieving his one and only stolen base. And since Preston had been there at Shea Stadium the day that photograph had been taken, he couldn't help but wonder if saying a few words to that effect might be as good a way as any for the two of them to break the ice—that was, providing this guy ever stopped screwing around with that damn Venetian blind.

But Preston's bromance with this guy's sports stuff ended when Mitchik turned around. A cynical no-bullshit smile, heavy lidded film-noir eyes, neatly trimmed Van Dyke beard, not to mention that sitting atop this man's cluttered desk was a half-eaten bagel, a cup of coffee, and a copy of the *New York Post*—spread open as befits a private snoop, to page six, the gossip page—combined to say that ice-breaking conversation was not required when a man had an unlit stogie crammed into the corner of his mouth as he leaned across his desk to shake a prospective client's hand, because if this guy wasn't a real-deal private detective, he sure as hell could play one on TV.

"Like the place? Simon Mitchik, and you are?"

"Preston … Preston Stoner," he answered.

Mitchik, coffee cup now in hand, leaned back in his swivel chair. "So, Stoner, what's up?"

"I want MUMS to find my mother."

Mitchik slowly rotated his chair ninety degrees. "So, what we have here is a gentleman who wants to find his mother," he said to a sagging window blind. "That it? You got more to give us, or what?"

Preston cleared his throat, somewhat bemused to find this bruiser of a man sipped his coffee pinky finger extended. "Yeah, well, I'm afraid there isn't all that much to tell, except she left home when I was a little kid."

Mitchik slowly swiveled back around, leaned forward, elbows on desk, his fleshy eyes now piggy slits. "Hmmm. Not much, huh? Maybe you should let us be the judge of that."

"Hey, listen," Preston responded. "For your information, I was only *five* years old the last time I saw my mother. So how much *can* I remember? She left me with a neighbor for the day, saying she'd be back, and we never saw her again."

Mitchik studied him for a few seconds, then cupped his hands together and suddenly exploded them apart as if he were releasing a bird. "That's it, Stoner? Poof, your mommy up and disappears on you just like that?"

"That's it. You got it."

"And this was, what … when you were five?"

"That's right. Nineteen fifty-two to be exact. Not long after I turned five."

"And the police? No one went out looking for her?"

"My uncle *was* the police. The county sheriff, and I assure you, when he said there was no hint of foul play, there was no hint of foul play."

Mitchik stroked his chin. "*You* can assure *me*? Okay, sport, if that's the way you want to play it, be my guest. But how about a note? In my experience, women who run off from their families generally leave notes."

"You're right; there was a note. Though I never knew of its existence until my aunt confessed it to me a couple of years ago, just before she passed away. But it seems she'd never read it herself, so she had no idea exactly what it said. Only what my uncle told her, which wasn't much. Supposedly, he kept it locked in the safe at the jail, but once he retired she had no idea what became of it, or even if it ever existed at all. She told me that the most my uncle ever said to her about the note was that it revealed things about his sister that should never see the light of day."

"Soooooo," Mitchik drawled, "things not fit to see in the light of day. Sounds like your mama might have been walking the wild side … sooooo, you want me to do what?"

"Find her, of course. Or what happened to her, because by now my mother's probably long dead."

"That depends. How old was she when she ran off?"

"She was born in nineteen twenty-four, so that would have made her …?"

"Depending on date of birth, twenty-seven or twenty-eight," Mitchik chirped in. "Which'd make her a tad over eighty today, so it's not all that improbable she's still alive."

"She was a Pisces, born March thirteenth," Preston added, shocked to realize how young his mother had been. "You might say that losing her has been this giant hole in my life ever since. Frankly speaking, it's something I've only recently worked up the nerve to face up to," Preston added, aware of his quickening pulse and totally unaware he kept crossing and re-crossing his legs.

"Stoner, relax, my man. You're doing fine. Better than most. But where was your father in all of this?"

"At work, I suppose. He was the editor of the local paper."

"Yeah? So why didn't he fill you in?"

"Because he never had the chance. The thing was, that same day … that night, actually … my father succumbed to a fatal heart attack in his sleep. According to my uncle, he was pretty darn sure my father went to bed that night clueless that his wife had run off on him."

Mitchik whistled. "Jesus, kid, that's some kinda fucked-up shit."

Preston glanced out the window as a fire trucked screamed down Flatbush Avenue. Across the street, a bus pulled into the stop. He imagined himself down there, waiting politely for an eighty-something women to get off.

Mitchik crushed his coffee cup into a ball and slam dunked it into the circular file. "You say that sheriff uncle of yours personally looked for her … really looked for her, right?"

"You bet … called in the state police and the Nebraska Bureau of Investigation. Nobody seemed to know for sure how she managed to slip through the cracks. My uncle's best guess was that she'd hopped a freight train back east. I was in high school when he told me that. At the time he didn't sound all that sure about it, so I figured it was only a hunch."

"A hunch, huh? And you left it at that? Stoner, listen up. MUMS don't do hunches. We do reality. So, what I'm dying to know is, what's up with you that it took so long to get it together to start looking for her?"

Preston's vaulted soul sank deeper in his chair. "As the years passed, I gradually became aware of a few things. Like when I was a kid back in grade school, the other kids used to ride me pretty hard because the gossip around town had my mother running off with some dirty old hobo. That was until I started punching them in the nose to get them to shut up. Of course, I don't remember all that much about things that far back, but I do vaguely recollect someone hanging around our house who may or may not have been a hobo who did odd jobs for us. The guy I have in mind I remember mostly because he could really play the harmonica. I wish I had a name to give you. Best I can do is something Irish sounding: Mulligan, maybe, Mulvaney, Mooney. But as to whether my mother ran off with him, or anybody for that matter, as far as I'm concerned that's why I'm here talking to you, isn't it? Because I'm sick and tired of not being able to forgive what I can't forget. Sick and tired of pretending it doesn't matter, because goddamn it, it does. So, what do you think? We got enough to go on here, or what?"

"Stoner, from what you've given me so far, we've got *bubkes* to go on. But then again, most people who show up here for the first time give us *bubkes* to go on. But rest assured, if you're up for it, MUMS is more than willing to get on the trail. Shit, this is what we do. Somebody's lost, we do our best to track 'em down. But all kidding aside, missing person cases can get expensive. Naturally, we charge by the hour. Keep in mind, anytime you call us on the telephone, the meter's running the moment I say hello. On the other hand, anytime we call you, that's on our dime. As for our rates, we tailor them to size. Your story's a real heartbreaker, and since you're obviously not a rich fucker, just to be nice, we'll take you on for one ninety-five an hour. Plus expenses, of course. In case we have to go out of town—to God forbid, Nebraska, is it?—that'll be at a flat rate of three hundred a day plus expenses. For all of that, you're gonna get a preliminary report and maybe an update or two along the way before you get your final report. Just remember, you can put a stop to this merry-go-round anytime you please. So that's it. The rest is up to you. You out or in?

Preston's carefully prepared answer to this question was supposed to have been *Let me think it over, and I'll get back to you*, but how could he, with Mitchik balancing a pencil by its point on the end of his finger? Because the man was not only damn good at it, he was absolutely mesmerizing. Hand held rock steady underneath. Pencil elevated motionless at the perpendicular, as if capable of staying that way forever, until seconds later, he flipped it with a flourish and snatched it from the air.

"So? You look puzzled, Stoner. Something bothering you?"

Oh no. Nothing was bothering this Stoner guy, except for teetering on the brink of entering into a contract with a detective agency based solely on the strength of a cheap cocktail-party trick. His eyes now closed, momentarily racked with indecision, wondering how he was going to explain it his wife; it was almost like what he was waiting for was for Mitchik to come around from behind his desk and place his hand on his shoulder.

"Buck up, my friend. You're not going to be one of those weepy guys who fall apart on us, are you? Look, you don't have to break your balls over this. All we need from you is for you to go home, sit down, and make a list of everyone, living or dead, who might know or might have known something about your mother's disappearance. Phone numbers and addresses may save us a lot of time and you a lot money. I'm assuming you have a photograph?"

Preston nodded.

"There you go," Mitchik said. "Listen, believe it or not, I assure you, you're going to remember a shitload more about that day than you think. The key to it all is to relax and let it flow. I don't know, but if I were you, on my way home, I'd pick up a six-pack of beer or a bottle of Jim Beam, or cop some hash or weed, you know, whatever best floats your boat. Once home, close the blinds, dim the lights, and settle back. A little music. Maybe some Frank Sinatra, Bobby Hackett, Blossom Dearie. You came

185

in here looking like fright night at the Bijou, for Christ's sake. Loosen up. You're going to do fine. I see from your ring finger you're married, so see if you can swing a blow job from your wife. Yeah, smile away, but nothing's better for a man's ego than his woman going down on him; and, if you don't mind me saying it, maybe that's your problem here, Stoner. You got yourself one big-time, infantilized ego, my friend. You're still five years old, Stoner, and who wants to be five years old all his life?"

Somewhere between Frank Sinatra and that blow job from Joellen—which Preston didn't think likely anytime soon—as he spoke, Mitchik sort of sashayed to the center of the room, one arm extended, the other folded across his chest, ghost dancing to some inner disco beat. An admitted *klutz* as a dancer, Preston had always been a sucker for groovy moves, and here was Mitchik mamboing a pas de shoe with a deft little bob and a back-kick twist of his heel, as if deftly tapping shut the open drawer of a filing cabinet were Twyla Tharp or Bill T. Jones choreography.

"Not to worry about it, pal," Mitchik then said, now perched on the forward edge of his desk. "MUMS sticks to a case like a rat on a glue pad. You're grinning, Stoner, which means you appreciate my style. So, listen up. Stick with MUMS, and whatever we end up costing you—even if we have to go to whatever the fuck is the name of that town you're from in Nebraska, and don't bother to tell me now; include it with the stuff you're going to write down—but sure as shit MUMS'll be a whole lot less expensive than what you'd pay some wacko shrink to give you half the peace of mind. That's assuming, of course, you don't get cold feet and go cheap on us—and by the way, what the hell you people eat out there in Nebraska besides beef steak? You guys ever heard of pastrami or lasagna? Anyway, let's pray it never comes to that. Hell, for all we know, your mother, right this minute, could be drooling baby food all over herself within shouting distance of the Verrazano Bridge."

Naturally, by this time Preston was totally on board with anything and everything Mitchik, from his diamond pinky ring and gold wristwatch with a poker-chip dial, to the cherrywood hairbrush the man withdrew from his desk drawer to attend to his hair, to the dark-chocolate, belted, leather car coat with attached hoodie he'd taken down from the coatrack.

"Okay, Stoner. Chop, chop. On your feet. Time to get it in gear. I'm overdue for a rendezvous in Sheepshead Bay. Got me a date with a redhead, two-dozen oysters, and a jeroboam of champagne. Once you say the word and come up with five hundred as a retainer, we'll get to work finding your mother for you. Give us a week and a half—no, make it two—before you can expect your first preliminary report. The IRS has already exacted its pound of flesh from us for this year, so let's do this one off the books, okay? Anyway, I hope you've figured out by now, MUMS don't shit around. You play chess, Stoner? A brainiac like you has got to play chess, so consider us Kasparov thinking nine, ten moves ahead. Anyway, my boy, on your feet. Any questions, ask 'em now, 'cause you and me are as good as outta here."

Mitchik hit the light switch and held open the door.

Of course, Preston had questions. Many questions. Who wouldn't have questions? Especially the one that had been nagging him ever since he walked in: "So, Mitchik, what's up with your partners, Uribe, MacDonald, and Shumsky anyway? You got only one office here. You guys work shifts or what?" he said.

Mitchik did a phony double take. "Okay, Stoner, you got me. I'm busted. You ask. I tell no lies. We got no Uribe, no MacDonald, and no Shumsky. They're just made-up names to complete the fucking acronym. Consider us a one-man band, a conjuror for hire with less personal baggage than a whore checking into a cheap motel. Uribe, MacDonald, and Shumsky don't exist, just like your mother doesn't exist 'til I find her, just a man's whole fucking life doesn't exist 'til he gets balls enough to live it. Life's an illusion, Stoner. My real name's Contini, same as my secretary, whose real first name is Dawn. She's my niece, and her tits are silicone. And, oh yes, before I forget, the streets of Flatbush are paved with gold, and my other car's a Lear jet. You ever hear of quantum physics, Stoner? Yes? Okay, enough farting around. Time for us to make like a couple of neutrinos and get the fuck out of here."

Preston surfed Mitchik's wake downstairs to the street, watched him whip a metallic-silver, Mercedes-Benz SUV into a rubber-pealing one-eighty—the GPS no doubt set for Sheepshead Bay.

Arriving home to drop off his car before catching the bus to work, lining up his Outback for a serious attempt at an outrageously tight parking space in front of 87 Pioneer, infused with the heuristics of what once was and might still be, Preston climaxed his day by nailing that sucker in one fell swoop, scarcely inches to spare, fore and aft.

20

Beatrice, 1952

The Debate
"Is Theism a Logical Philosophy?"
Mr. E. Haldeman-Julius,
Philosopher, Author, Publisher
from Girard, Kansas
vs.
The Reverend Julius Watkins,
Pastor of the First Presbyterian Church
Beatrice, Nebraska

Positioned out of sight in the lee of a platform he'd finished building less than two hours ago, seated on a rickety folding chair, Moody found little solace in the thought that should things get too boring, he could always take a nap. Unlike Mr. Stoner, whose mission in life seemed to be to do battle with the injustices of the world—and understood so poorly what little chance he had of setting them right—political and theological discussions left Moody cold. In fact, once he'd finished with the setup, he'd have been long gone but for his boss imploring him to please stick around.

"There's been talk, Moody, of a planned disturbance tonight. I'll be keeping watch somewhere up front, so if you don't mind, I'd feel a whole lot better having you on the lookout at the rear of the church, just in case some idiot with mischief on his mind decides to come at us from behind."

Of course, Mr. Stoner could very well be right. The last time Moody'd snuck a peek, among those still streaming in, he'd spotted a suspicious-looking group of eight or nine led by the Reverend Mr. Digby, who instead of looking around for a place for them to sit as a group, had set about scattering themselves throughout the church. Whatever, the business end of the old hickory-wood ax handle balanced across his lap, he'd scrounged up in the basement of the church, would come in mighty handy should push come to shove and there was trouble.

Moody didn't know beans about debates. His best guess was, they were some kind of watered-down trial, where the guy who loses doesn't get carted off to jail. Still, he expected a dull affair. Certainly, nothing on par with the high jinks and fun displayed in Stephen Benét's *The Devil and Daniel Webster.* The only thing he knew for sure about tonight was that Mrs. Stoner, this being her last night ever with her kid, wouldn't be in attendance. And speaking of the devil, the church had now gone silent. Mr. Haldeman-Julius was due up first, so he must be about to speak.

"Are all ideas that men have devoutly held, all notions in which men have believed and which men have even died for, therefore true? Surely not. Imagine it! What I think is true. What Dr. Watkins thinks is true. What Mrs. Mary Baker Eddy thought was true. What John Wesley, who believed in witchcraft, thought was true. What everybody thinks is true—which means that truth is equivalent to the sum of all absurdities?"

Truth—the sum of all absurdities? Moody stifled a laugh. And he thought he had that old fart all figured out. That for sure, he'd start off like gangbusters, rolling his *r*'s and pontificating bombast to beat the band, instead speaking even-toned sense, common man to common man. And Moody had to admit, he kind of liked the idea of putting truth on trial right off the bat, questioning humankind's slavish tendency to worship things that didn't exist. Things all the way from the Holy Trinity, Mary, and all them holy saints, to dragons, unicorns, fairies, genies, Santa Claus, and the tooth fairy. Except, the problem was, if Haldeman-Julius's aim was to slick talk believers into not believing, he had about as much a chance of getting that done as convincing them to stop breathing.

"There are many other theistic arguments," Haldeman-Julius continued, "but all, on examination, are seen to be mere assumptions, bare sophistry, adroit evasions of obvious facts, rendered in metaphysical balderdash to refute a realistic approach to life …"

Sophistry, metaphysical, balderdash. Gilded prose delivered in a deeply sonorous, well-articulated, baritone voice. Moody's smile blossomed into a full-blown grin. He rose from his chair, took a quick peek and sat back down. Indeed, the place was packed. Standing room only in the back. Every face rapt to Haldeman-Julius as he pulled out all the stops: arms akimbo, the thrust of his jaw oddly reminiscent of a photograph of Benito Mussolini Moody'd once seen pictured in *Life* magazine.

"The arguments for theism are heated and numerous, but the results are always the same. They cannot show us the slightest evidence for the God idea [*thunk*]. They cannot show us the finger of God in any period of man's history [*thunk*]. They cannot show us their God in nature [*thunk*]. They cannot show us that God exists [*thunk*] …"

The first *thunk* had Moody tightening his grip on his club, the second had him rising for another peek. Satisfied it was only Haldeman-Julius knocking his fist against the podium for punctuation, he sat back down as Haldeman-Julius' commentary continued on.

"… that there is any method for man to save himself except through his own efforts [*thunk*]. A man must fight with his own sweat and blood and tears [*thunk*]. If he is winning a measure of joyousness … and gladness … and laughter out of life … it is because of his faith in his own powers … and not in some mysterious entity beyond the cloudsssss."

Haldeman-Julius's elongated esses tappered to silence as Eulaylia Smithworthy signaled times up by tinkling her antique silver dinner bell. Applause being forbidden, Haldeman-Julius returned to his seat on the dais in silence. Though in Moody's opinion, there wouldn't have been any anyway, since whenever reason dared speak truth to belief, belief rarely listened.

Not that Moody cared who won or lost tonight. This whole affair was a bunch of hooey. In fact, in his opinion, Eulaylia Smithworthy herself was nothing less than the town's reigning queen of hooey. President of the Eastern Star Lodge, relentless in her campaign to rid the Beatrice Public Library of filthy books and communist propaganda, a frequent contributor to the Letters to the Editor section of the *Courier-Eagle*, this stubby dumpling of a woman, renowned for flashy jewelry and outlandish hats, was, without doubt, not only the official timekeeper for tonight's debate, but Mr. Stoner's nemesis as well—harridan and hypocrite being but two of the nicer names Mr. Stoner had for "a woman, who cares more for her precious rose garden and her husband's personal wealth than the teachings of Jesus Christ." Presently seated tonight front row and center, pew-mate to the Right Reverend Mr. Digby, she as he, seemingly united in their opinion of the goings-on so far, scowling like a pair of angry pug dogs.

And the king of hooey? Moody chuckled because that'd be J. Herman Smithworthy, Esquire, the President of the First National Bank of Girard, Kansas, equally disdained by Mr. Stoner as nothing less than "an ample-bellied rooster of a man, whose sartorial splendor ran to bow ties, Panama hats, and bespoke seersucker suits, rich as Croesus and doesn't know his ass from a hole in the ground."

Moody chuckled again. Old tight-ass Herm, as no one in town dared call him to his face. The reputed ghostwriter of his wife's scathing diatribes that Mr. Stoner dutifully published in the Letters to the Editor section of the *Courier-Eagle.* This being poker night at the Lions Club, for sure, "old tight-ass" wouldn't be in attendance tonight.

The Smithworthys. The very thought of having to deal with them on a regular basis was enough to prompt any man to cling to the traveling life. For sure, riding the rails in a boxcar, there wasn't a snowball's chance in hell of rubbing elbows with anyone of the Smithworthys' ilk. Or, for that matter, letting themselves get involved in pain-in-the-ass situations like last week, when ole Herm cornered Mr. Stoner in Monte's Barber Shop, fit to be tied to find someone to come put his lawn into fit condition for another of his wife's famous Sunday-after-church garden parties because his own gardener had broken his leg, and what the hell, if Mr. Stoner hadn't gone and volunteered Moody's name.

Of course, he could and should have said no. Except it was pretty much common knowledge around town that the *Courier-Eagle* was deep in hock to Herm's bank, so out of respect for Mr. Stoner's situation, Moody decided to play it cozy, declining the offer by pricing himself out of the game. Except, damned if J. Herm didn't blink twice at a price at least twenty bucks above the going rate for cutting lawns—which only went to show a guy how much that stingy old bastard was under the control of his wife.

Even so, Moody had thought the deal pretty fishy at the time. Since with the drought and all, and Bat Gintzel's citywide watering ban, nobody's grass around town was doing all that well. Then again, nobody's grass wasn't the Smithworthys' grass, because once through their big gate, and out of sight behind the dense hedge that fronted the Smithworthy place on North Summit Street, damned if Moody didn't find the sprinklers full on, watering what looked to be a full half acre of luscious green lawn sorely in need of a haircut. But the thing that really pissed Moody off was that all the time he spent push mowing that lawn in the hot sun, neither the lord nor the lady of the manor had the common decency to send their cook out to offer him so much as a glass of the stuff.

Moody shifted uncomfortably in his seat. Doctor Watson was due up to speak. According to Mr. Stoner, the good doctor tended to long-windedness, and since the timekeeper for the night was Mrs. Smithworthy, she'd be loath to cut him off.

"If and when you get sick of the God talk," Mr. Stoner had suggested, "try stuffing your fingers in your ears." Except Doctor Watson was proving to be much more than Moody expected. No Holy Roller screaming from the pulpit, he. His message was non-hysterical, factual, and reasoned.

"Mr. Haldeman-Julius draws a distinction between the spiritual mind and the scientific mind that does not seem to me valid. At least, in my own thinking it is not valid. It is a very common assumption that the spiritual has nothing to do with the real, with facts, with life as it is. I am surprised that my worthy opponent should be betrayed into making this distinction, because everything that has to do with truth, beauty, art, literature, and science is spiritually minded, and I maintain that he himself is a profoundly spiritually minded man if for no other reason than he is interested in all the beauties of the world. And I maintain that I am no less scientific in thinking if I have a little strain of spirituality in my own being. It is a mistake for my colleague to call the Buddha an atheist …"

And now Moody's interest was really piqued. While he didn't know all that much about the Buddha, according to lore, this holy man had spent a good, long stretch of his early adult life as a wandering beggar, living a life not all that different from Moody's own.

"And few familiar with the Buddhist hymns," Doctor Watkins continued, "and Buddhist philosophy, who recognizes the Buddha for the mythical and mystic character he is, would dare to call him an atheist. Not only was the Buddha actuated by a desire for contact with great mystery, he was a great humanist. Therefore, for these reasons alone, God-fearing Christians should feel themselves free to acknowledge kinship with the Buddha. Humanity, at its core, is mutually mystic."

Kinship with the Buddha? Humanity at its core, mutually mystic? Certainly, Dr. Watkins's line of reasoning was a whole lot easier to follow than Mr. Stoner had led Moody to expect. And certainly, much, much easier on the senses than the sight of Mrs. Smithworthy's stocky calves and pudgy ankles, peeping out beneath her pew—blessed though they be in their capacity to endure heavy loads. Oh yes, that day Moody'd cut her grass all right and, in so doing, taken extra pains to make sure to eliminate for all time, any likelihood of working for them again. Knowing full well they preferred scum like he never to darken their door, he'd requested permission to use their bathroom, knowing at least they'd have to grant him that, and in so doing, allow him the opportunity to leave in his wake the hobo's calling card in the form of a massive turd lovingly coiled atop the mound of toilet paper he'd, first, stuffed into the bowl. Accidently forgetting to flush, of course, so that when Eulaylia Smithworthy ordered her maid to go flush away that nasty man's disgusting mess—because she'd be loath to take care of it herself—the bowl would overflow turds and shitty paper all over the floor. And oh, the look on poor Mr. Stoner's face when Eulaylia's next missive arrived later in the week. His poor boss totally in the dark from where her vitriol sprang, balling up her letter, pronouncing it "unfit to print, a veritable letter from hell," then hurling it into the wastebasket. And, wouldn't you know, hell just happened to be what Dr. Watkins was speaking of next.

"Now, Mr. Haldeman-Julius says that I don't believe in hell. Well, there's hell, and then there is *hell* …"

The good doctor paused to allow a wave of partisan laughter to pass. "I seem to recall once … what was it? … maybe fifteen, twenty years ago … back in the days when Sy Stoner's father was still editor of our newspaper … a letter sent to me by one of our colored brethren—who, tonight, shall go unnamed—regarding an article of mine that had recently appeared in the *Courier-Eagle* concerning the lasting damage visited upon the American psyche, back in the twenties and thirties, by a hell-and-damnation preacher from Chicago, an ex-baseball player by the name of Billy Sunday. So, in closing, I would like to leave you with our colored friend's memorable words: 'Reverend Watson, I don't know about Hell and Damnation up there on them boulevards where you folks live, but if that Billy Sunday fellow ever showed up down where I live preaching his unholy brand of racist fire and brimstone, I suspect come sunup, folks up where you live wouldn't have any clothes left on your lines or chickens in your coops."

A snort. A stifled guffaw, followed by a wave of laughter. Moody, however, was not amused but appalled by Dr. Watkins's distasteful joke. Those white folks out there had no idea what in the world they were laughing at. Hell and damnation, preached Billy Sunday style, was what white preachers scared white folks with to keep them on the straight and narrow. But the poor, especially the colored poor, had no need of sermons on hell. An unjust, two-tiered legal system, a lifetime sentence of wage slavery, eating humble pie and saying *yessems* to the boss? It'd be a mighty cold day in devil town before any of them got so much as a whiff of the heavenly life that people like the Smithworthys took as their God-given right to live. But, at least, the good doctor had this much going for him. Instead of running over like Moody expected, he'd finished right on time, so factoring in a ten-minute rebuttal for each contestant, this horseshit dog and pony show was only twenty minutes shy of being done.

Of course, Moody was curious how Haldeman-Julius was going to respond. Once the house quieted down, the spokesman for the devil opened his rebuttal with a hearty laugh. "Well, sir, from the sound of things, at the end of this debate, Dr. Watkins won't be getting off his knees any more than I'll be getting down on my mine." The words had hardly issued from his mouth when suddenly, somewhere off to the left, a male voice shouted out, "Atheist, go back to Kansas."

Moody jumped to his feet just as the first tomato struck, quickly followed by another and another. Two miscreants in the organ loft who'd somehow got past Mr. Stoner. One of them with the athletic build and throwing style of a natural center fielder, whom Moody recognized as someone he'd seen come in with Digby.

"Dirty Jew," that same voice on the left called out as tomatoes continued to pelt the stage.

"Communist," a lady shouted from the center section.

"Pornographer," a male voice chorused from the right. "Godless bastard. Tar and feather the son of a bitch and run him out of town."

Oh, yes, Digby had scattered his troops well. The House of the Lord had become a house of pandemonium. Nothing, but nothing, would have given Moody more pleasure right then than to be up there in that choir loft ax handling the living bejesus out of those two tomato-throwing nut balls. But he'd been charged to guard the rear. Which, he assumed, included looking after Haldeman-Julius and Dr. Watkins as well, who—instead of being front and center, exhorting folks to get a grip on themselves and behave—was, interestingly enough, nowhere in sight. As for Haldeman-Julius, having tucked himself into the recessed backside of Dr. Watkins's massive pulpit, he seemed to be having himself a grand old time, grinning like a little kid at a paper-wad fight.

And Mr. Stoner? It'd be just like him to pick this moment to slip outside for a smoke. Or for that matter, where was the goddamn sheriff? Or that numbskull deputy of his? And Blue Jay, the local town cop? This time of day, he'd be over at the East Side Café, thumbing girlie magazines and pigging out on apple pie. Moody hunkered down to take stock of the situation. Those idiots were due to run out of ammunition soon. Once that happened things were due to calm down. He was considering if he ought to go check in case someone was trying to sneak in by the back door, when the first egg struck, exploding shell and yoke all over the platform. Fearing the worst was yet to come, Moody leapt onto the platform.

"Come on, sir, we got to get yew out of here," he said, crouched at Haldeman-Julius's side as an egg whizzed overhead.

"Leave?" Haldeman-Julius roared in delight. "And miss the fun? Not on your life. Those scalawags up there in the balcony think they're doing the work of the Lord."

"Sir, I promised Mr. Stoner to see after yew. It's eggs now, but who knows what's next?"

"Listen, Moody, I stirred this pot. I intend to enjoy the stew, and since the two of us are now, as it were, comrades in the same foxhole, please can that *sir* and *mister* stuff and call me Manny."

Moody shrugged. No doubt about it, this Manny guy was loveably insane. But given the first lull, they needed to make a break for it—which, come to think of it, no more eggs flying their way for the past few seconds—might have already arrived. Moody peeked around the corner of the pulpit. The coast seemed clear. Digby's minions seemed to have deserted the organ loft. The church pew itself, now a hastily vacated war zone—that late tonight or early next morning, Mr. Stoner would have him here doing cleanup.

He was in the act of helping Manny to his feet when he realized those two assholes from the choir loft had started down the center aisle, one of them toting a bucket that Moody figured contained nothing good. Smiling broadly, his club firmly in hand, he dropped from the platform to block their way.

"Fun's over, my friends. Life's full of choices, and these here are yers. Either set that bucket down nice and easy and we part friends, or one of yew is gonna be the fool running up that aisle with an ax handle jammed up his rear end."

Because the man holding the bucket had skittery eyes and gone out of his way to pretty himself up real nice for church, Moody concluded he wasn't likely all that keen on having an ax handle up where the light don't shine. The other man, however, the younger of the two, the one Moody had admired for his graceful follow-through, had bad news written twenty-three different ways all over him; so, if things came to it, he'd the one to take out first.

"So which is it, gents? Take yer lumps, or set that bucket down nice and easy and walk away? I'm a gonna give yew a count of three, and lest there be any misunderstandings, nothing, and I do mean nothing'll give me more pleasure than for one or both of yew to up and call my bluff."

"One" was no more out of Moody's mouth than the man with the bucket put it down, arms spread, opened handed, like innocence itself. As for the other guy, true was, Moody had no intention of stretching his count to "two." No, he'd do as he used to do when he was a boy sent to bring in the cows. "Yeeeeee-haw! Go on now, git," he yelled with a sudden jump forward, swiping his club back and forth in the air. The pair immediately turned tail, jostling to be the first up the aisle.

Haldeman-Julius broke into applause. "Good show, Moody. Way to go. Two against one, and by Jove you've sent 'em packing."

But Moody knew that now was not the time for celebrating. Fearing that bucket contained bleach or some other bilious swill, he dipped his finger, then tasted it with his tongue—then laughed. "Hey, Manny, I do believe this here is just good old-fashioned tap water, and yew know what? I'm a-thinking that what these boys was aiming to do was baptize them a Jew. But now we're rid of them clowns, don't you think it's about time we ring down the curtain on Mr. Stoner's one-ring circus?"

"Not on your life, Moody." Haldeman-Julius called back. "I intend to finish delivering my rebuttal even if it means preaching to an empty church."

Moody hopped back onto the platform and gently took Haldeman-Julius by the elbow. "Listen, Manny, my mama told me once if she told me a thousand times: 'Hughie, the most difficult lesson to learn in life is knowing when it's over.' And the way I see this here debate, yew done given it your best shot, and a damn good shot it was. As sure as God's little green apples, come sunrise yew can bet yer bottom dollar, atheism'll be none the worse for wear."

To Moody's relief, Haldeman-Julius allowed himself to be escorted out the back door. However, once outside and revivified by the somewhat cooler night air, noticing the sheriff's cruiser driven clear up onto the sidewalk near the front of the church, where a relatively large knot of people stood gawking at the ignominious spectacle of two men spread-eagled over the cruiser's hood, like a moth drawn to a porch light, Haldeman-Julius swung a hard right to go take a look-see. Moody, however, having anticipated as much, stepped in to block his way.

"See here, Manny, Mr. Stoner's instructions were that if things tonight got too out of control, I was to see you straight back to his office, and from the sound of that ruckus up there in the front of the church, I don't think yer presence helps matters any. And since it looks to be like Mr. Stoner's gonna be busy for quite a while, gathering up stuff for a write-up in tomorrow's paper, why don't we just do as the man said and hie ourselves the hell back to the *Courier-Eagle* building?"

Moody, hoping soon to be rid of his ward, opted for a shortcut across the courthouse lawn. Neither of them cared to speak. How could they with the main event still going on behind them? Two comic voices standing out over the din: Digby's shrill tenor insisting that what had just transpired inside that church was a true act of God, and Sheriff Kneebone's booming basso profundo barking for everyone to, by God, calm down or he'd run the lot 'em in.

Approaching the bench where Moody had sat with Mrs. Stoner earlier that day, Haldeman-Julius slowed to a halt.

"See here, Moody, I see no reason to wait for Sy in his stuffy old office when we could just as well bide our time out here in the open air. Surely, sooner or later, he's bound to pass our way."

Not all that keen himself on the idea of being cooped up inside with a man who loved nothing more than hearing himself talk, Moody agreed.

Haldeman-Julius removed his suit jacket and draped it over the back of the bench. Then, undid his tie, loosened his collar, sat down and inhaled and exhaled deeply.

"Ah, Moody, such are the transient blessings of life. I speak, of course, of the familiar musk of freshly milled soybeans that graces this evening's air, which I find to be highly redolent of summer nights back in Girard, Kansas."

Rather than indulge in the redolence of soybeans, Moody closed his eyes and leaned back. When it came to the presumption of scents, he'd prefer the aroma of Lifebuoy soap given off by Mrs. Stoner earlier in the day, and the acrid fumes of diesel switchers busy shunting freight cars into what, for her, would be tomorrow's flight-to-freedom train.

"Behold, my friend …," Haldeman-Julius then said.

Curious, Moody opened his eyes. Haldeman-Julius had his head tilted to the sky.

"… truly, planet Earth is but an insignificant speck of dust in a vast and mighty universe. The briefest of grace notes amongst the eternal music of the spheres. The loneliest corner of the cosmos. As above, so below, on warm summer nights during that period of the new moon best described as a riotous festival of stars and stars and stars, that even cities ablaze with streetlight can cancel out."

There was a short pause. Moody wondered if he was expected to reply.

"Moody, to quote James Agee: 'Let us now praise famous men.' Specifically, those men who were hurling eggs and tomatoes with abandon tonight. Though hopelessly misguided in correctness of purpose, they proved themselves to be the very spirit of the Great Plains. For they are men of resolute action, are they not? Men of passion, partisans of independence, celebrants of freedom in all things. Judge them not, for they are the salt of this earth, the very stuff that makes America, America. The only difference between them and us is that you and I have figured out a few things along the way they've yet to think about. And who can fault them, knowing what they know of the world, which is mostly fixin' things, breakin' things, growin' things, fornicatin', and gettin' shit-faced on Saturday nights? But don't ever take them for fools. Consider them fledgling rrrecruits to our cause, Moody," he proclaimed, tracing an elegant arabesque with his hand in the air, suddenly back to rolling his *r*'s again. "Truly, the tomato throwers of this world are but the patrrriotic kin of Shay's rrrebellious frrrontier farmers of Western Massachusetts. They are the Minutemen of Concord, self-appointed defenders of every man who's ever been hoodwinked, cheated, or had his pockets fleeced by scheming politicians beholden only to money-grrrubbing oligarchs. While the complete collapse of the capitalist system may never occur within our lives, Moody, rrrest assured that fall it will. Marx, I deeply believe, had the message rrrright; only his timing was bad."

"Yeah, yew bet, Manny. Like maybe something called World War II got in the way," Moody said, mildly amused by H-J's self-affected ways. And the man hadn't rolled his *r*'s once during the debate.

"Rrright you are, Moody. Indeed, the Grrreat Deprression had the powers that be all but pooping in their pants, deeply in fear that the abject poverty that had stricken our land might prompt the wrathful poor into violent rrrrevolution. It is rrrecorded fact, is it not, that it was only by strrressing this exact point that FDR was able to muster the rrrequisite number of Rrrepublican votes in Congress to pass the New Deal. Because, as you know quite well, the big boys with the bucks knew only too well that an angry populace had found them out. For who better than a man on a soup line to know whose brrread the butter gets sprrread on? While men may hate many things, the thing every man hates most is injustice, and what grrreater example of injustice could there be for the workingman than the catastrophe of a worldwide economic deprression? Do you not agree?"

Did Moody agree? Agree with a man who didn't seem to give a hoot whether other folks agreed with him as long as they were listening? Just for fun, he decided to jump in.

"Tell me something, Manny, yew ever been in a real fight? Yew know, kicked the shit out of somebody just for the fun of it?"

As Moody expected, the great debater's reply was deliciously slow in coming. "Noooo," Haldeman-Julius drawled. "Can't say I have."

"Pity," Moody said, "'cause 'til you do, you won't understand beans about revolution or war. Fact is, when you get right down to it, it's violence and cruelty that really gets a man's pecker hard. You're way out of line thinking, deep down, each of us is of equal worth. Face it: some folks are just no damn good. Like those two fellers throwing tomatoes in that church? Yer gonna trust yer revolution to scum like that? Why, I do believe Stalin and Hitler, at one time in their lives, were poor, ignorant boys just like them. And speaking of death and destruction, how about the Old Testament, the way it's chuck full of stories of God's people neglecting His word and going sour on Him? Meaning what? Meaning man's inconstant nature can't sit still long enough to think before he acts. That it's more or less set in stone that the scumbags of the right and the scumbags of the left will always be at each other's throats, leaving the otherwise good folk of the world hotfootin' it in the frying pan, wishing things was otherwise."

Haldeman-Julius clapped his hands in glee. "Touché, Moody, touché. 'Hotfootin' it in the frrrying pan.' I do believe you've missed your calling. You turn an excellent phrase, my friend."

"But I'm not just turning phrases here, Manny. I'm not strivin' fer fancy oratory. I'm just saying in plain words that people don't come into the world all the same. That you can't judge a dog's temperament by whether or not it's wagging its tail. And I guess right about now you must be dying to know just where I place myself in the general scheme of things. The answer is, Manny, I don't. Why? Because the stars in my firmament don't have no fixed locations. That's why those men in the church were afraid to mess with me. In their arithmetic, I don't add up, 'cause I don't take sides. Think of me as Nietzsche's Zarathustra masquerading as a poor man. I don't truck with good. I don't truck with evil. I don't hold grudges, and I don't act out of anger. Those men in that church turned tail tonight for one reason and one reason only: they knew they'd run into a man that was the real deal, a cold-blooded fucker who loves nothing more than to kick ass, and that once he starts in, there's no way he lets up 'til the job is done."

Moody sat back, curious to see if Haldeman-Julius had it in him to continue their debate. But the man just sat there, staring up at those stars as if he hadn't heard a thing. Which was fine with Moody, because things seemed to be breaking up at the church. People dribbling away in twos and threes, but so far, no Mr. Stoner.

Out of respect for Haldeman-Julius's privacy, Moody turned his attention to the hypnotic interplay of flashing red and white light emanating from the sheriff's cruiser through the leaves of the trees. At the same time, he had an uneasy feeling that somewhere out in the darkness, something or someone was keeping watch on them. And once he raised his hand to shield his eyes from the chattering light, there it was, the shadowy form of a dog lurking beside an elderly elm tree.

As best he could make out, it didn't wear a collar, so it wasn't anybody's pet. Weight? Maybe forty pounds. More likely than not an ole yeller, as folks call 'em down south, it's shorthaired pelt the dun color of a worn-out shoe … so it could very well be the same dog he'd run into a couple of days ago rummaging for doughnuts from Zettl's trash … a breed noted for keeping to themselves … some say the kind Indians used to keep … who preferred barn life to being cooped up inside … this one a bitch with swollen dugs … so there's got to be hungry pups somewhere nearby. He felt under the bench for his uneaten ham and cheese sandwich from earlier in the day. Sure enough, the bitch dog's ears shot forward the moment his fingers brushed the paper sack.

"Who's your friend?" Haldeman-Julius said with a sly grin.

"Dunno; some stray, I suppose."

"Well, you can see she's in a family way. It's a pity we don't have something to give her to eat."

"Well, there's this old sandwich that was under the bench. Maybe we ought to give it to 'er and see."

Moody crept forward a few steps. The bitch dog licked her chops as he laid the sandwich on the ground, with her back muscles rippling shoulders to tail as if she suspected a lowdown dogcatcher trick. Car doors could be heard closing in the distance. An engine started, and the duty lights on the cruiser went out. Pru and Kneebone must be shutting up shop. Likely as not, Mr. Stoner would be along soon. And for some reason all her own, that dog still chose to hold herself aloof from that damn sandwich.

But leave it to a man of many words to put a dog's mind to rest. "Come on, mama," H-J said, clucking his tongue against the roof of his mouth. "We're on your side, girl. Nothing wrong with that sandwich, 'cept it's a mite dried out."

The dog responded like a trophy bass taking bait: a lunge, one violent snap of its jaws, and the sandwich disappeared. Moody fully expected that having eaten, the dog would disappear as well and not do as it then did: stretch itself out sphinxlike on the ground some three or four feet from where they sat: head erect, eyes and ears alert to a happenstance night that seemed to be holding its breath.

Haldeman-Julius laughed softly to himself. "Do you feel it, Mr. Moody? There's magic in the air tonight. You and me and this dog, Caliban, Prospero, and Ariel. *Et en Arcadia ego.* Even in Arcadia am I," he said, then paused. "You do know your Shakespeare, do you not, Mr. Moody?"

Moody shrugged. "No, sir. Can't say as I do. I tried reading that *Romeo and Juliet* once but didn't get too far. Way too many of them fancy words that nobody uses anymore."

"Well, don't feel so bad. Shakespearian language takes some getting used to. For your information, Caliban, Prospero, and Ariel are thrrree characters from *The Tempest*, which in my estimation, is one of Shakespeare's grrreatest plays."

Intrigued, Moody looked from the dog to Haldeman-Julius, then back to the dog again. "Okay, I give. I know yer dying to tell me. So what's yew and me and that dog got to do with a bunch of characters in an old-time play?"

"Well, of course, I speak in whimsy. *The Tempest* is far too complicated to explain in detail tonight. Let's just say that while we thrrree bear scant rrresemblance to characters in an early seventeenth-century play, considering the mischief prompted by my appearance here tonight, even though I make no claim to be a magician who delights in turning the elemental rigors of life into a rollicking carnival, I think it apt for me to reference myself as Prospero, because I am, at my best, a show-offy oratorical, conjuror of words, marooned by the machinations of fate to dwell on a rhetorical island of faded glories. Just as you, as Caliban, bear little resemblance to a trrruculent slave who is the deformed son of an evil witch named Sucorax, I do detect in you a contrary spirit that stands free of any man's bidding, an admirable trait that is both your strength and weakness. As for our doggie friend here—seated happily for the moment at my feet as if I were its master—I do not think it a stretch to consider her, just for fun, as a blithe, quirky natured, servant-sprite of the night named Ariel. You see, in some odd way, much as in the play, the way the three of us have been cast together on this warm summer's night somehow reflects the phantasmagoric, tragicomedic tenor of the play. Not wishing to put too fine a point on it, Moody, while I, in no way, take you for a coarse, base man, you seem to have limited yourself to addressing your basic wants and needs and leaving it at that. While you've self-educated yourself to an admirable degree, the plain fact rrremains, you have only educated your doggy self. Caliban, you see, in my opinion, rrrepresents a bestial man whose sense of humanity has yet to experience the trrranscendent. Despite your earnest attempts to pull yourself up by your bootstraps, you can do no better than elevate one foot."

Intrigued, Moody spoke up. "Jesus, Manny, no need going fancy on me. Just say it like it is: to you, I'm no better than a dog with its leg raised, pissing on a fire hydrant."

"Oh, Moody. I do admire your rrready wit. But what I'm trying to get at here, my good man, is what do you know, I mean trruly, trrruly know of Mozart, Beethoven, Goethe, Shakespeare, Rrrembrandt, Vermeer, Michelangelo, Eurrripides, or Homer, save what you read in books? *Reading about* is simply not enough to temper an aggrieved soul. Art must be experienced whole, ingested utterly, gluttonously devoured. It's not until you've thrilled to a Beethoven symphony rendered in live concert under the baton of a famous maestro like Toscanini; or witnessed, in all its heart-wrenching wonder, a crackerjack stage production of *Hamlet*; or stood in tears entranced by the way Rrrembrandt nuances shadow and Verrrmeer nuances light; or stood momentarily gobsmacked in the presence of Michelangelo's *David*, certain that something made of cold, hard marble is about to draw brrreath. For these are the transcendent moments of which I speak, the lack of which enables a man such as yourself to shamelessly prrroclaim that you are a 'cold-blooded fucker.' It is man's ability to crrreate and apprrreciate high culture that separates him from the lesser beasts, that enables him to strike a balance between—as Emerson's Unitarians would have it— 'the interdependent web of life' and 'the inherent worth and dignity of every man.' Survival of the fittest is a battle cry for losers, Moody; it's the Calibanesque rallying cry of the warriors of Sparta. Though in the end they succeeded in defeating and humiliating the glorious Athenians in war, I beg of you, Mr. Moody, to consider which of their cultures influenced the world more?"

Moody was duly impressed by *the interdependent web of life* and *the inherent worth and dignity of every man.* "Whew boy, Manny. And to think yew come out with all that highbrow stuff off the top of yer head. I hardly know what to say except that for a Jew boy, yew sure got a whole lot of the Irish in yew."

The bitch's ears shot forward, her head canted to the side, seeming confused by the sudden outburst of two men laughing.

"Indeed, indeed, Moody. As they used to say back in the Philadelphia slum where I grew up: a Jew and an Irishman sitting side by side in a bar makes for a long and merry night. But highbrow blather aside, I too, over the years, have taken note of the fact that one doesn't have to consult the dusty tomes of history to come to the conclusion that rrrevolutionaries, once awarded the upper hand, end up abusing their newly won power to rrrule and subject. In fact, one doesn't have to rrread history at all; George Orwell's little allegorical novel, *Animal Farm*, lays out the truth of the matter quite nicely. As a youth, you see, I once mistakenly thought that bettering the lot of the downtrodden was as simple as publishing the finest in literature and philosophy at a price the least of our brethren could afford. But alas, lo these many years, having published and sold fifty-four, yes, fifty-four million, that's *millions* of my *Little Blue Books*, nothing has changed. Why, I kept asking myself, until finally it came to me that the missing element in my equation was art. Art, Moody. Art experienced in all its fabled glory. Art that brings forth that good that refines the human soul. That same good, by the way, that your nasty friend, Mr. Nietzsche, would have us believe does not exist. And while I shall ever remain an unrepentant atheist Jew, that is not to say that I am a man without faith. A faith not of God, but of that good that Shakespeare's Prospero sums up like this: 'How many goodly creatures are there here! How beauteous mankind is! O brave new world that has such people in't.' To embrace these lines, my dear Moody, is to understand the essence of divine creation."

For a long moment neither man nor dog stirred nor spoke. A long moment that concluded with Haldeman-Julius withdrawing his watch from his pocket to check the time.

Moody stood up and extended his hand to help Haldeman-Julius to his feet.

"Yew know what, Manny? I'm a thinking yew look plum used up— that maybe yew ought to skip meeting up with Mr. Stoner and go on back to your hotel."

"Maybe so, Moody. Maybe, so. Still, 'Oh brave new world'—stirring lines, are they not? For, all in all, somewhere deep inside we *are* all goodly creatures, and tonight, I must confess this goodly, but tortured, soul is particularly tired beyond its years. My health is failing. My darling wife is dead. My son and heir an incompetent nincompoop. My once-glorious publishing business teeters on the brink. I was a man who once numbered among his friends such illustrious personages as Eugene Debs, Will and Ariel Durant, and Carl Sandburg. A man who, together with his wife, had the honor of being Charles Darrow's personal guests at the Scopes Monkey Trial. A man who is now but a sad footnote to the history that has passed him by, besieged by both the IRS and the FBI. In short, all the great lions of my youth are dead, and tonight may very well have been my last hurrah. Therefore, I beg of you, please deliver Simon my deepest regrets for going back to my room to the Woods Hotel. For, as sayeth the Bard of Avon: 'We are such stuff as dreams are made on, our life is rounded in sleep.' My train leaves tomorrow for Kansas City at five past twelve, so please extend my invitation to Simon to, say around ten, drop by my hotel and breakfast with me, which should give us plenty of time. And for you, Mr. Moody, my dear, sweet Caliban, be advised that Girard is serviced by both the Santa Fe and the Katy lines. So if ever in your railway travels, you should happen to stray my way, consider yourself a more than welcome guest. My little farm lies on the eastern outskirts of town, less than a half mile from the railroad tracks. Just ask anyone to point out where I live. Since my wife died, I reside alone with my dear housekeeper. Seven swans swim upon my pond. The high hedge surrounding my property allows me to bathe nude in my swimming pool anytime I please. It may be a good long while before we ever meet again, so let us call it a night. And it *has* been quite a night, has it not, Mr. Moody? A night of countless stars and, dare I say, countless words uttered to no end."

Moody watched Haldeman-Julius, then the bitch dog seconds later, mosey off in the direction of the Woods Hotel, the tail of that damn dog curled over her back like a question mark, which was another of those odd quirks of breed that set old yellers apart, much like taste in art sets folks apart. Because when the chips were down for hungry men and dogs alike, fancy pictures in glided frames were a piss-poor excuse for a ham sandwich and a bowl of soup.

21

Early December 2004
Red Hook, Brooklyn

As far as Joellen was concerned, developing neighborhoods were best judged by the quality and variety of their eating establishments. On the foodie scale, the best she could say for Red Hook was that it still lagged far behind. Sure, there was the Hope and Anchor, where the food was good, but the ambience was way too dinerish and noisy to suit an elitist husband who insists on dragging his wife out of the house on a night she'd rather stay in, claiming he has something *important* to tell her.

She admired her husband for many things, but the ability to wind down the day sipping wine at the Red Rose Restaurant on Smith Street in Carroll Gardens while perusing the menu was not one of them. Unfortunately, his idea of relaxed conversation was that it always had to be "about" something—preferably something read recently in *The New Yorker*, the *New York Review of Books*, or the op-ed page of the *New York Times*. But, if she turned out to be right, and this night out had something to do with that kooky shyster detective of his, why didn't he just get on with it instead of jawing on and on about how Jean-Paul Sartre's idea of hell was other people?

"Dear," she said, in an effort to get him to cut the crap, "I thought you said you had something important to tell me?"

Arrested midsentence, her man winced and blinked twice. "Well, I heard from Mitchik today," he said.

Bingo, she thought. "Really," she said, feigning surprise, "so …?"

"Oh, nothing earthshaking. He's in Beatrice. Says he's hot on the trail. Got several good leads and should be back in Brooklyn by the end of the week."

"Really," she said, because, really, what else was there for her to say other than, perhaps, some news was better than no news? At that late date, she should complain? After all, it was her idea to engage a detective in the first place. "So, nothing more? Your man just left it at that? I have to say, I do wonder. It's been such a long time since your mother disappeared. I shouldn't think a trip to Beatrice would be worth his while."

Preston's eyes narrowed. "Come on, Joellen, get off it. Say what you mean. You think Mitchik's juicing the bill."

She laughed at his testy reply, telling herself that thin-skinned exchanges between spouses must have been what Sartre had in mind when he equated hell with other people. "Relax, Preston. You misread me. Mitchik's your chosen man, and I'm okay with that. I was just wondering—that's all."

"Yeah, well, don't think I haven't been wondering the same. Only now, at least he seems to have come up with a few names. There's some old geezer he found in a rest home. Reginal something-or-other, who seems to have had some pertinent stuff to say about my mother. Not to mention a whole bunch of other stuff he apparently happened onto in Omaha before driving his rental car down to Beatrice. Mainly, while he says it's too early to get excited, it could very well be, as I suspected all along, my mother might have made it all the way to New York City. Which is kind of exciting, isn't it? But all that stuff is not why I insisted on bringing you here tonight. We're here because I want to say *thank you* for enabling me to do something I should have done years ago. You were absolutely right, although I didn't buy it at the time, when you insisted that just the *prospect* of restoring a few vital pages to my life story would do wonders for me. We're here because, above all, I want to thank you for putting up with me all these years. We're here to toast goodbye to the fog of my assholish *meshuggaas* years and hello to the dawning of whatever is to come."

If only, she thought. A tear rose to the corner of her eye as his glass of Perrier clinked her Chianti. Her husband, just another *happy-go-lucky bipolar* as he often jokingly described himself, for this night at least, seemed to be firing on all cylinders, so she'd drink to that. And, though normally, they split the bill when they ate out—her money, his money; from the very beginning they'd maintained separate accounts—tonight, she'd grant her knight-errant the boon of paying the whole check. Because that night, if any did, rightfully belonged to Preston, the man, even though, in all probability, because he'd insisted parking on a dark side street in lieu of the well-lit metered space that had been available out front, it was highly possible when they returned to their car—because, naturally, he would have neglected to lock it—they'd find the contents of the glove compartment strewn all over the place by thoughtless teenagers seeking to score toll and meter money and enough to finance a pizza and a couple of six-packs of beer. Which was, by itself, the sort of upsetting event that normally would set him to brooding for hours if not days, which somehow she was sure he would not do tonight, because the little boy now signaling the waiter for the check, who normally careened through life as if hell-bent on self-destruction, had reduced them both to tears, because that's what aging lovers did when the years left before them would never be years enough.

22

Last Day: Beatrice
Thursday, August 14, 1952

Moody figured he'd laid in bed long enough. He groaned his bones upright, mumbling to himself the question that had been posed to him last night by his boss, when finally showed up looking like hell: "Moody, what the devil you still doing here in Beatrice? By now, you got to know, my brother-in-law's got half the town, half-convinced you killed that man out at Johnson's Creek. Lordy, one'd think you'd be long gone by now."

"I don't know, Mr. Stoner; misery loves company, I guess," Moody said to himself as he zipped up his fly, this being the answer he'd given last night as his boss pulled a bottle of Old Crow and two glasses out of his desk, and quipped back in return: "Well, my friend, misery do love company all right. Pull up a chair, Moody. No time like the present to salute and recognize tonight's folly for what it was: a profane reenactment of the closing scene to Wagner's *Twilight of the Gods.*"

But, Moody told himself, he'd been in no mood for watching anybody, much less his boss, drink himself blotto—assuming that's what Mr. Stoner had in mind with his Twilight of the Gods bullshit. Nope, no way. Screw the booze, firetrap or no firetrap, in that moment his only thought was to get back to his cot to ingest a little weed. Still, while he may be marking time until conditions were ripe for clearing out, there was no way he was going to leave his boss in the lurch, especially with that church to clean; consequently, since he had a full day staring him in the face, after he splashing a little water on his face, then wandering up front and helping himself to a cold cup of yesterday's coffee, seeing as how the Kelly twins were notorious for sleeping in, in order to get that platform disassembled and out of that church ASAP, he'd have to make a point of stopping by Maggie Gillard's boardinghouse and rousting 'em out of bed.

***

"Last time," Polly told herself, as she swung her legs carefully out of bed, lest she. disturb the snore machine she'd slept next to for the past seven years. Seven years of battling him for the covers. Seven dreary years where the brightest moment of the day was Bill Beezley—dressed in milkman white and black leather bow tie—jingle full bottles up the walk and rattle the empties back,

In fact, the past evening had been nothing but a whole bunch of *last times*. All those things a body ordinarily never paid attention to, suddenly a big deal. Everything an adios of one kind or another, from feeding the dog down to scouring the pots and cleaning the burners on the stove. From little Preston running naked around the house after his bath—with her chasing after him like she was the cook and he was the gingerbread boy, his little rubber penis going flippity-flop—to the inordinate amount of time she'd spent sorting the family album for a few photos she'd want to take, before settling on only one she'd snapped herself of him at Farlington Lake: her proud son holding aloft a two-pound catfish he'd managed to reel in all by himself. Then, there'd been the event she'd been dreading the most, the reading of that last-time-ever bedtime story to her darling son, then that last-time-ever goodnight kiss bestowed on his forehead as she tucked him in—that mercifully, by the time those two last times came rolling around, her storehouse of feeling sorry for herself had pretty much emptied out.

Then, later that night, lying there awake in the dark, waiting for Simon's headlights to sweep the ceiling as he turned into the drive, knowing because she'd already heard from Mrs. Turner that the debate had been a disaster, how, even though Simon wasn't exactly her favorite person in the world, she'd felt his pain as she listened to him sit with the motor running for a good long time, before finally coming upstairs with whisky on his breath. And if seven years of marriage had taught her anything, it was how to fake being asleep while your husband fought for balance as he tried to extricate his legs from his pants, cursing under his breath and cracking his big toe on the dresser in the process. After all, being tipsy wasn't like him. What *was* like him was once he stripped down to his skivvies, he crawled into bed whispering in her ear for sex, but when she didn't respond, it wasn't long before he was snoring to beat the band, arms and legs skewered this way and that, like strewn things wanting reattachment.

She rose from the bed and headed for the bathroom. "Let him sleep in. Little Preston as well," she told herself as she hiked up her nightdress and sat down to pee. It wasn't her fault she was a failure at being a good wife and mother. It was the Lord's failure to provide her with the natural instincts necessary to get the job done.

***

Moody was helping himself to a cold cup of stale coffee when Nancy showed up. Instead of her customary, cheery "Good morning," she snatched the cup from his hand. "Dang it, Moody, leave off that stuff. Don'cha know, sure as God's little green apples, it'll drill holes your stomach?"

She had no more put fresh coffee on to perk than Mr. Stoner, ashen-faced and unshaven, walked in with that day's supply of Zettl's freshly made doughnuts in hand. A minute or so later, the linotype men, Gar Davis and Petey Evans walked in. They'd chosen to go fishing up to Farlington Lake over attending the debate. Nevertheless, their slightly embarrassed, hushed demeanor were a dead giveaway of being fully aware of the disastrous doings of the previous night.

Mr. Stoner mumbled something about relieving congestion in the tiny space between Nancy's desk and his doorway that Gar and Petey jokingly referred to as the employee's lounge, then retreated into his office. Moody, on the other hand, having spent most of his adult life so far, regimented and confined, one way or another, in the company of disgruntled men without feeling any degree of attachment to them, was perfectly comfortable where he was. In fact, given the brief time he'd known Gar and Petey, he'd become somewhat fascinated, perhaps even awed by the relationship that existed between them, as if they were something more than just friends. Middle-aged bachelors, neither of them known to express the slightest interest in the other sex. Petey renting a room on the top floor of the old Victorian house on Carbon Street that Gar shared with his mama, the two of them same as lived together. Who, when they weren't chumming around cracking jokes at the other's expense, bickered and nitpicked like they were man and wife. Far be it from Moody to jump to conclusions, but considered in the light of the amorous relations that sometimes existed between men in prison, coupled with what he'd learned the previous day concerning Mrs. Stoner, he couldn't help asking himself, just how many queers were out there in the big wide world anyway?

In addition, from where Moody stood, he held full view of his boss, seated behind his desk, staring out the window. His boss, whom he'd once overheard yell at his wife that he would "by God, educate this town as to the true facts of life or go down trying." Who, apart from his autocratic tendencies, had somehow been able to it make to his office on time the morning after a night when everything that could go wrong, had gone horribly wrong, and still sit there in plain view of the hired help as if nothing happened, totally ignorant to the fact that his wife was about to up and disappear on him.

Once Nancy pronounced the coffee fit for consumption, Moody poured two cups, balanced a paper plate with a couple of doughnuts on it, atop one of the cups, and went in to sit with Mr. Stoner, who acknowledged his thanks with a tired little smile, broke a doughnut in half and dunked it.

"Moody, you got to pardon me for not saying good morning when I came in. I woke up with a hangover and fought with my wife before leaving the house. So, in an effort to get the day turned around right, I want to ask your pardon for failing to hold up my end of the bargain last night, leaving it to you to take care of those hooligans, for which I am eternally grateful."

"Mr. Stoner, yew don't ever have to apologize or thank me for doing what yew hired me to do," Moody replied, wondering if "fought with my wife" meant Mrs. Stoner had suddenly had a change mind and owned up to her husband that she was leaving him and why. But then again, he was already too mixed up in the lives of these people as it was. Whether she had or hadn't was no business of his. As his mother used to say, "Stickin' yer nose in where angels fear to tread's a sure path to trouble."

***

Polly stood backside propped against the kitchen sink. The breakfast dishes were drying in the rack. Directly over her head was the second-floor hallway register where too often her son had lain, calling down like a broken record, "Mama, mama, mama, do you love me, mama?" which, thankfully, he was not doing that day, else she wouldn't have been able to bear it.

"Last cigarette," she vowed to herself, as she tapped one from a pack of Kools. Yes, smoking was a filthy habit, but it sure helped with the stress. Really, she ought to give it up before her fingers were as tobacco stained as those of her two-pack-a-day husband, the asthmatic. A Camel man just like his father, who, to no one's surprise, died of emphysema.

But right now, smoking was the least of her problems. During the considerable amount of time she'd spent last night lying awake, no matter how hard she tried to poke holes in the logic of what she was about to do today, the formula for getting done what had to be done always came out the same: drop off the boy at Lorraine's for the day before doubling back home to change into her Salvation Army, nondescript traveling clothes; grab her already packed and waiting war-surplus rucksack from where she'd hid it in the garage; make sure the dog's water bowl was topped up when she tethered him to the clothesline before riding her bike to the train station—sited conveniently across the street from the bus station to throw them off the track—followed by a twenty-minute hike to a place she'd scouted out not far from Johnson's Crick, where the trains ran slowly enough for even rookie hoboes to hop a ride.

Yes, she was going through with this, even after Moody, bless his heart, had done his best to warn her away from jumping on and off even slowly moving trains—something nigh on impossible to envision, much less rehearse, a feat either pulled off first try or spend the rest of a maimed life wishing you had.

But Moody needn't have worried. Sure, she was scared but not that scared. If a person didn't want anyone chasing after them, hopping a train was the next best thing to catching a ride on Wonder Woman's invisible airplane. Besides, it wasn't like she hadn't spent most of her childhood climbing and jumping into and out of things. Really, about the only hitch she saw in her plan was passing herself off as someone she was not as she rode her bike through town. Still, dressed in bib overalls and light denim work shirt, the floppy brim of Sy's old fishing hat worn low on her eyes, that and a little luck and she'd be taken for just another eccentric old fart from the county poorhouse, who, for want of better transportation, either hoofed it or bicycled into town.

Polly ran the tap to douse her cigarette. Time to get the show on the road and the boy over to his Aunt Lorraine. If he pulled another of his fits about being too tired to walk, she let him ride his tricycle. And if that didn't do the trick, she'd get him there by pulling him all the way in his little red wagon. As for the little spat she'd gotten into with Simon this morning, she regretted it happened, regretted it tremendously. But was it her fault he'd showed up for breakfast this morning claiming to have a killer headache capable of etching metal, then, without so much as a good morning, started in on *her*, like *she*, as Digby's church organist, had something to do with the riot the previous night? Damn right, she'd let him have it back.

***

When Moody and the Kelly boys arrived at the church, as expected, Dr. Watkins's wife, Ruth, greeted them with a cold, hard stare. What Moody hadn't expected was for the scene of the crime, seen in the full light of day, to be in better shape than he had imagined it would be. Thankfully, the platform seemed to have taken the brunt of it, so that in little over an hour, he and his crew had disassembled and stacked the lumber, as per Mr. Stoner's wishes, out beside the alley, apparently, as some sort of charitable donation to the African Methodist Episcopal Church for some sort of building project Pastor Whitcomb had in mind, who'd be stopping by later that day to cart it off with his mule and wooden wagon.

That done, once he'd sent the Kelly boys off to collect their wages from Nancy, Moody joined up with Mrs. Watkins's little troop of not-so-happy-to-be-there lady volunteers, on their hands and knees, picking nits of dried yolk and crushed eggshell out of a heavy pile carpet. He had no more than settled into this routine, when, out of the corner of his eye, he noticed the silhouette of a man framed in the doorway by the glare of the morning sun that he strongly suspected would turn out to be none other than the second least likely person he cared to see.

Nevertheless, he kept his head down, determined, no matter what, to stick with what he was doing. However, when the dusty tips of Pru's cowboy boots intruded themselves into his limited view, Moody looked up innocently amused. The deputy, who until now had never seemed the sort to go out of his way to prettify himself, now carried about his person the unmistakable after scent of a late-night visit to a whorehouse.

"Mr. Moody, I'm a thinking it's about time we have ourselves a little talk."

Rather than disgrace himself in the House of the Lord, in front of all these fine church ladies, by telling Pru in so many words just where he ought to go and who to talk to, Moody politely excused himself to Ruth Watkins and willingly allowed the deputy to lead him outside, toward a stone bench sited under an ancient elm tree that dated, some said, clear back to before Beatrice was a town.

Pru propped his boot on one end of the bench and motioned for Moody to sit down. Then, like he was taking a page out of his boss's playbook, rather than come right out with whatever was bothering him, he began to dally like he had all the time in the world, popping his knuckles one by one, fooling around with the brim of his hat, interspersed with an inordinate amount of time spent vigorously scratching himself under the chin like a hound dog getting after its fleas. Which bothered Moody not one whit. It was plain to see, it was unlikely that this short and stubby agent of the law had come there today aiming to arrest somebody at least eight inches taller than he was.

"Pity," Pru finally said.

"Pity, what?"

"This here old elm. Up there near the top, don'cha see? Dutch elm disease, I do believe they call it."

"So what's that got to do with yew and me and the price of tea in China?"

"Well, fer starters, that disease ain't natural to these parts. Traveled here from someplace else I do believe."

"So?" Moody said.

"So, yew wouldn't be thinking of putting down roots here in Beatrice now, would you, Mr. Moody? Finding yerself a nice woman, say? Getting a little place all yer own?"

"No sir, I am not," Moody said, wishing to rid himself of this man's low-grade foolishness.

"Well, then, if that ain't the be-all, 'cause if yew was to up and leave, don'cha know life would suddenly be a whole lot simpler for everybody all around?"

Moody deemed the question hardly worth answering. Deputy Pru gave the flushed skin under his chin a couple more digs.

"Aftershave, Mr. Moody. Yew know my girlfriend, Marlene Roper, clerk over there at Sell's Appliance? Well, she's been nagging my butt to begin using some of that man's perfume stuff she gave me last Christmas, and darn if I didn't go and put some on me this morning. Guess I must of overdid it, 'cause it's like to driving me crazy, like I got me an allergy or something."

"Well, come down to it, yew do smell right nice. But surely, a man yer age has got to know by now, it ain't always easy being in love."

Pru yukked and slapped his bent knee. "Right you are, Mr. Moody. Indeed, being in love's truly got its downside. The things men have to go through just to get laid."

Moody stirred his legs like he needed to go. He'd pretty much had it with this idiot lawman.

Pru held up his hand. "Whoa, there, partner. You best hear what I come to say. First off, the sheriff and me got to hand it to you for facing down those tomato-throwing boys last night. Heck, we'd a-been there doing it ourselves but for Sy Stoner insisting we keep our noses out of his debate. Anyway, that's neither here nor there. The thing is, Moody, you're a smart man. Smart enough to know the sheriff's had me keeping a close eye on you ever since you came to town. And much as it pains me to have to say it, he didn't take any too kindly to the idea when I told him yesterday about catching you and his sister sitting like a couple of love birds all cozy and nice together in the park."

"Meaning what?" Moody said.

"Meaning, lay off the sheriff's sister if you know what's good for you, bub. That even though the state police over there in Ottumwa, Iowa, claim they got some damn hobo in custody confessing his head off, making yew pretty much off the hook for that evil business out to Johnson's Crick, the sheriff's still got you on his most wanted list for tryin' to diddle his sister."

Moody grinned and nodded toward the church. "That it, Deputy? If so, I'm much obliged for the warning. Next time you get the chance, tell your boss as far as his sister's concerned, my fly's zipped up. Now, we about done here, or what? In case yew haven't noticed, we got Mrs. Watson standing in the doorway wondering why the hell I'm wasting time by dithering with the likes of you."

"I'm just saying, fella, don't go pushing yer luck. Me, far as I'm concerned, yer welcome to diddle any woman in town whenever, wherever, and however many times yew want, long as yer partner in sin ain't below age, my Marlene, or Mrs. Stoner, and come to think of it, when and if yew ever do get around to letting down that zipper of yers, make sure yew wear a rubber, 'cause heaven knows, 'bout the last thing this town wants or needs is a couple of yer little bastards infecting our town's noble bloodline."

Moody stood up. He'd heard enough. It was either leave now or pop the little bastard in the mouth to shut him the hell up. "Relax, Deputy. No need getting testy on me. Yew've said your piece and I appreciate yew taking time out of yer busy day to stop by. But yew and the sheriff are reading Mrs. Stoner and me all wrong. Ain't nothing's going on between us. Further, this big boy been around and can take care of hisself."

"Relax yerself, Moody," Pru called after him as he walked away. "I love the sheriff and know him like he was my own kin. Yew gotta know he's been looking out for that little sister of his since day one. You best keep mind, he's got him an anger that's mighty quick on the trigger, and he'd as soon kill scum like yew to keep yew from ruining his sister's life. And, frankly, I ain't come here today out of the goodness of my heart. Despite what some people say, the sheriff's a straight shooter who plays by the book. So, if he was to up and kill ya, for sure he wouldn't try to cover it up, he'd turn himself in. With the end result being, he'd end up in prison and I'd be out of a job just when I'm getting mighty fond of deputy sheriffin'. Heck, I'd gladly kill yew myself if it weren't for the effort of reloading my gun."

Moody laughed to himself. Just a couple of days more to give Mrs. Stoner a decent chance of putting some daylight between her and her past, not to mention making it twice as hard for anyone to start jumping to the conclusion that the two of them had run off together, and he'd be only too happy to absent himself forever from this crumb-bum town.

***

Polly's heart sank when Lorraine failed to answer the door chime right away. It nearly skipped a beat when her sister-in-law finally appeared, still in her nightdress, a tissue pressed to her nose and a box of them under her arm.

"Oh, honey, you gotta forgive me. I shoulda called, but I woke sick as a dog and plum forgot the two of you was coming today. And I promised, didn't I? But honey, what can I say 'cept I just can't take the boy today. I've got me one of those dang summer colds. My head's stuffed up like it's in a vise. I hate like sin saying this, but is there any chance of us putting things off 'til next week?"

"Don't fret yourself none, Lorraine," Polly said, determined above all not to let this *last time* go sour. "You poor thing. Don't worry none about it. Course, we can wait, can't we, Preston? That bunch of stuff I had to do today is just a bunch of nothing," she said, thanking her stars that just to be on the safe side, she'd taken the precaution of checking in with Mrs. Bacacci to make sure she'd be available as a backup. Because the die was cast. She had to go and today was the day. Otherwise, Simon, Otis, little Preston, Lorraine, eventually, one way or the other, the cat would be out of the bag, and then she'd end up having to leave anyway. The very thought of standing her ground and fighting for her rights when all the odds were stacked against her made her want to puke. As a last resort, her husband would drag her to court in an effort to get the judge to commit her to the nuthouse, where men in white coats who call themselves *doctors* resort to such horrors as shock therapy and lobotomy to rid homosexuals of their "disease," when if anyone was stricken with madness it was them, a madness called plain, old-fashioned bigotry.

But her son, twisting and turning about her legs, still clinging to the paper sack that held his swimming things he had insisted on carrying all by himself, simply didn't give a hoot whether his aunt was sick or not. Today was the day he and the aunt, who never got out of sorts with him, were supposed to be having a whale of a time together in Winston Park. His aunt, who now had crouched down to inch open the screen door. "Hey there, young man," his aunt singsong teased to him, as she snaked her arm out, "please don't tell me the reason for that big old frown on your face is because of this mean old cold of mine. Because, I swear, child, if I don't see a big smile on that cute little smacker of yours pretty darn quick, I do believe I'll just have to *kitchie-kitchie-koo* one right out of you."

Polly reached down to ruffle her now giggling son's hair. Once again, Lorraine had saved the day with her magic. A magic Polly wished she had but sorely lacked. A magic that would enable her to fake a breezy, see-you-tomorrow goodbye to a person that during the seven years they'd known each other, a truly harsh word had yet to pass between them. A person who, whenever things seemed darkest, never failed to find a way to bring the light. A hug, perhaps—a peck on the cheek—anything, please God, that didn't spell farewell and breaking down into a big fat sob.

But Polly needn't have worried. As always, Lorraine remained in command. "Go on now, child. Take the boy and be on your way so's I can get back to bed," she said, and suddenly *this last time* was as simple as the sound of Lorraine's door latch. A sound not unlike something small and hard striking a linoleum floor. Lorraine's linoleum. Lorraine's kitchen floor the day Polly first realized the true depth of the love she bore for this woman, the innocent act of the two of them bending down at the same time to retrieve a fallen fork that turned electric when her fingertips accidentally brushed a stray lock of Lorraine's hair, a moment of hesitation when their eyes met that easily could have and should have yet failed utterly to prompt two lovers to kiss.

***

Once he finished at the church, Moody made a beeline for Bud Decker's Diner. A once-accused man now freed from suspicion, he was hungry, truly hungry for the first time since he and Kneebone had their dustup at the jail, and what better way to celebrate a reprieve than to gobble down a big bowl of Bud Decker's chili. "You again," he called to the bitch dog from the previous night, lounging in the shade of Decker's awning as he mounted the steps to go in, who responded to this courtesy, by raising her head and thumping her tail.

It was lunchtime. The joint was crowded. Even so, his favorite waitress, Bud Decker's daughter, Rachel, stood waiting behind the counter, idly tapping the eraser end of her pencil against her front tooth, grinning like she'd been saving the empty stool in front of her just for him.

"Come on, Moody. Order up. Whatcha havin'?"

"How's about a bowl of chili and glass of milk?" he said with a grin to a comely, hazel-eyed, barely turned seventeen lass, waitressing the summer for her dad. One button too many unbuttoned on her blouse, stacked as the farm boys liked to say: like a brick shithouse, her salty tongued, flirty ways so reminded him of his mother. "And don't stint on the crackers the way you did last time. Tell your old man he can retire on somebody else's dime."

Rachel rolled her eyes, then her hips as well, as she traversed the few steps it took to reach the service window, where, as usual, her overly anxious father stood casting ill-humored darts Moody's way because he didn't take too kindly to older men getting chummy with his teenage daughter.

Out of respect for Bud's ability to rustle up a decent plate of grub, out of respect for the red bandanna tied loosely around the man's neck, and the little soda-jerk hat that sat cockeyed on his head, Moody swiveled his stool to alter his line of sight out the window behind him. The bitch dog, he now noticed, for some obscure reason of her own, had altered her line of sight as well, to a sweeter spot of shade on the other side of Summit Street.

Moody's feigned interest remained with the dog until a chili bowl clunked down behind him. Rachel was ready for him when he turned back around, right bosom cushioned atop the jukebox remote, left bosom cozied next to a stainless-steel napkin holder. "Daddy says, you best keep your eyes to yourself if you intend on getting served around here," she said as she bonked his nose with the eraser end of her pencil.

Keith Handshaw, chief chicken killer over at Maish's Poultry House, who occupied the stool to Moody's right, waited until Rachel had moved on down the line to take another order before he leaned over and said: "Seeing as you're new around here, mister, ain't none of my business, but you ought to know, some folks around here aren't all that comfortable having persons of your questionable background hanging around this town, and Bud's probably one of them, so maybe you ought to think about watching yourself around his daughter."

"Maybe so, maybe so," Moody replied because he figured Handshaw to be an all right guy. "I ain't lookin' for trouble. I'm strictly here for the chili. Far be it from me to begrudge a man his concern for his daughter."

"I'm just sayin', that's all. Anyhow, I'm due back to work," Handshaw said as he shoved back his plate and stood up. "But just between you and me, no doubt about it, that daughter of Bud's not only gonna go far, she most probably already has, cruising the square late Saturday nights with farm boys in their daddies' pickups."

Mindful of Bud's heavy hand when it came to chili, Moody spanked the catsup bottle a couple of times to sweeten the taste before adding a dash of vinegar to cut the grease. Rachel, bless her sweet young heart, had served him up with a whole burger basket full of saltines. He crushed a liberal handful into his bowl, fully aware that his tenuous position in town was due to a general misunderstanding of the joys of renegade life.

As they say, to each his own. Could he help it if that was the kind of life that appealed to him. He couldn't speak for his now-deceased brother, but as near as he could reckon, he'd had the idea of never quite fitting in ever since their father took them out on their first coyote drive. Shotguns only, a ring of men and teenage boys spaced out twenty yards or so—his father toting a twelve gauge, his brother a twenty, and he with the pip-squeak four ten—forming a perimeter around a square-mile section of mixed pasturage and woods, waiting for the gunshot signal that told them to step off together and start closing in toward the middle so nary a one of those pesky varmints could escape, as few did. The way he remembered it, four were shot and killed and left to rot on fence posts that day. However, true to the old saying, *it's the one that gets away you never forget*. In his case, the coyote he'd been first to spot hid out in a brush pile, not more than six feet from where he stood. He looking it, and it looking at him, lips curled to a coyote grin. Two beasts of the wild they were, in a frozen moment of neither being sure what the other was going to do next. Least of all what he did next, which was probably as big a surprise to that coyote as it was to him: lowering the barrel of his gun and easing on past instead of pulling the trigger and giving cry. As if the two of them were of similar mind about the shameful game of killing for vengeance or sport. And *hello friend, you go your way, I'll go mine* had defined his life ever since that day, much as this bowl of Bud Decker's chili defined his stay in this town: black as sin and twice as greasy. Moody reached for his glass of milk.

"Come on now, Bobby," he heard someone in the booth directly behind him say, "stop jerking my leg. Combinin' milk and chili ain't poisonous. Can't be. No how, no way."

"Suit yourself," was the second man's immediate reply, "but my Great-Grandma LaRue—I've told you about her, haven't I? The one down in

Oklahoma, with Otoe blood, who knew a thing or two about the old ways? Well, if it weren't for her being dead and gone, she'd be here telling you the same. Combine chili and milk and the contents of your gut transmogrifies into concrete, and as you know full well, a man who can't shit is shit out of luck. You laugh now, but it's a guaranteed scientific fact of life. Lactose, doncha know, acting as a bonding agent. But then again, best I remember, back in high school, you flunked Mr. Saccani's chemistry class two years in a row, so I guess that explains the dumb look you got on your face. But swear to God, I'm not just making this up. Why, just a couple of months ago in the *Courier-Eagle*—you must have seen it—that story they ran about some old witch down in Pratt, Kansas, doing her husband in servin' him nothing but chili and milk for a whole week? Lord have mercy, when they opened the poor fool up, his intestines totally seized up with ossified chili beans."

Moody spooned up the last of his chili. He needn't look. He knew who those voices belonged to. Bobby would be Bobby Streeter, head of produce over at the IGA; the other guy, without the brains God gave a goose, some fella who specialized in washing shop windows, known around town as Fishworms. Moody laid a dollar on the counter. He reckoned the bill at eighty-five cents. The remainder he'd kick in for Rachel's tip.

He stood up to leave, conscious of the fact there very well may be a dog waiting for him outside, so he bundled up the uneaten remains of Handshaw's burger and fries into a couple of napkins and shoved it in his pocket. There was enough of the ham actor in him to consider gilding the lily on Bobby's joke by making a kind of show out of chugging the last of his milk, then suddenly collapse to the floor and make like he was dead. But then again, his better half was telling him that this wasn't his but Bobby's joke. Besides, why run the risk, aggravating Bud's limited sense of humor to the point of getting himself banned from the premises for life, especially since tonight's dollar fifty blue plate special was listed on the blackboard as meatloaf and gravy, biscuits, taters, and peas?

***

Polly mounted the steps to Mrs. Bacacci's back door, figuring she was more or less worn out, worrying if things were going to turn out the way she wanted them to. Still, to her relief, the old women appeared promptly at the door, hands dusted with flour.

"*Si, si.* Leave-a the boy. We bake a-pie," she said, then whisked the boy inside almost before Polly could give him a farewell hug and kiss.

Minutes later, clad in bib overalls and work shirt mufti, rucksack secured over the rear wheel of her bike, she was pedaling down Prairie Street into the teeth of a hot, dry wind. Her only stop along the way was to post a farewell letter to her husband in a mailbox with a late enough pickup time so there'd be no chance of it getting delivered that day. Of the few pedestrians she passed and the few cars she met, no one gave her so much as a second glance. And when she parked her bike near the entrance to the train station, her luck still held. The area was devoid of human activity like the good Lord himself wanted it that way. And since she'd worked hard all week on her man-walk, using Moody as her guide, when she set off walking the old streetcar line west out of town, it was as if she were truly aloft in an invisible flying machine: her loping stride, cocksure and lackadaisical at the same time, rucksack casually slung over one shoulder, upper body erect and taut, arms jangling at her side.

So that in less than forty uneventful minutes after leaving home, she found herself only a quarter-mile hike through a cornfield away from the place she'd scouted out, nearest the triple-tracked Burlington Line, as good as any for hopping freight trains. Nothing but nothing could stop her now. Certainly, nothing as minor as ripping her overalls and scratching her knee getting over that damned barbed-wire fence—something she had probably done a zillion times when she was kid. In fact, she rather relished this minor setback. Nothing worthwhile should be this easy.

Besides, like the good little Brownie Scout she'd once been, she'd come well prepared. Once she'd reached the stand of Osage orange hedge that bordered the tracks, the first thing she did was to search her rucksack for a quart jar of water and box of Band-Aids to tend to her knee. Of course, Moody had advised her to carry way more water than that, but she had no fear of running short. The way she'd planned it, there wouldn't be any long train rides. Her idea was to travel west only as long as it took to arrive at a town that looked big enough to have regular bus service to Omaha. From Omaha, she'd catch an express bus to Chicago, then another headed for New York City.

In the far distance was the ever-growing sound of an approaching train, unfortunately headed for, not coming from, Beatrice. Yet her heart sang as the lead diesel hove into sight. Her son loved trains, her husband loved trains, and now, here she was loving trains. Was there anything so stirring as a blissfully discordant, bestial concatenation of multihued freight cars? White Goose Flour, Pabst Blue Ribbon, Lehigh Valley, United Fruit, Santa Fe, Sinclair Oil, she chanted their names as they paraded by. The pungent smell of diesel fuel, the rickety-rack of steel wheels clacking over jointed rails, it was easy to see why Mr. Moody eschewed the humdrum of city life.

And then, as the caboose receded into the distance, she discovered a second treat as the delicate sounds of nature began to reawake: the buzz of bees, a nearby meadowlark trilling to its mate from a fence post, a scissor-tailed flycatcher giving voice on the wing, the distant bark of a bored farm dog, a raucous band of crows chorusing to her as they passed overhead: *Who do you think you're fooling down there? Caws we know your game. Caws we see you crouched down and ready to dash out and hop a ride on the next westbound train.*

And yes, the time had come for her to dash out and take up position beside the tracks as four westbound bright and shiny GP 7s, straining mightily to a mile-long train up to speed, groaned into view. For her to then stand in awe, scant feet away, the earth actually trembling under her feet, Moody's voice echoing into her ear how best to hop aboard one of these lumbering beasts. He, of little faith, who had never seen a seven-year-old Polly Kneebone leap and mount in a single bound her father's giant old plow horse, Chesterfield, then gallop him bareback down to the creek and back—his mane and tail and her pigtails streaming in the wind.

One boxcar passed, then another. *Wait 'til you got the rhythm in your bones*, was the way her mentor had put it. She stood just as she had imagined it, lying awake the previous night: lightly balanced on the balls of her feet, face-on to the rear of the train. And then, possessed by an unforeseen familiarity as if she had done this many, many times, she reached forth and locked her hands onto the leading edge of an open boxcar door, arced her left leg up and into the opening as the rest of her went tumbling inside.

She rose to her elbows in utter delight, waited as her eyes adjusted to the relative darkness of the car. And indeed, her prayers were answered, for she was riding alone and the train was gathering speed. And what was she doing lying on the floor of this boxcar, when the doorway was where she needed to be, laughing and clapping her hands as Simon's raggedy fishing hat blew away in the wind, as Beatrice's pathetic excuse for a skyline shrank from sight, because this often-hoped-for day had finally arrived, and come what may, she'd be the one calling the shots for the rest of her life.

***

Simon Stoner—learned editor/publisher of the Beatrice *Courier-Eagle*, ardent idealist and devotee of a simple life, replete with wife and child and mongrel dog, whose estate included a 1948 Packard Super Eight Sedan and a moderately priced two-story house with detached garage, who ascribed his splitting headache to the copious amounts of alcohol he'd consumed subsequent to the disastrous events of the previous night—not only had somehow summoned the wherewithal to show up in time to escort Haldeman-Julius to his train, but mission accomplished, he exited the station pondering the sheer futility of the row he'd gotten into with his wife as they breakfasted on bitter coffee, hard-boiled eggs, and burned toast. Of course, she would take umbrage when he dared to suggest that bigoted, fat little toad of a minister of hers had conspired to put the kibosh on his debate. He should have known better, of course. Poor thing. Sunday after Sunday, listening to the beguiling claptrap that came out of the mouth of that evil little man, it would have been a minor miracle for her not to react negatively when he dared suggest that the minister of her church was a sanctimonious disgrace to the Christian faith.

Bewildered though these cobwebbed thoughts may have been, they came to a screeching halt at the sight of a suspiciously familiar bicycle propped against the station's red brick facade. That nick in the rear fender, twin rattan baskets rigged front and back, a rust-flecked bell— unquestionably, yes, the bike was Polly's ... and if so, where the hell was she? That she suddenly decided to come and say goodbye to a man she had no use for was simply out of the question. More importantly, was the bike there when he and Haldeman-Julius arrived? If so, they must have walked right past it.

Or she might have stopped in to use the bathroom; Simon went back inside to check. But neither the railroad stationmaster nor the bus station supervisor across the street had seen hide nor hair of Polly. His wife's recent strange doings were beginning to wear thin. As far as he was concerned, to hell with her goddamn bicycle. If the damn thing was broken, as soon as Moody finished at the church, let him come fetch it.

Ten minutes later, Simon was sitting at his desk in the office, when Doctor Watkins called, wishing to thank him for all the trouble he'd gone to in putting on the debate, not to mention, sending his man Moody over this morning to help with the cleanup. Under normal circumstances, this gesture would have gone a long way toward soothing Simon's general state of disquietude, if only the good doctor hadn't continued on to say for Simon "not to worry. I'm on your side in this. I keep telling them not to hold you to blame for what happened last night." *Them*, of course, meaning Doctor Watson's church board was lathered up to the point of blaming the previous night's fiasco on the Jew.

Simon, however, being a seasoned recipient of racial insults, smiled to himself and hung up. The best way to deal with Doctor Watson's church board was to do it in print. And to get the ball rolling, he needed to place a courtesy call to the not-so Reverend Eugene Digby, to inquire if he, as a reputable man of God, cared to comment on the accuracy of the story the *Courier-Eagle* was to run in its very next issue, stating that the two men arrested for, first, throwing tomatoes, then eggs from the church balcony last night, together with a few rabble-rousers busy catcalling obscenities from the church floor, were, indeed, all prominent members in good standing of his congregation.

The reverend responded in sepulchral mode. "My dear, Mr. Stoner, 'Whoever speaks against the Spirit of God, it shall not be forgiven him': Mathew 21. 'I will heap mischief upon them': Deuteronomy 23. 'I will spend mine arrows upon them': Judges 2:14."

"But, Reverend," Simon said, his splitting headache momentarily forgotten as he scribbled furiously to get everything down, because he had the answer to every editor's prayer on the end of the line: a nut ball eager to make a fool of himself, "what are people to think? What does it say about your church when some of its members show neither respect for freedom of speech nor freedom of worship?"

"'Let him go for a scapegoat in the wilderness': Leviticus 16:10," Digby replied in a voice cloaked with sinister intent. "Publish what you will. You and your commie newspaper are sordid agents of the devil. By the will of God, shall thou be silenced."

The line went dead. Simon's headache resurged with renewed vigor. He lowered the receiver slowly from his ear, wondering if he should call Otis and lodge a formal complaint. But Nancy, who naturally had been listening in, popped her head around the door and said: "Don't you worry none, Mr. Stoner. That reverend's a good man. Really, everybody says so. Just ask your wife. Heck, my brother Kenny and his family attend that church. Me, I've been there myself dozens of times. Sure, the reverend's a real Bible thumper and gets kinda melodramatic at times, but really, most everyone thinks inside he'd just a big old pussycat. I betcha a few minutes from now he'll be back on the line, taking back a lot of that kooky stuff he just said."

Digby? Call back? An apology from a man reputed to have been an insurance adjuster in Omaha before he moved to town—or was it a used car dealer? Simon loaded up for bear by rolling a fresh sheet of paper into his typewriter. *He* had an editorial to write.

Except, come the middle of the afternoon, some four hours later, despite his best efforts to get down on paper a succinct and cogent version of all the stuff he had teeming around in his head, the avowed editorial to end all editorials remained wadded balls of rejected copy tossed into a wastebasket. The more he thought about it, the more it seemed that Digby was way craftier than he ever supposed. A no-holds-barred attack on the man in print would only serve to further the image Digby wanted to project as a fearless defender of the Christian faith. Not to mention that in this town of gossip and lies, where everyone was second or third cousin to everyone else, it would be all too easy to ignite a whisper campaign of *blame it on the Jew*. From there, it would be a simple matter to organize an advertising boycott—which, if only mildly effective, would be enough to bring the paper to its knees, and was this not the exact scenario his wife had been squawking about for the past month or so?

"Mr. Stoner, why don't you just go on home, for God's sake."

How long Nancy had been standing in the doorway, watching him wallow in misery, Simon couldn't be sure. But oddly enough, he had to admit that his little-slow-on-the-uptake secretary had unwittingly provided him with his first, and probably only, laugh of the day, because "for God's sake," hadn't this atheist heard enough of the goddamn *God* word these past two days to last him the rest of his godforsaken, godless life? As for Digby's threats, he and his father had accumulated boxes of threats over the years. So, for the time being, he'd leave off *employing the vorpal sword on his manxome foe and stand awhile in thought.*

***

Simon arrived home earlier than usual, neither surprised nor disappointed to find an empty house. The pity was, Polly wasn't around to show him where she hides the aspirin. No matter, he'd strip down to his boxer shorts, grab a Schlitz from the fridge, and take his insufferable headache into the living room and bask in the breeze of the floor fan until she returned.

Thus, ensconced in his rocker, eyes closed, sipping a bottle of beer, a man who rarely napped or read novels for pleasure, for whom non-fiction was stock and trade, whose mind was rarely at rest, found himself suddenly besieged with venomous thoughts. His wife's bicycle at the train station … how long had it been since he'd last had sex with his wife … Haldeman-Julius, the inveterate braggart, was also a notorious advocate of free love … ergo … ergo … ergo … what the fuck? Could it be, Polly snuck unbeknownst onto that train? Ran off with a pedantic, self-absorbed, melodramatic, alcoholic twice her age? *No! Absolutely not.* He blinked his eyes open and took a deep breath. *Whoa, there fella, what's wrong with you? Call Lorraine. If Polly and little Preston aren't with her, they're probably off shopping somewhere on the square … or, for that matter, they could be next door, visiting with Mrs. Bacacci.*

Lorraine failed to answer the telephone. Simon dressed quickly. He was in the act of mounting the steps to knock on Mrs. Bacacci's back door, when, from somewhere close behind, he heard the muffled voice of his son, singing "ipsy-wipsy spider."

Where? There just beyond the Bacacci's pear tree. Facedown to a gap between two ancient wooden planks that covered the Bacacci's' old well. The goddamn well he'd been trying to get the Bacacci's to fill in ever since his son was born. The goddamn well he had forbidden his son ever to go near, so he wouldn't end up like those kids you hear about on the national news, hopelessly wedged at the bottom of some old abandoned well, awaiting a long and complicated rescue that all too often, proved fruitless.

Simon sprinted to the boy and angrily jerked him upright by the arm. "Preston, I told you never to go near this well," he screamed as he squeezed his son tight. "Where is your mother? Where is Mrs. Bacacci? Boy, answer me. I said, where's your mother? Where's your mother? Your mother?"

"She ran off with Mr. Moody, the dirty old man," the boy finally managed in between sobs.

Simon drew the kid closer, telling himself to *stop yelling at the boy. He had no idea where his mother was, or for that matter, what could possibly be wrong with dribbling balls of spit on a spider web. Be grateful, you fool, your son's escaped what might have been. The very idea of his Polly running off with Moody was utterly absurd—nonsense from the mouth of a babe. Except for time spent cleaning up at the church, Moody'd been busy around the paper all day.*

"Come on, Preston," he said, taking his son by the hand. "Daddy's sorry he yelled at you. I'll bet your mother's inside with Mrs. Bacacci."

But she wasn't with Mrs. Bacacci, and to make matters worse, once he let the old woman know, in no uncertain terms, what had almost happened outside, in addition to being badly shaken himself and having a badly shaken son to deal with, now he had a highly distraught, senile old woman on his hands, who simply wouldn't shut up with the *kvetching*: "I'm a-sorry I fell asleep." "I thought-a the door was a-latched." "I'm a-gonna fill-a that a-well in."

It took quite a while to get everyone calmed down, and Simon was able to cross his backyard with his son in tow. For certain, he told himself, as he unsnapped the poor, suffering dog from the clothesline, he'd have Moody here tomorrow mixing cement to cap that well. And his wife, who must have taken leave of her senses to leave a dog chained up outside during the heat of the day, must be made to understand that she is to never, ever leave little Preston with Mrs. Bacacci again.

Simon's headache soldiered on unabated. What was once a dull ache was now a throbbing constant that had him seeing floaters. Once inside the house, with the help of his son, he finally succeeded in locating the aspirin, whereupon he suggested for the boy to please go amuse himself "because Daddy's mean old headache wants him to spend some quiet time in the living room with a wet washcloth draped over his face."

Naturally, Simon's quest for soothing bliss lasted fifteen minutes at best before the boy was back, whining to Daddy: "I'm hungry."

"Not now Preston, please."

"Where's Mommy?"

"She'll be back soon." *And dammit to hell, where* was *the kid's mommy?*

"When are we going to eat?"

"Okay, okay, I'll fix you something," Simon said, although he'd never cooked a real meal in his life. But then again, any idiot could open a can of baked beans and boil up a couple of franks.

Unfortunately, though it seemed an appropriate palliative at the time, tossing back shots of brandy while one's son gobbled down beans and a frank did little to lessen a headache. Nor did it help when he attempted to call Lorraine again and Otis answered: "Polly was here, but she's not here now. Lorraine was supposed to look after your boy today, but she's laid up with a goddamn summer cold." Then a pause and a chuckle: "What's the matter, Simon? Afraid that little wife of yours has lit out on you?"

Simon cringed and hung up without comment rather than respond to another of his brother-in-law's stupid non-jokes. Besides, it was beginning to grow dark outside, and next up on the menu was the ordeal of corralling a rambunctious five-year-old into bed. Even though, for the moment at least, his son seemed content, playing quietly, stacking and restacking three years' worth of *Life* magazines, arranging them by month, propped against the sofa cushions as if he were racking them for display in O'Reilly's Drugstore—no two ways about it: no matter what his wife said, there was something odd about that boy.

Figuring that he'd hit the hay himself as soon as he had the kid in bed, Simon went to the back door to make sure Polly wouldn't find herself locked out. Because she *was* coming back. Like it said in the lyrics to that lullaby Polly used to sing to her baby boy when she put him down for the night: *the wheels on the bus go round and round; the babies go wah, wah, wah; and mama always comes back.*

Mercifully, for this motherless night at least, the boy showed zero interest in employing any of the thousand and one little aggravations kids put their parents through before going to sleep. Consequently, Simon was soon stretched out buck naked atop the sheet, fitfully sweltering in spite of the window fan, waiting for the dark and silent night to welcome him into sleep and perhaps to dream as he had many times in the past of he and Esther Bloom in their glory days of reckless, carefree passion. The two of them, just a couple of Columbia University undergrad Jews riding a crosstown bus to 118th Street to catch Bird and Diz at Minton's Playhouse. But just as Simon was destined to never again wake up in the morning with Esther Bloom nestled in the crook of his arm, on this most pitiful of all pitiful nights, he was fated never to wake up again, because in this, his hour of greatest need, that something that he seriously suspected was wrong in his life was an occluded artery that was about to spawn the massive heart attack that would make his destiny complete, though Dr. MacNaught would not pronounce him officially dead until 6:47 the following morning.

***

His work done for the day, Moody stepped into the alley and smiled. That darn bitch dog was scrounging Zettl's trash again. When she trotted away with a doughnut in her mouth, having nothing better to do, he decided to tag along to see where it was she kept her pups, little realizing, three blocks later, he'd be crawling under the loading dock behind Sell's Appliance, where the presumed pups turned out to be only one.

Cute as all get out, maybe five weeks old, the pup was blessed with markings wholly unlike its mother. Floppy eared, longhaired coat a tricolor mix of white, black, and tan spoke to a daddy Cocker Spaniel. The mother didn't so much as stir, and her pup could have cared less, when Moody rolled onto his side and began to stroke it as it worried its doughnut. Rex had been the name of the family dog his mother put down the day they were forced to give up the farm, saying: *it's cruel to force a barn dog to go live in town.*

Damn them bankers. Damn the laws that made it possible for them to get away with the things they did in them days. Bossing people around, messing up folks' lives. But, just suppose, just suppose, he was to save up and make a down payment on a few acres somewhere? Shoot, it'd be easy enough to do. There was plenty work for him here in Beatrice. Take this bitch and her pup to come along and live with him. Call 'em Rex and

Regina. Call 'em all the family he'd need—that and a few cows, a stand of corn, a vegetable garden, some chickens, and a pig or two.

When Moody woke up from his unplanned nap, he crawled out from under the loading dock into what proved to be another stunningly glorious, starry night, not surprised in the least that his newfound family members had got themselves off somewhere. Probably on the prowl for something to eat, he told himself, as he brushed dried leaves out of his hair. And come to think of it, he was feeling a mite peckish himself. He was walking the alley, headed to Decker's for that blue plate special, thinking mostly about nothing, when a shadowy figure came rushing past him, carrying what looked to be an empty gas can.

There was no mistaking that roly-poly gait, and it certainly didn't take long for Moody to find out what old Digby had been up to. He had no sooner turned onto Summit Street than he met the town fire truck coming down the street, siren wailing like the hounds of hell, and the next thing he knew, he was standing alongside Pete and Gar watching their jobs go up in smoke.

"Word is, that fire ain't natural. That it may've been set. What do you think, Moody?" Gar said.

"Not much," he replied, knowing full well this was probably the doing of the nasty little man who'd fled past him in the alley. Knowing that this was pretty much it for the forty-dollar wad of five-dollar bills he'd saved up so far in his kit bag, not to mention the bulk of his Mexican gold he'd been looking forward to enjoying tonight, and that truly, the time had come for him to make like Mrs. Stoner and say *adios* to Beatrice, hop the next train east and take that red rose to his mama.

***

Beaten down from the bullshit hours he'd spent dealing with the aftermath of that damn debate, crotchety as hell with a sick wife upstairs in bed who'd left her husband with no other choice but to feed himself, thoroughly exasperated with a brother-in-law who'd, first, call him up whining how he couldn't find his wife, and then, for no fool reason other than the man couldn't take a joke, abruptly hang up him, Otis and his TV dinner had barely settled down in the living room to watch *Dragnet*, when the faint, real-life sound of a siren sounding from somewhere up near the square told him that this was pretty much it for relaxing tonight.

He had no more than strapped on his prosthesis and pulled up his pants when the telephone rang, with Pru on the other end, calling in to report that not only the *Courier-Eagle* building, but the whole damn west side of the square was in peril of going up in flames. Pausing only long enough to grab his hat and shout a what's-up to Lorraine, he was backing his car down the drive, when it occurred to him that maybe he ought to swing past his brother-in-law's place on his way up to the square, on the slim chance that no one had thought to clue the man in that his paper was on fire.

Sure enough, Simon's old Packard was sitting in the driveway. The rest of the house was dark, but the kitchen light was on, so somebody must be home. Otis rang the bell and knocked several times. When no one answered, he went around to the back door. Finding it open, he stuck his head in and called out. Getting no response, he walked in.

The butt end of a hot dog bun left unattended to on the kitchen table, a half-eaten bowl of baked beans, an empty milk glass and another reeking to high heaven of brandy was so unlike Polly, Otis decided that maybe he ought to poke his nose around. The living room was also a fright, so Polly had to be off somewhere and Simon was in charge. Upstairs, he found his nephew peacefully asleep in his little bed. But Lord Almighty, the boy's normally night-owl father, who, for some reason must have gone to bed early as well, was not so much asleep, as to be unawakenable to the point of barely clinging to life.

What seemed like forever, probably wasn't more than a ten-minute wait for the ambulance to arrive. During which time, the Sheriff of Gage County, faced with a medical emergency far beyond his rudimentary Red Cross skills, unlike the Marine medic who'd tended to him on that beach, who'd known exactly what needed to be done, Otis raced downstairs to call his wife to come over and sit with the boy until his AWOL mama came home. He was on his way back upstairs to reassure himself that Simon was still breathing when the phone rang. Thinking it must be the boy's mother, he thumped his way back downstairs. But it wasn't his sister; it was Pru.

"Son of a gun, Sheriff," his deputy said, after learning the dire state of affairs on his boss's end. "If that don't beat all. No wonder I've been calling this number off and on and nobody answered. I'm damned sorry to hear Simon's in a real bad way. Anyway, you'll be glad to hear that, for the time being, at least, it's looking more and more like Tubby Frakes's crew'll be able to keep the fire confined to the *Courier-Eagle* building." Which pretty much was all the sheriff needed to know concerning where his official presence was best needed tonight. Playing spectator to a fire that was destroying his brother-in-law's livelihood paled by comparison to sitting bedside with that same brother-in-law as, in all likelihood, his life ebbed away.

Otis returned upstairs filled with dread. The last time he'd been this up close and personal with death he was lying on some godforsaken South Pacific beach in a doped-up state of shock and partial dismemberment. But, at least in this instance, Sy, whether he knew it or not, unlike those poor devils who'd breathed their last on that fucked-up beach, actually had close family standing by as he clung to life, family who actually gave a shit whether he lived or died.

***

The next day dawned as it had nearly every day that month: stifling hot without a cloud in sight. Otis exited the hospital, nostrils flared by the acrid after scent of last night's fire. He was so damn tired, his eyeballs hurt. The best to be said for yet another day spent in the low-plain hell that was Nebraska was that Simon had met a gentle and peaceful end.

He glanced at his watch, opened the cruiser door and labored his prosthesis inside. He was savvy enough about the Jewish faith to know their dead were supposed to be buried within twenty-four hours. Since Sy Stoner was, as far as anyone knew, the only Jew for hundreds of miles around, even though Otis sincerely doubted the funeral people would go for it, what he'd *like* to do right then was head over to Dorsey's Funeral Home to find out how amenable folks there would be to giving his brother-in-law immediate internment. Unfortunately, what he *needed* to do was get on over to whatever was left of the *Courier-Eagle* building ASAP, because the state fire inspector could very well already be on site, poking the ashes, trying to figure out if that fire was set or not.

His deputy's mind, of course, was already made up. Gung ho for blaming it on Moody, even before all the specifics got filled in. But now that it's turned out that somebody else did in Sam Gerkin out there at Johnson's Crick, Otis was determined this time to keep an open mind. Much as he couldn't stand Moody, the man, and wished he'd never showed his face around town, there was no getting around it: the law was the law and a man was innocent until proven guilty. Still, it was hard not to speculate. The thing was, where was the motive here? Moody had it knocked working for an easy boss like Simon. Which made it kind of hard to fathom the man suddenly gone so far off his rocker as to do such a heinous deed. Digby, on the other hand, was another possibility. He, like a bunch of other nutty-as-a-fruitcake folks in town, seemed to have got themselves plenty lathered up over that damn debate. But everything in due time. As things stood now, barring anything more conclusive turning up, solving this case, providing there was a case to be solved, might just boil down to whose prints would be found on that empty gas can Pru claimed to have come up with snooping around in the alley last night. If they proved to be Moody's, well, the man could run, but he couldn't hide. Sooner or later, trouble had a nasty habit of rooting out its own kind.

Besides, Otis had his sister to worry about. But, once again, when Pru called the hospital late last night, according to him, since neither she nor Moody had been seen around town since, there was plenty of reason to believe that one or the other of them might have set that the fire to cover up them running off together, which was enough to make a man's blood boil. Except the only problem with that theory was that he simply couldn't imagine his sister so callow as to cut out from her marriage and kid without leaving at least a goodbye note or something behind. And since the post office lay conveniently up ahead, it wouldn't take more than a minute to pull in and sort through today's *Courier-Eagle* mail.

Sure enough, there was a letter. Addressed to *Simon Stoner, my husband*. The brute force of its message tempered by his sister's pleasingly elegant script.

> Simon, please do not try to find me. I do not want to be found. If found and forced to return to Beatrice, rest assured, I will only run away again. Explain my actions to our son anyway you'd like. When it comes to choosing the right words to fit the occasion, you, my dear husband,

are so much better than I. But know this: odd as it may sound, strange as it seems now for me to be actually writing these words down, do know that I love you both very much. The tragedy is that it's just not in me to love the two of you the way you both deserve and expect. Please believe me when I say that despite the immediate pain I may be causing you, I firmly believe that we are all going to get over this just fine. Remember those lines of Wallace Stevens you kept repeating to yourself as you cranked the ice cream freezer for our son's birthday? *Let be be the finale of seem. The only emperor is the emperor of ice-cream.* Well, for me, "let be be the finale of seem" means the time had come for me to confess that the reason for my leaving is that the true love of my life is my brother's totally unsuspecting wife, Lorraine. I know this comes as a shock to you. But I hazard to say that neither of us has ever fully been the person we *seemed* to the other person to be. Therefore, goodbye and farewell. Though in all likelihood we may never meet again, for what it's worth, I will always consider you my emperor of ice cream.

Otis resolved to take her at her word. Aside from the poetry crap—which he made no claim to understand. If his sister didn't wish to be found, then he would make no effort to find her, save only to convince himself she hadn't come to a bad end trying to hop a freight—for that had to be the way she'd done it, always thinking she was smarter than anyone else.

But, Lorraine, his wife, Lorraine—the object of his sister's desire? Jesus, it had been bad enough to have had a deadbeat brother who drank himself to death, but now he had a sister who'd suddenly got it in her head she's a dyke? According to modern medical science, homosexuality was a treatable, mental disease. The poor woman needed help. Help she'll never get. Help to keep her from cursing herself to the end of her days.

Otis's instinct was to destroy the letter to protect the family name. Yet God knows why, but a little voice deep down inside kept chirping: *not now, not yet.* That apart from the horrid truth it contained, this little note of hers, taken on its own, was a perfect example of his purposeful, always considerate sister at her misguided best. Something that ought to be hung onto, a kind of reminder of the carefree and promising young scholar she'd once been, seated at the kitchen table after doing the after-supper chores, dipping the nib of her pen into a bottle of Script's blue-black ink as she strove to master the whorls and loops of the Palmer Writing Method. Refusing to give up until she got it right, in much the same way she went about teaching herself to play the piano—not to mention all those fancy circus tricks she used to do on her bike. The shame of it was, if only his sister had the sense to listen, back when her brother tried to warn her away from getting herself mixed up with a Jew who harbored atheistic, pinko-commie tendencies. If only … if only … if only, she'd had the sense to pick herself a man more in harmony with a woman's true physical needs, she might have remained true to the way nature had designed a woman to be and spared herself the grief.

Anyway, for now, he'd keep her letter locked up in the safe down at the jail. Yes, Lorraine was going to bitch and moan about wanting to read it, and God forbid, she ever did, because she'd never be able to get past the lesbian bit. As for their poor nephew, for starters, they'd keep the story simple. Embellish it only as needed over the years. Tell the lad his mother had to go away for a while but not to worry because he'd be staying with them 'til she came back. And, who knew, perhaps for the first time in recorded history, time *would* succeed in healing all wounds and the boy grow so accustomed to the way things were now that he'd leave off fretting about a mother who never came back. Still, all in all, Polly must have been out of her mind thinking that someday, all of them were going to be all right, which was about as likely to happen as an amputee suddenly growing himself a brand-new leg.

23

Red Hook, December 2004

The week before Christmas, a nor'easter dumped seventeen inches of snow on Red Hook during the night. Preston Stoner awoke once to pee, but instead of returning directly to bed, despite an ominously scratchy throat and the chill of a hardwood floor under his feet, he made his way to the front bedroom window, where he stood for way too long, admiring snowflakes by streetlight, driven crazily aslant by a rattling wind. Naturally, a few hours later, he awoke to the fullness of the day feeling absolutely lousy.

"Sick," he informed his ever-sensible wife at the breakfast table when she inquired. "Sick, but not sick enough not to go to work."

Of course, she wouldn't hear of it. "Who do you think you are … Admiral Byrd?" she said pressing her palm onto his forehead. "Don't be an idiot. You've got a fever. Stay home. What are you trying to prove? You got snowdrift outside up to your eyeballs."

"Nope, my dear, away with such bullcrap," he remonstrated to his needlessly anxious wife. "Admiral Byrd, you say? To hell with Admiral Byrd. Now, Amundsen, he's my man. Do not be misled, my dear, by the briefcase I carry daily to work. The man you married is the half-breed scion of redoubtable, sub-Nordic, Jewish extraction. Need I remind you that relatives on my father's side of the family survived Hitler's death camps? Have you forgotten that on my mother's side, I have a great-grandmother who was raised in a sod house? Therefore, I assure you, I shall be going to work."

Thus said, half an hour later, Preston, girded for polar adventure in fleece-lined boots and mitts, the fur-trimmed hood of a down parka drawn tightly under his chin, with Aunt Ranie's hand-knitted, heavy woolen scarf wound around his neck, eased open the front door to confront the artic wonderland outside.

Nor was he the neighborhood's first brave soul to venture out. There was the Sarge, already hard at work, shoveling to clear the Stoner sidewalk. Across the street, his buddy Snowball was shoveling as well. No doubt, come midday, their entrepreneurial endeavors will have earned them sufficient cash to party the rest of the day on pizza, pork fried rice, and a couple of gallons of cheap wine.

Regrettably, in his haste to get out of the house, Preston had taken a pass on a second cup of coffee. Nevertheless, determined and unbowed, Preston fought his way to the middle of the street in order to wallow in the footprints of those who had ventured before him—which, considering the low-energy state he found himself in, proved to be an awkward but amusing game. Nevertheless, he found it extremely pleasing to be out and about, doing what needs to be done, unlike his buddy Richie, no doubt still curled up in bed, tortured with regret for passing up on that windsurfing trip to Tenerife he'd planned for this week.

True to form, the wait for the 61 bus was as if it might never arrive, and when it did, Preston was unable to find a seat. Consequently, by the time he debussed for the F train at Jay Street, lagging rearmost among a clot of fellow corporate sheep crowding the entrance to the subway, feverish and queasy and weak kneed as well, his inner resolve teetered on the breaking point. *He should have listened to his wife. At least half the office will be out today. That old fart Duncan, for sure, would be off somewhere, snowshoeing or cross-country skiing.*

While it was in no way remotely akin to the joy Roald Amundsen must have felt sighting St. George's Island through his telescope from the prow of a lifeboat, when Preston noticed a Red Hook–bound B-61 lumbering into the stop across the street, getting on that nearly empty bus was probably the easiest, if not the most joyful, decision Preston had ever made. He flopped into the first handy window seat and dozed with his head slumped against the window all the way back to Red Hook. Rousing himself barely in time to exit the bus at King Street, he was momentarily lost in a cloud of swirling spindrift like he was one of Jack London's wretched Klondikers.

While he fully expected Pioneer to have remained unplowed, the single, freshly plowed lane that now stretched to his end of the block beckoned like a superhighway. Hesitant of step, buffeted by the wind this way and that, he was no more than a quarter of the way home when he became aware that some sort of fracas seemed to be taking place in front of his house.

Two men. Could it be? Yes, it was, the Sarge wielding a snow shovel like a battle-ax. So that had to be Snowball defending himself with a goddamn garbage can lid. Preston hurried as best he could. *Stop them*, he would have shouted if not for a sore throat and the fact that whatever sound the snow didn't soak up would be lost to the wind.

His arrival swelled the number of onlookers to five, and now he understood why no one wanted to get involved. The Sarge, bareheaded and unshaven, once and for all, had totally lost it. A veritable, slavering Tweedledee scything the air with a fucking snow shovel. His buddy, Snowball, now his ebon Tweedledum, well up to the task of defending decapitation with a garbage can lid.

Bundled up and snow encumbered as these two were, neither seemed in mortal danger. Preston was of a mind to remove his sickly self indoors and leave them to their insanity. Still, it irked him to no end that the person he now stood next to was none other than that lowlife creep who'd recently moved into 188 Pioneer—reviled by one and all for bringing onto their block one of those parking-space-hogging, urban-war-machine Hummers, festooned front to back with World Wrestling Federation stickers, now in the process of making a general asshole of himself, laughing and jeering at the Sarge and Snowball for being a "couple of wino retards." Despite his sore throat, fever, and generally weakened condition, Preston's foremost desire in that chaotic moment was for someone, anyone, maybe even himself, to step forward and once and for all, set this bozo straight.

But apparently, Fate had a different sort of fun in mind, because suddenly the Sarge's legs went out from under him and Snowball pounced on him as he went down. And coming around the corner of Richards and Pioneer, who should be breaking trail for the rest of the Sarge's adopted crew, but Brutus, the noblest Rottweiler of them all, who, taking immediate note of the situation, scarcely paused before leading the whole damn pack on a let's-go-rescue-the-boss vengeance attack. A writhing mass of fang and fur, chorusing every imaginable note in the canine scale, blindsided poor Snowball as he sat pummeling the Sarge.

Preston lunged to retrieve the garbage can lid from where it now lay in the snow, hoping somehow to beat off the dogs. But before he could actuate his probably lamebrain plan, the blurred figure of Ritchie interjected itself through a gap between two parked cars, brandishing above his head the aluminum softball bats he kept handy just inside his front door for occasions such as this.

Ritchie's first swing caught the German Shepherd broadside and sent it reeling in pain. Three whacks more rendered senseless the pit bull. The end seemed near. Mildred and the rest of the pack were now in full flight bounding through the snow down Richards Street. Ritchie was about to whip his bat above his head to administer Brutus a coup de grace. Only, he too then managed to slip and fall.

Preston moaned a non-denominational, "Oh, God." His buddy was momentarily helpless, splayed on his back in the snow. Brutus's hindquarters now dropped for the charge—the deep-throated growl issuing from his throat like the late-night D train lumbering over the Manhattan Bridge— he was about to lunge once more for the garbage can lid when, to his amazement, somehow the Sarge had managed to wriggle out from under Snowball and lock his arms around Brutus from behind and then stagger to his feet with the writhing beast raised above his head. A shot-putter's spin. An Olympic heave. Brutus ricocheted off the telephone pole in front of 87 Pioneer like a crate kissing pavement from the back of a delivery truck.

"Holy shit," Ritchie screamed as he leapt to his feet.

The Sarge stood triumphant: legs apart, head back, fists thrust into the air, as he gave forth a victory *schrei* of such sustained voluminous power that it neither rose in pitch nor fell. There was no doubt now who was the alpha male. The Sarge was Hulk Hogan. He was Brian Boru. He was a howling primal like Attila the Hun.

Preston tried to get to his feet too, but his fever demanded he remain sitting in the snow. Not ten feet from where he sat, Brutus was also unable to stand, most likely because his back was broken.

"It's like WrestleMania, man," Ritchie announced with the full-throated gusto of a sports nut gone off his rocker. "Did the helicopter, for Christ's sake. Threw a beast as heavy as a small man against a frigging light pole. At least fifteen feet," he proclaimed as he finished stepping it off.

People came pouring out of their houses to see what all the hubbub was about. The young woman from 122—whose name Preston could never remember—made like Florence Nightingale, rushing out with a blanket to keep the, undoubtedly, badly mauled Snowball warm until the ambulance arrived. And most unbelievable of all, someone had gone to the bother of calling the cops … and they'd actually showed up.

Preston felt a hand on his shoulder.

"What gives, Prez?"

"Ah shit, Richie, I think I got the flu."

"Here, my man, take my hand. Let's get you inside. Get some Tylenol in you and into bed."

Ritchie steadied him up the stoop. Joellen took over from there, whisked him upstairs, helped him out of his things, and drew him a hot bath. Robed and slippered, before he took to his bed, he couldn't resist one last peep out the upstairs window. Sure enough, just as he'd suspected, the scene below was the block party he and his neighbors had talked about for years but had never been able to pull off. Hell, even some of the junkies from the methadone clinic were down there partying in the street. *Sarge, Sarge, Sarge.* The Hummer man was leading a chant. *Whang, whang, whang,* as Ritchie kept time, hammering his bat on a garbage can lid. And the Sarge, the man of the hour for maybe the first and only time in his besotted life. Making like Zorba the Greek, doing the hora with a beer can in either hand. And for the first time in Preston's passive-aggressive life, everything seemed reasonable and just. Brutus, Ritchie, and especially the Sarge, each in their own way, epic heroes all.

Later that evening, unbeknownst to Preston, the temperature in Red Hook plunged to a record low. Which mattered not to him, snug in bed, his little wife in dutiful attendance, plying him with vitamins C and D, zinc lozenges, and echinacea tea. Nor to Snowball, safely ensconced twenty-six stitches later and on the mend at Long Island College Hospital. Nor Ritchie, who had gone to the Bait and Tackle and finally succeeded in getting laid. Nor the remnants of the Sarge's pack, balled up for warmth in an abandoned sugar factory. The only Hooker to whom it truly mattered was the Sarge, as usual the odd man out, left to tough out his most epic of nights, alone in his van.

***

Two days later, Preston was still in bed, weak but getting stronger, when Ritchie called.

"Figured by now you'd be on the mend. I didn't want to disturb your misery, else I would have called sooner with the news about the Sarge. In case you haven't heard, it's a goddamn crying shame. I mean, who could imagine, if only our neighborhood Samson had had his dogs with him, he probably wouldn't have frozen to death the night of what had to be the greatest day of his life. Anyway, for what it's worth, you know our bodega guy? Closing up for the night, he caught the poor bastard taking shelter in the bus stop, fingers wrapped around a cup of coffee, shivering his ass off but grinning like he was feeling no pain."

When Ritchie then went on to point out that freezing to death was more like going to sleep, so it was probably not all that bad a way to go, Preston mumbled something about what a shame it was for someone to die alone, excused himself and hung up. Talk about getting scythed by the Grim Reaper. The thing that bothered him most was that the Sarge's family never gave a rat's fuck about him when he was alive, and sure as shit, they weren't about to cough up the necessary cash for a proper casket and funeral. So they'd refuse the body, which'd mean a sloppy autopsy performed by some bumbling coroner's assistant who could care less that the Sarge's butchered remains would be unceremoniously dumped in a pine box, slated for burial among all the other down-and-outs awaiting Judgment Day on Hart Island, that was, assuming the city felt the effort was worth the expense of backhoeing frozen ground, which was not only a shame; it was a fucking outrage.

Preston reached for the glass of water Joellen had set out for him the previous night—she'd been using the spare bedroom ever since he'd fallen sick—thinking that perhaps the rejuvenating powers of the best city water in the world might do for him what it had never done for the Sarge: give him the strength to go forth and rejoin the human race.

Unfortunately, when he stood up, he managed only a few steps before his heart fluttered out of control. Feeling somewhat dizzy, he sat down on the edge of the bed. But rather than just sit and wait for his A-fib to sort itself out, he retrieved the, as yet, unopened number ten envelope his wife had also left out for him on the side table last night—from Mitchik, no less, delivered two days ago.

He picked up the envelope, thinking it might be just the thing to calm his chattering heart. He remarked at its weightiness. Could it be? Surely not. So soon? The final report? And if so, was it something he needed to tear open and read right away? Particularly, if it might contain things better left unsaid?

Remembering something else his wife had left for him to check over as soon as he felt able—something to do with the Red Hook Civic Association needing her help in composing fitting texts for a pamphlet of historical neighborhood photos in anticipation of that far-off day when Red Hook might suddenly burst forth as an authentic NYC tourist destination—Preston exchanged Mitchik's envelope for her envelope, fumbled in the bedclothes for his reading glasses, then began to read:

> *Named after its red clay soil and hook-shaped, peninsular harbor, the Dutch established the village of Roode Hoek in 1636.*
> *This map from the 1760s shows a developed village at a time when there was little else in Brooklyn.*
> *In the 1850s the active piers of the Atlantic Basin made Red Hook one of the busiest ports in our nation.*
> *Grain barges from the Erie Canal wait at the mouth of the Gowanus Canal to discharge their wares ...*

Preston smiled. The tone was not to his liking, but then, pamphlets always were a bit dry. Still, he found himself touched deeply, mainly by the things left unsaid. The years leading up to the Civil War, for instance, were quite a bit more turbulent than just active piers and busy ports. But wasn't that the way it always went with history writ large? The lives of common folk, like great unrecorded jazz solos, lost in the ether to the overwhelming turmoil of watershed events. If he remembered correctly, the middle to late

1850s marked not only the blossoming years of Walt Whitman's *Leaves of Grass*; they also chronicled the regrettably tragic, terminal years of America's original crusader for women's rights, Margaret Fuller. But then again, as old give-'em-hell Harry Truman liked to say, "the only thing new in the world is the history you don't know." Meaning what? That societal bullshit always takes a backseat to grand design? That the homeless will continue to freeze to death for want of adequate shelter, that mothers, at wit's end, will continue to abandon their sons, never to see them again, just as our nation, seemingly oblivious to the lessons of Vietnam, will continue to send our youth off to war for God and country in faraway, storybook lands like Afghanistan and Iraq?

Preston closed his eyes and took a deep breath. Irregular heartbeat be damned, reason and order in the universe was his wife, singing in the shower. *When you're passin' by, flowers droop and sigh, and I know the reason why, you're much sweeter goodness knows, Honeysuckle Rose.*

He smiled: his wife, making like a siren, luring him to come join her so that she might scrub him clean.

Ticktock, ticktock.

And that damn clock, he laughed softly to himself. That silly Felix the Cat wall clock he'd given Joellen two years ago as a birthday joke. Gussied up with rhinestones, clock-face stomach, top hat, and red bow tie. Meant for a kitchen, it was her idea of a joke to hang it in a bedroom. He opened his eyes and yes, indeed, Mr. Felix's pendulum tail and Joellen's beat were marking time together in perfect sync.

The thing was, when Ritchie had called with the terrible news about the Sarge, Preston had been lying with the covers pulled over his head, torn between the foul, toxic scent of disease and the fetid memory of an event that occurred many years before. No one had been around to hear when the junkie next door put a shotgun in his mouth and pulled the trigger, and how, before the stench of that poor man's death ripened to the point where Preston was prompted to call the cops, death first presented itself as a mysteriously sweet odor, faintly redolent of his mother's prize honeysuckle bush back in Nebraska …

***

246

Joellen entered their bedroom fresh from her shower, slippered and robed, a heavy towel turbaned around her head, to find her husband seated on the floor, slumped against the bed, eyes shut, mouth loosely agape, head lolled slightly to the side, as if he were, but obviously was not, deeply asleep. She rushed to his side. Called him by name. Shook him by his shoulders. When he failed to respond, she ran to the telephone to dial 911 before hurrying back to his side and rolling him prostrate onto the floor to better initiate her best-guess approximation of CPR that she was resolved to keep up until the doorbell let her know the EMS had arrived.

"My husband," she said, pointing upstairs. "In the back bedroom. Please hurry."

Two highly capable young men bounded past her up the stairs. Their sense of dedicated urgency no less than her own. Except when she turned to follow them, suddenly it was as if she were wearing ankle weights, her role in this business now that of a helpless spectator who needed to stay out of their way.

The two men rarely spoke as they went about their well-oiled drill. Still, it wasn't long before she knew each man by name. It was Roy who snaked the breathing tube down her husband's throat to hand pump precious oxygen into his lungs, leaving it up to Phil, to rhythmically compress her husband's chest.

A minute ticked by, then another. "How's it going?" she finally ventured the strength to ask, because she simply couldn't just stand there dumb and numb, the sour aftertaste of her husband's spittle lingering on the tip of her tongue from her own feeble attempts at mouth-to-mouth respiration.

"Ma'am, fact is, we're kinda scrambling here," Roy replied calmly—so as not to raise her alarm, she supposed. "Our best guess is your husband's suffered a serious stroke. Unfortunately, before we can transport him to the hospital, we got to restore his vital signs. But rest assured, once that happens, we're gonna be moving fast. So, if you're maybe thinking of riding along with us in the ambulance, you better get yourself dressed."

She couldn't have been gone long. A minute or two at most of trying to keep the faith as she fished the hamper for yesterday's jeans, sweater, bra, and panties. However, try as she might, she couldn't fight back the obvious. What *trying to restore vital signs* really meant was that they'd figured Preston to be a goner from the moment they'd walked in.

Nevertheless, she returned to the doorway fully prepared to take that express ride to the hospital, because, she kept telling herself, these guys specialized in bringing 'em back to life. Besides, apart from the occasional bout of flu or the rare episode of asthma or A-fib, her husband was as healthy as a horse and way too goddamn stubborn to die.

Except, while Roy continued to methodically hand pump air into her husband's lungs, using his free hand, he was also speaking with someone on his cell phone. An emergency room physician, no doubt. Something having to do with the amount of time her husband had been without vital signs. She watched and waited as Roy listened attentively, fingered his bottom lip for a moment, before gently laying the bulb to rest on Preston's exposed chest.

"The defibrillator," she suggested. "Have you tried the defibrillator?"

"Sorry, ma'am, defibrillation requires a heartbeat to defibrillate. I'm afraid we've arrived too late. Most likely your husband passed on sometime while you in there taking your shower."

Yes, but, she wanted to say. *But what? But nothing.* She felt a fool in the presence of these lovely young men. They had to be wondering, *What's wrong with her? Where are her tears?* Indeed, why wasn't she pulling her hair and shrieking with grief the way she had the day Tiddles the Cat met his maker under the wheels of that delivery truck? Yet here she was, a paralyzed block of frozen silence who'd stepped from her shower thinking her husband on the mend, only to find the world as she knew it, suddenly flipped upside down.

And now, here was Roy, come to her, taking her hand gently in his—*as if*, she thought, *he were my very own son.* "Mrs. Stoner, you're probably wondering what's going to happen next," he said. "Rest assured, we're not about to leave you alone and just drive off. The way it works is, we're gonna be hanging around for as long as it takes for an officer from the seven-six precinct to show up, whose duty it will be to remain with you until someone from the coroner's office arrives."

"The coroner? You mean there's going to be an autopsy?"

"It's the law, ma'am. Absent the presence of a medical authority licensed to attest to cause of death, New York State dictates an autopsy."

She nodded. Of course, some sort of verification was in order. She'd seen enough bad cop and hospital shows over the years to acquaint herself with humankind's slavish adherence to procedural routine. And the man she'd been nursing with chicken soup these past three days, to whom she'd been married for thirty-plus years? Look at the poor thing, sprawled helpless on the floor—jowls unshaven, unkempt hair badly in need of a shampoo, robe shoved roughly askew exposing his woolly chest, peacefully departed and gone to his just rewards while his wife cleansed herself in the shower. An autopsy. Imagine that. Talk about irony. An autopsy for a man who, knife in hand, had been a veritable one-man wrecking crew of holiday roasts and fowls, whose oft-expressed desire was to die peacefully at home, and the penalty for getting his wish, was to get carved up himself. *Well honey*, as he liked to say each time another of his innumerable acts of clumsiness resulted in another broken tchotchke of hers, *nothing lasts, so let's not get ants in our pants*. Well, she thought, as she nodded permission to Phil to pull a sheet off the bed to drape over her husband's now lifeless body, they'd run the whole megillah together, for better or worse, in sickness and in health, 'til death do us part. And what to say about marriage to a man as predictable in word and deed as the rising sun, whose original bent in life had been to save the world but who ended up selling it soap powders and breakfast cereals instead. A lover unto whom she had borne a son. As faithful to her unto death, as regrettably, she, in a moment of great weakness, was not. Who, for starters, turned out to be far less the heroic archetype she'd originally supposed him to be, yet her love for him had remained fundamentally the same from those days when she supposed him a brave young Lochinvar who *rode all unarmed and rode all alone, faithful in love, and so dauntless in war*. What *could* be said of such a marriage? That it was rockier than some but smoother than most? That somehow, in spite of the inner workings of her husband's mind always remaining a mystery to her, somehow, they'd always found a way to make it work? Made it work like the time Roger once asked her: "Deep down, what's Dad really like?" And she'd brushed it off with laughter because really, she didn't know. And now that the final results were in? Apart from their shared familiarities, her husband died as much a stranger to her as the day they wed. So maybe Preston's gloomy old Kierkegaard had it right when he claimed the *individual* to be *incommensurate with reality*. Certainly, in her current emotionally bereft state, overburdened as she was with the incommensurate realities of death, she had a heck of a lot of calls to make: Roger and Cheryl in California and Bunny in Ecuador, for starters. Her cousins in Milwaukee and, of course, the guys at Preston's office. Later that day, once she had her wits about her, she might start inquiring around about cremation. Keep it simple, just family. Anything public such as a memorial service could wait maybe until spring, late spring. Something casual, but no fuss. Preston hated fuss. As for Mitchik and that letter of his—that from the looks of it over there on his dressing table, he never got around to opening—sure, she was curious, but really, whatever information it contained concerning Preston's mother was more Bunny's and Roger's business than hers, so she'd best leave dealing with it to them. Anyway, standing there, she had to look a sight. Those two boys looked utterly exhausted, like they'd been up most of the night. If she felt sorry for anyone, she felt sorry for them. After all, they were trained to save lives, not lose them. So, if anything, this moment had to be almost as hard on them as it was on her. "Tell you what," she suddenly heard herself say with the unexpected ease of a rudderless craft drifting free of its mooring. "Since the three of us will be keeping company for a while, I'll bet you two could use some coffee. What say I scrounge up some bagels and put the kettle on while you two finish up collecting your things?"

"Sure, ma'am," Roy replied, "but you don't have to do that. I don't expect we'll be waiting around all that long. Fifteen, twenty minutes tops."

"But I want to do it, Roy, and my husband would want me to do it. Which reminds me, while you're at it, it's one of those silly little quirks my husband claimed he inherited from his mother that used to plague him to no end whenever someone neglected to do it, but once you finish packing up, would one of you please be so kind as to switch out the light when you come down?"

Printed in the United States
By Bookmasters